Out in the lightless gulfs of space, two great powers coiled around each other like monstrous serpents. And, like monsters, they fought and tore.

A week before, Ellis had watched the blood of the two serpents spread across Colonel Carter's starmap in a series of vivid splashes: a brilliant, icy blue for the Wraith, a gory scarlet for the Asurans. Each splash, Carter had told him, was the site of a known engagement. Between these battle markers lay the serpents themselves, twisting wildly through each other in three dimensions—an approximation of the two powers' battle lines.

The whole map, in fact, was an approximation, and therein lay the danger of it. "Most of this information is days old," Carter had told him, pointing vaguely at a cluster of splashes. "At best we find out about one of these engagements a few hours after it's over and done. Really, we've got no idea exactly where the fighting is going on."

Ellis had peered closely at the map, a gnawing feeling of worry under his sternum. Carter had scaled the display to take in dozens of star systems, and already half of them were enveloped by the serpents and their terrible wounds. "Is there anything you *can* be certain of?"

"Just this." Carter had touched a control, and a small green dot had blinked into life in the centre of the display.

"Let me guess." Ellis straightened up. "Atlantis."

STARGATE
ATLANTIS™

ANGELUS

PETER J. EVANS

FANDEMONIUM BOOKS

An original publication of Fandemonium Ltd, produced under license from MGM Consumer Products.

Fandemonium Books
PO Box 795A
Surbiton
Surrey KT5 8YB
United Kingdom
Visit our website: www.stargatenovels.com

STARGATE
ATLANTIS™

METRO-GOLDWYN-MAYER Presents
STARGATE ATLANTIS™
JOE FLANIGAN TORRI HIGGINSON RACHEL LUTTRELL JASON MOMOA
with PAUL McGILLION as Dr. Carson Beckett and DAVID HEWLETT as Dr. McKay
Executive Producers BRAD WRIGHT & ROBERT C. COOPER
Created by BRAD WRIGHT & ROBERT C. COOPER

WWW.MGM.COM

ISBN: 978-1-905586-18-9
Printed in the United States of America

PROLOGUE

Fire from Heaven

The sky was dark, and death was in the air.

The Father could smell it, taste it on his tongue. The sun was high, but he couldn't see its light—the clouds of smoke and dust were too thick. A sluggish, sickly night-time was sprawling towards him from the far horizon, lit with stuttering flashes.

Those sparks were getting closer, he knew. Some of them were lightning, static electricity ripped from the skies by all the particulates in the air. But many of them, the brighter, straighter ones, were not electricity in any form recognized by nature.

They were anger, those lights. They were rage and revenge, and they were directed at him. For what he had done.

He turned away. He had a cloth held to his mouth to keep out the worst of the stink, but the miasma of burned rock and roasted flesh was getting too strong. The last city had been immolated just minutes before, the bright beams lancing down from the sky to lay open its protective mountain and boil what lay inside. How many of his children had vaporized in that searing attack, he wondered? A hundred thousand? More? It was impossible to tell. He had spent a year in that city and had never explored one tenth of it.

There would be no more exploring now. The city didn't even exist as rubble any more, its citizens could not even be called corpses. They were dust and smoke and a foul taste in the air, and that was all.

He would be next. The beams were getting closer.

The attackers had shown not the slightest trace of mercy, not a second's hesitation. There had been no attempt at communication, no warning, no negotiation. They didn't want anything from the planet or its people, they simply wanted them *gone*. And they had gathered all their energies to that one end, and sent them stabbing down from orbit in a storm of light.

The planet had fallen in hours. There was no defense. The people had relied on their mountains to protect them, had hidden their great works underground for millennia. The cities had sprawled under the hills and the cliffs and the great peaks, unseen, for thousands of years, and it had been enough.

But this was a new enemy, sending down their fire from heaven, and stone was no match for their weapons.

A beam snapped down a kilometre away, the sound of its passing a horrid ripping noise, deafening even from this distance. The Father felt the heat of it, the sizzle of its electricity over his skin, and it nearly knocked him off his feet. As he stumbled, he saw, briefly, the circular hole it left in the clouds, before the beam cut off and the smoke roiled back in to close the gap.

Where the beam had touched ground, a cone of grey was rising.

A thousand tons of pulverized rock and soil spat up into the greasy air, the initial blast from the beam's transfer of energy. It came up in a tall narrow fountain, almost smooth from this distance, regular, until the upper edges of it slowed to a point where they began to surrender to gravity. But even as the cone started to unravel, light was growing at its base. That gush of powdered rock was little more than a cosmetic effect. The beam had penetrated kilometers down into the planet's crust, and a powerful reaction was growing there.

Behind him, another beam speared the clouds and violated the world. And another.

There was no chance he could get to his sanctuary now. The facility was too far away, over the next hill, and it would take too long to prep the starhopper anyway. The machine had slept for too long. He had never even been sure it would still work.

He hadn't expected to need it.

He steadied himself, ready for the end.

Where he had seen the beam strike, a sphere of light was rising, swelling, insanely bright. Mass became energy in the centre of that sphere, matter ceased to be. Hell was being born in front of his eyes.

Finally, the ground itself reacted to the light, and heaved, rippled into a titan blastwave that erupted outwards from the sphere, hid it in an expanding disc of flying rubble. It spread terrifyingly fast, the heat of a new sun driving it onwards.

The Father knew it was going to kill him. He spread his arms in the face of it, his eyes open, daring it to take him.

The sound of it was thunder, battering his ears.

And the rolling blastwave seemed to shrink back from him, to coalesce, its edges solidifying and hardening into planes of dark gold. The sky above it turned black, the ground beneath it shrank away. The entire scene focused and attenuated and became metal.

He was inside the starhopper.

He stared, blinking into the darkness of space. The optic portal was set to full transparency, and a panoramic starfield surrounded him. Above his head and to either side, status boards pulsed calming mandalas of data, while the controls under his fingertips were slightly warm; the subtle exchange of energy between his body and the mechanisms beneath.

The screams of burning children, the thunder of the beams, all were gone, stilled. He was alone.

He raised his hands from the controls, ignoring the hopper's gentle complaint, and turned them over. They were as they always were—the lines across his palms, the whorls of his fingerprints, all as they should be. But the transition from the dream to reality, the unbidden jump from a slaughtered world to the still womb of the starhopper, had jarred him terribly. The vision of the dying cities had been so real, and waking up hadn't felt like waking at all. Had he really been asleep so long?

How, indeed, could he have slept at all, with the cries of his people so fresh in his ears?

He looked over to the storage alcove, where his *visios* hung from a levitation clamp. The mask seemed to glare at him, accusing, the glossy gold reflecting his own face as he studied it. The empty eyeholes gaped, lifeless. When he reached out to touch the *visios*, it felt cold enough to burn.

As his fingertips met the metal, the control board began to chime plaintively for his attention. The proximity alarm was sounding.

There was another ship approaching. They had found him.

He laid his hands flat against the vector cascades, and thought the starhopper's drives into searing life. As the acceleration pushed him back into his throne he concentrated on the sensors, ordering a tactical map onto the portal. Threads of light appeared in front of him, sewing themselves into twists and skeins, globes and planes that rotated dizzyingly in the air above his hands. And there, finally, in the midst of those dancing graphics, a pulse of brilliant white, shining like a jewel.

His objective. At last, that which he sought was drawing near.

Hope rose in him, for the first time in as long as he could remember. Perhaps, if he was quick enough and strong enough, he might survive.

Whether he lived or died, he decided suddenly, he would go to his fate appropriately dressed. He snatched the *visios* from its alcove and settled it onto his face, felt the cold metal hug his skin. His gaze narrowed behind the eyeholes, and he returned his hands to the controls, spurring the hopper to maximum speed. It resisted for a moment, then leapt forwards.

Weapons fire erupted from behind him, scoring the hopper's phase-shield. But the little ship was already opening up a hole in the dark, its hyperdrives reaching out into the night and wrenching spacetime open in a burst of silver-blue light.

The hole billowed in front of him, filling the optic portal. Putting all memories aside, he let it envelop him, knowing that his pursuers would be close behind, but somehow at peace with that.

The jewel on his tactical display still pulsed. Atonement was within his grasp.

CHAPTER ONE

The Fall

Horrors often start off small.

A suggestion of a footfall outside the bedroom door, late and close to sleep, and the careful testing of a handle. The far-off sheen of ice on a night-time road. A tickle behind the eye. Little things, caresses at the edge of consciousness, too subtle to fear. It is only when these horrors have been given time to grow and fester that they become known for what they are.

The handle turns, and the door swings inwards.

The ice is an oil-sheened slickness under tires that no longer grip.

The tickle grows into a grinding headache, resistant to drugs, resistant to prayer, steadily building day on day...

So it was with the horror that took Atlantis. It began small, almost too small to see, but it was only awaiting its chance to metastasize. Despite later recriminations, no-one could have foreseen it. Even Colonel Abraham Ellis couldn't, though the horror began with him.

He never saw it coming. It was too far away, at the end of a tunnel made from swirling blue light.

The tunnel was an illusion, Ellis knew; some weird artifact of the hyperdrive engines. He had no idea why the strange, supercompressed universe his ship was flying through should appear the way it did, no more than he could explain the careening sense of headlong motion he had experienced the few times he had been through a Stargate. In fact, while he knew the specifications and capabilities of his ship down to the last kilo of thrust, Ellis could claim no real knowledge of how the hyperdrives even worked, let alone how *Apollo* appeared to be lit blue and silver by a light that probably shouldn't be there.

The mystery didn't bother him. As long as the drives did their job, flinging the great ship between the suns at untold multiples of lightspeed, he was quite content to let them get on with it. Let fuller minds than his ponder the true nature of the light flooding his bridge. The Asgard had, in all likelihood, taken its secret with them to their collective grave.

No, what was really bugging Ellis was the unmistakable, and quite ridiculous feeling that *Apollo* was falling.

He closed his eyes momentarily, settled back in the command throne, took a long breath. All the familiar sensations were still there—the faint vibration of the deck through the soles of his boots, the cool metal edges of the throne arms, the click and chatter of the systems surrounding him. Somebody walked across the bridge behind him, and he heard their footfalls on the deck. But with his eyes closed and his senses grounded, the falling sensation wasn't there at all.

He opened his eyes. Through the wide forward viewport, between the weblike support braces, the hyperspace tunnel soared and shone. And once again, Ellis was dropping down into a pit of blue light.

"Dammit," he muttered, very quietly.

Major Meyers glanced up from the weapons console, one eyebrow raised. "Sir?"

In response, he just nodded curtly at her panel. Meyers' attention hastily returned to the firing solution she'd been working on.

She hadn't looked up at the viewport, Ellis noticed. In fact, she'd tilted her head, almost unconsciously, as if to *avoid* looking at it.

Did she feel it as well?

Ellis had heard of the phenomenon, but he'd always dismissed it up until now. Something that civilians might experience, perhaps, or the kind of mess-hall backtalk that went around when the ship was on a long haul and the usual bitching about drills and shore leave was wearing thin. As far as he was aware, there wasn't even a name for it.

Just a feeling that some people had, when looking too hard and too long at the hyperspace tunnel effect, that it either tilted up towards the heavens or dipped right down to the depths of Hell.

Ellis shook himself, angry at his own weakness, and got up. It was nothing, just a failure of perspective, a trick of the eye. Nothing that should be on his mind now, not when he was flying his ship into the middle of a war. "ETA?"

"Seventeen minutes," Kyle Deacon reported from the helm.

"Good. Meyers, get me the bomb bay. No…" He frowned. "Second thoughts, I'll head down there myself. Give McKay a scare."

"Yessir. I'll call you before we break out."

He walked past her console to get to the hatchway, and as he did, leaned down and tipped his head towards the viewport. "What do you think?" he breathed. "Up or down?"

"Down sir," she replied, eyes fixed steadily on her readouts. "Definitely down."

Out in the lightless gulfs of space, two great powers coiled around each other like monstrous serpents. And, like monsters, they fought and tore.

A week before, Ellis had watched the blood of the two serpents spread across Colonel Carter's starmap in a series of vivid splashes: a brilliant, icy blue for the Wraith, a gory scarlet for the Asurans. Each splash, Carter had told him, was the site of a known engagement. Between these battle markers lay the serpents themselves, twisting wildly through each other in three dimensions—an approximation of the two powers' battle lines.

The whole map, in fact, was an approximation, and therein lay the danger of it. "Most of this information is days old," Carter had told him, pointing vaguely at a cluster of splashes. "At best we find out about one of these engagements a few hours after it's over and done. Really, we've got no idea exactly where the fighting is going on."

Ellis had peered closely at the map, a gnawing feeling of worry under his sternum. Carter had scaled the display to take in dozens of star systems, and already half of them were enveloped by the serpents and their terrible wounds. "Is there anything you *can* be certain of?"

"Just this." Carter had touched a control, and a small green dot had blinked into life in the centre of the display.

"Let me guess." Ellis straightened up. "Atlantis."

Carter nodded. "Trying to get a true picture of events over these kinds of distances is hard. Information travelling at C or below means that simultaneity is bunk—you can't tell if two things are happening at the same time because in relativistic terms there's no such *thing* as the same time. And information above C, like gate or hyperspace travel, plays havoc with event ordering."

"So we're screwed." Ellis rubbed his chin, still glaring at the map. "We can't get a true picture of what's going on, and what we don't know could kill us."

"Yeah," Carter said grimly. "If the Wraith find out where Atlantis is, they'll swarm us. If the Replicators find out, they'll do worse. The city's long range sensors are great at picking up moving objects, but as for what those objects are doing… Right now I feel like a kid caught up in a bar fight, hiding under the table. I can hear pool cues on heads, but I don't dare stick my own head out to see where the danger is."

Ellis had been in a few bar fights in his time, although he had normally been wielding the cue. "But McKay says he's got a plan?"

"Hasn't he always?" Carter had smiled at him, briefly. "He's gone all retro on us. A series of early-warning sensors, dropped into these systems here…" She touched another key and a chain of yellow dots flared into life and started pulsing. The map turned around on itself, stars swimming past each other as the galaxy rotated about the Atlantis marker, and Ellis could see how the yellow dots were spread evenly around it; close to, but never quite touching, the two serpents. "The sensors are stealthy—scanner absorbent, mostly passive… They spread out to form VLAs, then communicate with their relays through narrow-beam communications lasers. That's old technology, but they'll be pretty hard to spot."

"And they send data back to Atlantis via subspace?"

"Yes, but only through an encoded network. Basically a lot

of dummies, really short messages and some fancy coding." She tapped the map's surface. "If anything bad happens within three light-years, we'll know about it thirty minutes later."

Ellis had nodded, lost in thought. "Not bad... Although if something did pop in your backyard, what would you do? Move the city again?"

Carter had given him a lost look. "That's the part we haven't worked out yet."

The bomb bay was cold. Ellis could see his breath as pale vapor as soon as he keyed the hatch open.

McKay's stealth sensors were a strange mix of the old and the new; naquadah generators and pulsed communications lasers, subspace encoders and liquid-fuelled rockets. Had the scientist and his team been given longer to work on the units they could probably have functioned perfectly well at room temperature, but in the panic of watching the Asurans and the Wraith tearing at each other across dozens of nearby star systems, some features had fallen by the wayside. A suitable cooling system for the superconducting circuitry was one such omission.

In the deep cold of space, this wouldn't be a problem. Here in the bomb bay, Ellis decided he'd better be careful not to touch any bare metal.

He walked briskly out into the bay, between the launch racks. The racks had been lowered just after *Apollo* had left Atlantis, so McKay could make final adjustments to his sensors, and Ellis wasn't surprised to see them still down. McKay, despite being a genius, couldn't keep time worth a damn.

Either that, or he just worked best under pressure. As long as he kept coming up with the goods, Ellis didn't care much which it was. "Doctor McKay? Are you in here?"

"Yes!" McKay popped up from behind the next rack along, clutching a laptop, his jacket fastened tightly up to his neck. "Please don't tell me we're there yet."

"Not yet."

The man sagged visibly. "Thank God."

"You've got twelve minutes."

"Twelve?" McKay stared at him, then at the laptop screen,

then at Ellis again. "You're joking!"

Ellis folded his arms. "Not something I do on a regular basis, Doctor."

Abe Ellis had met few people who were as completely opposite to him as Rodney McKay. Physically, they were poles apart; Ellis dark-skinned and compact, where McKay was pale and half a head taller. While Ellis could remain still and quiet for as long as he needed to, McKay seemed almost unable to *not* move, and once he started talking it was often difficult to get him to stop. He was nervy and animated and ever-so-slightly out of control, or at least he always had been in Ellis' presence.

Ellis knew that McKay possessed an intellect that exceeded his own by an order of magnitude, and that he was one of the most valued and respected members of the Pegasus expedition. Despite this, if he was honest with himself, he didn't like the man much. Besides, the thought of a civilian calling any kind of shots made him uncomfortable.

McKay was waving the laptop at him. "It's too soon! Look, these calculations are extremely complex. I mean, twelve *minutes*? Couldn't you just go around the block a couple of times?"

"Doctor, we've already *been* around the block." A very long way around, in fact; in order to throw any potential observers off the scent, *Apollo* had been backtracking in and out of hyperspace for two days. "We arrive at M3A-242 on schedule, like it or not."

"I know, I know." McKay sighed, breath steaming. "Okay, I guess they're probably good to go anyway. I'm not sure about some of these vectors, but there's a margin of error built into the software just in case any of my mass readings are out of whack…"

"Error?"

"Let's call it wiggle room. Colonel, this isn't easy. If all we had to do was drop these things and go home, we'd be done by now. But each cluster has got to align into a Very Large Array using nothing more than a couple of thruster burns, mimic pre-existing orbital dynamics and keep in relay LOS over distances of millions of kilometers. Even for me, that's not exactly a walk in the park."

"Not to mention doing it under the noses of both the Wraith and the Asurans."

McKay paled slightly. "Yes, well. Quite frankly I'd been trying not to think about that part. How long now?"

"Not long enough." Ellis jerked a thumb over his shoulder. "Move it, Doctor. Unless you want to be here when I depressurize the bay."

McKay snapped the laptop closed. "Fine. I'll just tell everyone to keep their fingers crossed."

Ellis moved back slightly to let McKay past, as the man began to head towards the exit hatch. "Doctor, M3A is in spitting distance of Atlantis, and the Wraith might be on their way there right now. Believe me, we've *already* got our fingers crossed."

They almost made it back to the bridge before *Apollo* was hit, but not quite. Meyers had just warned Ellis that the ship was about to leave hyperspace, and rather than risk being caught off-balance when *Apollo* decelerated he had stopped in the bridge access corridor. McKay, sensibly, had done the same. Both men felt the ship lurch as it returned to realspace; that was quite normal. There was no way that several thousand tons of metal was going to rip a hole in the universe without a jolt.

The second impact, however, caught Ellis quite off-guard. "That's not good," he growled.

McKay gave him a quizzical look. "What was that? Did we go back into hyperspace?"

"I don't think so. That felt almost like—"

The deck shook again. As it did so, Ellis' headset crackled. "*Sir?*"

"Meyers, what the hell?"

"*Colonel, you'd better get up here…*"

They ran the last few meters onto the bridge. Ellis keyed the hatch open, quickly skirted the tactical map and stopped dead when he saw what was outside the viewports.

He heard McKay swallow hard. "That's, ah… Is that what

I think it is?"

"Yeah." Ellis sat down slowly. "We're too late."

There was a Wraith warship directly ahead of the *Apollo*.

It was close, a dozen kilometers away or less, and it dominated the view from the forward ports. *Apollo* had broken out of hyperspace in high orbit around M3A, and Ellis could see the dark glitter of that world's nightside to the right of the viewport. The Wraith ship filled much of the rest of his view.

It was canted at an odd angle, well off the ecliptic, and embers of orange light glowed fitfully over its hull.

Ellis narrowed his eyes. "Meyers?"

"Unknown type, sir," the Major reported, tapping out commands on her board. "Bigger than a cruiser, smaller than a hive ship."

"*Everything's* smaller than a hive ship," snapped McKay, but Ellis threw him a warning glare. "List it as a 'destroyer'. What else can you tell me?"

"It's dead. Massive weapon hits all over, power system failure, hull's opened up along the port side. We hit some debris as we broke out, sir. One of the engines."

"Damage?"

"To us? Superficial."

Ellis nodded, relieved. *Apollo*'s shields were up, standard procedure upon dropping out of hyperspace, but large solid objects could hit a shield hard enough to batter a ship to pieces. Shields protect against small, powerful impacts in localized areas, like Kevlar body amour stopping bullets. Hit a man in Kevlar with something big and heavy enough and he'll die, amour or no amour.

Apollo was drawing closer to the Wraith ship now. The space around it was full of twinkles, as fragments of debris turned over and caught the sunlight. Ellis could see that some of the closer twinkles had arms and legs, although not always in the correct number.

"There's another one," said McKay.

As *Apollo* neared the stricken vessel, a second wrecked ship had emerged from its shadow. Like the first, this ship was broken, tumbling, alive with internal fires, but it was very different in form; faceted where the Wraith ship was smooth, absorbing sunlight where the other reflected it from the glossy bone of its hull.

"Replicator cruiser." That was Deacon. "Looks like they blew it clear in half."

Meyers half-turned to Ellis. "Sir? I'm picking up more. This system's a scrapyard."

McKay snorted. "So I guess we won't be deploying our little sensor array then, huh?"

"Not much goddamn point now." Ellis rubbed a hand back over his scalp. "Run a sensor sweep. Is *anything* alive out there?"

"I hope not," Deacon replied. He wore spectacles, and it was a nervous habit of his to push them back up his nose even when they hadn't slid down. He did so now. "I'd hate to do any fancy flying in this mess."

"Noted," growled Ellis, and sagged back a little in the command throne. "Meyers?"

"Working on it, sir." She tapped out a command chain on her board, ran her finger quickly down the list of results. "Okay… I'm getting a lot of interference from the debris, and the LIDAR is picking up more traces than it can handle. But I'm not reading anything that's changing vector, or anything that isn't cooling down. I think we're on our own out here."

"That's a good thing, right?" McKay leaned down to scan Meyer's results over her shoulder, then turned back to Ellis. "Whatever happened here, at least we missed it."

"Looks that way," Ellis agreed. "Doctor, is there any reason for us to stay?"

"Hmm? Me?" McKay pointed to himself, eyebrows raised. He seemed genuinely surprised to be consulted. "Er, no, I don't think so. I mean, we've all seen dead Wraith before, and frozen Replicators are even more boring." He shook his head and put his hands in his pockets. "I'd say we're done here."

"That's good enough for me. Deacon?"

"Sir?"

"Find us a clear area to jump out. I don't want any of this crud ripping a hole in the shield when we go to hyperdrive."

"Yes sir." Deacon began tapping at his own board, then paused and frowned. "Er…"

"'Er' what?"

"Colonel?" McKay was staring out of the viewport. "I think we're in trouble."

A point of silver-blue light had appeared to the right of the port. Something was breaking out of hyperspace ahead of *Apollo*'s starboard bow.

Ellis jumped to his feet, watching the light billow out into a whirling cloud. "Weapons hot! Shields to max power!"

The hyperspace emission shrank in on itself and vanished, spitting a brilliant shard of metal as it faded. As Ellis watched, the shard glowed at one end and began to accelerate smoothly towards *Apollo*. "Meyers? What have we got?"

"It's small, sir. I'm not reading any weapons signature."

"A missile?"

"Unknown."

If the shard was a ship, it wasn't much bigger than a puddle jumper. "Distance?"

"Three thousand meters and closing."

"If it gets within a kilometer, burn it."

As he spoke, the comms screen on Deacon's board lit up. There was a burst of static, then a brilliant flare of pixels that, in a second or two, resolved themselves into a face.

No, not a face—a *mask*. A construct of gleaming, polished gold that was part Greek, part Roman, and part something Ellis had never seen before. Something ghostly.

Behind the mask, dark eyes gleamed in fear. "*Tau'ri, egoo sum sub incursis! Comdo, egoo indeeo templum!*"

"What?" McKay was shoving his face into the comms screen, almost clambering over Deacon to do it. "*What?* Did you hear that?"

"Yeah, I heard it. Didn't understand a damn word. Now get off him!" Ellis shoved the scientist aside, sending him scurrying away, then turned his attention back to the golden apparition on the screen. "Unidentified pilot. Do you require assistance?"

Light, reflected from the golden mask, spilled through the screen. At the same instant a similar glare washed through the viewport.

"Another hyperspace window," said Meyers. "Either he's brought some friends, or—"

A stream of sparks arced out of the darkness. One of them struck the mask's ship, flaring off a shield but hitting the little vessel hard enough to change its vector. It slewed sideways.

"Not friends," gasped McKay. "Definitely not friends."

The second burst of blue was further away, but larger. The vessel it was vomiting out was huge; a hunched, faceted thing, studded with weapons emplacements. A Replicator cruiser, its drives glowing blue-white as it began to accelerate.

"Okay," muttered Ellis. "Now it's on."

The comms screen flickered. For an instant, it showed a different face, one that looked human, but then that was gone too. Ellis was left looking at a panel of fluttering static. "We've lost comms."

"We're being jammed," someone reported from behind him. "All frequencies are down."

The Asuran ship must have locked onto *Apollo*'s communications, Ellis thought grimly. They didn't want anyone shouting for help. "Make sure our firewalls are up. I don't want them feeding a virus through that static. Deacon, get us between the Replicators and that first ship. I didn't get what Goldie was saying, but it sounded like he was asking for help."

"He was," said McKay quietly.

Ellis felt the ship move under him, saw the view from the forward ports tilt and slide as *Apollo* began to vector between the two other vessels. The main drives were throttling up under Deacon's control, the ship's speed increasing.

Sure enough, the other ships were reacting. The shard was drawing closer, the glow from its blunt end dimming fitfully. It had crossed *Apollo*'s bow and was now on the low port side, trying to put the battlecruiser's bulk between it and the pursuing Asurans. And the Replicator ship was swinging about hard, impossibly fast for something so big, trying to bring its prow to bear on the shard.

Streams of energy were still hosing towards the smaller ship. A few shots caromed off *Apollo*'s shields—Ellis saw pinpoint glows appearing above the hull, illuminating the hazy dome of the shield, and felt the distant hammer of their impacts—but most of the fire was still directed at their first target. Any ordnance hitting *Apollo* seemed an afterthought.

He didn't like it, though. "Get us in closer, and ready the missiles. Let's teach them to pick on somebody their own size."

McKay blinked at him. "You didn't actually just say that, did you?"

"Shut up."

Meyers keyed the missile launchers online. From the corner of his eye Ellis saw power bars on her board filling up, but his main attention was on the viewport. The masked man's ship was drawing level, now; almost *Apollo*'s entire bulk was shielding it from the Asurans.

"Replicator ship has lowered its shields," Meyers said suddenly. "It looks like they're diverting power to a primary weapons system. Sir, they're going to—"

Lightning erupted from the Asuran's bow, a twisting river of raw energy that cavorted out towards the shard and sent it whirling. The lightning carved a leaping track through *Apollo*'s shield, forks snapping through it to scorch the hull, multiple strikes ripping down like a storm in the desert. Even when it faded out a second later, Ellis felt the ship shivering, saw sparks the size of buses crawling across the upper armor.

"What the hell was that?"

"Whatever it was," Meyers said, "it looks like all they had. Main power systems on the Asuran are down, they've gone into some kind of recharge cycle."

"Then let's finish this before they get their breath back. Open fire, all forward railguns."

Space lit up.

Multiple weapons emplacements mounted along *Apollo*'s forward hull had come to abrupt and terrible life, directing streams of hypervelocity ingots towards the Replicator cruiser. The vessel seemed to shudder as the railguns carved into it, ripples of vibration coursing along its flank as the weapons blowtorched through its outer plating. The ship's hull blistered, shedding metal and great gouts of burning atmosphere.

Its engine glow faltered, flickering as the power began to fail. Whole lines of windows began to glow horribly bright as fires engulfed its decks.

Ellis took no pleasure in watching the slow death of an enemy. "Missiles," he ordered.

Apollo was passing under the Asuran vessel, Deacon pouring power into the thrusters, swinging the ship down in a sharply angled burn. As the Replicator's shadow passed over the viewports, Meyers triggered the missiles. Four sparks appeared at *Apollo*'s bow, rose, then darted back along the ship's hull. Ellis resisted the urge to follow them with his gaze as they passed over him and out of sight.

A second passed, and then—for a brief time—night turned to day.

It took some time to get the shard on board. It had been rendered inert by the Asuran attack, and was drifting amongst an expanding cloud of debris from the cruiser. Meyers had some difficulty finding it amidst all the scrap metal.

Eventually, though, the ship was located. Deacon, despite his earlier misgivings, was able to execute some very fancy flying indeed, even surrounded by the shattered corpse of the Replicator vessel, and matched vectors with it. With the doors to the bomb bay open, *Apollo* was able, very slowly and very gently, to scoop the little craft aboard.

Now that it was close enough to see, the vessel was certainly striking. Partly because of its design; it was at once cluttered and graceful, sinister and effortlessly elegant, as though a predatory insect had been frozen halfway through changing into a musical instrument. But the ship also caught the eye because of what it seemed to be made of.

Ellis, standing with McKay just outside the ring of armed marines he had posted around the ship, was having a hard time taking his eyes off it. "Is that what I think it is?"

"What, gold? Yeah."

"Who would have a gold spaceship?"

"Somebody rich."

There were technicians checking the ship out, scanning it

for radiation, toxins, or any sign it was about to blow up and take half of *Apollo* with it. They had been checking for several minutes, but no-one had started running yet. Ellis was almost hopeful.

"So you've not seen anything like this before."

McKay shook his head. "No. Nothing like this design at all. It's not Goa'uld, not Asgard, certainly not Wraith… I've checked through every database I can lay hands on, but I've got nothing."

"But you recognized the language he was speaking."

"Maybe. No. Yes. Ehh…" McKay made an exasperated gesture. "It sounded a little like Latin. Look, I'm not the languages guy, okay? Maybe I'm wrong."

"And if you're not?"

"If I'm not, then I think we're in a whole heap of trouble." The scientist cocked his head to one side, still looking at the ship. "Interesting trouble, but still… You know…"

"We live in interesting times." Ellis puffed out a breath. "If those guys don't give me an all-clear soon, I'm going to go over and start kicking that thing anyway."

As if on cue, the lead technician turned and gave him the thumbs up. Ellis gave McKay a grim smile.

"Let's see what we've got."

"Just… Don't kick it."

The two men crossed the bay, passing between two of the marines and drawing close to the ship. McKay's stealth sensors clung above their heads, almost forgotten, their launch racks raised and retracted. It wasn't even certain if they were going to be deployed at all, now. *Apollo*'s new acquisition had thrown everything into question.

There were round, glassy protuberances at the forward end of the ship that Ellis had thought might be viewports, but he was disappointed to find them totally opaque when he studied them. He noticed McKay walking away from him while he was trying to peer through, looking agitated as he focused his attention on the vessel's flanks. It took him less than a minute to make a complete circle of the craft, after which time he rejoined Ellis and shrugged. "If there's a door in this thing, I can't see it."

"Doctor, there's at least one pilot in this ship, and he might still be alive. If you can't find a door, I'll give the order to cut through the hull."

"I'd really rather you didn't do that…" McKay frowned. "Dammit, there's got to be a way in. What's the point of a spaceship you can't get- Jesus!"

"What?" McKay had jumped back, holding one hand in the other as if he had burned his fingers on something. "What did you do?"

"Nothing! I mean, I don't know. It just started moving!"

Ellis stared. A section of the ship's hull had separated into a filigree of intricate metal plates, sliding under and through each other like some bizarre puzzle. He could hear the faint whisper and click of the mechanism that moved them, a distant chiming…

The plates snapped apart, vanishing into concealed recesses in the hull. When they were gone, they left an open hatchway.

The two nearest marines were right next to Ellis, gun muzzles nosing ahead of him. Boots rang on the bomb bay floor as the others ran into position. Ellis looked down and realized he had drawn his own sidearm on reflex.

He left it in his hand as he put his head and shoulders into the ship.

The interior of the vessel was as complex and unfathomable as the outside. The space Ellis was looking into was quite small, so he guessed there were compartments fore and aft, but he couldn't see any obvious hatches or openings. He grimaced, wondering whether he would need to be as lucky as McKay to find the right control and get to the pilot before he died.

"Hello?" he called, feeling slightly out of his depth. "Anyone?"

To his left, the front of the ship, something moved. He heard it, quite clearly. A moment later, the wall between him and that compartment split into dozens of randomly-shaped panels and hinged away to nothing.

The man in the mask lay near the front of the ship, on a couch that was half *chaise longue*, half dentist's chair.

Ellis clambered in to crouch next to him. He could see the

man moving, one slender arm lifting fitfully from under the golden robes he wore. The masked head turned towards him, slowly, as if borne down by the weight of the metal.

McKay was standing in the doorway. He nodded at the mask, urgently. Ellis reached up and lifted the lustrous thing away.

As he did, the pilot smiled. "Thank you, Tau'ri."

Ellis set the mask down. It really was quite heavy. "Are you injured?"

"Yes."

"Can we help?"

"Yes."

McKay stepped closer. "What can we do?"

"Take me to Atlantis," the man whispered, his dark eyes closing. "Take me home."

CHAPTER TWO

...For I Have Sinned

There were days when Atlantis enjoyed quite glorious weather, days when the waters around it lay so still and clear they rivaled the sky for blueness. There were days when the winds blew in sweet from the mainland, gentle and warm, bringing almost imperceptible scents of forest and mountain. There were days when those within the city yearned to be out, and those outside could think of nothing but raising their faces to the open skies and basking in air so fresh that nowhere on Earth could match it.

The day that the golden ship came down was not one of those days.

Samantha Carter was out on the balcony, the railed platform jutting out from behind the control room. The bulk of the tower was providing some shelter from the elements, but she was still perched some nine-tenths of the way to the top, and at this height there was no such thing as a warm breeze. She looked up at a sky that was all wind and clouds, and screwed up her face against yet another blast of cold drizzle. "I don't see it."

"Give 'em time." John Sheppard was next to her, leaning out over the balcony wall and squinting down at the waves, a dizzying eight hundred meters below. "This isn't something they've done before."

"Yeah, I know. Wouldn't be easy, even in good weather." Carter cupped a hand over her eyes and frowned up into the scudding grey. "We certainly picked a day for this, didn't we?"

"Bracing," he grinned. "Come on. You can't tell me you're not looking forward to this just a bit."

"I'm not sure that's the phrase I'd use." The wind gusted, and Carter ducked slightly in the face of it. "John, I've been over your reports—to be honest, in the past couple of weeks

I've not done much else. But what I mean is, there's a precedent for this, and it's not a good one."

"Ellis could be wrong."

"Ellis isn't saying anything, one way or the other. He's being cagey, and I don't blame him. But what if it's true? What happens then?"

"I guess we'll find out before long." He shrugged. "Hey, how bad could it be?"

Carter narrowed her eyes. "Did I ever tell you how much I hate it when you say things like—?" She stopped. There was a sound, faint, a wasp-whine at the edge of hearing, almost lost to the wind. Carter tilted her head, trying to place it. "Do you hear that?"

Sheppard straightened. "I hear it. I just don't believe it."

The sound grew suddenly louder, and as Carter looked up to track it she saw an irregular fragment appear below the clouds. A moment later it was gone, obscured by grey, but it returned just as quickly, bobbing slightly as it approached.

"Oh my God," breathed Sheppard. "They're actually doing it. The crazy sons of bitches are actually doing it!"

He sounded amazed, and not a little horrified. Carter didn't quite understand. "You knew they were going to do this."

"No I didn't! I thought they were just going to beam it in…" He pointed, as if unable to believe that the shape above them was actually there. "What are they, insane?"

Carter gaped. "This was your idea!"

"It was my *plan B*, okay?"

"I guess they never got that focusing problem sorted out." The sound of the approaching puddle jumpers wavered abruptly, and Carter snapped her gaze back up to find them again. Her heart was drumming in her chest. "Come on," she whispered into the wind. "You can do this…"

The jumpers were close enough to see clearly now, three of them, coming in obliquely to the tower. They flew in tight formation, with barely a few meters between those on either side and the third vessel keeping slightly to the rear. And between them, webbing the three vessels together, were black threads against the grey sky; a haphazard tangle of steel cable.

The golden ship, Abe Ellis' prize, was slung between the three jumpers.

Even from this distance, Carter could see that the little cluster of ships was frighteningly unstable. The cables between the three jumpers were tough, heavy-duty woven steel, but their strength was finite. If any of the active ships went more than a meter or so out of formation, the cables would simply shear through. At best, the golden vessel would be dumped into the sea, but it was far more likely that such an event would cause catastrophic damage to some or all of the ships involved.

And yet, despite the shifting weight of their cargo and the battering they were taking from the elements, the three puddle jumpers were keeping it together.

A few hundred meters out they turned directly towards the tower, losing height all the way in. When the reached a level with the balcony Carter saw the golden ship rise a little as the formation spread out and the cables stretched, but then the pilots bunched their ships close again and once more the prize dangled like an orange in a mesh bag.

"I can't look," said Sheppard, not taking his eyes off them.

"They will take the crosswinds into account, won't they?" In bad weather, the upper levels of the tower could be prey to some vicious and unpredictable changes in wind direction. Carter knew enough about puddle jumpers to realize that one of the ships on its own wouldn't even notice atmospheric conditions, unless it was flying through a tornado. But three of them tied together and hauling several tons of inert spaceship about were a very different story.

"Sure they will," Sheppard replied, sounding unconvinced. "I taught them everything they know."

The jumpers lurched sideways.

There was an angry twanging sound, almost drowned out by the sudden rise in engine pitch as the three vessels struggled to keep together. The jumper on the left twisted, dipped as the wind caught it, and Carter gasped as a cable snapped free. The golden ship—now almost directly below the balcony on which she and Sheppard were standing—bobbed wildly.

The formation hung agonizingly in the air, engines whistling, and then as one they darted forwards into the tower and out of sight.

There was a moment's pure, open silence.

And then a heavy, complicated sound, multiple impacts of metal, a shrill, short cacophony of scraping. Distant shouts.

Sheppard winced. "That doesn't sound good."

"No sirens, no explosions…" Carter smiled. "Good enough."

As she spoke, her headset crackled into life. "*Colonel?*"

That was Palmer, one of the control room techs. "What is it?"

"*Unscheduled gate activation, Colonel. It's the IOA.*"

"That was fast. Okay, I'll be right up." Carter made a face. "Our master's voice."

"Okay then…" Sheppard squared his shoulders and turned to go back into the tower. "You know, I'm still not sure if I'm going to buy Lorne a drink or have him committed."

"After that?" Carter's eyebrows went up into her hairline. "He's a genius."

"He's insane."

With the Stargate activated, a wormhole was forged between two galaxies. Across three million light years, radio signals streamed through the event horizon and brought the face of Richard Woolsey to Atlantis.

He was just settling himself in front of the camera. In her office, standing in front of the wallscreen on which his magnified image was being displayed, Carter watched as Woolsey sat down, straightened his tie, and leaned forwards to adjust his glasses in the reflection from a display that was obviously not switched on yet.

Carter gave Sheppard a sideways look. "*Don't,*" she mouthed.

"*What?*" he replied soundlessly. He was trying not to smile.

The view tilted for a second, then stilled. Woolsey frowned and nodded to someone out of shot, presumably the tech who had moved the camera. Then, after the faint beep of a monitor being switched on, Woolsey saw that he was being watched.

"Ah, Colonel!" His smile switched on like a lamp. "It's good to see you again."

"Likewise," lied Carter.

In truth, she didn't dislike Woolsey. He had a tendency to meddle, certainly; to assume greater knowledge of a situation than he actually possessed, and occasionally to panic at the worst possible time. But he was a man of some integrity, and had proved himself to be at least nominally on the side of the angels.

No, this wasn't personal. It was simply that the feeling of being supervised by a civilian committee, especially one so distant, made her slightly uncomfortable. Carter was used to taking orders from people who were either of a higher military rank, or in what she regarded as a justifiable position of authority. The International Oversight Advisory was neither.

On a good day, they were merely ineffectual. But there had been times when their vacillations had made them a dangerous liability.

Still, while Carter had no time for the kind of political games that fuelled the IOA, she knew the rules off by heart. So she put on a smile, dipped her head ever so slightly forwards, and said: "Always a pleasure, Mr Woolsey. Of course you know Colonel Sheppard."

"Indeed I do," replied Woolsey. Somewhat warily, Carter thought. "I was told Colonel Ellis would be here too?"

"Colonel Ellis will be joining us shortly, Mr Woolsey. In the meantime—"

Light flared behind her, a column of brilliant blue-white that seemed to drop, momentarily, from the ceiling. When it vanished, Colonel Ellis stood in its place.

"Well, actually he's here," said Carter, flatly.

"Sorry about that." Ellis glanced around quickly, as if to get his bearings. "I got held up."

"Better late than never," said Sheppard quietly.

Carter nudged him. "Colonel Ellis, it's good to see you back. Where's Rodney?"

"Thank you, Colonel. And Doctor McKay asked to be beamed directly to the hangar. He wanted to look at the ship, make sure it had survived the journey intact." Ellis cleared his throat. "I did, ah, suggest that he might like to ride one of the jumpers down, but he declined my offer."

Carter chuckled. "I'll bet."

"Excuse me?" On the screen, Woolsey was looking puzzled. "Hangar? Surely you didn't store that ship in the jumper bay?"

"No, not there," Carter replied. "There's an open area a couple of levels down from here. It wasn't being used for much, just storage, and some of the outer walls are modular. We managed to get them retracted temporarily to make a kind of, well, parking garage. Major Lorne and his team flew the ship in on tethers."

"It couldn't be beamed in?"

"No," replied Ellis. "Our transport sensors couldn't get a complete lock on the hull. We're not sure why, possibly a defense mechanism or a property of the hull. But Doctor McKay didn't want to risk it arriving in pieces."

"Very wise. What about your guest?"

"He's undergoing a last couple of tests in *Apollo*'s infirmary," said Ellis. "When my people are sure it's safe for him to be moved, we'll ship him down to Doctor Keller, nice and gently."

"What's wrong with him?"

"Concussion, mainly. His body does seem to be healing itself to some extent. But whatever the Replicators hit him with, it hurt. He took some serious knocks up there."

"I see." Woolsey had gestured to someone offscreen, and in response a folder was passed to him. He opened it. "Thank you," he muttered, not looking up. "So, Colonel Ellis, what has he told you?"

"Very little so far. Partly because he's been unconscious some of the time, but I'm sure he's deliberately holding back, too. Basically…" There was a pause, and Carter noticed that Ellis was looking distinctly uncomfortable. "Basically, he says his name is Angelus, and he claims to be a corporeal Ancient."

That roused Woolsey from his folder. "A Lantean that didn't ascend? That would make him, what, ten thousand years old?"

"Give or take," said Sheppard.

"Well, that's news," replied Woolsey dryly. "How's he looking?"

"Pretty good for his age," said Ellis. "I know this sounds wild. Believe me, I'd be the first to advise extreme caution. All I'm giving you is what he gave me."

"And the ship?"

"Like nothing I've ever seen before." Ellis folded his arms. "Doesn't quite match any of the Lantean ship designs we have on file, but it doesn't resemble anything else we know about either. It's a new one on me."

"Colonel," began Carter. "Surely your medical team have done some preliminary tests on this… Angelus. Do they confirm what he's saying?"

Ellis shrugged slightly. "To be honest, we don't have nearly the research facilities you do here. We were able to confirm the ATA gene, and his anatomy doesn't look much different from what Lantean bodies are supposed to be. Then again, I could say much the same about Doctor McKay."

Sheppard grinned. "Hey, can I quote you on that? Rodney'll be thrilled."

"Colonels, please…" Woolsey closed his file, looking perturbed. "Look, this Angelus could be anyone. Until we've got more information, it's impossible to make any kind of decision."

Now there's a switch, thought Carter. "Mr Woolsey, the only thing we can do at this stage is find out all we can. Speak to him once he's recovered, do tests… If Angelus is, somehow, what he claims, then some serious decisions will need to be made. You know what happened the last time there were Ancients on Atlantis."

"I do," said Woolsey grimly. "I was there."

"So from your point of view, wouldn't it be best to start formulating preliminary plans based on the possible outcomes? If he's for real, Plan A, if he's not, Plan B, and so-on?"

"If he's a Wraith in disguise, Plan C, throw him to Ronon," said Sheppard, largely under his breath.

Woolsey nodded. "Yes… yes, I'll put that to the Advisory. Probably best to start now… The IOA's decision-making process can be a little, well…"

"Thorough?" ventured Carter. Woolsey smiled.

"I was going to say 'torturous', but 'thorough' will do."

Ellis stepped forwards. "And the *Apollo*?"

"Personally," said Sheppard, "I'd feel a whole lot better with *Apollo* still in my sky for now. From what Colonel Ellis here says… You're sure about that, Colonel? The Replicators actually dropped their shields?"

"Absolutely. Damnedest thing I ever saw."

"So whoever this Angelus is, they were prepared to sacrifice a whole cruiser just to get one decent shot at him. I don't know about you guys, but that makes me just a little nervous about having him around."

"I concur," said Woolsey. "Colonel Carter?"

Carter shook her head. "Actually, I disagree. As far as we know, the location of Atlantis is still a secret, and I'd like to keep it that way for as long as possible. I'm sorry, Colonel, but that means not having *Apollo* around right now."

Sheppard leaned slightly towards her and dropped his voice. "Doesn't that leave us a tad, you know, exposed?"

"Sure it does. But come on, if the Replicators want him that badly and they knew he was here, they'd be all over us right now. I'd rather have *Apollo* seeding those stealth sensors. The more information we have about who's in our neighborhood the better."

"I'm with Colonel Carter," said Ellis. "Even without Angelus in the picture, the Wraith and the Replicators are still at each others' necks. If their war threatens to spill over into this system, you need to know about it."

Woolsey slapped his folder in exasperation. "But Colonel Carter can't spare McKay! Not if she's going to investigate Angelus and his ship!"

"McKay's done all he needs to on the sensors." Woolsey opened his mouth to speak, but Ellis put his hand up. "Yes, I know he'll tell you differently. But you know what he's like. You all do. He'll tinker until the last possible moment if you give him the chance, but if you take that chance away, he'll come through. At least, he always has so far."

Woolsey looked for a moment like he was going to keep on arguing, but then he leaned back pushed the folder away from him. "Colonel Carter, it's your call."

"Thank you," she replied. "Colonel Ellis, is there anything else you need before you head out?"

"Nothing that can't wait until we get back."

"Very well." She smiled. "As soon as Angelus is out of your hair, I'll let you get out of ours."

Ellis ran a hand back over his smooth scalp, and gave her a rare grin. "My pleasure, Colonel."

Looking at Angelus, Sam Carter found herself incapable of judging his age.

He was lying on a bed in the infirmary, screens drawn up around him for privacy. He was quite still, his eyes closed, arms folded lightly across his chest in the manner of a Pharaoh. The medical gown he wore hung from him like a robe, and his hair—long, darkly curled, peppered with grey at the temples—spread in a halo over his pillow.

He could have been some ancient king, laid out for burial, if it hadn't been for the blood-volume sensor clipped over one forefinger.

But his face… That was where Carter's intuition failed. His features were oddly fine, the closed eyes deep, the nose long but slender. His skin was pale, but unlined. He could, Carter realized, be any age between thirty and sixty, and she could not trust herself to make a guess which was closer.

Of course, if his claims were true, she could add ten thousand years onto any age she came up with.

"How long has he been like this?" she asked.

Jennifer Keller was on the other side of the bed, looking at Angelus with the same kind of slightly perplexed expression that Carter guessed she'd probably been wearing. "Hmm?"

Carter gestured to the sleeping man. "Has he woken up at all? Said anything?"

"Ah, yeah. He woke up just after he was brought in, asked who I was."

"Anything else?"

Keller put her head to one side. "Yeah, now that you mention it. He asked if he was home."

"*Home…*" Carter barely whispered the word. Of course, to a Lantean, Atlantis would be home. The human expedition occupying it now were only interlopers. Before today, it had seemed completely natural for Carter and her team to be here in this alien city; necessary, even. Now, with the possibility that one of the original owners was here, her whole perspective was threatening to come unglued. Suddenly, she was no longer sure of how she saw herself.

Charitably, maybe she could call herself a guest. From another point of view, though, little more than a trespasser.

If Angelus was truly an Ancient, she wondered, which view would he hold?

She shook herself. "All right, what else can you tell me?"

"Okay, I've run a full series of MRI scans, done blood tests, taken tissue samples… EEG and ECG too." Keller was nodding to herself slightly as she spoke, as if running through a list of her own actions in her mind. "Pretty much everything I can do with what I have here."

Carter hadn't known the woman for long, but could already see that while Keller was a competent doctor, she could be uncertain of herself. "I'm sure you've been thorough," she told her.

Keller half-shrugged. "I've probably forgotten something… Anyway, I've run the results against everything we know about the Lanteans. As far as I can tell without a complete genome-sequence, I don't see anything that disproves his story."

"You're sure?"

"Look, I'll show you." Keller pointed to a nearby table, outside the screens, and when Carter moved over to it she followed her there. "X-Rays here, brainwaves here… I'm still waiting on final analysis of the blood samples, but the gross chemical makeup is a match. See?"

Carter rubbed the back of her own neck, trying to loosen up a niggling stiffness there. "I was right, you've been thorough."

"Thank you."

"So what do you think?"

"Me?" Keller gave that little half-shrug again. "Honest opinion? I think- Oh!"

The woman's hand had flown to her mouth, and she was staring at Angelus.

The man was sitting up.

Carter walked quickly over to him. "How are you feeling?" she said quietly.

Angelus was blinking repeatedly, a slightly puzzled expression on his face. His eyes, now that Carter could see them, were very dark, with almost no difference in color between iris and pupil. "*Luxis est valda perspicuous*... Excuse me, I mean that it's very bright here. The light."

"We can turn them down..." Carter nodded to Keller, who went over to a panel and dimmed the lights. "That better?"

"Yes, thank you." He looked up at Carter. "In answer to your question, I feel quite well. Where is this place?"

"You're in Atlantis. We call this section the infirmary, it's where we heal our sick."

"And injured..." A frown darkened his features for a moment, then he seemed to gather his thoughts. "Please, forgive my rudeness. My name is Angelus."

"I'm Colonel Samantha Carter. Do you remember meeting Doctor Keller?"

"Of course." He bowed slightly to Keller, then fixed Carter with a strange, intense look. "Colonel? Is that a signifier of authority?"

"It's a military rank."

"I see. And is there anyone of higher rank here in Atlantis?"

"No, I'm in charge of this expedition."

Angelus nodded slowly, as if taking the information in. "Very well. In that case, Colonel Samantha Carter, I have a request to make of you."

"Me, personally?"

"As leader, it should be no other."

Carter took a deep breath. "What do you need me to do?"

"I need you, " said Angelus, "to hear my confession."

A second passed, while what Carter had been expecting to hear and what she had actually heard collided in her mind and then dodged around each other for a while. Finally she mastered her surprise enough to say: "Excuse me?"

Angelus got to his feet, and as he did Carter saw that he was very tall. When he reached out and took her hands in his, his skin was cool, and oddly smooth. "You, Colonel," he said quietly, "shall be my confessor. I have done things, things you need to hear about. I must confess to you."

"What?" Carter whispered, in spite of herself. "What did you do?"

The Ancient gave her a sad smile. "I killed my children," he said.

CHAPTER THREE

Suffer the Children

It was dark, and someone was crying for help. He could hear her screams even through the weight of sleep, scratching at him, over and over. But his arms were like lead, too heavy to move, and no matter how he tried he couldn't reach her. He couldn't even shout back, to let her know help was coming.

If he had, it would have been a lie.

Sheppard blinked awake, staring up into the dark. His alarm clock was chirping at him, an insistent two-tone whine, and the display was flashing plaintive green digits into the gloom. Sheppard turned his head, squinted at the numbers, then reached out and hit the alarm button hard.

Harder than he should have done. There was a dull cracking sound from the clock's innards and the numbers went out.

"Snooze," he muttered.

Silence was preferable to the sound of the alarm, but Sheppard was already regretting the destruction. He'd have to requisition a new clock, now, and lie about what had happened to the old one. Still, a story about how the thing had mysteriously fallen off the table and broken sounded better than the truth. He couldn't have told anyone that.

He sat up, shaking his head to clear the last vestiges of dream from his mind. Maybe the next clock he was given wouldn't have an alarm that sounded so much like distant cries.

Or at least not ones in a voice he remembered so well.

Carter was waiting for him outside the conference room. She was looking at her watch as he walked towards her, and for a moment he wondered if he was late. His sleep had certainly been disturbed—he had lost count of the number of times he had woken during the night—but he couldn't remember lapsing back into slumber after he had murdered the alarm. Perhaps, he thought, the clock had exacted a final revenge on him, stealing a few minutes to make him look bad at the briefing.

Then again, he wouldn't have been the only one not at his best. Sam Carter looked as if she hadn't slept at all during the night, or at least had gotten up in even more of a hurry than he had.

"Morning," he said as he drew close.

"Colonel." She smiled, but he could see that her hair was just a little unkempt, odd strands of it sticking out at random angles. The folder under her arm was in a similar state, with printouts and scraps of paper jutting from it.

Sheppard jerked a thumb back over his shoulder. "Look, I'm sorry, but my alarm got busted... I must have—"

"What?" She gave him a blank look, then glanced down at her watch again. "Oh, I see! No, it's not you, it's Rodney."

"Rodney's late?"

"No, he's early. Dragged us all in there twenty minutes ago. I'm surprised he wasn't knocking on your door too."

"He knows what I'd do to him if he did." He frowned at her. "Sam, are you all right?"

"Hm? Yeah, I'm fine. Just a lot to take in, that's all." She gestured towards the doors. "Come on."

"Hey, wait a minute." He put up a hand, peeking slightly around her as he did so. The doors were open, multiple panes hinged apart as one, and he could see part of the conference room past Carter's shoulder. A shadow moved there, changing shape as it crossed the wall, the table... Sheppard felt himself tense for a moment, until he saw that the shadow was just McKay, prowling nervously with a data tablet in one hand.

He felt a chill. Maybe he hadn't shaken the dreams off as thoroughly as he'd hoped. "Listen, this Angelus guy. What's he been saying?"

She held up the folder. "I was, you know, kind of planning on telling you in there..."

"No, this 'killing his kids' thing he's got going on. Is this something we should be hearing?"

Carter took his arm, quite firmly. "It's more complicated than that," she hissed, and propelled him through the doors.

He always forgot how strong she was. Sheppard went into the conference room a little off-balance, almost stumbled, but righted himself just before McKay walked into him.

"Hey," he said, feeling just a bit foolish.

McKay blinked at him. "What kept you?"

"Traffic." Sheppard glanced quickly around the room. As well as McKay, and Carter following him in, Teyla Emmagan was there, perched on a chair at one of the table's flattened corners. Ronon Dex, too, lolling back in his seat with his arms folded.

Angelus was not in the room. Sheppard hadn't really expected him to be, but still found himself strangely relieved. "Hey guys."

"John." Dex nodded a greeting. "I'm glad you're here. McKay's going crazy."

McKay glared. "I am not!"

"Sorry, I meant to say 'driving the rest of us crazy'."

"Play nice, boys," said Carter, sounding tired. "John, sit down and I'll run through this. Rodney, you too."

"Can I, you know, not?" McKay waved his data tablet. "I'm still trying to get my head around some of this and I can do that better on my feet for some reason."

"Rodney?"

"Yes?"

"Sit down. You're driving me crazy."

He sat. Sheppard flashed him a quick grin, then found a chair alongside him and dropped into it. He swung around to face Carter. "So, what's the verdict?"

She slid the folder over to him. "Okay then. Long story short; so far we've got nothing at all to say Angelus is anything other than what he claims."

"Really?" Sheppard realized he was actually surprised at that. He hadn't been consciously expecting Angelus to be a fake, but now that he was being told the opposite, something in him was jolted. He pulled a sheet of printout from the folder, and squinted at the network of colored bars that covered it.

"What's this?"

"Genome comparison," Carter replied. "Rodney, what about the ship?"

"The ship is, well, frustrating." McKay looked sour. "I haven't been able to get into it."

"I thought you opened it up on *Apollo*."

"Yes, yes I did." The scientist stared at his data tablet for a moment, and then dropped it onto the tabletop in disgust. "But I don't know how."

"You don't—"

"It just opened up, okay? I have got no idea what I did to get it to do that… I spent three, no four hours last night poking the damn thing in every conceivable place and all I've got to show for it is sore fingers. So I'm sorry, but for the moment I've got nothing to add to this conversation."

Dex leaned forwards, arms still folded, a predatory grin all over his face. "That's why he's cranky."

"Mm." Sheppard was looking at a side-on X-ray of a human skull, the contrast of the image altered to show soft tissues, nerves, blood vessels. The bones seemed unremarkable, but the space behind the eyes seemed more densely packed than he would have expected, a complicated network of whorls and convolutions.

There was a scratch on the printout, a line of dead pixels diagonally along one corner. Sheppard traced it idly with his fingertip. "That still doesn't explain how he's not ten thousand years old, not ascended and not dead. Ship or no ship, this doesn't add up."

"Well, actually, yes it does," said Carter. "According to what Angelus told me, he would have been in stasis for almost that whole time."

"Stasis?" Sheppard glanced up from the next printout. "Where?"

"He called the planet Eraavis," she replied. "He said it was in a system on the far side of Replicator space."

Sheppard glanced over at Teyla, but the Athosian shook her head. "It is not a world I am familiar with," she told him. "But given its location, perhaps that is not entirely unexpected."

Another scan result, this time in three dimensions, an oblique view across the Ancient's skull and spine. The folds compacted into that skull looked like none Sheppard had ever seen, and the sight disturbed him oddly. He wasn't a squeamish man—he had seen the damage that weapons could do to flesh, more times than he cared to count—but on the whole he preferred people's insides to stay on the inside. Even this image, computer-enhanced and false-colored as it was, gave him a visceral reaction, and he found his attention straying to another scratch in the printout, just like the X-ray. Keller was going to need to change her printer cartridge. "So what was he doing there?"

"Looking after his children."

He put the scan back down. "Are we actually talking about kids here?"

"No." Carter shook her head. "He regards the population of Eraavis as his children."

Sheppard closed the folder and slid the whole thing along to McKay. "Okay, I'm listening."

"Back before the war with the Wraith, Angelus was a scientist. Split his time between physics and some kind of experimental sociology. He says he'd devised a way of increasing a population's intelligence by behavioral influences... What did he call it? 'A programming language that functioned in terms of geosocial interactions'."

McKay snorted. "Does that make *any* sense at all?"

Carter cocked her head to one side. "It wouldn't be the first time an Ancient's tried to play God."

"True. But how long would that take? I mean, even if he was going to artificially advance their intelligence by modifying their brains, it would take, what decades?" McKay shook his head. "And what you're talking about, it seems, I dunno, a lot more subtle..."

"That's why he was in stasis," Sheppard guessed out loud.

"Right," Carter agreed. "He had a kind of lab hidden underground, mainly built around a series of expert systems and a stasis facility. Whenever his computers thought he needed to wake up and screw around with the Eraavi they'd get him online, and the rest of the time he'd be frozen. He was planning this experiment to last about a thousand years, but only to be awake for about fifty of those."

Sheppard whistled. "Talk about being in for the long haul."

"Yeah, but he was a little too successful. He advanced the Eraavi too far, and the Wraith got a scent. He was in stasis when they attacked."

"His children were culled?" whispered Teyla.

"He doesn't know exactly." Carter ran a hand back through her hair. "Whatever happened, it must have been bad. Either his computers decided to keep him frozen until they thought it was safe, or they took a hit and malfunctioned. He was in stasis for almost ten thousand years."

"Holy crap," breathed Sheppard.

"Is that even possible? " McKay asked. "I mean, the Ancients we found on the Aurora had been in stasis for that amount of time, but they'd still aged. They couldn't even survive outside the tubes."

"I don't know," Carter replied. "Maybe he had a more advanced version, or he tinkered with it somehow. He didn't say."

"So that's what he meant by killing his children," said Sheppard. "Advancing them to the point they became Wraith food."

"No, that's the odd part. He says the Eraavi were alive when he got out of the lab. The thing is, that's as far as we got. Keller pretty much threw me out of the infirmary."

"Just when you were getting to the good part," Dex said grimly. "John, what do you think?"

"Sounds crazy enough to be true. Just don't ask me to believe a word of it." He turned back to Carter. "We need the rest of the story. Once we've got that, maybe we can start checking it out."

"Agreed." She stood up. "Rodney, I need you back with the ship. Anything you can tell me about it, even from the outside, could help. If you can figure out a way to get back into it that'd be great too, but start off with the broad strokes. Teyla?"

"Yes, Colonel?"

"Get together with Ronon. See if you can't get a lead on the Eraavi. Somebody must have heard of them. And John? You're with me. It'll take two of us to get past Keller."

There was a series of self-contained living spaces a couple of levels under the infirmary, not entirely unlike the kind of rooms one might find in a small hotel. Like most of the city's components, their original function remained a mystery, but Doctor Keller had recently extended the medical team's territory downwards to included them. Since then, the rooms had proven very effective quarters for those who might need quick access to medical facilities, but yet didn't warrant a bed in the infirmary. Or, in the case of Angelus, people who required a comfortable and closely-monitored form of house arrest.

There were two marines posted on the door. Sheppard knew them; Kaplan and DeSalle. Perhaps not the pair Sheppard would have chosen, but competent enough.

They snapped to attention as he and Carter arrived, but Sheppard gestured at them to relax. "At ease, guys," he said, then nodded at the door. "How's he been?"

"Quiet, sir," Kaplan told him, pushing his cap back on his head. "Really quiet."

"Yeah?"

Concern must have shown on his face, because Kaplan immediately tried to reassure him. "It's okay, sir. He's wearing biomonitors, so if there was anything wrong Doctor Keller would know about it. But no, so far he's not caused any trouble."

"Glad to hear it." He looked over to Carter. "Shall we?"

In response, she waved her hand over the lock control. The door sighed open, and Sheppard saw Angelus for the first time.

There was a big window in the far wall of the apartment, an asymmetrical panel of something that wasn't quite glass, with a sprawl of the city's towers and spines rearing behind it. The Ancient stood silhouetted there, a tall, slender figure, his back to the door. He had one hand raised, the long fingers pressed flat against the window, and if he heard the door open he didn't respond to it.

Carter went in first. "Angelus?"

"I had forgotten what it was like," he breathed. "The city. I never thought I would forget this, of all things…" He turned, a lost expression on his face. "How could I have forgotten?"

"You've been away," she replied, sounding wary.

"I have. But still…" He looked back over his shoulder, as if to get one last glimpse of the towers ranged out behind him, then seemed to steady himself. "Forgive me, Colonel. I'm proving a poor guest."

"Angelus, I'd like you to meet Lieutenant Colonel John Sheppard."

The Ancient bowed slightly. "So many new faces. Welcome, Lieutenant Colonel."

"Nice to finally meet you," said Sheppard. He kept his voice neutral, and didn't move any closer to the Ancient than he had to. It was easier to gain an initial impression of someone, he always found, from a slight distance.

Angelus was very still; that was Sheppard's first thought. Even when he had turned around he had done so with the minimum of effort—not so much a grace, but a kind of efficiency, as though he was unwilling to waste even the slightest movement. He wore a long robe of what looked like pale gold, and the reflections from this seemed to pull all the color from his skin. That, and his stillness, gave Sheppard the unnerving impression he was speaking not to a man but to a statue, all white gold and ivory.

His dark hair and eyes were the only contrast about him.

"I'm sure you have many questions," said Angelus. He gestured to a set of padded forms nearby. "Would you like to sit down?"

"Not right now."

A brief smile crossed the Ancient's lips. "Of course. Doing so would restrict access to your sidearm."

"Hey," started Carter. "He didn't mean—"

"Please, Colonel. I fully understand, and I bear John Sheppard no malice for his mistrust." Angelus spread his hands. "No physical test you could subject me to will be exhaustive.

My story cannot be verified. I am sure there are many species in this galaxy capable of pretending to be something they are not. In all truth, why *should* I be trusted?"

Clever, thought Sheppard. "Look, either we find a way of proving you are who you say you are, or we're just gonna be doing this dance forever."

"Agreed. So, how can I assist you?"

"Well, let's start with the rest of your story. What happened when you woke up?"

"Ah," said Angelus. "That."

There was a period of silence. The Ancient was simply standing, outlined in light from the window, his gaze seemingly fixed on a point midway to the floor. It wasn't until Sheppard looked over at Carter, hoping for some signal as how to proceed, that he spoke again.

"You understand," he said, his voice barely louder than a whisper, "that this is... Difficult. During my time with the Eraavi, I..." He paused, took a breath. "I became very fond of them."

"Your children," Sheppard prompted.

"Yes, that is how I began to think of them. More and more as my time with them went on. I must admit, when the experiment began, that is all they were to me... An experiment. A complex system on which to test my theories. But it didn't take me too many years before they became something far, far more."

He half-turned back to the window, and stood gazing over his shoulder at the city's spires. "I think that was, partly, why my guiding hand became known. My intention was to remain completely hidden from the test subjects—to do anything other would have compromised the purity of the experiment. Over the years, however... As I guided them through the earliest algorithms, I found I could not keep such a distance."

"How did they regard you?" Carter asked him. "Did they resent you?"

He turned his haunted eyes to her. "They called me Father."

"Okay," said Sheppard, slowly. "So you realized your experiment wasn't valid anymore, but you stayed around anyway. Did you think they needed you that badly, or did you just get used to the adoration?"

"I don't know. Honestly, I do not. I had begun to ask myself the same question… My own motives had become a mystery to me, and there is no comfort in that. I had decided to resolve that question when I was next roused from stasis, but of course I never got the opportunity. The Wraith robbed me of it."

"They must have hit the Eraavi pretty hard."

Angelus smiled grimly. "It is a matter of some pride to me that they survived at all. Suffice to say that when I finally escaped my stasis chamber, things on Eraavis were very different."

"We've seen some post-Wraith cultures," Carter began. "I know—"

"Colonel, you know *nothing!*" the Ancient snapped. He spun to face her, his face dark with sudden rage. "You have seen cultures beaten into submission by the Wraith, not steeled against them. You have seen primitives, no better than cattle, not a surge in art and culture and technology… You were not there, Colonel Samantha Carter, and you do *not* know!"

Sheppard had taken a step back, and his hand, unconsciously, had dropped to the butt of his pistol. "Easy, tiger," he warned, keeping his voice flat and calm. "You're right, we weren't there. We need you to tell us."

Angelus glared at him, dark eyes flashing beneath his brows. And then, abruptly, he was still again. "I apologize," he said, bowing to Carter very slightly. "That was unforgivable.

"John Sheppard, I *will* tell you. Ah, if only I could have shown you… There were cities, you see, cities to rival Atlantis itself." He closed his eyes, raised his face to some unseen wonder. "The Wraith had blasted the Eraavi back to the invention of the mud brick, but over the millennia they had recovered, and used what I had taught them. Cities, the like of which you have never witnessed, and every tower and garden and library and home built utterly below ground. They had extended existing cave systems, digging deep and far… When I awoke, there was barely a mountain on Eraavis that didn't hide a city beneath its peak."

"That's incredible," muttered Sheppard.

"Truly. And they were not ignorant of the Wraith's danger, either. They had developed a sacrificial culture, entire villages on the surface, living as though they knew nothing of the cities under their feet. When the Wraith came, time after time, they found scattered groups of primitives, subsistence farms, iron tools. They never saw the teeming millions, just the devoted few…" His eyes, open again now, gleamed. "This is what I found when I awoke. If my experiments had still been a priority, they would have been validated beyond my imagination."

"What did you do?" asked Carter, sounding a little stunned.

"At first? I walked the land."

"Meaning…"

"I spent ten years walking among the Eraavi," Angelus replied. "Learning their history, their culture… I had arrived with every intention of building a society in my own image, but I now found myself exploring a whole new one."

"That must have been amazing…" Carter pulled a seat close and sat down carefully. "You must have been very proud."

"I think I was beyond pride at that point, Colonel." Perhaps following Carter's lead, Angelus sat too, perching on the edge of the bed. Sheppard watched him sit down, judged how quickly the Ancient could get to Carter if he went for her, calculating how many shots he could get off if that happened. *Enough.*

"When was this?" he asked. "Our time."

"I finished my travels a year ago, John Sheppard. Believe me, I could have spent my whole life travelling there, and would have done had I not learned two things. Firstly, that I had been remembered. The Eraavi still revered their Father."

"And second?"

"That the Wraith were coming back." Angelus raised his hands, a strange gesture, and sat looking at them for a moment. "The Eraavi were too numerous, I could see that. If there was another cull, they might not be able to remain hidden. Their expansion and that of the Wraith were on a collision course. Sooner or later, all this wonder would be brought to ruin."

Something in his voice lodged a shard of ice under Sheppard's sternum. "What did you do?"

"I did what any loving father would have done," the man replied. "I gave them the means to destroy the Wraith."

"We need to get back to IOA," Sheppard told Carter a few minutes later, as they walked back towards the tower. "Jesus, if they knew about this—"

"If they knew about this they'd throw eight kinds of fit," Carter said quickly. "Listen, John. Be careful about who you tell for the moment, okay? Believe me, IOA could really go the wrong way on this one. We're going to need confirmation at the very least."

"How are we going to get that?"

"Give me time."

"Sam, if what he told us is true we might not *have* any time!"

She stopped, and put her hands up placatingly. "Look, we've been over this with Ellis, and the situation hasn't changed. If they knew he was here, they'd be all over us already. If we get this wrong, shoot our mouths off to IOA before we've got all the facts, then yeah, we could find ourselves up to our ears in bad guys before we could spit. So we've got to be careful."

Sheppard pointed back towards Angelus' room. "Like he was careful?"

"He didn't know about the Replicators. How could he have done? If he did, maybe he wouldn't have been so quick to do what he did. But one way or the other, John, we need to know."

He took a deep breath, tried to calm the angry slamming of his heart. "Okay. Okay, maybe you're right. Question is, what do we do now?"

"We get back with the others, tell them what we know and see if they've gotten any results. And we get a message to the *Apollo*. We'll need Ellis on this one."

"Right." He put his hands to the back of his neck, fingers linked, trying to stretch out a sudden knot of tension there. "I'll light a fire under 'em."

"Good." She gave him a quick, grin. "And try not to panic."

Despite himself, he chuckled. "Sure. Hey, Sam?"

"Hm?"

"You don't think it could have worked, do you? What he was trying to do?"

She shrugged. "I have no idea. But that's one of the reasons I don't want IOA in on this yet. If they even get a taste of this…"

"They'll be all over us, I get it." He stretched his arms out, fingers still woven, and cracked his knuckles. "Okay, let's see how far across the hangar I need to kick Rodney."

CHAPTER FOUR

The Sixth Circle

A pollo jumped into the M4T system with shields set to maximum, all forward railguns live and eight missiles, including a pair of tactical nukes, hot in their tubes and ready to fire. Even though the Replicator ship he had encountered the previous day had been an easy kill, Ellis was in no mood to take chances.

He was on the edge of his seat, quite literally, as the ship broke out of hyperspace. Despite the inexorable downward slope the tunnel effect seemed to have these days, he had fixed his attention on it for the past several minutes, his eyes narrowed, staring down that silver-blue throat as if he could force himself, by sheer will, to see what lay beyond. Foolish, he knew, but if there was anything waiting for him at the other end, he didn't want to blink and miss it.

There wasn't. *Apollo* lurched out of hyperspace and into still, silent darkness.

"Stay frosty," Ellis growled, glaring out at the starfield. "We thought it was gonna be quiet last time, too. Meyers?"

"Yessir?"

"Full sweep. Deacon, shut down the main drives. Thrusters only while we try and shed some heat."

Deacon tapped at his control board, and Ellis heard the faint grumble of the drives attenuate as they were throttled back. *Apollo* still had plenty of forward momentum, even after leaving most of its velocity in hyperspace, and would continue to coast forwards forever until some other force was applied to it. That suited Ellis just fine for now: the heat from the main drives would light *Apollo* up like a torch against the freezing background temperatures of space, and while the battlecruiser could never shed enough thermal energy to become invisible, every degree lost could be an advantage, however slight.

Trying to stealth any kind of ship without a cloaking field was damn near impossible; Ellis was all too aware of that. But he wasn't going to advertise his presence in the system any more than he could help. Besides, if trouble did arise, *Apollo*'s main engines could be brought back online within moments.

"Meyers, how's that sweep coming along?"

"Still building up a picture, sir, but no significant returns yet. So far, it looks like we're all alone out here."

"Just how I like it. Okay, let's get McKay's program running."

Behind him, two technicians began the process of loading Rodney McKay's guidance program into *Apollo*'s computers. The stealth sensors, still chilling on their racks down in the bomb bay, needed to be dropped at a very precise location in the system. Their operational range was vast, several Astronomical Units in radius, but the arrays needed to mimic the orbits of existing debris. McKay's program would, the scientist had claimed, take charge of *Apollo*'s own sensors, map out a gravitational diagram of the system in precise detail, and work out exactly where to drop the sensors. McKay had boasted of the program being accurate to within ten kilometers, but Ellis wasn't buying that. Still, on an interplanetary scale, even distances in the thousands of kilometers became vanishingly small.

The sensors would be dropped in the right place, he had no doubt, or would find their way there.

Within a few moments, Deacon's control board chirruped, and a tactical display flowered open on his centre screen. Similar readouts sprang to life on the weapons panel, too. "*Damn*," said Ellis. "That guy's scary. Okay, people, looks like we have our drop point. How long to get there on thrusters?"

Deacon ran through a swift set of calculations on his panel. "About two hours. We'll need to swing around the second moon to grab enough extra velocity, but that will set us up for dropping the sensors at the right speed, too. We'll only need to make a couple of course corrections before we set them free."

Ellis nodded slowly. "Outstanding… Helm, let's do this."

"Into the hands of Rodney McKay," he heard Deacon mutter, "I commend my spirit." And with that, the thrusters began to fire.

Just as predicted, the journey took over two hours. With Deacon monitoring the ship's course, Meyers keeping a watchful eye out for potential threats and the rest of the bridge crew making sure *Apollo* and the program kept in synchronization, Ellis allowed himself the luxury of taking some of that time away from the bridge.

Touring the ship was a habit of his, but one he seldom got to indulge in. *Apollo* was a big vessel, over one hundred and fifty meters from prow sensors to drive bells, and even to walk from one end to the other could take more than an hour. Had the distance been in a straight line, Ellis could have jogged it in a couple of minutes, but the interior of the ship was almost unimaginably complex. Split into dozens of rooms and compartments, connected by hundreds of meters of corridors, gangways, service ducts and bulkheads, *Apollo*'s innards formed such a maze that new recruits to the ship were given photocopied maps as soon as they set foot aboard.

To be seen actually using one was to invite ridicule, but they were a fact of life, nonetheless. Ellis still had his, somewhere, as a souvenir. Nowadays, of course, he could have found his way around the ship blindfold.

Given the situation, Ellis decided to restrict his wanderings to the rearmost section of *Apollo*—that way, he could be back on the bridge in the shortest time should anything warrant his attention. He stopped off at the wardroom to grab a mug of coffee, setting the dispenser there to produce a brew both darker and sweeter than should technically have been possible, then took off down one of the aft gangways. One that would lead him, via a series of other compartments, to the 302 bays.

He was halfway there when he realized there was something wrong with the ship.

At first, he couldn't even be sure what made him think so. The deck seemed steady under his feet, the constant background noise of the air-circulation and heating systems was uninterrupted, and there were no warnings or alerts. In fact, for a few minutes, Ellis remained convinced that his intuition was deceiving him. If there really was something not right with *Apollo*, surely he would have been informed by now?

It wasn't until he was making his way through one of the aft service areas that he discovered what had tipped him off. It wasn't something that could be easily seen in the open gangways or the more brightly lit sections, and even in the relative dimness of the service compartment it was hard to be sure. Ellis stood quite still, coffee mug in hand, for a long minute before he was certain.

The lights were flickering.

The flicker was amazingly subtle; not constant or obvious, but a momentary variation in brightness occurring once every forty seconds or so. Almost impossible to see. If Ellis hadn't known the ship as well as he did, if he hadn't made himself learn every quirk of its design and every idiosyncrasy of its operation, he would never have noticed it.

But yes, there it was again. A fluttering dip in brightness, then a slight surge, then normality again. Not random, but regular. He reached up with his free hand and keyed his headset. "Meyers?"

"*Sir?*"

"How's everything up there?"

There was a slight pause, probably while she checked her readouts. "*All quiet, sir.*"

"Good... Look, Meyers, get one of the techs to run a power diagnostic."

"*Will do, Colonel. Is there a problem?*"

He took a gulp of the coffee, but it didn't taste all that good any more. "Looks like an intermittent fault in the lighting system. Might be nothing, but if there's a pulse in the power grid I want to know about it."

"*I'll get somebody on it right away, Sir. Will you be long coming back?*"

"No," said Ellis. "I won't be long at all."

True to her word, Meyers had the results of a full diagnostic check on the grid ready for Ellis when he returned to the bridge.

There were no faults. The grid was totally clean.

Someone less sure of himself might have put the flickering lights down to imagination, or set the problem on the back burner until a less critical time, but Ellis didn't do that kind of thing. He was acutely aware of just how dangerous an environment space could be, and even the thousands of tons of weapons, armor, systems and personnel that made up a ship like *Apollo* could be brought low in a moment if even the slightest fault wasn't checked out immediately. Ellis studied the diagnostic for a while, then decided to ignore it and do things the old fashioned way. He called up a team of engineers and told them to deal with it.

The next hour passed quickly. *Apollo* swung around the second moon on the course Deacon had plotted, smoothly transferring a fraction of the planetoid's momentum to the battlecruiser. It was, in accordance with the physical laws of the universe, an equal swap: the moon slowed down while *Apollo* sped up. Of course, the moon was millions of times more massive than the ship, so while *Apollo* almost doubled its velocity, the impact on the moon was all but undetectable. Perhaps the day it finally surrendered to the gravity of its parent world had been brought forward by an hour or so, but Ellis knew he would be dust a billion years before that mattered to anyone at all.

McKay's program warned them in good time before the sensors were due to be launched. Back when the system was being designed there had been talk of an automatic activation, but Ellis had vetoed that without a moment's hesitation. He didn't mind McKay's computer program letting him know what should be done and when, but there was no way he was going to let it take over his ship. Ellis believed, very firmly, in the human element.

Which is why it was Major Emma Meyers who fired the first sensor array out into space. Ellis watched it go from the command throne, on a tablet computer slaved to cameras in the bomb bay. He saw the rack descend into position, slow on its hydraulic rams, and the clustered sensors dart free as McKay's program sounded its alarms.

Moments later, they were gone from sight, too small to make out with their matte surfaces absorbing the meager starlight. The tiny thruster burns that would spread them out into an array thousands of kilometers across would take many hours to complete, but *Apollo* couldn't stay around that long. Ellis had a report to make, and for that he needed a Stargate.

"Phase one is complete," he told Sam Carter, just over an hour later. "You should start getting test returns from the array within a day or so."

"That's good to know, Colonel. I'll make sure we're listening for that."

Apollo was in a new system, one several light years from M4T. Ellis had chosen it quite carefully; it was reasonably far from any predicted Replicator or Wraith activity, hopefully distant enough to avoid any confrontations. But it was also part of the Stargate matrix.

Although the battlecruiser was fitted with a subspace communications system, Ellis had decided at the beginning of the mission that he would not be using it. Subspace communications could be detected more easily than burst transmissions through a Stargate, and M4T was too close to the enemy battle lines for him to chance that. Retreating to a safe distance and using a local Stargate was the safer option by far—he'd not open subspace communications unless absolutely necessary.

Ellis had hoped that negotiations with the local populace for use of their gate would be swift. Despite what some of the Pegasus expedition seemed to think, neither he nor anyone else had a right to simply beam down to the surface of an alien world and activate a Stargate. However, as it turned out, there were no negotiations to make. The landing party reported no signs of life when they arrived, and were able to dial back to Atlantis unmolested. Still, Ellis remained nervous, and found himself trying to keep the conversation as brief as possible. The sooner *Apollo* was away from here, the better.

The problem with the lights had unsettled him, far more than it should have done.

"So far we've detected no enemy activity, and apart from

a slight technical problem we're good to go here, Colonel. I'd like to be underway as quickly as possible."

There was a pause. "*What problem?*" she asked.

"It's nothing to worry about. Minor pulse in the power grid, but I've got a team on it."

"*Would it stop you making a slight detour?*"

Ellis rolled his eyes, and tried not to sigh audibly into the pickup. He should have known. "What kind of detour?"

"*We've traced our new guest's point of origin,*" she said, and he could hear the wariness in her voice. "*There are some elements of his story which we're having a hard time getting to grips with.*"

"And?"

"*And we need visual confirmation. Colonel, it shouldn't take much time—I'll upload the jump solution directly to your helm terminal, but trust me, it's not too far from where you are right now. I just need you to drop out of hyperspace in low orbit and make a cursory scan of the planet.*"

Ellis glanced over at Meyers, but she just gave him a kind of facial shrug. "Can't you send someone through the gate?" he asked Carter.

"*Not any more. Colonel, I wouldn't ask if it wasn't important. But believe me, this is vital. We need to know what happened down there.*"

"The more I hear about this, the less I like it." He sat back. "Very well, upload that solution. I'll have Deacon check it out, but if there's no problem we'll jump there as soon as I get my landing party back."

"*Thank you.*" She sounded genuinely relieved. What was going on back there? "*Lower your firewalls and I'll send the data through.*"

The audio feed shut off. Ellis heard a series of faint sounds from Deacon's board as the hyperspace flightplan was uploaded, then a chime that meant the firewalls were back up. There was almost no chance that anyone would be able to tamper with the radio signal from Atlantis, but almost no chance was not the same as none at all. The Replicators, machines themselves, were masters of electronic warfare, and there was no telling just what the Wraith's biomechanical data systems were capable of. A piggybacked computer virus could be as deadly a weapon as a railgun or a nuke if it was allowed through *Apollo*'s defenses.

The thought didn't give Ellis much comfort. Not a lot did, in these troubled times. "Well?"

Deacon tapped a few keys on his board, then frowned and pushed his spectacles a little higher on his nose. "M19-371," he replied. "Colonel Carter was right, it's not too far out of our way. But it is on the other side of Replicator space."

Ellis stared at him. "We'd need to go through the Replicator battlelines?"

"No, not as such. This jump solution's been worked out pretty thoroughly." Deacon nodded. "I think we'll be okay."

Ellis could feel his teeth clamping together. "'Slight detour' my ass," he muttered. "Okay, plot it out on the tac map. If—and I mean *if*—I like the look of it, we'll go on Carter's goddamn goose chase. In the meantime, call the landing party. I want them off that rock and shipboard right now."

Much to Ellis' chagrin, the jump solution was sound. He could find no real objection to the diversion, or at least none he could safely vocalize. He wasn't sure if the crew would think less of him if he did express his disquiet, but now was not the time to find out. Instead, he gave the order for *Apollo* to re-enter hyperspace, and tried to put his nameless fears to the back of his mind.

The engineering team he had sent to work on the power grid came back during the flight, reporting that they could find nothing at all amiss with the generators, the power distribution grid, or any of the associated batteries or capacitor banks. Ellis could do nothing but accept their findings—he trusted his engineers implicitly, and if they said there was nothing wrong with those systems then the fault, if there was one, lay elsewhere. Somewhat against his instincts, Ellis was forced to put the problem aside, and told the engineers to stand down, with the proviso that they monitored the grid at regular intervals.

Meyers spent some time reconfiguring the ship's sensors for ground analysis, while Deacon ran simulations of the course home. Carter would need to know Apollo's findings as soon as possible, but although M19 had originally been part of the Stargate matrix she seemed certain this was no longer true. Ellis, despite his feelings about the woman, saw no reason to doubt her on that, and had Deacon plot a jump solution that would allow them to call back to Atlantis without raising the wrath of either of the two great serpents.

He could only guess what the map of those two twisting battle lines looked like now, and how many systems had drowned under those bright splashes of monstrous blood.

It was a disturbing notion, and one that threatened to bring back the disquiet that had troubled him earlier. He shook it away. "Deacon, what's our ETA?"

"We're four minutes out, sir."

"Right. Meyers, fire up the sensors as soon as we break out. Tactical sweep first, then orbit-to-ground as soon as we know we're not going to get jumped on. Helm, have we got an outward-bound yet?"

"It's queued up and ready to run, sir."

"Good work." He sat back in the command throne, reached down to grip the seat arms. The solidity of the metal there, the cool, hard edges under his palms, seemed to steady him. Steel was something he could rely on; smooth tempered steel and trinium armor and the cold iron ingots in the magazines of the railguns. That was something he could put his faith in, right there. It was all the strength he needed, and his fears retreated in the face of it.

"One minute and counting," said Deacon.

"Weapons hot," said Ellis calmly. "Shields to max."

"Forty seconds- What the hell?"

Something on Deacon's board was buzzing, a low, insistent drone. "Helm, what am I hearing?"

"Glitch in hyperspace navigation," Deacon said quickly. He was already tapping out command chain, fingers flying over the keys. "I'm compensating... There!"

The drone stopped abruptly. Ellis glared at Deacon. "A glitch?"

"Minor, sir. A percent off on the timing... Breakout in three, two, one."

The hyperspace tunnel grew an end, a disc of black nothingness that raced towards *Apollo*, flared, and vanished into darkness. Ellis felt the deck shudder slightly under his feet as the ship re-entered normal space. "Check our position. Run a stellar overlay, make sure we are where we're supposed to be."

"Sir?" Meyers had turned towards him. "Tactical sweep shows us clear. Shall I go to ground-sensing?"

"Wait until we know there's some ground to sense. Deacon, don't make me come over there…"

"It's fine, Colonel," Deacon shoved his glasses back so hard the frame squeaked. "We're right on the money. Just a fractional rotational anomaly, that's all. I'm correcting that now."

"Are we in orbit around M19-371?"

"Should be coming into view now, sir."

Sure enough, the starfield outside the viewport was turning. *Apollo* had come out of hyperspace in the right place, but tilted about twenty degrees off the ecliptic with a sizable yaw. To get the ship back on course Deacon was swinging the ship to starboard and executing a long-axis roll at the same time—the visual effect, with no sense of movement to back it up, was mildly disorientating. "Meyers, factor the rotation in and begin ground-scanning."

"I just have…" She sounded hesitant, which wasn't like Meyers at all. Ellis saw her lean towards Deacon. "Kyle, are you sure we're in the right place?"

"Sure, why?"

She shook her head. "This can't be right. Colonel, didn't Atlantis say this world was inhabited?"

"They said it was where Angelus came from."

"It can't be," she breathed. "It can't be."

Ellis opened his mouth to ask her what she was babbling about, but then the planet rolled into view, and he forgot what he was going to say. The strength he took from steel faded, lost in the sight.

He stood up. "My God," he whispered. "It's on fire."

There might have been a time when the planet could have supported life. According to the readouts on Meyers' tactical display its gravity was near Earth normal, its rotational period at roughly thirty hours, its orbit in the sweet spot between the boiling and freezing points of liquid water. There could have been life on M19-371, once. It might have been a garden world, a paradise.

There was no way to tell. The planet was a charred ball, blackened and blasted, cracked through with threads of livid red. There were no land-masses he could see, no polar caps, no green, no blue. Just black and gray and the flickering, liquid orange of distant magma.

"No breathable atmosphere," Meyers said dully. "Traces of oxygen in the upper layers, but not much. Nitrogen, carbon dioxide, methane, some exotics. Mostly particulate carbon."

"Radiation?"

"Off the scale."

"Analyze it." Ellis stared down at the planet, watching black clouds the size of continents roil sluggishly beneath him. Where the clouds were parted he saw spots of dull light, overlapping rings, hundreds of them. Craters, no longer burning but glowing hot, vomiting up more smoke into the dead, poisoned air.

"Sir?" That was Meyers again. "I've got the radiation signature."

"Spit it out."

She took a deep breath. "Asuran weapons fire, Colonel. It was the Replicators."

"Tell me one thing, Colonel Carter," Ellis asked a short time later. "Were you expecting that?"

He heard her sigh. "*No. Angelus told us the planet had been attacked, everyone killed, but that level of destruction is just...*" She trailed off.

"What would make them do that?"

"*Hit it so hard? My guess is they discovered most of the cities were underground, hidden from the Wraith, and just pulverized the crust to make sure they got everybody.*"

Ellis leaned back in the command throne, covering his eyes with his hands for a moment before wiping them down his face. He felt tired, exhausted, his eyeballs gritty and his neck muscles shiveringly tense. The warmth of his hands over his eyes for a moment helped a little, but that wasn't the only reason they had found their way there. There was a part of him that wanted to shut out the image of that burning world, even though it was long gone from the viewport. He could still see the clouds, the craters, the glowing fracture lines. It was all there, behind his eyes.

He'd even authorized use of subspace comms in order to make this particular report. He needed to speak of this quickly, as if doing so would somehow lessen its horror. The sooner it was gone from him, the better.

"No, I meant why did they hit it at all?"

"Oh, I see…" Carter paused, as if gathering her thoughts. *"That's the part we needed confirmation on."*

"But it was to get Angelus."

"Partly. From what he told us, he'd realized that the Wraith couldn't be fooled by the Eraavi much longer, so he decided to give his children a fighting chance. He started designing a weapon; we don't know quite what, something extremely powerful. Not nuclear weapons, something far worse than that. The way he was talking—before he clammed up again—he didn't seem to think that hive ships would have been a real threat any more."

The military side of Abe Ellis perked up at that. "Really? Are you sure he didn't say anything else?"

"Yes, I'm sure. Thing is, he never got to finish it. The Asurans must have picked up some kind of energy signature from his tests and realized what he was doing. Maybe they got so freaked out by it that they decided to burn the entire planet and everyone on it."

"And our boy Angelus just made it out, huh?" Ellis folded his arms. "All on his own."

"The Eraavi weren't spacefarers. That kind of research must have been forbidden—it would have attracted the Wraith faster than anything."

"Makes sense." As much as anything did any more, Ellis thought glumly. "Okay, there's nothing more we can do here. If there's no objection, I'll take *Apollo* on to the next drop point."

"No objection at all, Colonel. The sooner those sensors are online the safer I'll feel."

Ellis cut the connection from his end. He'd given up on feeling safe. "Deacon?"

"Course is queued up and ready, sir."

"That's good to hear. Okay, get us back in the pipe. And then stand down—you've been on for two consecutive watches already. That means you too, Meyers."

"Yes sir, if you insist. Hyperdrive is ready on your command."

Ellis nodded. "Do it."

In front of the viewscreen, a spot of silver-blue light appeared, raced towards the ship and spread open like a maw to engulf it. Ellis caught a glimpse of the stars at the edges of the hyperspace vortex streak into comet-tails of light as the ship accelerated out of the normal universe, but they were gone in an instant. Within a few seconds, *Apollo* was diving down the endless blue tunnel once more.

"All systems optimal," Deacon reported. "Estimated time to the next drop point is five hours seventeen."

Ellis stood up and stretched. His first instinct was to tell Deacon not to rush, to throttle the hyperdrive back a few degrees and let the crew have a little downtime, but he suppressed that urge as soon as he felt it. Atlantis needed those sensors, and fast. Besides, Meyers and Deacon were not the only bridge crew he had. They had stayed on watch of their own accord, and he had let them out of a desire for continuity on the mission, but they would need to be relieved soon anyway. Their replacements could handle the next watch or two.

"I'll be in my quarters," he muttered. "Any change in status, you know the drill."

"Colonel?"

"Deacon, I told you. Get some rest."

"Sir, I would. But—"

"What?" Ellis turned towards him. "But what?"

Deacon swallowed, staring at his board. "There's been a change in status."

Ellis was at his side in two strides. "Show me."

"Here." The helmsman pointed at a set of figures on his board, then used the keyboard to bring up a second set. As soon as the new digits appeared, Ellis could see they were deviating.

"We're off-course?"

"Not as such. All I've brought up here is the time until we're due to break out, accurate to a thousandth of a second. Obviously that's not nearly accurate enough, but all I need to do is see it, you know? The nav system brings us out at the right time and place."

Ellis frowned. "But the time you just put up is the real time?"

"According to the ship's clock, yes. There's a compound error that's causing a disparity between the two countdowns. I can compensate at the moment, but the bigger it gets the harder it'll be to keep on top of it. At this rate we could break out too early or too late, and that could be, well…" He pushed his glasses up. "Not good."

"So what's causing it?"

"I have no idea." Deacon slid his seat back on its rails and stood up. "Sir, I'd like permission to head down to the control core. If there's a fault, it's more likely to be in one of the primary systems, given that none of the secondaries seem to have picked up on it."

"Fine. Get down there and see if you can clear this up before we break out. I'd hate to have to dry-dock the ship right in the middle of all this." He stepped back to let Deacon go past, then noticed Helen Sharpe, *Apollo*'s Third Officer, put her head through the aft hatch. Deacon stopped at the hatchway, and there was a swift conversation that involved Deacon pointing at the helm and Sharpe nodding a lot. Ellis couldn't hear what they were saying, but he knew a situation update when he saw one. A moment later Deacon ducked out of sight, and Sharpe walked quickly onto the bridge and up to Ellis. "Third Officer reporting for duty, sir."

"Deacon told you about the anomaly?"

"He did."

"Good. Let me know if there's any change in that glitch." He went back to the command throne as she sat down, and dropped wearily into it. Meyers turned to give him a quizzical look, but he just shook his head at her, very slightly. There was no way he would go back to his quarters when there was a situation, even if it was just a data error.

He saw Meyers dip her head and speak briefly into her headset, then continue what she was doing. A few minutes later, one of the bridge techs brought him a mug of coffee.

Ellis didn't normally like food or drink on the bridge, but in this case he was prepared to make an exception. The caffeine boost was extremely welcome—no substitute for a couple of hours sleep, of course, but in the circumstances it was the best he could hope for. After a few gulps of the stuff, he almost started to relax a little.

He should have known that was a mistake, letting his attention wander.

There was a sudden, urgent buzzing from the helm, followed instantly by a muttered curse from Sharpe. Ellis set the mug down on the deck and leaned towards her. "Status."

"The glitch just jumped by a factor of ten," she reported curtly, already working at the keyboard. "I've got something else… Hold on… Dammit!"

"What?"

"Power slide. Colonel, if I can't get on top of this we could lose hyperdrive."

Ellis keyed his headset. "Deacon, what's the situation down there?"

There was no answer, just a rustle of static. "Deacon? Major Deacon, report immediately!"

This time there was a response, although not in words. It was faint, softer than the static; a sigh or whisper drawn out longer than any throat could sustain. There was a metallic, ghostly quality to it that made Ellis' skin crawl. "What the hell?" he breathed.

After that, silence. Ellis gave up and switched channel. "Security, get a team to the control core. Locate Major Deacon immediately."

"Colonel?" That was Sharpe, sounding something close to terrified. "I think I'm going to lose this."

"Stay on it, Captain."

"I'm not sure…" Her fingers were rattling off the keys, insect-quick. "It's jumping, there doesn't seem to be any pattern. If the error gets past a certain point the core—"

Apollo dropped out of hyperspace.

The breakout was unscheduled, uncontrolled, and sickeningly violent. Instead of the usual gentle lurch there was a massive impact, a twisting, as if the entire bridge had been hit off-center by something huge and impossibly fast. There was an awful noise, stunningly loud, a shriek of overstressed metal, and the ship seemed to drop away like an airliner in turbulence, the deck falling several meters before rebounding heavily back upwards. Ellis felt it come up and hit the soles of his boots, jarring his spine and almost sending him clear out of the command throne.

There was a second, grinding jolt, this time in a direction he couldn't even name, and then it was over. The ship was still.

Ellis opened his eyes. He hadn't been aware of shutting them, but now—after some frantic blinking to clear the sparks from his vision—he could see in just what a mess the impact had left the bridge.

The lights had dimmed to half-brightness, but something behind him was sparking, the fitful bursts of light making the whole scene even more chaotic. He saw Helen Sharpe getting up, steadying herself on the helm console—she must have been flung right out of her seat. Meyers had been sent in the same direction, but the edge of her console had gotten in her way. She was slumped over it, unmoving.

Groans and curses sounded from behind him, over the hateful spitting of whatever electrical failure was sparking back there. Ellis turned his head, wincing at the pain in his spine, and saw people getting up. There didn't seem to be any serious injuries, but everyone had been hammered off their feet.

"That," he grated, "was one bitch of a breakout."

"I'm sorry, sir," Sharpe replied, holding her head. She sat back down in her seat and slid it forwards. "The cumulative error got too much for the core to handle, and it shut down the hyperdrive."

"Yeah, I know what happened." He straightened himself up, rolled his head around a couple of times to free up his neck and shoulders, then got up to see to Meyers. "But it still shouldn't have been that hard."

"That was the error. Core gave us what it thought was a smooth exit, but it's timing was already way off. Charlie foxtrot, sir."

"You got that right."

Meyers was coming around, grimacing. "Whatahell?" she slurred.

"Take it easy," Ellis told her. "Wait until the medics get up here."

"No time," she groaned, and slumped back into her seat. "They'll be busy. What happened to the lights?"

"Not sure. Can you run a sweep with this power?"

"Gimme a minute."

"Outstanding." He patted her shoulder, gently, then moved back across to Sharpe. "Anything?"

"Not much. Half the systems are down… Anything that requires fine-sensing is out, hopefully not for long, though. Auto-recalibration."

"Looks like one of the generators is out, Colonel," called one of the techs, already back at his board. Ellis glanced up and saw that the man had a track of dark crimson spilling down one side of his face. Scalp wound. "Capacitor banks three and five discharged, could have blown their breakers."

"Shields are out, sir," someone else told him. "Comms too."

"Wonderful. Meyers, can you *please* give me some good news?"

She shook her head, and then winced and put her hand to it. "Ouch," she hissed. "Note to self, no head-shaking. Okay, the bad news. I have no idea where we are. The stellar database is out."

There was something in her voice that told him she wasn't quite finished. "And?"

"And, I think…" She leaned closer to her board, squinted. "Oh crap," she whispered.

"Don't tell me. We're not alone."

"No sir." She looked up at him, her face bleak. "I think it's the Wraith."

CHAPTER FIVE

Creator

"Chapman," Sam Carter muttered to herself. "Russel Chapman." Then she lashed out, hard, with her right foot.

The kick was perfect, a *dhe dhad* roundhouse that impacted the punch bag solidly at waist height. Had Chapman actually been the target of the blow he would have crumpled around it like a loose sack of grain.

Carter bounced back, regained her stance, and then darted in to pummel the bag with a series of vicious elbow and fist strikes, ending the sequence with a *mud dhrong* punch that would have broken a strong man's jaw. The bag, suspended top and bottom with heavy bungee cords, rattled and bounced, swaying to a slow halt as Carter backed off.

She wiped the back of her hand across her forehead, letting the bindings mop up some of the sweat, shook some more out of her hair. She hadn't planned on working the bag for as long as she had, and the sustained assault she had unleashed on it was beginning to take its toll. There was a continuous ache across the back of her shoulders, now, and the dull muscle-memory of repeated impacts in her knuckles and shins. Maybe, she thought, this hadn't been such a great idea.

Then again, ever since the IOA had called to deliver their decision she had needed to hit something. And doing so, over and over for almost an hour, had felt good.

It wasn't a realization that she was especially proud of. In truth, she recognized it as a failing. She should have been prepared for what the Advisory was going to decide: knowing what she did about them and how they worked, she should have expected it. But the decision, when it came, surprised and distressed her far more than she had expected. She hadn't been able to think of another way to get rid of the effects of that call other than to make her way down to the gym, set up a punch bag and beat the living daylights out of several imaginary members of the IOA.

There was no-one else in her section of the gym. From the next room, though, the sounds of heavy blows and occasional grunts of pain issued. Ronon Dex and John Sheppard were in there, sparring again. It seemed to be something they did frequently—Carter had only been on Atlantis for just over three weeks, and she had already noticed them in there several times.

They were talking as they fought, but she couldn't quite hear what they were saying. Perhaps Carter wasn't the only one getting rid of some aggression.

She left the punch bag to dangle, and walked across the gym to where her towel lay folded neatly on a bench. She picked it up and dried her face with it, and when she brought it down Angelus was standing in front of her.

It took an effort not to start. She'd not heard him at all, and she was sure she'd only had the towel over her face for a second or two. Either he could move very fast, or very quietly, or both. In any case, it was something she would have to watch for in the future.

"Angelus," she said, as calmly as she could. "What are you doing here?"

"I was told I could find you here," he replied. Then he tilted his head, very slightly, gesturing over his shoulder. "Pleased don't be alarmed. I have my chaperones."

Carter glanced behind him, and saw DeSalle and Kaplan by the door. "I see. Well, it's good that you're up and about. You must be feeling better."

He was looking at the punch bag. "What are you doing?"

"Exercising."

"By attacking this… Object?"

She nodded, feeling oddly embarrassed. "It's called *Muay Thai*. The fighting style, not the bag… It's a martial art from my world."

"Art…" he repeated softly. He walked partway around the

punch bag, watching it, as though waiting for it to impart some deep insight.

"In the room next to this one," he said after a few seconds, "I noticed Lieutenant Colonel John Sheppard and a tall man with very distinctive hair. They were fighting too."

"That was Ronon Dex." Carter made a slight, fluttering mime around her head. "With the hair. They're sparring, sort of pretend-fighting. Keeps them in practice."

"They seemed to be taking it very seriously. Are you sure it wasn't some kind of dominance ritual?"

Carter smiled. "No, I think they just like hitting each other."

He didn't answer. Next to him, with his stillness and calm grace and the smooth, liquid tones of his voice, she started to feel awkward. "Look, Angelus. This isn't something I normally do."

"It isn't?"

"No. I mean, you probably think it's pretty…" She grimaced slightly, unsure of how to go on, but his expression urged her to continue. "Pretty childish," she said finally.

He looked at her oddly for a moment, then a slow smile spread across his pale features. "Ah, Colonel Carter. Do you think me too enlightened to see the value of this? You think my people were any better?"

She shrugged wordlessly.

Angelus shook his head. "No. Oh, to hear us talk, you would think us beyond the need for such pursuits. Noble, we were, and full of high ideals… We knew all the answers, Colonel, and we shouted them like anthems, to anyone who would listen. But still." He lifted his hands strangely, his long fingers crooked. "We are gone, and yet you remain."

There was the sound of a heavy impact from the next room, and a series of muffled curses. Somebody had hit the mat, hard, and Carter didn't think it was Dex. "Maybe not for much longer," she said grimly.

Angelus lowered his hands. "What do you mean?"

She sighed deeply. "You know I take my orders from a group on Earth, right?"

"I thought you had autonomy here."

"On some matters, yes. But not wholly. And not when it concerns you." She began walking back towards the punch bag, and then realized that she still had the towel in her hand. She balled it up and slung it back towards the bench. "I presented them with my report last night. All my concerns, *Apollo*'s sensor logs from Eraavis, everything."

"Your concerns?"

She rounded on him. "Angelus, I'm sorry. But it's my opinion that you represent a clear and present danger to Atlantis. The Replicators obviously consider you public enemy number one, and they've already shown they will stop at nothing to destroy you—not genocide, not suicide, *nothing*. Right now they don't know where you are, but if they find out they will destroy Atlantis and everyone in it to get to you."

"That's a logical assumption. But your superiors do not share your concerns?"

"Oh, my *superiors*?" She spat the word. "They consider you an acceptable risk. I've been ordered to give you full access to any facilities you need here. They're even going to send an observer to make sure I do."

There was a long silence. Then Angelus said: "I don't understand."

"Sure you do." That was Sheppard. Carter looked around to see him standing by the door. He had a towel draped over his left shoulder and a long bruise purpling the side of his face. He looked sour.

"You know damn well what's she's talking about, Angelus," he went on. "And don't try to tell us it's not what you wanted."

"Not against your wishes," Angelus replied. "And believe me, Colonel Carter, I share your concerns. I watched the Replicators destroy everything I loved, and I will share the blame for that until the day I die. But trust me, I have no intention of hastening that day."

"Trust you?" she began, but he moved towards her, very quickly and very silently. Before she could step back, he had her hands in his.

They were cool, like before, and gentle against her skin. "Trust me in this, Colonel Samantha Carter. Whether I am here or not, one day they will come for you. They hate you too much not to do so. But if you let me complete my work, you need not fear them. Not them, nor the Wraith, nor any threat that might arise against you or your homeworld. I promise you this.

"Let me finish my weapon, and I will rid you of the Asurans forever."

Carter knew that McKay would react badly to the news, but she had misjudged just how fast that news would travel. It must have reached him in less time than it took for her to shower and track him down to the mess hall—when she found him there, she only had to look at him to realize he already knew the IOA's decision.

He was sitting slumped at one of the tables, near the one of the big panoramic windows but not looking out of it. His head was forwards, resting on his arms, and she could hear him muttering to himself.

Despite her feelings, the sight raised a smile in her. He looked like a cartoon, drawn to define dejection.

She walked across the mess hall, returning the greetings of several people scattered around the place, and sat down opposite McKay. "Hey Rodney," she said brightly.

"Spare me the false jollity, okay?" He spoke without raising his head, giving his words a muffled quality. "I know about Eraavis, I know about the IOA, and I know what's going to happen."

"Really?"

He lifted his head and fixed her with a slightly manic stare. "Yeah, really. Isn't it obvious?"

She forced brightness into her voice. "Something tells me you're looking at the worse possible case here."

"It's kinda what I do." He straightened up and sat back. "Seriously, I've seen what the Asurans are capable of. You weren't here when they hit us on Lantea—" He put his hands up as she started to speak. "Yes, I know you've read all the reports, seen the videos on YouTube, whatever. It's not the same, okay?"

Carter had to concede that. "I guess it's not."

"All they needed to drive us right off Lantea was one beam weapon. *One*. That was, what, a few hours after we'd nuked half their cities and all their shipyards? I was in the tower when a shaved edge of that beam hit us. God, the *sound*. Have you any idea how loud that kind of thing is? Just what kind of damage it can do? And the way it hit…" His voice faltered. She saw him swallow. "Threw her right back across…"

He fell silent again. He looked down at the table, eyes suddenly unfocussed, then out through the long windows and over the city. "One beam," he breathed. "How many do you think they've got now?"

"Rodney, listen to me." Carter leaned closer to him, and dropped her voice a little. "Look, I understand what you're saying. If the Replicators find out we've got Angelus they'll come after us with all guns blazing, I get it. And if he starts doing whatever he did on Eraavis they might find out all the sooner. But that doesn't mean things are going to pan out like that."

"At the moment, I don't really see a way out of it."

"You're not looking hard enough."

McKay frowned, but he looked back at her, and Carter could see she'd lit a spark of hope in him. "Tell me you've got a plan," he said. "Anything. Please."

"Stargate Command," she replied.

He gave her a blank look. "What, send him there? To Earth?"

"God, no… Angelus has made it plain he needs to be in Atlantis for this, and whenever he says 'jump' the IOA are begging him to tell them how high. Besides, if this weapon of his brought the Asurans running, it might send out the same call to someone unfriendly in the Milky Way."

McKay, held her gaze for a second, then looked away. "You're right. Bad idea."

"No, what I mean is, we get SGC to step in on our behalf and call a halt to the whole project."

"Not their call. Okay, I know you've not been here all that long, but the way it works is, IOA call the shots. They cut SGC out a long time ago."

"IOA has political control over the mission, but what if

things stop being political?"

"I don't—?"

"Rodney, what Angelus is talking about is weapons research, pure and simple. This isn't about contacting new alien races or making alliances, this is about a guy building a gun. And I'm willing to bet that a weapons project taking place in the city would get SGC involved." She lowered her voice even more, putting a conspiratorial tone into her words. "If I could convince General Landry that the expedition is being put in danger, he could override the IOA on military grounds."

"That's brilliant!" McKay's face lit up. "Of course! Okay, what, you just need to call them? You can do that now?"

"Calm down, okay? So far, I've got nothing to go to Landry with."

"What? Show him the surface of Eraavis, that should do the trick!"

Carter shook her head. "Cause and effect, Rodney. Sure, we all saw what happened to Eraavis, but we've only got Angelus' word that the planet was destroyed because of the weapon he was building. What if he was wrong? What if there was another reason? If I go to SCG with what we've got right now, they're more than likely to tell us the same thing the IOA did."

He sagged. "Crap."

"But that's where you come in. At the moment, we don't even know what this weapon is."

"You haven't asked him?" McKay's eyes went wide. "Ah, come on!"

"Rodney, just asking him isn't the issue. I'm going to need a detailed report on this thing, whatever it is. Full specs. You're going to have to work with him, analyze any research he has, and then come back to me with a file I can send to Landry."

"I could do that." He nodded vigorously, then paused. "Hold on. How am I supposed to make a report without him building the weapon and bringing the Replicators here?"

"He's not going to be able to do it that quickly, is he?"

McKay shrugged nervously. "He's an Ancient, and he's on home turf. Anything's possible."

"Well, just get it done as quickly as you can."

"That's it? That's your plan?" He let out a nervous laugh. "What am I supposed to do while he's putting together the Death Star in our basement, keep knocking stuff over to try and hold him up?"

"No. But think about it, he's going to need a lab, right? So the first thing you'll need from him is enough information about what he's doing to be able to choose a suitable facility."

McKay tilted his head, obviously weighing that one up. "Right…"

"And then find him somewhere, well, like you said. In the basement. Maybe if he's lower down in the city, it might block a signal that might otherwise alert the Replicators."

"Um, correct me if I'm wrong, but didn't the Eraavi build all their facilities under mountains? What have we got that that several million tons of solid rock hasn't?"

"That's easy. We've got you." She got up. "Come on, let's go find him. The sooner we get this ball rolling the sooner we can kick it right out of our park."

The security detail Carter had assigned to Angelus had never been entirely for the Ancient's benefit.

It was in part. She certainly believed that the man needed protecting—whatever he may or may not have done in the past, Angelus was an extremely valuable asset. There was every possibility that he was the last of his kind; the Ancients as a species were either long-dead or had transcended flesh and given themselves over to the ageless, bodiless existence they called Ascension. His knowledge and insight could, if he was willing, advance the cause of the Pegasus expedition by untold amounts.

So the marines guarding him were partly to make sure he came to no harm. Carter would not have been popular with the Advisory had Angelus, still recovering from his injuries, taken a tumble down some steps and broken his elegant neck.

But of course, there were other concerns. As Angelus himself had pointed out, there really was no way his origins could be completely verified, and Carter had learned enough during her time in SG-1 to be deeply, reflexively mistrustful. There were simply too many threats in the universe to take anyone or anything at face value. The Ancient had arrived on her doorstep, and was now offering gifts. Despite the awful danger he represented, he still seemed too good to be true.

In response to these concerns, Carter had assigned a small detail of guards to Angelus, just enough to provide him 24-hour supervision. And, of course, to make sure he didn't get up to any mischief while she wasn't around.

That arrangement might have to be revised now, though, given the new turn events had taken. And for that, Carter would need to go to John Sheppard.

When called, Sheppard revealed that he was in the infirmary. He didn't sound all that happy about it, and when Carter and McKay arrived the man looked anything but glad to be there. He was sitting sideways on a gurney, his legs dangling, while Jennifer Keller dabbed at the side of his face with a gauze pad.

Ronon Dex was there too, watching Sheppard's treatment and looking faintly amused. He often did, Carter had noticed.

"I should strap this up," Keller was saying. Sheppard glared at her sideways, without turning his head.

"Strap it up? My *face*? How could you strap up my face?"

"You broke your cheekbone!"

"No, Ronon broke it. And you haven't answered my question."

Keller dabbed quite hard, making him wince. "I could put a giant pressure bandage around your entire head," she snapped.

"Wouldn't that stop me talking?"

"It would stop you doing a lot of things."

"Plaster," suggested Ronon, not at all helpfully. "We could leave little air holes—"

"Not funny, okay? Jeeze…" Sheppard gave Carter a plaintive look. "Colonel? A little help?"

"Looks like you're getting all the help you can handle," she replied. "John, are you going to be off active duty for this?"

"What? No!"

Keller sighed. "Broken cheekbone, chipped tooth, possible concussion," she reported, putting the gauze down. "And a lousy attitude."

"Well," McKay muttered. "At least that's intact."

"*Fractured*," Sheppard replied, shrugging his way out from Keller's ministrations and standing up. "Just a hairline, okay? And no, I'm not concussed either."

"Great. This is all I need." Carter ran a hand back through her hair, wishing she'd spent more time hitting the punch bag. "Doctor Keller, in your honest medial opinion, does he need to be off duty?"

Keller made a face. "Honestly? No. Not for the injuries, anyway."

"Thank you," growled Sheppard.

"Oh, don't start thanking anyone yet, Lieutenant Colonel," Carter told him. "Believe me, you and I are going to have a *very* serious chat about how to play nice in future, understood? In the meantime, follow me. You too, Ronon."

She spun on her heel and stalked out of the infirmary, McKay on her heels. By the time she got out into the corridor, Sheppard and Dex had joined her.

"Sorry," Sheppard said quietly, as he drew close. "Wasn't thinking."

Carter shook her head disbelievingly. "How did he manage to break your face?"

He threw Dex a glance. "Lucky shot."

She heard the Satedan chuckle in response, but put her hand up before the exchange could continue. "Okay, fine. Like I said in there, we'll continue this later. In the meantime, we've got more important things to deal with." She walked off, down the corridor towards stairs. "Angelus is going to need some extra protection."

"What kind of protection?"

"The kind that's more about protecting us from him."

"Ah."

"We're going to get a lab set up for him, and once we do I'm going to need a full surveillance kit installed. Audiovisual, motion-sensing, data-taps, the works. Plus we'll need to at least double the number of marines on duty, and to make sure they report back to us at the end of every shift. Can you do that?"

Sheppard nodded. "No problem. Where's the lab going to

be?"

"We don't know yet. Rodney and I are going to have a chat with Angelus now, and try to work out a gameplan from what he tells us. Once we know more about the weapon, we'll have a better idea of where we need to put him."

"Understood." They had reached the top of a stairway, one that led down to the accommodation units where Angelus was staying. Sheppard stopped there. "Does this mean we're actually going to let him build this thing?"

"No, it means we're going to play along with the IOA for now."

He smiled. "That sounds like the best idea I've heard all day. Okay, you go talk to Angelus, I'll get started. Come on, Ronon. We can cut back down here to the transporter."

The two of them turned, and began to walk away. As they did, Carter called out after them. "Ronon?"

The Satedan paused, and looked back over his shoulder. "Yeah?"

"Next time, pull your punches."

He snorted. "Where's the fun in that?"

Angelus was back in his room. Carter could tell because there were two marines guarding the door. She recognized them as Clarke and Bowden—Kaplan and DeSalle must have been off-watch. They came at attention and saluted as she stopped at the door.

"At ease," she told them. "How's it going?"

"Just as always, Colonel," Bowden said. "Quiet as a mouse."

"Keep me posted," she replied, and opened the door.

Angelus was on the bed, his long frame stretched out perfectly straight, perfectly still. In addition to his robes he was wearing the heavy gold mask Ellis had told her about. She guessed it must have been brought to Atlantis with the rest of his meager possessions, but she hadn't seen it before.

The profile of the mask was unearthly, eerie. It was beautiful, that golden face, but its beauty was that of a corpse. That, coupled with the blackness of the empty eye-holes and the silent stillness of the room, sent a shiver down Carter's back.

Not for the first time, the Ancient looked as if he had been laid out for burial.

He must have heard her and McKay come in. One moment he was as motionless as a statue, and the next he was sitting up on the bed, the golden mask transfixing her with its hollow gaze. "Colonel Carter," he said.

"Angelus," she replied. "I'm sorry to disturb you. Were you sleeping?"

"Not at all. Please, come in." He stood, then reached up and removed the mask from his face. It seemed to come away with some small resistance, as though it fitted snugly. "And your companion?"

"This is Doctor Rodney McKay," said Carter. "Rodney is one of our civilian specialists. I think he's the person best suited to help with your project."

McKay raised a hand, rather nervously. "Hello again."

"Of course, you were in the starhopper." A small smile of recognition crossed the Ancient's face. "I let two people in, I remember now. You were one of them."

"You *let* us in?"

"Yes." He put the mask down, carefully. "I very much doubt you would have gotten inside if I hadn't."

"Well, that explains a lot," McKay said sourly.

Carter stepped in before he could say any more. "Angelus, we've been asked by the IOA to provide you with laboratory facilities for you to research your weapon, but at the moment we don't know what you might need. Can you help us?"

"Of course. If you like, I can provide you with a complete list of my requirements. Can you furnish me with a means of recording data?"

"Sure. I'll have a tablet sent down for you."

"That would be kind."

McKay was wandering around the room. He seemed to find keeping still more difficult the more nervous he got, and something about Angelus was making him very edgy indeed. Carter started to wonder if even bringing him along had been a good idea. "Rodney? Anything you'd like to ask?"

"Hm? Oh yes, sure. Ah, Angelus?"

"Yes?" The word was enunciated carefully, hesitantly, as though the Ancient was unsure of where his question might lead.

"I was just wondering if you could give us a quick run-down of the weapon's principles. You know, just a preview?" He put his hands in his pockets, a nervous gesture that made him look rather boyish. "It would, ah, be a really big help in ascertaining what kind of lab we need to set you up in."

"Very well…" The Ancient's smooth white brow furrowed very slightly. "I must warn you, the principles are rather obscure."

"I think I can handle them."

"I have no doubt. I'm just not sure my grasp of your language can." He took a step backwards to the bed, and leaned on the edge of it, not taking his feet from the floor. "There are two fundamental principles; the first concerns the… *Vindicio ratio*… Method of sending, for the second."

"Delivery system?" ventured Carter.

"As good a phrase as any. The first principle is that of a certain particle, one of the family of *plenus verto proprii*, which forms its interactions under the *validus vis nuclei*…"

McKay held up his hands. "Wait, wait, wait a second," he said quickly. "*Plenus*… turn, turning? Fully turning… Full turn particle?"

"Oh!" said Carter. "A particle with a full spin!"

"A boson? And then *validus vis*… Oh, wait! I know this one… Strongest force! We're talking about mesons!"

"That is your word for them?"

"Yeah." McKay nodded. "Bosons are the family of particles that have an integer spin, as opposed to fermions which only have a half spin. Mesons are strongly interacting bosons. It's pretty basic quantum chromodynamics."

Angelus smiled, quite broadly. He looked, for the first time, almost happy. "These are terms I must remember, Doctor McKay. It will facilitate working with you in the future, as will your grasp of my language."

"Well, the Ancient language isn't a million miles away from

Latin, and I kinda got that drummed into me back at school. Before I got taken out of school, anyway…" He glanced at Carter. "Where was I?"

"Mesons."

"Oh yeah. The delivery system."

"Indeed. The system begins with a beam of mesons, fired at extremely high energy levels and pulsed at high frequencies. This causes a… How might you say it? A susceptibility in the planes most basic to *tracto vicis*, the dimensions, those planes associated with *vis fluctuates*. There is a vibration which-"

"You're losing me," said Carter, but McKay shook his head. "No, I got it. Keep going."

"Very well… Ah, this susceptibility can be exploited if enough energy is fired along the meson beam in a single pulse. This energy, which I calculated to be roughly the equivalent of a single *lacuna navitas fabrica* released in no more than one millionth of a second… This burst of energy then travels along the meson beam until it interacts with the plane instability and causes a *perturbo una locus* of the *agri totalis vulgus propria*. You see?"

There was a long silence. Finally, McKay shook his head. "Sorry. You lost me at *lacuna fabrica*."

Angelus pointed at the floor. "The city requires three of them to provide its power."

"Oh," said McKay. "ZedPMs!"

"Hold on," said Carter. "Each shot from this weapon requires a whole ZPM?"

"Yes," Angelus replied. "Did you realize you both pronounce that phase differently?"

"He's from Canada. Look, we can't go around shooting ZPMs off into space! What happens to the city?"

"Please don't concern yourself with that, Colonel. I'll show you how to make more."

It took another half an hour of gradual translation and explanation before McKay told Carter he was satisfied. He was sweating by the time he said it, and Carter couldn't blame him. The intricacies of the Ancient's plan might have been under-

standable had they been laid out in languages Carter was used
to, but instead of Angelus adopting more English terms,
McKay had started to use more and more Latin, until the conversation between the two of them had become an indecipher-
able morass of bilingual theoretical physics.

That branch of science was more McKay's specialty than
hers. Even so, the conversation seemed to have taken something out of him.

Once Carter had excused herself and McKay, she walked
with him in silence until she was completely out of the Ancient's
earshot. Then she stopped. "What do you think?"

"I think that's probably the most scary discussion of quantum electrodynamics I've ever had," he replied. "Jesus, Sam...
If he's right about this... I mean, I can see why the Replicators
came after him, put it that way."

"How do you mean?"

McKay took a deep breath. "How far did you get?"

"Just give me the basics."

"Okay... You generate a high-energy meson stream, pulsed
at an ultra-high-frequency. Tune that to generate a specific form
of instability in the spacetime dimensions most closely tied
to quantum fluctuations. And then you unleash one almighty
energy surge up the meson beam, again tuned to the exact same
frequency but in anti-phase to the waveform of the initial beam.
That rips open a series of dimensional rifts in a kind of cascade, but concentrated into a tiny space. About half the size of
a hydrogen atom, or the effect dissipates."

Carter frowned. "That's a lot of energy in one space."

"No kidding. Spacetime can't handle that kind of energy-
load, so it breaks down. And what you get is a localized desta-
bilization of the Higgs-Boson field."

She stared at him. "That's *insane!*"

"See what I meant?"

She did indeed. The Higgs-Boson field was, according to
recognized theories of high-energy physics, one of the most
fundamental forces in the universe. It was what gave particles
mass. Without it, the universe would never have evolved out of
its most early form—that of a searing sea of undifferentiated

elemental protomatter.

Switch off the Higgs-Boson, Carter thought wildly, and all matter ceases to be. That part of the universe returns to how it was a billionth of a second after the big bang. Angelus had devised a method of turning bits of spacetime back into primal Hell.

The destructive power of such an event would be unimaginable.

"Rodney, can you start that report right away? If we can get across to General Landry what Angelus is trying to do, I think we've got a good chance of stopping this before it gets dangerous."

"Sure. Hey, Sam?"

"Hm?"

"Something just occurred to me…" He glanced over his shoulder, quickly, as if to make sure no-one was close by, then leaned closer to Carter. "What we saw on Eraavis, that mess back there. Crust scored, all life burned away, lava everywhere…" He nodded back towards the Ancient's room. "What if *he* did it?"

"Angelus? How?"

"An accident? Look, if he was messing around with fundamental physics, what if something went wrong and he melted his own planet?"

Carter thought about that for a moment. "No. *Apollo*'s scans showed up clear signatures of Replicator weapons fire. Besides, if he'd set off a weapon like that anywhere near a planet, there wouldn't have been enough of it left to sweep up and send back to us in an envelope."

"I guess." McKay seemed to brighten. "When you put it like that, the thought of an explosion on a scale unseen since the Big Bang seems almost comforting."

Suddenly, looking at McKay, Carter found him very strange. Almost as alien as Angelus, although in a totally different way. Out of the two, she found herself abruptly unable to decide which frightened her more.

"Okay," she said. "Take comfort in that while you put the report together. I'm going to find Angelus a lab. One that he's not going to do any work at all in."

CHAPTER SIX

Blood and Gold

Rodney McKay had a kind of epiphany, two days after Angelus had begun work on the weapon. He realized, quite suddenly and without any particular provocation, that he was being torn in two.

It was an intellectual quandary he really hadn't anticipated. The realization, when it came, literally stopped him in his tracks, in the middle of the corridor that lead to the control room and Sam Carter's office. He halted so abruptly that somebody almost collided with him: a female technician must have been walking quite closely behind him, and McKay saw her stumbling around him to get past, clearly thrown off-balance by the sudden stop.

Dimly, he watched her go, feeling disconnected. At that moment, he could have been viewing an abstract image moving past him and felt no more recognition. The knowledge of just how deeply conflicted he felt had stunned him.

The only thing more surprising was that he hadn't noticed it before.

McKay stood there for a moment, still clutching the data tablet he had been taking to show Carter. After a few seconds he set off again, but more slowly this time, and only after making sure no-one else was in the corridor with him. And when the way branched, he diverted from his original path and instead set off towards the nearest transporter.

There was a lot to think about, and he couldn't do that while giving Carter his report. That would have to wait.

The transporter took McKay to the mess hall. Once there he found an empty table near one of the long windows and sat, placing the tablet on the table in front of him. He found himself looking at it as though not entirely sure what it was.

"Wow," he breathed, blinking as though clearing his vision would help to clear his mind. "Wow."

It had taken quite some time to get the lab set up properly, which could almost certainly be put down to deliberate delays on Carter's part. She wanted Angelus to hold off starting anything fundamental before she had all her methods of surveillance in place. But Angelus was eager to work, and despite the delays had been frantically calculating from the outset.

And since the start of this, McKay had been swept along by the Ancient's plans.

He had been working with Angelus almost that entire time, and had only taken short breaks away to eat and sleep. For a while he had remembered his instructions from Carter and followed them diligently—gain as much information about the weapon as possible, collate everything, and report back on a regular basis. Together with the data being recorded from the surveillance suite, the case against building the weapon had really started to come together.

It wasn't a duty that McKay took lightly, either. He held his position in the Atlantis expedition in high regard, and while he would be the first to admit that there were those among his team-mates who were, perhaps, more instinctively loyal then he, McKay liked to believe that he could at least be counted on. Letting people down wasn't something he liked to do at all, even when their demands were, as was so often the case, petty, small-minded, distracting or just plain difficult. Although those people frequently failed to appreciate just how vital his work was, and how annoying being pulled away from it to fix the most simple faults could be, he still tried, as hard as he was able, to come through.

To do otherwise, at least in the eyes of those making such continuous and unjustified demands on his time, would be seen as failure. McKay was a sensible enough man to accept that failure was an intrinsic part of human existence, but there was no denying that it made him look bad.

Not only that, but he had friends here. Perhaps not *close* friends—feelings of that nature weren't ones he felt especially comfortable with, and he tended to avoid them if at all possible. But there were some whose company he found agreeable. Others he respected, for various reasons. If he was honest with himself, there were probably more people in the city that he respected and *didn't* like, but that was beside the point. He didn't want to see any of them—with no more than a handful of exceptions—immolated in a Replicator assault.

And far more importantly, Rodney McKay did not want to see a hail of energy beams crashing down onto his own head, either.

The danger represented by Angelus and his continued residence in the city chilled McKay to the core. The video footage *Apollo* had sent back from Eraavis had been truly horrifying. He had seen destruction before, but never on such a sustained, determined level. If the Replicators had somehow blown the planet apart, that would, in a way, have been less frightening. It would have been an instant of violence, a sudden unleashing of fury. It would have been comprehensible.

But to do what they had done to Eraavis, the Asurans must have fired on the planet, continuously and mercilessly, for hours.

The longer Angelus remained in the city, the more likely it became that Atlantis would suffer the same fate; McKay was in no doubt of that. And if the Ancient began actually reproducing his weapons experiments, there really wasn't any hope at all. He'd attracted the Asurans once. There was no reason to assume he wouldn't do so again, for all his promises to the contrary.

All these factors made for a compelling case. And, for a few hours, McKay had been honestly compelled.

It hadn't lasted, he knew now. And it couldn't have lasted. The science was just too seductive.

McKay knew he was being tempted, that was completely clear to him. What wasn't clear was how he could possibly avoid giving in to that temptation. He had been fascinated by theoretical physics since childhood—the interactions of subatomic particles, in all their sublime and boundless variety, awed him. It was the foundation on which everything vital about himself was built—his intellect, his skill, his thirst for insight into the most fundamental properties of the universe. It wasn't simply that McKay liked to know how things worked, he *needed* to know how. It was a hunger, one that had pulled him onwards almost all his life: from the school science project that had brought his abilities to the attention of the CIA, through his time at Area 51, and then to Antarctica and finally across the gulf between the galaxies themselves, here to Atlantis.

His dreamed of theoretical physics, on occasion. That is, when the dreams weren't shudder-inducing nightmares about his own impending doom, which tended to be the norm. But on the good nights, he would find himself in vast libraries, the bookshelves groaning with heavy tomes; each a wealth of answers, only needing to be opened…

Angelus, for all his dangers, was holding a book open for Rodney McKay. The science he was offering went beyond any experiment or study in history. The principles behind this weapon made even the Stargates seem mundane.

The Ancient's weapon could, in one blast of unimaginable cosmic violence, recreate the Big Bang itself.

How could he resist that? How, after searching his whole life for the answers, could he give them up? It was impossible.

The dream-books were being opened for him, and they were almost close enough to read. And if McKay had been asked, at that moment, whether the secrets held within were worth dying for, he could not have honestly answered: "No."

His reverie in the mess hall lasted an hour. When he finally felt ready to return to the world, McKay called Carter on his headset and told her he had nothing worth bothering her with, and would be staying in the lab with Angelus until something interesting happened. Then he opened up his latest report on the data tablet, thought for a moment or two about simply deleting it, and then let his conscience get the better of him. He opened up an encrypted folder and stored the file there.

Then he went back to the lab.

The journey took some time. McKay had deliberately chosen a location that was away from the core of Atlantis, out on the west pier. On the one hand, that kept it away from the most vital areas of the city, but it also made getting there a chore. The nearest transporter was several hundred meters away, through a series of corridors that, like much of the city's internal architecture, all looked very much the same, and finally along a covered gallery that ran along a long, open slot in the pier's upper surface. Whenever he returned to the lab, it was always something of a relief for McKay to reach the gallery. Not only was it a welcome exposure to fresh air, but it also meant that he hadn't gotten lost again.

By the time he got back to the lab this time, his legs were starting to ache and the tablet was feeling a lot heavier than it should have done. He noticed that his pace had slowed considerably as he came in off the gallery, and picked it up a little as he approached the guard station. There were two marines sitting behind the armored glass of the station, and they nodded to McKay as he drew level. He smiled briefly back at them as he strode past, arms swinging, trying to make it look as if he had been pounding along since leaving the transporter. As soon as they keyed open the lab doors, though, he practically staggered inside and dropped the tablet on the nearest table.

There was an ache in his chest. Was that from breathing too hard, or was it something else? He rubbed his sternum nervously, and then noticed that Angelus was watching him.

The Ancient was wearing his golden mask. It could only have been a trick of the light, but the eyeholes seemed frighteningly empty.

McKay dropped his hand. "Hey."

"Welcome back, Doctor McKay. You seem out of breath." Angelus reached up and took the mask off, set it down on the terminal next to him. He was sitting at the image processor, a hexagonal ring of terminals that bulked at the center of the lab. The processor terminals surrounded a holographic projector, and McKay could see a series of gridded planes whirling in the air above it.

He found a nearby swivel chair and sank into it. "It's quite a walk."

"Back to the tower?"

"What? No, to the transporter." McKay squinted at the

Ancient's slender form for a moment, then down at his own torso. There was a quite a difference. "Well, I've never been much of a hiker, you know?"

Angelus turned to him. "You surprise me."

"I do?"

"Of course. You seem to think well on your feet, Doctor. I have seen you walk around this space many times when you have been trying to define a concept or solve a calculation." He touched a control, without looking at the panel, and the holographic image faded out. "I could easily see you covering many *stadia* in your quest for answers."

"I guess I'm more of a pacer." McKay took a breath and held it, checking on the feeling in his chest. It didn't spike, so he decided that he was probably okay. He stood up and moved over to join the Ancient at the display.

The lab was in the same state of slightly chaotic activity as it had been for the past two days. A trio of technicians had been assigned to work with Angelus, but according to Carter they were still being 'vetted'. Their eventual arrival had been catered for, though: several laptops, data tablets and pieces of test equipment had been arranged on folding tables along two of the lab's walls. All the screens McKay could see, including three big flatscreens on the wall above the tables, glowed with animated graphics and streams of raw data. The calculations involved in the weapon design were immense; beam power and pulse frequency exhibited in fractally recursive forms so complex that several of the most powerful processors on Atlantis had to be wired up in parallel just to handle them. Along another wall, four squat blocks of metal sat humming, surrounded by electric fans: multiple disc drives, running far beyond their normal capacity in order to store the processed data. If it hadn't been for the fans, the drives would have melted in their towers.

There was a lot of equipment here, and Angelus was pushing all of it to its limits. So far, though, the only work being done here was calculation, so Colonel Carter had been content to let it continue as long as she was kept updated. Perhaps McKay shouldn't have been helping this phase of the Ancient's project take shape so enthusiastically, but he had accepted, during his introspective hour in the mess hall, that he could not stop himself. It was unfair of Carter to make him try.

McKay got to the image processor just as the Ancient brought a new series of forms into being above it. "What's this now?"

"This simulates the target point instability during the initial delivery strike." Angelus tapped out a series of commands on a portable keyboard, his fingers moving with startling speed. "Some of the values required are still estimates, I'm afraid. The recursions are not yet at a suitable level of iteration to provide the accuracy we need."

McKay knew all about the level of accuracy. Considering the amount of energy delivered by the meson pulse, and the tiny amount of space it had to be compressed into, it was a wonder that conventional mathematics could even describe the required precision. "How may iterations have they been through?"

"Ninety-three."

"Right. We'll need, what, twice that? And with each recursion taking exponentially greater processing power to process…" McKay glanced around, feeling slightly frantic. "We're gonna need a bigger lab."

"I believe what we have should be sufficient. Once we pass one hundred iterations I shall deploy an inverse compression algorithm. That will limit the amount of data overflow in direct proportion to the level of accuracy we reach."

"Neat trick." There were no seats around the image processor. McKay thought about dragging one closer, but decided it would make him look foolish. He leaned against a terminal instead, trying to take the weight off one foot at a time.

The golden mask was resting next to his arm. It looked cool and heavy, its gleaming face reflecting the holographic light in strange curves. He found himself, not for the first time, studying it from the corner of his eye.

It was an odd thing, both sinister and beautiful, and the Ancient's habit of wearing it so often was intriguing. McKay had almost asked about it before, several times in fact, but until now had always held back. He couldn't quite decide why, but there was an air of privacy about the mask, a kind of intimacy that had made him uncomfortable broaching the subject .

And, bizarrely, there was something about Angelus that made McKay loathe to upset the man.

But now, maybe for the first time, the mask was closer to McKay than it was to Angelus, and the proximity of it was strangely heady. He reached out, hesitated, then leaned forwards and picked it up.

It was actually heavier than he had anticipated. "Sorry, Angelus. I never asked… What does this do?"

"Do? The *visios*?"

"Yeah. You wear it a lot, and I just wondered what it's function was."

The Ancient looked at him, a strange, slightly haunted expression on his face. "It does nothing, Doctor. Except to remind me of happier times."

"So it's just a mask, then." McKay felt almost disappointed. He had been expecting the golden artifact to have some kind of exotic property — for it to induce hypnotic states, maybe, or aid concentration. He hadn't really thought that Angelus might just have been sitting around with a mask on.

"I suppose it is," the Ancient replied. "To anyone but me."

McKay found himself feeling rather embarrassed. He had obviously strayed into deep emotional territory; not a place he felt comfortable about going. He decided to change the subject. "Anyways, the simulation. Even with the estimated values, it's looking pretty detailed."

Angelus' gaze stayed fixed on the *visios* for a moment, then he returned his attention to the holo display. "At this point, the simulation is running more as a test of its own capabilities than a true indication. There are some elements that I am storing in order to refine them later, though." He pointed at the edges of a stack of planes, the way they rippled through each other in a series of perspective-defying loops and whorls. "These waveforms, for example, seem common to all levels of simulation. I believe we will encounter them under full test."

"Brane interaction? That's going to send instability phases right through the incursion space." McKay straightened up.

"That could be bad."

"Indeed. At worst, such an instability could reflect the field effect back down the transmission beam."

"Oh lovely." McKay stalked away from the processor, turning the *visios* over and over in his hands, then spun on his heel and walked back. Angelus was right, he always did think better on his feet, even if they did hurt. "You'd end up with the Higgs-Boson shutdown occurring at the point of firing, not the target."

"Which would be, as you say, *bad*."

Angelus turned back to the processor, and began typing again. McKay watched him for a while, then wandered away, deep in thought, images of the instability simulation spinning in his mind. If he concentrated, he could almost *see* the network of calculations and crumpled dimensions needed to destabilize the spacetime plane, but only in abstract. If he tried to pin it down it simply slipped away from him. There was something here he was missing, he was certain, something that was only just out of his reach. Perhaps if he could see some of the simulated data after the compression algorithms had done their work, it would all become clear.

He rubbed the bridge of his nose, wincing at a sudden needle of pain there. "Oh man, is the air dry in here? Is it the heat coming off those stacks?"

Angelus glanced around at him. "Is anything wrong, Doctor?"

"I dunno. Something's starting to play hell with my sinuses, that's all." He walked over to where the storage blocks had been set up, putting his hand out to feel the warm air wafted off them by the fans. "Damn. Yeah, it's these things."

"Perhaps you would benefit from a walk outside. Call it pacing in a single direction."

The thought of walking again so soon didn't really appeal, but the pain in McKay's forehead was getting worse. He didn't answer Angelus, but instead wandered away from the stacks.

The mask in his hands was still invitingly cold, despite the dry heat of the air. He flipped it over, studying the interior for the first time. When he had seen Angelus wearing it, it had always seemed to hug his face securely, but he could see no mechanisms inside. Just cool, polished metal.

Through the eyeholes, the floor seemed to waver, as though through a heat-haze. "Yeah, maybe," he muttered absently. "Thing is, if I go out there, get a good dose of cool sea air, then come back in here, my head's going to explode."

"Then perhaps you should—" Angelus halted in mid sentence. Then he said: "Doctor?"

McKay lifted the mask, trying to see more clearly through the eyeholes. As he did, the wavering seemed to increase. "Yeah?"

There was no answer. He raised the mask to his face, and suddenly he was flying backwards.

A folding table hit him in the back. He bounced off it, awkwardly, sending a couple of data tablets flying, and just about regained his balance before he went over. He reached out and grabbed a nearby terminal for support, and as he did so realized that he didn't have the mask any more.

Angelus was holding it, in both hands, protectively. He must have launched himself from the processor like a cat, and grabbed the mask as he hurled McKay into the tables. How could anyone move so fast?

And more to the point, why? He didn't look angry. If anything, his face was a picture of fear and confusion. His dark eyes were wide, staring at McKay.

"Are you all right?" he gasped.

McKay opened his mouth and tried to speak, but there wasn't any air in him. He dragged in a breath, and managed to nod.

"Are you certain?"

"Yeah, I think so… Angelus, what the hell?"

"I am sorry…" The Ancient shook himself, stared down at the *visios*. "There was no call for that, it was… Unforgivable."

"I don't understand."

Angelus shook his head. "I- You must not…" He took a deep breath of his own, and that seemed to calm him slightly. "The *visios* is the only thing I have left to remind me," he explained. "It is for me alone. I am sorry, Doctor. I should not have struck you. But you cannot wear this."

"Look, I didn't mean to offend you, okay? But you could have…" McKay winced, put a hand to his chest. He was just starting to realize how much his ribs hurt. "Ow… You could have just told me!"

"I know." He stepped away, and seemed about to place the mask back down on the processor. Then he paused, and came back. He reached out.

McKay flinched, but Angelus was holding the mask out to him.

He laughed nervously. "Yeah, it's okay. Really. You keep it."

"No. Doctor, I believe… Maybe it is time to put this away. I have been dwelling on the past too long. Would you return this to the starhopper?"

"Your ship?" McKay took the mask from him, holding it nervously. "It won't open."

"It will now." The Ancient's expression had turned to one of gentle sadness. "Please, take it back for me."

"Okay…" The idea of getting into the golden ship was tempting, he couldn't deny that. So was the thought of getting away from Angelus for a bit. "It might take a while."

"Take all the time you need."

"Sure. Okay then, I'll…" He backed away, still very much aware of how fast the Ancient could move. "I'll put this back, right where it'll be safe..."

The door opened for him as he reached it. He turned, and hurried out into the corridor and past the guard station. Only then, quite out of earshot, did he call Sheppard on his headset and tell him to drop everything and meet him in the hangar.

The hangar was a wedge-shaped segment of the city's central tower, a two-story space that had been almost unused by the Pegasus expedition since they first arrived. Parts of the tower's outer wall in that area had been found to be modular, and could be convinced, under power, to fold away, leaving sizeable entranceways. The function of this was not known, but it was hypothesized that occasionally the city's builders had needed to store things bigger than could be ferried in through the Stargate.

In any case, once the equipment stashed there had been moved back against the rear walls and covered with tarpaulins, a space about twenty meters across had been available to house the starhopper.

There was a big double door at the thin end of the wedge, towards the tower core, and Sheppard was waiting there when McKay arrived. "Okay Rodney, what's up?"

McKay had been walking as fast as he could all the way to the hangar, via various transporters. By the time he got there he was quite out of breath, and his chest was aching. At least now, there was good reason for it to do so. "Give me a minute."

"You are so out of shape."

"I am not. I just got a punch in the sternum, okay? A minute." He bent over, stood with his hands on his knees for a few moments, breathing hard. Then he straightened up. "Angelus just attacked me."

"He *what?*"

"Look… Maybe attacked is the wrong word. But he sure hit me pretty hard."

Sheppard was looking at the *visios*. "Because you stole his mask?"

"No! Well, actually, yes." McKay held the thing up. "I was with him in the lab, we were talking about the simulations, you know… There's this neat algorithm he's going to use to shave the data down as it goes through multiple recursions, I mean it's some seriously cool stuff—"

"Rodney," said Sheppard warningly. "I have other things I could be doing."

"Sorry. But anyways, I'd picked this up, and there was something funny about the eyeholes. Or I thought there was." He held the mask higher and stared through its eyes, but there was none of the distortion he had seen in the lab. "Oh. Maybe it was the heat coming off the stacks. So I was going to put it on, and—"

"You were going to put it on?" Sheppard's eyebrows went high. "Don't you think that's a little, I don't know, rude?"

"It is?" McKay frowned, feeling as though the conversation was getting away from him. "Listen, *he's* the one who hit *me*!

Slammed me right across the damn lab!"

"Really." Sheppard pretended to look impressed. "That's a big lab. I'm surprised you're not getting Keller to check you out after such a mighty blow."

"All right, more like shoved." McKay rubbed his chest idly. "But he pretty much knocked the wind right out of me, you know? I never knew how fast he could move."

"You want me to pull it up on the surveillance?" As per Carter's instructions, Sheppard and a small team of specialists had fitted the lab with a network of cameras, microphones, motion sensors and taps into all the computers Angelus would be using. He had boasted at the time that the Ancient wouldn't be able to fold up a paper airplane without it being recorded. "Shouldn't be too hard, what with him throwing you around like a sack of beans."

"Something tells me you're not taking this entirely seriously."

Sheppard put his hands up. "Okay, okay. You just seem in pretty good shape after all this violence, that's all. But I'll get the recordings up, don't worry."

"I'd appreciate it. And yes, I'll be going to see Keller after I've checked out this ship of his." He stepped up to the door control and waved his hand across it. After a moment's hesitation, the doors parted, slid aside with a thin, metallic scraping.

Beyond them lay the golden ship, the starhopper. Just as it had before, the sight of it stopped him cold.

The ship was side-on to him, facing away from the modular wall and at a slight angle, evidence of the rather imprecise method by which it had arrived in the tower. The hangar was probably about the same size as Apollo's bomb bay, but somehow the ship had seemed smaller there. Here, it loomed, hunching slightly forwards, as though ready to leap away. The dim light of the hangar sparked off its strange curves and leant a glossy, organic sheen to the opaque domes at its prow, and the surface of it still shone with the subtle opulence that only brushed gold can lay claim to.

It looked like jewelry. No, McKay thought, wonderingly: it looked like a sleek, wingless insect, disguising itself as jewelry in order to get the drop on some unknown prey.

As McKay stood there, watching, Sheppard stopped next to him. "Really takes some getting used to, doesn't it?"

"No kidding."

"Rodney, you said you couldn't open this thing."

"I think it's under Angelus' control. He said to Sam and I that he let me in, back on *Apollo*. I think, if he wants me in there now…"

As if in answer, part of the ship's flank turned into a jigsaw of glittering panels and folded away to nothing.

"Okay," said Sheppard. "That's creepy."

"I forgot, you'd not seen it do that." McKay swallowed, then squared his shoulders. "Come on, where's your sense of adventure?"

"Left it in my other pants."

"Look, this might be the only chance I get to study this ship from the inside. Sam said we needed all the info we could get, right?" He set off towards the hopper. "And I'm damned if I'm going to set foot in this thing on my own, so get in gear!"

He had left his data tablet back at the lab, but he still had a PDA that he'd upgraded. He took it out of his jacket pocket and switched it on, setting the integral sensors to the broadest settings they could muster. He might not have long in the starhopper—only as long as Angelus let him stay, assuming he was right and that the vessel was directly under the Ancient's control—and he was determined to gather as much data about the ship as he could in whatever time he was allowed.

"Want me to go in first?" Sheppard asked him as they reached the open hatch. McKay shook his head.

"Much as my self-preservation says yes, my self-esteem says no." He peered inside, holding the PDA in front of him like a talisman. On its tiny screen, data began to accumulate. "Okay, let's see… When I was in here last, on the *Apollo*, there was this—" He stopped, frowning into the gloom. "Hold on."

"What?"

"It's different. There was a kind of bulkhead on either side of the door." McKay looked about, letting his eyes adjust to the gloom inside the hopper. Sure enough, not only could he see all the way to the control couch at the front of the ship, but the area that had been closed off to him before was now laid open too.

He climbed in, unsure of where to head first. The interior space of the vessel was shaped roughly like two elongated eggs, set end to end, with a cylindrical 'waist' where they joined. The smaller egg contained the cockpit—McKay could see the couch where he and Ellis had first seen Angelus, and beyond that the softly glowing panels of the control system. What lay in the larger aft section was more difficult to make out. The only light came from a double row of fist-sized jewels running along each side of the ship, pulsing faintly blue-green like the bioluminescent markings of some deep-sea fish. There was something taking up most of the hopper's aft space, some kind of engine or power module, perhaps, but its outline was complex, jumbled. With the lack of light, he couldn't really make out what it was he was seeing. "Sheppard? This mess at the back here? What does that look like to you?"

"What, that? Damn…" McKay saw him squint into the darkness. "From here, it looks like a bunch of gold-plated squid all trying to play the same trombone."

"I meant, what do you think it is?"

"Well how the hell should I know? Engines? Look, you go check the squid band out, I'll go up front."

"Okay. Here, stash this somewhere, will you?" McKay handed him the *visios*, then began to clamber gingerly into the rear egg. Even if the tangle of metal in front of him hadn't been taking up most of the hopper's interior, the vessel would have been cramped. It was hard to see how Angelus could have spent much time there without a serious case of cabin fever.

"You know what's weird?" he called back over his shoulder.

"What?"

"Well, you've seen Ancient technology before… Of course you have, we live in it… And okay, they built in a variety of styles, but they tended to follow a kind of basic pattern, right?"

"And none of this looks like Ancient tech, is that what you're trying to say?"

"Kind of."

"I guess. I mean, some of these controls, maybe... But you're the expert."

McKay nodded absently. "Yes, I am..." He held up the PDA, and watched it running through a series of basic scans. There was power in the ship, that much was obvious. Traces of heat, vibration, low-level energy output on a number of different bands. Nothing that was immediately surprising for a machine that was powered-down and left on standby. The emissions from a quiescent puddle jumper were not much different.

He put the PDA back in his pocket. It could work just as well from there.

For a few seconds he tried to get past the central mass and further back towards the rear of the hopper, but the space was too cramped. Even if he was as slim as Angelus, McKay decided, he'd not have been able to get back there without injury. Puzzled, he gave up on that idea, and decided to go back to the cockpit and see if anything there looked more familiar.

He turned. And froze, every hair on the back of his neck crawling to slow attention.

He was no longer alone in the aft section.

There had been no sound, no movement. The lights still pulsed in their soft, slow rhythm, their meager brightness rising and falling like moonlight on a sluggish sea. The interior of the starhopper was as cool and still and inanimate as it had been when he had first entered.

But McKay was being watched. He could feel it more certainly than he could feel his own hammering heart.

He tried to speak, but terror had robbed him of breath. Whatever was observing him was doing so with complete and utter malevolence, a cold rage and a hunger the like of which he had never even imagined. He was in this ship with something that was totally, utterly focused on his destruction.

"*Sheppard*," he hissed.

"Hm?"

"We have to leave..." He couldn't even blink. Every instinct screamed at him that to move was to die. "There's... Something..."

Sheppard was rising off the couch. He must have been sitting there while he was studying the controls. "Already?"

There was a sound, far away, a metallic fluttering…

The patch of light coming in through the hatchway was changing shape, growing ragged at the edges.

The spell broke. McKay found himself rocketing forwards, all the tension built up in his limbs released in a sudden, massive burst of energy. "Out!" he howled. "Get out of this goddamn thing now!"

Sheppard didn't question further, just launched himself towards the hatch. McKay, scrambling forwards on the slick floor, saw him dive out, the filigreed edges of closing hull snagging on his clothes, and then he too was barreling through the opening.

It snapped shut on him, the golden maw closing around him in a hail of razored teeth. He felt the blades of it on his legs as he dropped free, and icy pain as they cut through the skin…

The floor of the hangar hit him squarely across the shoulder blades. He yelped, collapsed in a heap, and rolled over, clutching at his leg. As he did so, he saw the hatchway vanish as if it had never been.

A moment later, and it would have had his foot off.

Blood was soaking out through his right trouser leg. There were long cuts in the fabric where the closing hull panels had caught him. Pain, a growing, throbbing sting, surged up into his gut. "Ow. Son of a… *Ow!*"

"Are you okay?" Sheppard was next to him, sitting up on the deck. "What the hell just happened?"

Mckay shook his head. "I don't know," he muttered. "But I think that ship just tried to kill us."

CHAPTER SEVEN

Fragments

Ever since she had decided to bypass the authority of the IOA, Sam Carter had been preparing three dossiers in parallel. The first was, of course, a series of compiled reports for the Advisory, detailing what progress had been made on the Angelus project. The second, Carter's dossier for General Landry, contained *almost* exactly the same information as the first, although the order and intent of its contents varied considerably.

The third, though, was very different. Its contents would have made no sense at all to anyone but Carter herself—in fact, they made little enough to her. And while the first two dossiers were purely digital in form, this last file was strictly old-school: a manila folder containing paper documents, many stapled together or held in place with paper clips.

There were printouts in there, photographs, scans and transcripts, reports and requisitions; a collection of papers that seemed to have no correlation to one another at all. Carter had been putting the file together for two days, now, and she still wasn't entirely sure why. It was as though the documents it contained were pieces of a puzzle, but a puzzle she wasn't completely sure even had a solution.

Still, she couldn't shake the feeling that the file's contents needed only to be laid out in the correct order for their meaning to become clear to her. And it was this order that Carter was trying to find when the IOA observer arrived on Atlantis.

Carter had been sitting at her desk, a piece of paper in each hand, trying to read both at once in the hope that somehow they would make more sense together than they did alone. One was a form from one of the Atlantis medical staff, one Nurse Rhonda Neblett, who was reporting the loss, possibly theft, of a series of blood samples. Apparently, even though the blood had been in test tubes and locked in up one of the medical labs, it had vanished overnight.

The test tubes had not. They were exactly as Neblett had left them.

The other sheet contained information that was even more obscure. When Colonel Ellis had reported back to Atlantis after jumping into the M19 system, all the sensor readings gathered during *Apollo*'s orbits of Eraavis had been compressed into a data packet and sent back through the Stargate. Most of the data was video footage, the now-infamous film of the planet's scorched and blasted surface. In addition to this, however, were the results of all the chemical, radar and gravimetric scans that the ship had carried out while it was filming. A part of this information, translated into a series of complex graphs and charts, was in front of Carter now.

Much of it was a mystery to her: the chemical sciences were not really her field. But even with her level of knowledge she could see holes in the data. There were elements that should have been in the atmosphere of that slaughtered world that, according to *Apollo*'s sensor suites, were quite absent.

Together, Carter was certain that the documents in her folder, especially these two, meant something desperately important. Part of her was almost afraid to know what that might be.

A distant rumbling broke into her reverie, making her start slightly. Carter often found the world around her shrink away when she was working on a difficult problem; her perceptions would narrow, collapse into a into a single point encompassing only the mystery she was trying to unravel. It could be useful, that sheer degree of concentration, but there was a downside. When the real world decided it required her attentions, the switch in focus could be startling.

The rumble turned into a rising, rushing snarl. Carter put the papers back into their folder and stood up as the Stargate activated, the growl of the forming event horizon dropping back into a liquid hum. The activation was scheduled, and should have come as no surprise: Andrew Fallon, the IOA's chosen observer, was on his way through.

Carter put the folder away, and went down to the gate room to meet him. The Stargate had shut down by the time she got there, leaving the observer standing in front of an empty, open ring of stone.

She trotted up to meet him. "Mr Fallon?"

"Colonel Carter." He extended a hand, and she took it to shake briefly. "That's an unusual experience, isn't it?"

"The gate?" Carter looked up at it. "Really? I don't even notice any more."

Fallon blinked a couple of times, as if trying to clear his vision. "Well, if you need reminding, it's like riding Space Mountain in a hamster ball."

The observer was, in terms of appearance, quite unremarkable; a man of middling height and build, clean-shaven, with graying hair. His voice was soft, and his accent hard to place. He was, Carter judged, a man who was quite used to having people not notice he was there.

To some, that can be a curse. A few, though, turn it into a career.

He had a small suitcase in one hand and a coat draped over his shoulders, which told Carter that he intended to be around for a few days at least. Carter's heart grew a little heavier to know that, but she should have expected it. Her hope that the IOA's observer would look around, make his report and then go home again could only have been a vain one.

She dismissed it. "Do you want to settle in? There are spare rooms on the accommodation level—if you like, we can get one set up pretty fast."

Fallon smiled. "I'd prefer that to happen in the background if at all possible. Midway has me a little stir-crazy, so maybe we could start right away?"

"Of course. My office is just up here."

She led him back up the stairs and through the control room. He waited at the door to her office for her to go in, and then stood until she sat behind her desk. Then he set down his case, folded the coat neatly on top of it, and sat opposite her.

Precise, thought Carter, summing the man up in that single word. She patched a call down to the techs in charge of the accommodation level and asked them to set a room up, aware that Fallon was watching her carefully the whole time.

"So," he said, when she was done. "Here we are. The seat of power."

"I don't exactly think of it like that."

"Well, it's not always a good thing. Like it says in the comics, with great power comes great responsibility. And you do bear a lot of responsibility here, Colonel." He folded his fingers together, settling back a little into his seat. Carter could feel him weighing her up.

She half-smiled. "It's very much a team effort. I've only been here three weeks, but I don't feel like I'm bearing the responsibility alone."

"And you've taken it upon yourself to manage the Angelus matter?"

Her smile died. "I'm not sure what you mean."

"Angelus has been working for two days now, but the Advisory are sensing a lot of reticence in the reports they've been getting back."

Carter felt herself go a little bit cold. Just how much did the IOA know? "He hasn't complained to me." *Not directly, anyway.*

"It took almost twenty-four hours to find some electric fans because the computers you gave him kept overheating. Longer to fit a bunk so he can stay in the lab and work around the clock, which is what he wants to do. He's got no tech team, apart from Doctor McKay. To be blunt, Angelus is starting to think you're deliberately holding him back."

"I'll admit there have been supply issues…"

Fallon just raised an eyebrow.

"Okay," Carter sighed. "Cards on the table. Like you said, I've got a responsibility. And I believe I'd be failing that if I let Angelus start building death rays in my basement unimpeded."

"Because of the danger to Atlantis?"

"Sure. You must have seen the Eraavis footage."

"According to *your* last report—two days ago—Angelus says he can develop this project without alerting the Replicators again."

"And I don't believe him."

"I see." Fallon glanced about, as if taking in the sight of the office. The office, the control room beyond it, and more... "Colonel," he said levelly. "Let me ask you this: what are you doing here?"

"Excuse me?"

"Simple enough question." He leaned back in his seat and gestured around him. "All this. The Pegasus expedition, Atlantis, everything. What's it for, Colonel? What are you actually doing here?"

Carter narrowed her eyes. "I'm sorry, Mr Fallon, I've really got no idea what you're getting at."

"Okay, I'll spell it out for you. Stargate Command had a clear purpose, at least in the beginning. Secure the gate. Make sure nothing bad came in from outside. Once they failed in that remit, and bad things started coming in anyway, the purpose was expanded—gather technologies, information and alliances to help protect Earth."

"I know," Carter grated. "I was there."

"Which is why I don't understand your position, Colonel. Seriously, what is Earth getting out of Atlantis? What new technologies developed here are making things better for the people at home? How many of Earth's homeless are you housing? How many hungry people are you feeding?" He nodded at the techs working outside. "Because from where I'm sitting, Atlantis is a drain on resources and personnel that could be better used elsewhere."

"You won't find that a popular opinion in these parts, Mr Fallon."

"I wouldn't expect to."

Carter leaned towards him. "Listen, right now Atlantis the only thing standing between Earth and the Wraith. If it wasn't for the alliances we've made here, the information we've gathered and the continual vigilance of the people in this city, then the Wraith would be on their way through the gate and everyone on Earth would find themselves on the menu. Hungry and homeless alike."

Fallon smiled. "I've heard some twisted reasoning in my time, but that about takes the cake."

She stared. "I beg your pardon?"

"Colonel, if there had never been an expedition to Atlantis the gate here would still be at the bottom of the ocean on Lantea. If Weir's people hadn't blundered into the Wraith they would never have become the threat they are. If your local braniacs hadn't screwed around with the Replicators' core programming you wouldn't be in the middle of an interstellar war." He shook his head, wearily. "Do you know what you're actually doing here, Colonel? Damage control."

Carter opened her mouth to yell him out of the office, but stopped herself. She took a deep breath and unbunched her fists. "Care to explain what you mean by that?"

"Colonel, you're no fool. You know exactly what I mean: ever since the first Stargate was dug out of the sand we've been in trouble. The Goa'uld, the Replicators, the Wraith... The universe has proved itself, over and over again, to be full of enemies. Enemies that didn't even know we were here until you people started poking them with a stick. And every time you wake some new species of cannibal psycho you stumble around, get people killed, and then find a way to hold them off for a while by blundering good luck. Tell me, does that really seem like an appropriate use of resources to you?"

"So what would you rather do, Fallon? Hide in a cave and wait for them to come to us?"

"Not any more. You've poked too hard. If the Stargate had been left under the sand, if O'Neill hadn't blown up a System Lord saving a few grubby throwbacks on Abydos, if Weir hadn't dragged this city up off the seabed and told the Wraith all about us, we'd probably have been left in peace long enough to come up with our own solutions. But not now."

He stood up. "This project has put the whole of Earth into deadly jeopardy, and now your job is to do something about it. And guess what? The opportunity has just fallen into your lap."

Carter was on her feet too. "I don't believe Angelus is a solution. Considering what happened to Eraavis, I think he's as dangerous as any enemy. Right now, he's the stick we're poking the Asurans with."

"Weir poked them long before you got here, Colonel. Thing is, you've got a chance to do something worthwhile here, to make Atlantis mean something. And it looks to me like you're doing everything in your power to obstruct that."

"*Mean* something? Are you insane?"

"Bottom line, Colonel—as far as the Advisory is concerned, Angelus is developing a weapon that can protect Earth from the threats you've stirred up. And if that costs us Atlantis, then that's a fair trade."

"You have got to be kidding," she hissed.

"I'm not. From now on, you'll not only offer Angelus every assistance, you'll also cease any attempts to impede his research. You'll assign him a tech crew and any expertise he'll require. I'm under strict instructions to report all progress back to the Advisory on a twice daily basis, and if I see something I don't like we'll pull Angelus back to Earth and set him up with a lab there."

"Earth?" Carter stared at him, horrified. "Fallon, he screwed up on his own planet and the Replicators melted it—"

"The Replicators are a long way from Earth. But you know what? You're right—if some part of this weapon does attract the bad guys, maybe it would be better if they came here rather than to Earth, hm? That way, only a few hundred people will die in flames and not six billion."

"If we kick him out of the damn city maybe nobody dies!"

Fallon shook his head. "He's too valuable. He either works here or at home. Your choice." He picked up his case and coat, turned away from her, and headed for the door. As he reached it, he paused. "This whole mess is your fault, Colonel," he said quietly, not looking back. "All you exploration junkies, spinning your Stargates just to see what would happen… Here's your chance to atone. Don't screw it up."

"Fallon?"

"Yeah?"

"This isn't over."

"Damn right it isn't. I'll go and see Angelus now, let him

know how things are going to be run around here."

With that, he was gone. Carter watched him making his way to the stairs, half of her hoping that he'd fall and break his spine.

The other half wondering if he was right.

She sat in the office for some time, listening to the soft chatter of the control room, trying to calm herself and failing. The conversation with Fallon had shaken her.

Three weeks, she thought. She had been in charge of the Pegasus expedition for three lousy weeks, and already she'd had the authority ripped out from under her.

Had she made a mistake? She had known that the Advisory wanted what Angelus was offering, but perhaps she'd underestimated just how badly. And seriously, she wondered, how could they trust her with a decision like that? She had proven herself to be an effective agent in her time at Stargate Command, sure. She'd been promoted, in the field; she'd fought and led men into battle and, on more occasions than she trusted herself to count, she had been instrumental in saving the day.

But she'd been in Elizabeth Weir's shoes for three weeks. It wasn't enough.

Her headset crackled softly, a certain sign that it was about to admit a call. Carter sighed, put her elbows on the desktop and her head in her hands, and closed her eyes.

As she did so the speaker blipped in her ear. She touched the control on its side. "Carter."

"*Colonel? It's Jennifer Keller, down in the infirmary.*"

Carter's eyes snapped open. There was something in Keller's voice she didn't like at all. "What's wrong?"

"*There's been an incident. Rodney McKay's been injured.*"

"Seriously?"

"*No,*" said Keller quickly, "*it's not serious.*"

In the background, almost out of range of the pickup, Carter heard McKay begin to disagree vehemently, and she puffed out a relieved breath. "Sounds like his voice hasn't been impaired, anyway."

"*Oh no, that's working just fine. But Colonel, he wants to talk to you. Alone.*"

"So put him on."

"*In person. He's extremely insistent.*"

"I'll be right down."

Carter hurried to the nearest transporter. She was most of the way there when she heard her name called, and turned to see Radek Zelenka running towards her.

Zelenka was the expedition's second expert in Ancient technology, just below McKay in the Atlantis scientific hierarchy. He was a slight, bespectacled man, a native of the Czech Republic. Carter hadn't really spent enough time in his company to know much about him, but he seemed extremely competent. Certainly, his soft voice and slightly withdrawn nature was often a welcome opposite to McKay's bombast.

He skated to a halt, slightly out of breath. "Colonel Carter? May I speak with you?"

"Is it about Rodney?"

He looked at her blankly. "*Should* I be speaking to you about Rodney?"

"I guess not. Look, I'm in kind of a hurry…"

Zelenka nodded. "I understand, but this is rather important. May I walk with you?"

"Sure." She gestured down the corridor. "I'm heading to the transporter, so I can go with you as far as there. What did you want to talk about?"

"Well…" He fell into step alongside her as she set off. "That report on the power fluctuations. Have you had a chance to read it yet?"

The report was one of the documents in Carter's mystery folder. For the past twenty hours, parts of the city's power grid had been experiencing unexplained drops in power. There hadn't been many—four at last count—but they had been noticeable. Carter had asked Zelenka to look into the problem, just in case anything was wrong with the ZPMs. "I have, yes."

"I think, perhaps, you should throw that report away."

Carter raised an eyebrow. "Why is that?"

"It's inaccurate. No, I'm sorry. What I mean to say is, it is no longer the whole picture. Um…" He scratched his head absently, brushed hair out of his face. "The fluctuations are different now."

"Worse?"

"Not as such. They are not as strong now. The level of the drops in power has now decreased to only one or two percent of what they were."

"Well, that doesn't sound so bad."

He gave her a slight shrug. "True. But they are now occurring once every forty-one seconds."

Carter stopped dead. "You're kidding."

"I am not. Where we were experiencing severe power drains at random, now the grid has settled into a kind of pulse. The drops are almost too small to notice—if I hadn't already been looking for them I wouldn't have known they were there."

"That's just weird." Carter got her feet moving again. They were coming up on the transporter now, and if Rodney wanted to speak to her alone she was going to have to dump Zelenka in the next few meters. "Have you tracked down a source for the drain yet?"

"No. It's system-wide as far as I can tell. And yes, that lab was the first place I looked. So far, I cannot pin it down to there."

Carter got to the transporter and stopped, turning to Zelenka as the doors slid open. "Okay, thanks for telling me. Radek, can you stay on top of this? Maybe it's nothing, a side-effect of the extra computing power we're feeding Angelus, but I've got a bad feeling about it anyway."

"You and me both." He was standing a little way from the transporter, and she realized, with some relief, that he wasn't planning to get in with her. "I'll keep you posted. Say hi to Rodney for me."

"Sure," she smiled, and stepped inside. And then, as the doors closed, remembered that she hadn't told him who she was going to see.

Obviously, she hadn't needed to. She chuckled softly,

touched the nearest activation dot to the infirmary and vanished in a flare of blue-white light.

.

McKay was alone in the infirmary when Carter arrived. He was on a gurney, sitting back against the raised backrest with his legs stretched out in front of him. As the door opened he started upright, then relaxed slightly as Carter came in. He raised a hand. "Hey."

"Hey yourself." McKay's right trouser-leg had been raggedly cut away just below the knee, and his entire lower leg was wrapped tightly in white bandages. Carter pointed at it. "What happened to you?"

"Got into a fight with Angelus' ship. Guess who won."

She pulled up a nearby seat and sat down. "It's not like you to go picking fights with starships."

"Trust me, I didn't start it." He sat up straighter, and swung himself around, wincing as he eased his damaged leg off the edge of the gurney. "Damn it, that stings. You know, I asked Keller for morphine, and she laughed. Can you believe that? *Laughed*. Does this look like 'just a scratch' to you?"

She could only shrug. "I'm not a doctor. Speaking of which, where is she?"

"Down in one of the labs. Something screwy with the MRI machine, or something." He stretched, as if he had been lying still for too long. "Sorry to drag you all the way down here, but Keller won't let me out just yet and I'm not entirely sure if I trust the comms, especially if that observer's around."

"Oh yes," Carter muttered. "He's around. But what about you, staying here because Keller said so? When did you start following other people's advice?"

He looked slightly hurt. "It's been known. Hey, I've been injured, okay? And, I might add, in the line of duty. Keller might not have the most wonderful bedside manner, but if she says she wants to run some more checks on me then I figure it's probably best to, you know, let her do it."

Carter could understand his aversion to leaving the infirmary. He probably hated being in here, but if there was any chance at all something might still be physically wrong with him he wouldn't take the risk. McKay was a legendary hypochondriac. "So what's your beef with the comms? Apart from Fallon."

"Let's just say I've already been physically assaulted by one inanimate object today." He took a deep breath, squared his shoulders a little. "Okay, here's the thing. When I was in the hopper, I managed to get some readings on a PDA before the door closed. And there's a whole bunch of stuff about that ship which doesn't add up."

"Like what?"

"Well... First I was concerned because it didn't look like an Ancient ship. The detail was all wrong, the shape of the thing... But I checked out the database and spotted a class of ceremonial vessel that wasn't completely different. And it turns out that the Eraavi blinged it up for him as a mark of respect, same time as they made him the mask."

"So, what then?"

"That's the problem. There's no way that ship came from Eraavis."

Carter tilted her head slightly, puzzled. "Say again?"

"I got some pretty detailed readings on the quiescent emissions from the drive system. I couldn't from the outside because there's some kind of shielding, but once I got in there... Anyways, it's got a hyperdrive, but a pretty pathetic one. If Angelus wanted to cross Replicator space in that thing, he'd need to do it in microjumps. Seriously, I don't think he could have done the trip in less than a month."

A cold knot had appeared in Carter's gut. "Can you confirm that?"

"My calculations? Yeah, as soon as I'm out of here. As for the readings themselves, I'm guessing I won't get another chance to get inside. Even if I could..." He screwed up his face, as though tasting something sour. "Thanks, but no thanks."

"I can understand that," she lied. There was something he wasn't telling her, something not right about the entire conversation. "Rodney..."

"You want to know what else?" he interrupted. "It's lost weight."

She blinked. "The ship? I don't—"

"I got mass readings on it when I was on *Apollo*. And while I was cross-referencing what I got on the PDA, I ran it through the load records on the jumpers that hauled it in. There's a discrepancy of almost fifty kilos."

"What does that mean?"

"I have absolutely no idea."

Carter remained silent for a moment or two, thinking hard. What McKay was telling her felt like more pieces of her mystery folder—strange, unconnected incidents that seemed as though they should fit together somehow. The chemical analysis of Eraavis had shown discrepancies, and if McKay's assessment of the starhopper's hyperdrive was correct, then that meant...

"You think Angelus is lying to us."

"I don't know," McKay replied, sounding oddly subdued. "If you'd asked me that before today, I'd probably have said no. In the time I've spent with him, I've never got the feeling that he's being anything but honest. Then again, my instincts aren't always one hundred percent accurate..." He sighed. "Sam, I swear I just don't know. Maybe it's the ship that's lying!"

Despite herself, she smiled. "I'll have it arrested."

"Well, you could maybe have Angelus arrested instead."

"Not a chance. If I tried it Fallon would just claim you were interfering with the ship and have it cordoned off. Or he'd have you reprimanded. Actually, both. Trust me, the Advisory want this weapon so bad they can taste it, and they don't care what happens to us as long as they get it."

"No big surprise there," McKay sighed. "Okay, I guess we'll just have to leave him to it for now. Until I can, you know, confirm what the Hell's going on."

"It's a risk."

"Well, he's contained. I spent a lot of time down there with him, you know? He's under guard the whole time, there's the surveillance... Sheppard installed guillotines in the lab's power feeds when he was setting the cameras up. If Angelus even looks like he's going to jeopardize the city with some kind of wild experiment, he can be shut down in a second, whatever this Fallon guy says. Hold on, I'm just going to try this..." He eased himself off the edge of the gurney, testing his weight on the bandaged leg. Carter saw him wince, but he didn't seem to have any trouble standing.

"Okay, that's not too bad," he muttered. "Anyway, back to Angelus. Why would he be trying to pull something? So far we've given him everything he wants, however reluctantly. Believe me, I've been over and over this. It doesn't make sense."

"You're right." She got up. "We haven't got all the right bits of the puzzle yet."

"Hm?"

"Never mind. Look, we have the sensor data from *Apollo*, we've got your PDA readings… Surely we could plug that information into the stellar database."

"To find out where he actually came from?" McKay nodded tentatively. "Yeah, I guess we could do that. There's only a finite number of bio-capable worlds, and the hyperspace trajectory data from *Apollo* could round down the point of origin even further… Yeah, that's do-able."

"Great." She got up. "Come on, we're leaving."

His eyes went wide. "What about my tests?"

"I'll have Keller book you back in later. Can you walk on that leg?"

McKay, as it turned out, was quite capable of walking. His wounds might have been painful, but they were by no means serious. Carter had already decided to call back on Keller and make sure before she put McKay through anything strenuous, but the fact that he kept forgetting to limp when he thought she wasn't watching clued her in.

They went back to the control room. McKay hauled himself theatrically in front of a terminal and set to work on the PDA data. Carter left him to it and went in to her office, opened a word processor on her computer and quickly typed out a summary of what McKay had told her in the infirmary. Then, without saving the file, she printed it out and deleted the text.

The hardcopy went into her mystery folder. One more piece of the puzzle, awaiting it's place.

By the time she was finished, McKay was already waving at her from his terminal, occasionally gesturing at his leg as if to let her know he was quite unable to walk the several meters from his chair to the office. Sighing, Carter got up and went across the gangway to join him. "Have you found something?"

"If by 'something', you mean our guest's true point of origin, yes I have," he told her, triumphantly.

"Wow, that was fast." She leaned closer to his terminal screen, genuinely impressed. "You got that down to one out of how many planets?"

"Well, okay, lets say *points* of origin."

"Rodney…"

"There's no way to be certain *exactly* which one it is, okay? There's too many variables. And this is assuming that he's telling the truth about how long he spent out there in the first place."

"Please don't make this any more tenuous than it already is. I can only imagine what Colonel Ellis is going to say when I send him off on- How many was it?"

"Four," said McKay, glumly.

"*Four* new detours."

He looked up at her. "You're not going to make me tell him, are you?"

"Not this time. I'll take the flak on this one. Just upload those points to my terminal."

She went back into her office, and then used her headset to call Palmer. "Simon, can you set up a subspace hail to *Apollo*?"

"*I'm sorry, Colonel, but didn't Colonel Ellis forbid patching into* Apollo *unless it was an emergency? He doesn't regard subspace as being secure.*"

"He's probably right, but I can't risk waiting until he reports in again. He's already overdue. Tell him it is an emergency. I'll take responsibility."

She cut the connection, and waited. A few seconds later an upload from McKay appeared. Carter opened it, quickly arranged the planetary ident codes into the order she would give them to Ellis, and then heard her headset crackle.

"Carter."

"*Colonel, it's Palmer. There's a problem. I can't raise* Apollo."

She stood up. Through the glass wall of her office she saw Palmer over by the comms board. He saw her looking and spread his hands. "*There's no return at all,*" he went on. "*The hail's going out, but it's not reaching anyone.*"

"That's odd." *And a little frightening,* she thought to herself. "Keep trying. They might be in a blind spot, or be having technical difficulties. Let me know as soon as they pick up the hail."

She sat down, slowly. There was a Plan B, of course—Carter knew she couldn't always rely on *Apollo* being at her beck and call, so she had decided some time ago what to do if the battlecruiser wasn't available. She would wait a short time for Palmer to work his magic on the subspace comms, but if Ellis continued to prove elusive, that secondary plan might have to be put into operation.

And McKay wasn't going to like it. Not one bit.

CHAPTER EIGHT

Insecurity

Radek Zelenka was alone in the ZPM lab when he heard the voices.

He hadn't intended to stay in the lab so late. Like every member of the expedition he kept long hours, and certainly wasn't adverse to working through the night when the situation demanded it. But the problem that was occupying him now had hardly seemed urgent. The fluctuation in the Atlantis power grid was puzzling, but in terms of actual voltage close to unnoticeable. The strange, rhythmic dips in electricity amounted to half a percent of the city's regular output at most. It wasn't even enough to make the lights flicker.

However, there were elements of the phenomenon that intrigued him, to a point where he had become thoroughly engrossed in cataloguing them. He had started to notice the anomalies at around six in the evening, Atlantis time, and had promised himself a couple of hours work on them before closing down his programs and heading out. Several of the tech staff who worked the later shift were due to head out then anyway, and Zelenka had planned to leave with them and join them for a meal in the mess hall. There had been talk of a movie. But, as the daylight outside had reddened into darkness, and the city lights had grown bright and golden in response, Zelenka had stayed at his terminal. Gradually, the rest of the tech team had left him; the group at first, no doubt following up on their meal and movie plans, and then other, less social members of the science staff. As each had gone Zelenka had muttered his goodnights, promising, without looking up from his screen, to be just a few more minutes. Another couple of cycles, just to confirm his readings, he would say absently, and then he would be done.

Eventually, there was no-one left to listen.

It was probably close to midnight when Zelenka became fully aware of his solitude. The ZPM lab was not a particularly large room, but complicated in form, and it was possible to sit in one part of it and be wholly out of sight of someone quite close by. For a few moments, as he leaned back and looked around, he wondered if anyone was still there, around one of the corners or behind a pillar, but he quickly realized he was totally alone.

He glanced at his watch, and smiled to himself. The movie was over anyway. Apart from the city's night staff—marines on guard, sensor operators on one of their constant shifts, anyone unlucky enough to have gotten cleaning duty—he was probably one of the last awake. There were few night-owls on the expedition. Work started early on Atlantis, and late nights were discouraged.

Zelenka shrugged, and went back to his work. If he was honest with himself, he rather enjoyed being alone here. The stillness helped him concentrate.

And the work required his concentration, there could be no doubt of that. Atlantis was big. Compared to cities on Earth, maybe, it wasn't exceptional—just over four kilometers from the tip of any pier to that of its opposite twin. Taken as a single structure, though, it was enormous, and ferociously complex. If every building in Manhattan, every streetlight, every hydrant and taxicab and TV and electrical socket, every single part of that entire conurbation was part of one single system, and controlled by one electronic authority, then it might rival Atlantis as a work of technological wonder. Such complexity was what made studying the place so endlessly fascinating, but also frustrating in the extreme. The power distribution grid alone had something close to six million output nodes.

Trying to find the source of the drain had seemed, at first, to be like looking for a single leaky pipe in a city-sized plumbing system, and when Colonel Carter had given Zelenka the task of tracking that leak down he had despaired. From the first few huge and unexplainable power drops, the problem had shrunk to its present, nearly-undetectable levels, which made hunting it seem even more hopeless. Zelenka had decided that his only hope of finding the drain was from the ZPM lab itself: it was directly connected to the main power chamber, and had uninterrupted access to the battery of Ancient devices monitoring the city's three Zero Point Modules. Each of those tiny power sources, despite being no bigger than a man's thigh, could power Atlantis for decades—or, if their energies were released all at once, reduce a planet to fast-moving rubble. Little wonder, then, that so much of the city's resident computing power was devoted to watching over them.

Zelenka had been siphoning off a fraction of that electronic attention to try and track down the drain for most of the day. One of his first ideas had been to poll a scattering of output nodes to see which were hit by the power drains earlier than others, and from this locate the source of the problem. The polling system uploaded its data to a core file: Zelenka, while running other tests at the same time, had watched the file grow in size for half a day, populating a series of graphs and maps and diagrams with its contents.

He had given up on that when he decided that the graphs were going to stay as flat as they started, and the maps as undifferentiated. There was no measurable lag between nodes at opposite ends of the city: the pulse was, quite literally, happening everywhere at once.

The exercise had not been a complete waste of time, though. While the data from the nodes showed no timing differences, they did show something else. Something that had filled the rest of Zelenka's day, and left him here alone in the lab.

There was a pattern to the drops in power that went beyond a regular forty-one second cycle, an underlying structure of breathtaking fractal complexity. It was subtle—as the pulses themselves had been almost too small to detect, so this structure was smaller still by a factor of a hundred. Only when the sensitivity of the node-sensors had been set as high as the grid would allow could it be properly seen. Zelenka had spent hours trying to filter the pattern out, writing algorithms to flatten any hint of electrical noise. System use, feedback from the sensors, even the microscopic flexion of the city's structure due to wave motion had to be eliminated.

The pattern remained. Now that he had found it, Zelenka couldn't make it go away.

Visually, it told him nothing. There was something of an eerie beauty to it, he couldn't deny that, and he found himself watching its slow, rippling fluctuations for several minutes. But there was a signal component to the structure that promised to be of far more use. Zelenka had spent the last half an hour, just before noticing he was alone, setting up a series of frequency analyzers and pattern-recognitions systems to try and make sense of what he had found.

The lab was very quiet. There was a faint humming from the city's air system, and the whirring of computer fans from the tech team's terminals and laptops, but apart from that there was nothing.

Perhaps that silence was what gave him the idea of translating the signal component to an audio output and listening to it.

The process was simple, a conversion of data that he accomplished almost reflexively. Then, with one more quick glance about to make sure no-one was around to hear this folly, he turned up his terminal's speakers and triggered the signal.

Breathy, sibilant sounds began to whisper out into the lab.

"*Hovno*," swore Zelenka. He had expected to hear static, or some meaningless pulsation, but the audio signal was something else entirely. It ebbed and flowed like waves on a distant shore, rising slowly in pitch and volume, then falling away in a series of melancholy echoes, only to hover at the edge of hearing for several long seconds before starting its inexorable climb again.

Zelenka leaned close to the terminal speakers, listening hard. There was another level to the sound, hidden by that lonely rushing, something more complex, more structured. The underlying pattern of the signal, he guessed, but even as that rational thought entered his mind it was swept aside. What lay beneath the sound, beneath the waves, was no mere pattern.

There were voices in there.

Suddenly, the lab was very cold. Zelenka found himself edging away from the terminal, straining to hear what the voices were saying but dreading making out the actual words. It wasn't easy; there were many voices, whispers, hissing over and through each other like the mindless sibilance of snakes. Dozens, hundreds of voices… He strained to hear, his skin crawling, trying not to remember the cold echoes of an attic in Prague as the whispers grew louder, edging towards comprehension.

It was too much. He moaned in horror, reached out to switch the speakers off and almost screamed as he saw the figure reflected in the terminal's screen. *There was someone behind him!*

He whirled. Sam Carter was in the lab doorway, a puzzled frown knitting her brow. "My God, Radek. What in the world?"

For a moment, Zelenka just sat there, heart bouncing, breath frozen in his throat. Then his lungs decided to release him, and he let out a shuddering breath. "Colonel."

"Are you all right?"

"Yes," he croaked. He turned down the volume. "Yes, I'm fine. You're up late…"

She drew closer, looking concerned. "I've been up arguing with Fallon about the tech team for Angelus. I was just going to get some sleep when the biosensors flagged somebody still in here, so I came down to check it out… What are you still doing up?"

"Working." He rolled his seat back on its castors. "Trying to track down the power drains. I guess I must have gotten caught up."

"Yeah, but what in?" Carter pulled up a nearby seat and sat next to him, peering at the screen. "What was that awful noise?"

He took a deep breath. "As far as I can tell it's what's underlying the forty-one second cycle of the drain pulses. There's a very faint pattern there that I've been trying to identify, and it's going through frequency analysis right now. I just thought I'd see what it sounded like." He shivered. "I wish I hadn't, now."

"I've got to admit, it did sound pretty freaky." Carter gave him a smile. "Let's hear it again."

"Do we have to?"

She nodded. Reluctantly, Zelenka raised the volume again.

He watched Carter's face as she listened, her forehead creased in concentration, light from the monitor playing patterns on her skin. "That's so odd," she breathed, finally. "It almost sounds like…"

"Voices?"

She gave him a startled look. "You hear that too? I thought it was just me."

"Whispering. And I think I may have…" He shook his head. "No."

"What?"

"It's nothing."

"Doctor, it may seem unimportant, but this situation is mysterious enough without us keeping secrets from one another. What were you going to say?"

He straightened his glasses. "Okay. But Colonel, if I tell you something strange, will you promise not to have Doctor Keller evaluate me?"

She raised an eyebrow. "How strange are we talking here?"

"When I was young… Younger, back in Prague. There was a fellow student of mine in the university. Bedřich, although we called him- No, never mind." He chuckled abruptly, then stopped, aware of how hollow his voice sounded. "One winter, Bedřich stopped turning up to his lectures. I became worried, so I visited him."

Carter was gazing at him quite intently. "Go on."

Zelenka shrugged. "His father had a large house, much larger than mine, in the Malá Strana. It had an attic… Bedřich was up there, he was spending all his time there, his father said. His wife, Bedřich's mother, had died, you see, and Bedřich had a tape recorder."

"A what?"

"One of those, what are they called? The old kind, with the big reels. He was disconnecting the microphone, letting the tapes record all the way through, and then listening to the tapes. Over and over again, listening to the blank tapes he'd recorded. Trying to hear…"

"Hear what?"

"His mother."

"Oh my God," she said quietly. "EVP."

Zelenka sighed. "Yes, I read up on it later, after Bedřich went to hospital. Trying to record the voices of the dead on tape… I even listened to one of his tapes. He said it had his mother's voice on it, but I didn't hear her. I heard…" He paused, and looked away.

"Radek… *What did you hear?*"

Zelenka nodded at the terminal. "That."

Carter looked at him for a few seconds, then reached out and turned the volume down again. "Okay, now that we've completely freaked ourselves out, what do you say we pick this up again in the morning? When the lights are—"

Half the computers in the lab went dark.

Zelenka jumped up from his chair. It went skittering back on its casters. "*Kurva,*" he gasped.

Carter was on her feet too, looking wildly about as the dark computers began to boot themselves up again. "What's happened? How did that happen?"

He shook his head. His heart was yammering behind his ribs, the pulse beating in his ears… "Oh, the *pulse!*"

"The what?"

"What I've spent all day working on!" He took the audio signal completely offline and brought up the timing track of the power drains. A quick look at his watch confirmed what had happened. "It's the power drain. It shut down all the computers that were running heavy loads. Their power supplies dropped out, so they rebooted."

"That must mean the drain's a lot bigger than it was," Carter replied, staring at the screen. "Yeah, there it is. Damn, Radek, that's a big jump."

"Almost ten percent below baseline."

"Not good. Let's see if the next one is as bad…" She straightened up, her eyes still on the screen.

Zelenka counted down on his watch. "Okay, we'll hit it again in three, two one…"

Nothing happened. This pulse was just as imperceptible as

the others.

They stayed where they were for another few minutes, waiting for a bigger spike, but none appeared. It seemed, for the moment, that the drain on the city's power had returned to its previous levels.

"That," Carter told him, "is the damndest thing. But if it's stabilized for now, I think it might be a good time to get some sleep."

Zelenka thought about lying in the dark, trying not to hear whispering behind the rushing of blood in his ears. "Yeah, maybe I'll stay up a little longer."

"This will keep for a while, don't you think?"

"I hope so. But right now, I need some fresh air."

There was an open area on the way to Angelus' lab; a long gallery, railed on four sides, surrounding a space in the pier amour. It was a kind of narrow cloister. McKay had mentioned it, while boasting to Zelenka about his rapport with the genius Ancient, but he had been characteristically dismissive. Zelenka, on the other hand, liked it a lot.

He could hear the sea from here, but it was a distant, comforting sound, not at all like the signal component and its tragic rushings. There must have been a fairly stiff breeze blowing across the city tonight—he was largely sheltered from it in the cloister, but if he listened closely, he could hear it whistle past some of the upper towers, and raise waves to slap against the pier's armored flanks. It made him think of the Vltava, and rain on streets, and suddenly Zelenka wanted very much to go home.

He glanced up out of the opening, towards the core of the city. Hundreds, thousands of lights were on there, studding the towers, outlining their jumbled, angular forms in dots of bright gold. The highest lights were misty, almost lost to the darkness, but the center part of Atlantis was awash with them.

It was a strange sight, alien. After years as part of the expedition, still oddly unfamiliar. It gave him no comfort to see it. There was a coldness to the city, an antiseptic, inhuman feeling that he had never experienced anywhere else. It was as though the structure of the place was completely apart from the people that lived there, unaffected by them. Sure, they could hang pictures or play movies or set up beds and bookcases, but the walls remained unchanged, the floors and ceilings stayed exactly as they would be if no-one was there at all. Zelenka gazed up at the city of Atlantis and knew that if it wished, if it gained the will, it could wipe all traces of them away in an instant.

Humans clung to its surfaces like germs to a toilet bowl. One flush, and they'd be gone as if they'd never arrived.

He turned away, an act that felt more like defiance than avoidance. As he did so, something moved at the far corner of the cloister.

Zelenka froze, one hand on the cold rail, peering out across the open space to try and see who or what was there. The cloister was lit, although not brightly; panels along its walls cast a sea-green glow that was gentle on the eye, but not very revealing. There was certainly more shadow here than light, and if something had retreated into the darkness it looked very much like it was going to stay there.

A minute passed, and then another. Zelenka stayed where he was, waiting for the movement he had seen to repeat itself, but he waited in vain. Eventually he decided that he had seen nothing after all. One of the disadvantages to wearing spectacles was the occasional reflection cast across their surface, especially when looking up at an alien city full of lights.

He walked on, feeling rather foolish, wondering if perhaps he should invest in contact lenses. On the one hand, he might see less in the way of ghosts if he did so. Then again, wearing contacts would necessitate starting each day by touching his own eyeballs. The thought made him shudder, and by the time he reached the end of the cloister he had dismissed it entirely.

There was an opening at the end of the gallery, leading into a short corridor. Zelenka looked down it, saw the guard station that had been set up there and thought about turning back. After all, what was he here for anyway? He had already determined that Angelus' lab could not be proved the source of the power drains. Was he really going to walk in and accuse the Ancient of sucking the city's power like some kind of voltage vampire?

It was ridiculous. Sometimes, Zelenka thought darkly, McKay was right to berate him. He could be a damned fool on occasion.

Then he noticed that the guard station was empty.

He walked up to it, puzzled. There should have been two marines posted there at all times. If either had to take a break for any reason the other would stay, and the post was supposed to be manned continuously, despite Fallon's objections. If the two marines there had both left at the same time, and Sheppard found out about it, there would be hell to pay.

The guard station was a prefabricated, collapsible structure from the city's stores. Unfolded and bolted into place it formed an armored box a couple of meters square, with plexiglass panels on each side. There should be no way that the post could appear empty when it was occupied, unless whoever was inside was on the floor.

He pushed the door slightly open, and peeked in. There was a small folding table there, set against the far wall of the box, and a couple of unoccupied seats, but that was all. No marines on the floor. There was a mug of coffee on the table, and next to that, an automatic pistol.

Zelenka grimaced. He didn't like guns. He had been given some extremely basic training in how to use them when he had joined the expedition, but he had found the entire process distasteful, and promised himself that he'd not pick a weapon up again if he could possibly help it. He left the gun where it was, and closed the door of the guard station.

Although the corridor was quite cool, being so close to the open gallery, the coffee hadn't been steaming. Zelenka wondered how long the post had been abandoned.

He walked on past it, towards the door to Angelus' lab. The door, he could see as he approached, was open, and warm light shone from within. According to McKay, the Ancient worked almost constantly, taking no more than an hour's rest a day, if that. Whether that was due to his evolved physiology or his obsession, no-one could say.

No sound, barring the hum of machinery, came from inside the lab. Zelenka slowed as he neared the door—maybe the

Ancient was asleep after all. The technicians assisting him would have gone back to their own rooms by now, surely?

He slowed, stopping just before he got to the door, and then leaned around it.

Angelus was inside. Zelenka had not actually seen the Ancient before, but there could be no mistaking who he was looking at. He was clad in a kind of loose robe or toga made from shimmering golden fabric, and his skin was as pale as marble.

The Ancient was standing in the middle of the lab, very still. He had his left hand raised, and he was looking intently at his own palm.

Zelenka frowned, unable to determine exactly what was going on. Angelus had an expression on his face that was part interest, part puzzlement, and part... What? Something close, Zelenka decided, to wonder. It was as if the mechanics of his own limb were somehow fascinating him—he was turning the hand very slightly, flexing the fingers just a little, as though to study the way it moved.

In the strange, shifting light from the display holograms behind him, Angelus looked to Zelenka almost completely alien.

He backed away, slowly, until he was certain that his footfalls wouldn't disturb Angelus in his reverie, and then turned and headed back towards the gallery. He could not interpret what was going on in the lab, but neither could he bring himself to interrupt it—partly through fear, but also from a sense that what he had witnessed was something desperately *private*.

But whatever was happening here, he decided, Carter would need to be told. Even if Angelus had not seemed so strange, the empty guard post could not go unreported. Besides, Zelenka wanted to be away, and soon.

The night had offered him enough strangeness already; it was a heady brew, and he could drink no more of it. It was making his head spin.

The thought of the city core, so alien and impersonal a few minutes ago, was now heartbreakingly comforting.

As he neared the guard post, he slowed. It was as empty as

before, the door slightly ajar. When he looked in through the plexiglass he saw the gun and the mug just as he had left them. There was a thought in his head, a nagging itch of a thought that was so unlike him, so out of character that he couldn't quite tell where it came from. But it wouldn't go away.

He was tired, that must have been the cause. Fatigue was finally catching up with him, he realized with a grim smile, and a heavy, muzzy feeling was taking hold of him from the neck up. Still, the thought was insistent.

You're a damned fool, he told himself. And as he did so he ducked into the guard station and grabbed the gun from the table.

As soon as he had done it, he regretted it, but his feet were already carrying him away. He found himself starting to run, the gun heavy and cold in his fist. It was a hateful thing to hold, but there was a seductive nature to it as well. Trotting down the silent corridor, almost overwhelmed by nervousness and fatigue, there was something about the weapon that gave him strength.

A stupid kind of strength, he knew. A foolish, false bravery that was more likely to get him into trouble than anything else. After all, hadn't he just stolen a piece of military equipment?

That thought struck him as he reached the end of the corridor, and brought him up short. He stopped, lifted the gun to stare at it. Almost, he realized with a shivering sense of irony, as Angelus had been looking at his own hand.

He was still looking at it when he heard something next to him breathe.

CHAPTER NINE

My Little Eye

If Zelenka's day had been one of disturbing revelations, he was certainly not alone in that. Teyla Emmagan was faring no better.

Things had started to go sour for her almost as soon as the day had begun, with her return trip through the Stargate. Teyla was used to walking out of the gate and into Atlantis; falling uncontrollably out of the event horizon was a bad way to come home. She'd not had any time to prepare herself for the trip back from Malus Rei, that was the problem. There had been no time to ready herself for the strange, headlong sensations involved in being flung between worlds. Instead, she had entered the rippling surface of the event horizon in mid-leap, desperately trying to evade a hail of Malan crossbow bolts.

Although there was a degree of subjective time between entering one Stargate and leaving another—enough to remember the feeling of being hurled about, at least—in terms of objective time the journey was instantaneous. Teyla came out of the Atlantis Stargate in mid-air, the other half of the frantic jump she had made back on Malus Rei, but the Malan gate had been neglected so badly it was leaning askew on its foundations. The change in perspective was startling in other ways, too; Teyla started her leap at early evening, and ended in morning light, tumbling uncontrollably along the gate room floor.

Dust, gritty and pale, puffed out along with her, as did several crossbow bolts. Thankfully, due to the angle of the Malan gate these whickered harmlessly over her head and clattered into the ceiling of the gate room.

Teyla scrambled up, dropping into a fighting crouch with her gun raised, in case any Malans came out after her. But as she did so the gate closed, the mirrored surface of its event horizon scattering into quantum foam and spinning away to nothing.

Half a crossbow bolt tumbled out of the foam and skittered forlornly along the floor.

Teyla straightened up, and then turned to those who had gone before her. "Is everyone all right?"

The rest of the team—three medics, two engineers and a handful of armed marines—nodded, raising clouds of gray powder as they did so. Malus Rei was prey to dust storms, and it was during a particularly violent one that the inhabitants had turned on them. Just like Teyla, all of them were covered in the stuff, and most had bits of cloth tied around their faces to keep the worst of it out of their lungs.

"Very well," she told them. "I will make my report to Colonel Carter. I suggest the rest of you take a shower and then get some rest. It has been a trying few hours."

She watched them disperse, trailing dust and grumbles, then wandered away from the gate. She stooped to pick up a bolt, and as she got up she saw that Carter was trotting in to meet her. "Good morning, Colonel."

"Teyla, it's good to see you back in one piece. What happened?"

Teyla coughed, tasting dust. "I am afraid things did not go well, Colonel. The Malans did not appreciate our efforts. Or our presence."

Carter was looking at the crossbow bolts littering the floor. "They attacked you?"

"Their offspring did… I have to admit, being chased out of town by crossbow-wielding children is not an experience I have any desire to repeat."

"I'll bet." She glanced up at the operations balcony, and then stepped closer to Teyla. "Listen, we need to talk. Can you come up to my office?"

"Of course." Teyla unwrapped the cloth from her own nose and mouth. "Right now?"

Carter smiled. "When you've gotten some color back."

As planets go, Malus Rei—Carter's people called it M2S-318—was largely unremarkable. It was dry, and dusty, and prone to storms, but it had a sizeable population, scattered in tough little townships that huddled around natural wells. During the previous day, Teyla had led her team through the Malan gate on a goodwill mission: the plan had been to visit several of the larger settlements and provide the inhabitants with medical supplies, food, and other material aid. Nothing would be asked for in return, but obviously there were benefits for the Pegasus expedition in terms of information and a growing network of local allies. Such missions had proved invaluable in the city's previous location, and the tactic had been adopted again, now that the new resting place of Atlantis seemed to be permanent.

The Malans, however, were simply not receptive to goodwill. Perhaps they had been culled once too often by the Wraith, or maybe the harshness of their dusty lives had made them naturally surly. Or perhaps, Teyla thought to herself, as she showered the powdery dust out of her hair, they were simply desperately unpleasant people. There were all kinds of humans in the galaxy, she knew. It would have been naïve to assume there were none who were, by their very nature, just plain bad.

She should have found the Malan attitude to children a warning, she decided. Any race who regard their own offspring as expendable has serious issues. Although, she had to admit, using the children as warriors had a certain twisted logic. After all, when one is being chased by hordes of filthy, dust-caked youngsters—even those armed with crossbows and jagged iron knives—it is hard to shoot back.

Well, from now on the Malans would be alone on their stormy little world, sending their children out into the choking dust to gather water and farm their tough, fibrous root crops. They had their way of life, and it would be folly to try and convince them it was wrong, even if it went against everything Teyla had been brought up to believe.

Besides, there were people in the galaxy who not only needed help but would welcome it. In future, she would direct her energies towards such folk, and let those who were just plain bad make their own way.

Carter was not alone in her office when Teyla arrived in the control room. She was talking to a young, dark-haired woman with glasses, and standing to one side of the office was a middle-aged man wearing what Teyla took to be Earth civilian clothing. She didn't recognize either of them, and the emotions of the man were hard to read. But the woman seemed agitated, even afraid.

Teyla found an empty seat and watched them, curious as to what was going on and unwilling to simply walk into what looked like a difficult situation. From what she could see, the woman had a request for Carter, and it seemed that the Colonel wanted to acquiesce. But she kept looking over to the man, and each time she did there was a tiny, almost imperceptible shake of his head.

Somehow, this civilian seemed to be in charge of the situation.

It was a puzzle. Teyla did not know Colonel Carter well—the woman had only been in charge of the Pegasus expedition since the loss of Doctor Weir, not much more than three weeks earlier. Since that time she and Teyla had not interacted much, and the few conversations they had shared had been models of stiff professionalism. But from what she did know about Carter, Teyla couldn't imagine her as someone who would give up authority easily. Whoever this man was, he must have been in a position of considerable power.

After a few minutes, the young woman appeared to realize she was getting nowhere. When she left Carter's office, the man went with her. Neither of them were talking, but the woman was plainly upset.

Teyla watched them pass. As they did, she heard one of the techs near her curse under his breath.

She turned to him. "Is something wrong?"

The man—bearded, somewhat heavy-set—shook his head. "No, it's okay. I'm sorry."

"Is there a fault with the Stargate?"

He was silent for a moment, his eyes fixed on the control board in front of him. Then: "It's not the Stargate. Look, perhaps I shouldn't say, but…" He glanced briefly over to Carter's office. "The girl who was just in there? She's a friend of mine."

"I see." Teyla moved her seat closer to the man. Franklyn, she remembered. "She seems troubled."

"Yeah, well… She's been assigned to the Ancient's tech team. Not like she's been given any choice in the matter, either."

That was unusual. From what Teyla knew about the technical assignments on Atlantis, there seemed to be considerable leeway in who ended up with any particular task. She had seldom heard of anyone protesting an assignment, and never being refused in the way she had just observed.

"So, your friend does not wish to work with Angelus?"

Franklyn shook his head. "She's won't tell me why. But I swear, something that she's seen down there has scared the living… Er, daylights out of her. I told her to see Carter, get reassigned. But it doesn't look like she's buying it."

Teyla looked over towards the office, and saw Carter beckoning her in. "I am due to see the Colonel now. Perhaps I could ask on your friend's behalf?"

He thought about that for a moment. "Let me talk to her again first. I don't want to speak for her, you know?"

"I understand. Thank you for being candid, Mr Franklyn."

She got up, and walked across the gangway to join Carter, pausing at the doorway. "Colonel?"

"Teyla, please come in." Carter was sitting behind her desk, and she gestured at the seat opposite her. Teyla moved it slightly away from the desk and sat, keeping her posture alert but neutral, hands folded in her lap. After what she had seen here, and heard from Franklyn, the atmosphere in the office was less than comfortable.

Carter seemed to sense this. "Staffing problems."

"I am sorry to hear that."

"You and me both. Anyway, the Malan situation. I guess it went badly."

"I will submit a full report, Colonel. Suffice to say that I do not believe we should return anytime soon."

"From what I heard, if you hadn't been on the ball things might have been a lot worse."

Teyla understood the expression, but she couldn't help wondering where it stemmed from. How could one be on a ball and yet alert for danger? The language of Earth people, she had decided some time ago, was a stew of words. How they understood each other was a mystery, much of the time. "Thankfully, there were no injuries. All we lost was some pride and some time."

"Right…" Carter nodded absently. She seemed lost in thought, her fingertips tapping at the desktop nervously. Teyla, slightly disturbed but not wanting to break into Carter's thoughts, simply waited.

Finally: "Teyla, you've spoken to Angelus, right?"

"Once, yes."

"How did he strike you?"

Strike? Oh. "He was… Polite."

Carter raised an eyebrow. "Anything else?"

"Intelligent. Extremely so. He seemed…" Teyla scrunched her face in thought, trying to put into words how Angelus had seemed when she had been with him. How could she effectively talk about the immeasurable sense of pain emanating from him? Or the regret, the loneliness? She had been talking to a man who had slept ten thousand years while his children built cities under mountains, and had seen them die in fire. Where were the words for that?

"He was sad," she said quietly.

Carter sighed. "I know what you mean. But listen, there's something else. When you talked, it was about the location of his homeworld, is that right?"

"It is. Ronon and I found no information about the Eraavi or their home, so I asked Angelus to help me locate it in our database."

"And he was okay with that? He didn't try to hide it, or give you the runaround at all…"

Teyla didn't like the way this conversation was going. "Colonel, what is this about?"

Carter looked at her hard for a moment. "I've got reason to believe Angelus might have been lying about Eraavis."

"Lying? To me?"

"To all of us. McKay is sure that Angelus couldn't have made the trip across Replicator space in that ship of his—it's just too far."

"That is... I mean, I am very surprised. I had no sense he was being dishonest with me. Just the opposite. Colonel Carter, I would swear that he was telling me the truth."

Carter shrugged. "Maybe there's been some kind of mistake. If Rodney's figures are wrong... All I'm saying is, we have to be open to the possibility that Angelus lied."

"In which case, we should confront him."

Carter snorted. "Oh, I'd love to. But that man who was in here earlier? He's an observer from the IOA."

"The group on Earth that tells you what to do."

"Yeah, them. Well, the Advisory want anything Angelus is selling, and they've sent that observer here to make sure we play ball. If I start accusing Angelus of screwing with us now, they'll hear about it and drag him right back to Earth. My hands are tied."

Teyla sorted out the stew of words in her head. People were afraid Angelus would accidentally summon the Replicators if he began building his weapon again, she was quite aware of that. So of course he couldn't be allowed to be taken to what was, by all accounts, a very populous world. The Advisory had made a highly effective threat. No wonder Carter had deferred to the observer.

The Colonel's hands were, metaphorically, tied. Her own were not. "I understand. This must be very difficult for you."

"I'll get by."

"I am sure you will, with help." She stood up. "I may have made an error when I located Eraavis. I think it would be useful if I did some... Research on the matter."

Carter smiled softly. "Thank you. Let me know as soon as you find anything. *Personally*."

The languages of Earth people were complex, it was true. And yes, sometimes it was hard to determine what they were saying. On the other hand, occasionally they could make themselves very clear indeed.

Colonel Carter was being spied on. To what degree, Teyla couldn't be sure, but given that Carter didn't feel able to speak freely even when the IOA man was out of the room, she must know that he was watching her very closely indeed. Which meant that although she didn't trust Angelus, she couldn't investigate him herself—the danger of having the IOA step in was too great.

But if someone else were to undertake such an investigation; someone, perhaps, with motives separate from Carter's... Someone who had been lied to, expertly and directly, by the Ancient, and wanted to prove it? Well, in that case, the Colonel could not be held responsible.

Teyla had heard Sheppard speak of such things in the past. He used phrases like 'plausible deniability.'

Whatever the concept was called, Teyla understood it perfectly. She also understood that she was being used, played quite effectively by Colonel Carter. She was quite aware that some people considered her proud, although she preferred to think of herself as simply confident in her own abilities. And when it looked as though those abilities had failed her, it was only natural that she would feel driven to learn all she could from her failure.

Carter, in only three weeks and with so many other things on her mind, had already learned that about Teyla Emmagan.

Later on, Teyla might get angry about that. But for the moment, Carter's plans and her own meshed well. She would play the new Colonel's games, for her own benefit. If Angelus was able to lie so effortlessly to her, and make her believe his lies so conclusively, then she needed to know how he had done it.

She spent some time writing and submitting her report on the Malan debacle, which also gave her time to mull over the situation with Angelus. It was a puzzle knowing what to do, at first. Her immediate thought had been to march down to the lab and confront the man, but she quickly realized that would solve nothing other than to alert Angelus—and his IOA guardian—to the fact he had been caught in a lie. If there was a quick way of having the Ancient taken to Earth and getting Carter into serious trouble, it would be the direct approach. Teyla, after giving the matter some thought, decided that caution would be better.

Her next idea was to ask McKay about his calculations, and exactly what he thought about the location of Eraavis, but the man was off-world, on some kind of mission with Ronon and John Sheppard. So instead, Teyla called Franklyn again, and asked his friend's name.

Later that afternoon, Teyla made sure she just happened to be in the mess hall at the same time as Alexa Cassidy. After some nimble maneuvering, she found herself sitting opposite the young woman with a tray of random food items in front of her. There was a shift-break in progress, and the mess was crowded: making sure she got close to the physicist had been difficult enough, without the distraction of paying attention to what she was ordering.

She sat for a few minutes, toying with a plastic bowlful of some sickly-looking dessert and watching Cassidy push food absently around her own tray. After a time the crowd in the mess began to thin out. The man on Cassidy's left finished his meal and walked away, then the one on her right. Teyla had anticipated that Cassidy wouldn't rush back to Angelus after her break, and she was right. It was only when the mess was nearly empty again did the woman push her untouched tray aside and stand up.

Teyla looked up at her, directly for the first time. "Alexa?"

Cassidy frowned behind her glasses—they were large, and made her look rather owlish. "Yes?"

"May I speak with you?"

"Ah, Ma'am? I've really got to get back." She was look-ing at Teyla warily, obviously unsure why she might warrant this sudden attention. They had never spoken before, after all. Teyla realized that if she didn't take control of the conversation quickly, the woman would bolt. She seemed the type to do so; bookish, unsure of herself.

"I am sorry, Alexa. I know you are busy with the Ancient's project—but I am here because of Mr Franklyn."

"Bob?" Cassidy sat back down, slowly. "What's wrong?"

"With him? Nothing. But he is worried about you."

"Damn it." The woman looked away. "I told him not to say anything."

"He knows you are unhappy with your current assignment. I believe he suggested you request a transfer."

Cassidy nodded miserably. "Fat lot of good it did me, with that IOA hawk standing right there. Look, I'm in enough trouble already…"

Teyla took a chance. "Alexa, please. What is it about Angelus that frightens you?"

The woman froze, and stared at her for a long moment. Then she got up. "I have to go," she breathed.

Teyla stood too. "Let me help you."

Cassidy didn't reply. She simply turned and walked briskly away, out of the mess hall.

Teyala watched her go, cursing herself. She had played that badly, and lost one of her main lines of enquiry. Now she would have to try something different.

Glumly, she put her finger into the dessert and brought it to her mouth. It tasted exactly as she had imagined it, which didn't improve her mood at all.

Much later, when darkness had fallen, she went down to the lab where Angelus worked.

She had been mulling Franklyn's words over in her mind, trying to make sense of his insinuations. He seemed certain that Cassidy was afraid of Angelus, or at least of something that had occurred in the lab, but what could that be? By all accounts, the Ancient was a model of politeness. Teyla herself had not perceived the slightest threat from him—he had been quiet, helpful, almost gentle. She could not find it in herself, even after all she had seen, to believe him so radically different with Cassidy than he had been with her.

There was his work, of course. The design of his superweapon would frighten most people, if they truly understood it. But again, Teyla couldn't quite reconcile what she knew of Cassidy with that kind of attitude. According to Franklyn, she was a most dedicated scientist, one whose enthusiasm for the applications of high-energy physics had not only seen her rise to the upper levels of a discipline that was thoroughly dominated by male academics, but had done so while she was still in her early twenties. If anyone would remain unafraid in the face of whatever the Ancient's weapon could wreak, it would be her.

Which left something else… Something Teyla could only discover by seeing it for herself.

The way to the lab was a little convoluted, but Teyla had an excellent sense of direction, and before long was entering the long, railed cloister. On the other side of that, and through a short, angled corridor, lay the Ancient's lab.

He would almost certainly be there. Rumor had it that a bunk had been set up in the lab for him, so he could take periods of rest without leaving his work. However, it was late. Teyla would be surprised if she found Cassidy and the other techs still at Angelus' side at this hour. She stepped into the cloister, shivering slightly at the sudden coolness of night air. And then, as she reached the first corner, she saw something move in the opposite corridor.

Warily, Teyla slid further back into the shadows, and made herself immobile. She could see shadows moving fitfully in the open corridor entrance. Someone was approaching.

She waited. The shadows grew more defined until, a few seconds later, two men in uniform emerged from the corridor. Teyla didn't recognize their faces, but they were marines, no doubt from the guard post Sheppard had set up at the entrance to the lab. Perhaps they were going off-shift, although she was certain she had seen no-one else going in. She relaxed a little.

But then, as the two men walked along the other side of the gallery, Teyla became aware that there was something very strange about them.

The cloister was long, but quite narrow. Although the marines were on its far side, when they came to the corner they would turn towards Teyla and see her. Watching these two, she suddenly had no desire at all for that to happen. Instead, she eased herself down behind the rail, crouching with her face to the gridded metal supporting the handrail. From there, hopefully, she could see and yet not be seen.

The marines were closer now, halfway along the gallery. And Teyla realized what it was about them that disturbed her so.

They were walking utterly in unison. Teyla had seen soldiers march before, and even the most highly trained warriors still retain a degree of individuality when they move. Everyone's bones, after all, are different, even in the smallest ways. Everyone's muscles are made and stressed and worked according to those bones. Two men, even if they were the exactly the same height, the same build, trained the same way, would not have moved so completely alike as these two.

Twins could not have moved so.

There was no communication between the two marines, either. Not a word passed between them as they walked along the gallery. And even when they reached the end of the cloister—turning towards Teyla's hiding place behind the rail—they didn't pause, or falter, or make way for each other. They walked back into the corridor as smoothly and as faultlessly as two machines.

After a minute passed, Teyla let out the breath she had been holding and stood up from her crouch. The marines would, at that pace, be well into the city's corridors by now.

She moved quickly along the cloister, keeping close to the rail. She was almost at the corridor entrance when there was a sound far behind her, a scuffling footstep.

It didn't sound at all like the steady, mechanistic tread of the marines, but Teyla froze anyway, then slid back out of the light again, scowling. Her attempt at a covert observation of Angelus looked like being thwarted at every turn. Maybe she should just give up, and come back on a quieter night.

There was a man on the gallery, on the same side as her, looking right at her.

No, she thought, he was looking *for* her. He had frozen in place, just as she had, and perhaps he had sensed her there. But he couldn't see her. He was peering, leaning forwards to see, the meager light of the gallery reflecting from his glasses.

It was Radek Zelenka. What reason could he have for being

in the cloister so late at night? He normally spent his time inves-
tigating the hidden functions of Ancient devices, or being ver-
bally abused by McKay. Often both. But here, now? There was
no sense to it.

She supposed it was possible that Carter had tasked more
than one expedition member to observe the Ancient for her, but
Zelenka would have hardly been Teyla's first choice for the job.
Far more likely that he was here of his own agenda.

Or that of Angelus.

It was a strange thought, but after seeing the two marines
acting so inhumanly it was not one she could shake easily. The
night's events had left her feeling unsure, almost disconnected.
Even Zelenka, a man she had known for some years and who
have never shown her the slightest malice, seemed wrong to
her, his very presence alien and malign.

For the moment, Teyla decided, she would remain hidden.
Better, in this lonely corner of the city, to be the observer rather
than the observed.

Zelenka began to walk towards her. By his stance she could
tell that he had not seen her, and it was a simple thing for her to
move out of his way and still not be spotted. In fact, he passed
within a few meters of her, completely oblivious. All the more
reason to think he was not part of Carter's surveillance plan.

Once he was into the corridor, Teyla peeked around to watch
him walking towards the guard station. She saw him pause
there, look into the open door. No-one was there to greet him: it
appeared that the two marines had indeed deserted their post.

Zelenka stood looking into the station for a few seconds.
What was he seeing there?

Abruptly, he backed away, glanced quickly over his shoulder, and then carried on along the corridor. He was moving
slowly, trying to be quiet. Teyla watched, just a little amused by
his efforts, as he walked up to the entrance to the lab.

When he got there, he stopped. Something inside had caught
his attention, but he seemed unwilling to go in. For almost a
minute he stood there, a perplexed expression on his face, intent
on what he was seeing.

In the deep, night-time silence, all Teyla could hear was the distant rustle of waves and her own hammering heart.

Suddenly, Zelenka turned away from the lab and began to walk quickly back towards her. Teyla moved back from the corridor entrance, hugged the gallery wall and listened to his footsteps get closer. There was a pause in the footfalls, as if he had stopped partway along the corridor, and when they resumed they were faster, more purposeful.

From the other direction, the other end of the gallery, Teyla heard more footsteps. Distant at first, but heavy, slow, perfectly regular. She cursed silently.

Zelenka was hurrying back up the corridor now, his pace increasing. He slowed as he reached the corridor entrance, though, and Teyla watched, perplexed, as the man halted, and then slowly raised his hand to stare at what he held.

It was a pistol. Teyla suppressed a gasp.

Too late. She saw Zelenka tense as he heard her. She snapped a hand out, grabbed the gun and twisted it out of his grip. He yelped in shock, a sound far too loud in the stillness of the gallery, and with the footfalls getting closer one she could not afford to have him repeat. She swung him around, pushed him quite hard against the corridor wall and clamped her free hand over his mouth. "Do not move," she hissed into his ear. "Please."

He struggled for a moment, but even with her hand gripping the pistol Teyla was strong enough to keep him in place with her forearm alone. Instead, he mumbled something high and frightened against her hand.

"I am sorry," she replied, her voice an urgent whisper. "I should have told you not to speak either."

He opened his mouth again, but Teyla increased the pressure against his chest just enough to make him reconsider. She could have held him there for as long as she wanted, but the machine-regular footfalls along the gallery were getting closer.

She leaned close to him, put her mouth to his ear. "You are going to do exactly what I tell you, yes?" she said.

Zelenka nodded.

"Good. Come on." She moved away, and pushed him, gently but urgently, towards the lab.

At her prompting, he began to move reluctantly back the way he had come, ducking reflexively into a sort of awkward crouch. Teyla came up alongside him, gesturing with the gun barrel. The footfalls were too close for speech, now. She couldn't risk the marines hearing her. In a moment they would be at the end of the corridor, and she and Zelenka would be in plain sight.

She grabbed his jacket and pulled him sideways, down behind the guard station, hoping he wouldn't stumble against it or make some other sound. Thankfully his skills at self-concealment were up to this particular task, and he folded himself into the shadows behind the station without fuss. Teyla squeezed in next to him, keeping her head below the level of the plexiglass, tensed and ready to leap, the gun held white-knuckle tight in her fist.

The footsteps halted. Teyla heard the door to the guard station open, movement from inside, the creak of a folding chair. Then the door was closed, and the second chair protested under weight. After that, silence.

The marines had returned to their guard duty.

As far as Teyla could see, there was only one place that Zelenka could have found a pistol in that corridor, and she didn't want to be around when the marines noticed it was missing. She turned back to the scientist and gestured again, miming a path low around the guard station. Zelenka, wisely, must have decided that compliance was the most sensible course of action, so when she set off, scampering silently away with her head still below the level of the plexiglass, he followed in kind.

When they were both around the far corner and into the gallery, quite out of sight, she stopped, pulling him to a halt close to the wall. "Radek, what are you doing out here?"

She heard him swallow nervously. "Are you going to put the gun down?"

"No."

"Teyla, you and I haven't exactly been the best of friends, but how long have we known each other?"

Her face hardened somewhat. "That remains to be seen. Now, what were you doing?"

"I don't know!" He was having a hard time keeping his voice low; it kept trying to rise into a nervous squeak. "I swear... Look, I was with Colonel Carter, we were working on something. I thought it might have a connection to Angelus or his lab, but when I looked in he was..." He shrugged helplessly.

"He was what?"

"Acting strangely. I don't know. But I didn't want to go in after that. So I came back."

Teyla lifted the gun, saw him flinch away from it. "And this?"

"It seemed like a good idea at the time..." Zelenka looked embarrassed. "Actually, no, it didn't. I really have no idea why I took that."

She narrowed her eyes. "That makes no sense."

"It doesn't?"

"No." She lowered the gun. "But neither does anything else tonight."

"I'm glad I'm not the only one who thinks that." He ran a hand nervously back through his hair. "Do you think we should—?"

A scream, high and sudden, cut through his words.

It had come from the lab. Teyla saw Zelenka spin away at the sound of it, a reflex reaction that would have had him running if she'd not grabbed the back of his jacket again and stopped him dead. "You are going the wrong way."

"That's a matter of opinion."

"I know that voice. Come on." She shoved him back in to the corridor, and followed him in.

She had been right in her assessment of who had screamed: Alexa Cassidy, clad in a white lab coat, was standing in the middle of the corridor. The two marines were standing in front of her, barring her way.

Teyla left Zelenka dawdling and ran up behind them, holding the gun low, out of sight. "What is going on here?"

Cassidy was sobbing in terror, incoherent, trying to speak past great gulps of breath. "Something's... They tried..."

"Alexa, please calm down. You are safe now."

"No." The physicist shook her head. "Not safe. Please let me go."

The marines were looking back at Teyla. Their eerie synchronous motion was nowhere to be seen now; they moved just as anyone would. Teyla saw one of them—a Lieutenant DeSalle, by his nametag—look past her as Zelenka walked reluctantly up the corridor.

"Please, Ma'am," he said flatly, "let us handle this."

The other marine reached out to take Cassidy by the arm, grabbing her as she shrank back. "Doctor, I think you should go back."

"No," she moaned. She looked despairingly at Teyla. "Please," she whispered. "Help me."

"Lieutenant, let her go." Teyla took a step closer, getting between the two marines. The one holding Cassidy had the name 'Kaplan' sewn above his breast pocket. "There is no need for this."

"Mr Fallon gave us express orders," Kaplan replied. "Doctor Cassidy has been assigned."

"I quit," said Cassidy quietly.

Teyla reached out to her. "Alexa, come with me. We will sort this out with Colonel Carter."

"Something's wrong," breathed Zelenka. "Teyla…"

"Radek, call the Colonel."

"I'm trying to, that's what I meant. There's no signal."

"What?" Teyla reached up to her own headset. "Colonel Carter?"

He only answer was static, and a distant, sinister rushing, like breathing. Or chanting. The sound of it was awful, filled with malign intent, and she shut the signal off to avoid hearing more of it.

As she did so, Cassidy dragged herself free from Kaplan's grip.

Teyla stepped aside to let the woman pass her, and then looked up to see that Kaplan had draw his sidearm. He must have done so terrifically fast; Teyla hadn't even seen him move. In a split second the pistol had gone from securely holstered to being aimed, one-handed, at Zelenka.

In response, Teyla stepped back and brought her own gun up.

"Lieutenant, you may stand down."

"Give her back," he said.

"I said *stand down*!"

There was a blur of movement: DeSalle, brutally quick, had reached out to grab the gun from Teyla. He was faster than she'd ever seen a man move—his entire arm was up and his hand clamped hard over the top of the gun in the exact same time it took Teyla's trigger finger to twitch.

The gun went off into DeSalle's face.

Bullets, despite what happened in the movies Sheppard insisted on showing her, do not fling people backwards. Occasionally people fling *themselves* backwards as the bullet strikes them, but that is only a reaction to the impact, not the impact itself. Teyla had seen enough men shot to know what bullets do.

Bullets kill. And dead men do not hurl themselves about. Dead men fall down.

Lieutenant DeSalle, despite the fact that the bullet had crashed clear through his skull, was *not* falling down. He was very much upright. His head was tilted back slightly, but as Teyla watched he straightened, and turned his ruined face towards her.

Light shone through the hole where his left eye should have been.

He let go of the gun. Teyla backed up, still aiming, utterly aghast. There was a part of her mind that was waiting for him to fall, waiting for his body to realize that half his brain was gone. *Fall*, she thought wildly. *Fall fall fall…*

He stepped back, calmly, his face still turned to her. He did so in perfect unison with Kaplan. Both men, moving as one, backed slowly and deliberately away from her.

They stopped partway up the corridor, and at the moment they stopped walking the floor shook faintly under Teyla's feet. There was a soft grinding noise, a metallic scraping, as diagonal slabs of metal emerged from the walls just ahead of the two marines. The metal slid inwards, drew close, slammed massively and irrevocably together.

And then all the lights went out.

CHAPTER TEN

What Lies Beneath

When *Apollo*'s navigation system failed, the ship could technically have broken out anywhere. The relationship between hyperspace and realspace is not a direct one: a journey of ten light-years might take an hour in one direction and two in another, and a timing error of thousandths of a second can account for spatial displacements in the millions of kilometers. Hence the enormous complexity of the navigational computers, and the awful consequences should they fail.

The ship's systems did, to their credit, make every attempt to ensure the survival of the crew. Even in the midst of a cascade failure they managed to send *Apollo* from one universe to another largely intact, rather than as a cloud of free and extremely fast-moving molecules. Not only that, but in a supreme effort of mechanical will they had held the breakout back just long enough to get the ship within range of a gravity well. This was the result of a deeply imbedded emergency protocol, one programmed to allow a vessel stricken with hyperdrive failure at least a fighting chance of survival. A ship lost in deep space, between the stars, is little more than a complex metal coffin.

That, though, was the limit of what *Apollo*'s systems could do. And it was hardly their fault that the system they had dropped the ship into was about the least survivable they could have found.

For one thing, the system was full of Wraith. By some minor miracle *Apollo* had broken out on the far side of a planet to the massing fleet, and at roughly the same time as a Wraith cruiser had jumped in to join its fellows. So far, it seemed that none of the alien ships had detected *Apollo*'s headlong emergence into their staging post, which was hugely lucky for Ellis and his crew. The battlecruiser was crippled. It could no more fight the Wraith than it could escape them.

The other flaw in the ship's choice of destination was the solar system itself. The emergency protocols might have found *Apollo* a gravity well to drop into, but there were no habitable worlds rolling around that well. The star shining at the heart of the system was small and hot, far younger than Earth's sun and racing towards a much earlier grave. It had planets, but none that could support life in the conventional sense; these were gas giants, jovians, titan worlds without land or water. If any terrestrial planets had formed around that hot little dwarf, the gas giants had long since swept them to dust.

Of the four jovians, the third from its sun would have been the most recognizable to terrestrial astronomers. In many ways it was much like Jupiter—like that world, it was sheathed in a thin curtain of crystallized ammonia, banded by storm systems and dotted with vast convection cells. It also shared a composition with that giant world, in that it was almost ninety percent hydrogen under the ammonia, with the remaining tenth a soup of helium, sulphur, phosphorous and complex hydrocarbons. And much like Jupiter the planet had a thin interphase layer of water clouds, at the point where the crystalline tropopause met the hydrogen-rich stratosphere.

This was *Apollo*'s hiding place, and had been for the past forty hours. Hovering like a bug between the hydrogen sea and the sheltering ammonia sky.

There was almost no light in the water layer. While the ammonia clouds were a mere skin in relation to the planet's bulk, they were still fifty kilometers thick, and heavily reflective. Every few hours a convection cell would spin close enough to stir the cloud layer near the ship and send dull shafts of ruddy light spearing in through the gloom, but for the most part *Apollo* drifted in darkness. Even its running lights had been shut down to conserve power.

Had the lights still been active, Ellis knew they would have dimmed disconcertingly whenever the drain pulse hit.

The pulse was impossible to ignore now. When he had first

noticed it, the dimming of the lights had been an almost imperceptible flicker. But it had been growing more serious ever since the breakout, slowly but inexorably, the power dipping lower with every pulse. It was as though the ship had a heartbeat, although a failing one.

Apollo was dying. And it came a little closer to death every forty-one seconds.

On the bridge, the pulse was impossible to miss. The lights were dim anyway—the ship was still on emergency power, and the darkness only made the regular drop in voltage all the more obvious. Most of the bridge crew had taken to using laptops and PDAs, rather than *Apollo*'s instruments. At least that way they could keep working for longer than forty-one seconds at a time.

Sharpe had two laptops taped to her control board, and was using them to constantly monitor the ship's position. It was a complex job; juggling the navigation computer's wildly inaccurate timings, trying to manually recalibrate them between each pulse, resetting the readings on the two laptops against each other and the board continuously. Ellis wondered how she'd managed to keep it up for so long.

Still, it was time for another status report. "Sharpe?"

"A moment, sir." Her fingers rattled over the keys, hands dodging between laptop and control board and back. Ellis saw her pause, look up slightly, and as she did the lights dipped. The hum of the aircon stuttered, then picked up again as the lights brightened. She knew when it was going to happen on reflex now.

They all did. It was like a water-torture, a continuous drip that wore into the senses, hour after hour…

Ellis forced the thought away. "What have you got?"

"We've dropped another two hundred meters, drifted six hundred bearing zero niner four. There's a current close by, sir. We're going to need a correction burn within the next twenty minutes."

"Okay, set it up." The burn, a series of thruster bursts intended to keep the ship safely in the water layer and away from any convection cells or storm currents, would have to be carefully timed. When *Apollo* had first entered the jovian a burn had been allowed to carry on through one of the power drains, and the results had almost been disastrous. A thruster had jammed on during the pulse, and almost sent the ship spiraling into the hydrogen layer. "Meyers? Any visitors?"

"Nothing on passive, sir." Meyers was using a PDA to keep her data calibrated, but even with that help she had only the most limited access to the ship's sensor suite. Much of it had been damaged or completely misaligned by the breakout, and those segments that still functioned could barely be trusted. It was all Meyers and Sharpe could do to keep the ship in place, let alone track what was going on above the ammonia clouds.

Ellis nodded, then closed his eyes briefly as the power dipped. When it was over he got up. "Anyone got any good news?"

"Maybe, Colonel." That was Copper, the tech who had opened his scalp on a panel when the ship had broken out. He'd been patched up by a medic a few hours ago, but the bandage taped to his head had spots of crimson soaking through, and he was pale in the dim light. Ellis hoped he'd be able to deliver his good news before he collapsed.

He crossed the bridge to join Copper and the rest of the tech team, behind the tactical map. "Okay, what have we got?"

"Compression, sir." Copper had a laptop open on one of the systems boards, and he swung it around to show Ellis what was on the screen. "These are the recorded data files from all the onboard systems—security, sensor logs, pretty much everything."

Ellis bent to look more closely at the screen. "All this stops at the breakout?"

"Yes sir. We got jolted so hard that we lost most of the recording systems, but auto-recalibration should have set them back up before there'd been any loss." He reached up to touch the bandage lightly, and winced. "Of course, we know that—"

The lights dimmed. Ellis sighed, waiting until the pulse was over. That, of course, was the reason *Apollo* was still crippled after all this time. All the systems needed for tracking down the ship's multiple faults had not only been hammered out of true by the violence of its return to realspace, but any attempt to recalibrate them had been rendered futile by the constant pulses. Every forty-one seconds, many of *Apollo*'s systems returned to their factory default settings.

So far, all attempts to track the source of the pulse down had failed for that precise reason. Gross physical searches could only achieve so much. The ship's technicians needed accurate data.

As the lights came back up, Ellis straightened. "But you think there's something you can do about this?"

"I think so. Mischa's been working on a compression routine that will break the recorded data into small chunks, and I've been programming a worm to get the routine into the data core between pulses."

"Hold on, a worm? Like a computer virus?"

Copper tilted his head. "Not exactly. They're synonymous with malware now, sure, but the first worm was developed to find idle processors on a network and give them jobs to do. It was a legitimate software tool."

Ellis frowned. He didn't really like the idea of rogue autonomous programs being given free reign in *Apollo*'s data core, but this was the first piece of hopeful news he'd heard in a long time. "So can this work?"

"I think so. I've got a copy of the worm on this laptop, off-network, and I've assigned it Mischa's compression routine as a payload. We're about to try it on a non-essential file, something that we won't miss if it hits a pulse and goes AWOL. We just need you to give the word."

"It's given. Let me know as soon as you have any results."

Copper saluted briskly, and Ellis saw his pallor deepen suddenly as the sudden movement jarred his injured head. He reached out to steady the man as he swayed. "Maybe we'll go easy on the protocol for a while, yeah?"

"That sounds like a good idea, sir."

Ellis left the technician to his programs, and headed back towards the command throne. As he passed the tactical map he saw Meyers look up and beckon him over, and continued past the map to join her.

Meyers half-turned in her seat. "Colonel, I think we've got a problem."

Her voice was low, little more than a whisper. Ellis leaned closer to her and responded in kind. "Another one?"

"Sorry. I know it's the last thing you wanted to hear, but…" She lowered her voice still further. "I can't be sure right now, not a hundred percent. But some of the sensor readings I've been able to get have shown something coming towards us. I'm picking up energy spikes like you'd not believe…"

"Wraith?"

She shook her head. "Sir, I think it's a storm front."

"How bad can that be?"

"Bad. The way the convection cells are starting to bunch up, the level of the spikes… We're probably talking about a wavefront of twisters about as wide as Mars, traveling at several hundred kilometers an hour and causing lightning strikes a thousand times bigger than anything we get at home. If we get hit by that, it'll shred us."

"Dammit. Sharpe, are you hearing this?"

"Yes sir. And before you ask, no, we can't get out of the way in time, not in the shape we're in now. The pulse is getting worse—at this rate it'll be impossible to make correction burns within eight hours, and with the main drives offline…"

"So unless we can fix the pulse before the storm hits, we're done for."

Sharpe nodded. "Our only alternative would be to go up and over it. We might just about be able to manage that, but we'd break cover. If any Wraith were looking in this direction…"

"Let's keep that as Plan B for now." He stepped back. Neither Meyers or Sharpe needed to be told to keep the information to themselves; they were quite aware of when such things should be spoken of in hushed tones and when they should be broadcast. Right now, there were only a few people that needed to know, and a lot more who would find the prospect of a ticking clock dangerously distracting.

Ellis found himself gazing out of the viewport. There was almost nothing to see, only the merest hint of glow from above, and the rest just gluey darkness. Even the stars were hidden from him, up above the ammonia. But out there, somewhere in the murk, was a raging storm front as big as a planet. When it arrived, it would bring light—sunlight as it scoured the cloud layers above and below, and an army of lightning strikes. There would be no missing it. When the storm was ready for them, it would announce itself.

All the better, then, not to be around when it did.

Copper's compression worm was not an instant success. Ellis watched it fail nine times before it successfully retrieved a file. Even on the tenth time, it was able to snatch just a piece of data before the pulse killed it.

But it was a start. Information had been downloaded from the data core. It might only have been a fragment of a backup of a mission log, but it represented a breakthrough. If Ellis could have given Copper and his team a few hours downtime as a reward, he would gladly have done so.

He couldn't. There simply was no time. He could feel the storm coming.

Instead, he set Copper's people to work. Over the next hour, thousands of worms infiltrated the data core, splitting files wherever they could find them, compressing the split chunks, and hauling the encoded fragments into protected areas. A dozen laptops logged into these areas between pulses, uploading and recombining the data. There was no orderly plan for the worms, no priorities or targeted areas. At the rate Copper's people were working, it was all they could do to keep replicating the worms and sending them, wave after wave, into the ship's memory.

There were casualties. If a pulse arrived before a worm had completed its task, the worm and anything it was interacting with at the time was lost. But with a success rate of over ninety percent, and more technicians working to recreate the lost data as the missing files became apparent, Ellis realized that he was almost starting to hope.

The first data he asked to see was footage from *Apollo*'s internal security cameras. Major Kyle Deacon was still missing, and no trace could be found of the man. Although he loathed to admit it, Ellis knew there was a very good chance Deacon's disappearance was not unconnected with the ship's plight.

The footage was uploaded into a laptop. Once this was done, Ellis thanked Copper and his team for their efforts so far, told them to keep at it until they dropped, and then took the laptop away with him. This wasn't something he wanted to view in public, at least not yet.

He didn't want to see it alone, either.

Ellis was in his cabin, connecting the laptop to the ship's power grid when Meyers keyed open the hatch. She raised an eyebrow. "Is that wise?"

"No alternative. These things are taking longer to charge all the time. The power feed won't be constant, but if the battery's charging between pulses it shouldn't take the laptop down when the lights go out."

"Beats swapping batteries, I guess." A small assembly line of battery chargers had been set up in one of the maintenance bays, with runners to make sure the various laptops and PDAs being used all over the ship stayed fed. "What have you got?"

"Internal cams." He moved his seat aside and dragged a second one over with his ankle. She dropped into it and peered at the screen. "That's the mess hall."

"I know. Hold on…" Ellis clicked out of the viewer application and brought up a list of available files. "Deacon left the bridge at, what, oh-three-fifty?"

"Yes sir." Meyers looked at him quizzically. "Colonel, you don't think—?"

"I'm not thinking *anything*, Major. But Deacon went missing just before all this happened, and no-one's got a damn clue where he's hiding. So yeah, forgive me if I'm interested as to where he went."

"Sir, Deacon wouldn't—" She stopped as he glared at her. "Sorry."

"Don't second-guess." He tapped the screen. "If the answer's anywhere, it's here."

She said nothing. Ellis went back to studying the files. "There, that's the bridge cam file. Let's start with that."

He dragged the file onto the player. There was a faint whir

from the laptop, and then the footage sprang to life; an instant of blurry color and then a jarring, static-riddled freeze-frame of black. "Goddamn it."

"Sir, that's the end of the file. All the recordings must have defaulted to the point they crashed out."

"Right." He squinted at the player's controls for a moment, then found the rewind and started to scroll the footage back. The bridge appeared, four times. There were four cameras installed there, and their output had been pasted into a two by two montage.

Ellis watched people move in jerky reverse for a few seconds, then saw Deacon appear in the helm seat. "Okay, got him."

He let the footage roll on. The internal cams were of quite high resolution, but there was no sound. Audio files were in a different section of the data core. In normal circumstances the pictures and sound would have been married and enhanced for playback, but all Ellis had right now was raw footage. He hoped it would be enough. "There he goes. Oh-three-fifty-two."

"Marked. So now we need the entry corridor? What the hell does that come under?"

"These filenames are hard to- Hold on, I think this is it." There were only two cameras in the corridor, but both showed Deacon leaving. Meyers marked the time again, and they moved to the next area.

Slowly, file by file, they tracked Deacon through the ship. The data core was in the forward part of the main hull, ahead of the bomb bay. The most direct route to it from the bridge was via the deck that ran over the bay, and that was where they saw him, with each camera they accessed. He didn't deviate, didn't slow down, didn't make a detour into any other part of the ship. He simply left the bridge and headed directly for the core.

He never made it. Between one pair of cameras and the next, somewhere above the forward edge of the bomb bay, he simply vanished.

"Doesn't make any damn sense," Ellis muttered. "What's off corridor nine?"

"Nothing he could get to without being picked up on another

cam." Meyers frowned. "Maybe there's a storage cupboard down there or something... Sir, can you run those last two again?"

Ellis brought up the last two files. As he did so Meyers leaned across to take control of the laptop from him. He let her get on with it—she seemed more at home with the player application than he was.

She quickly brought the two pieces of footage up together. On the left side of the screen, Deacon stood frozen, paused between frames. On the right was the place he should have appeared once he had left the field of the first camera.

He didn't. Just as before, when the player was activated, he walked out of the first camera's view and never entered that of the second.

Meyers paused the player, scanned back a few frames until Deacon's back reappeared. "What's this?"

Ellis squinted at the screen. "What?"

"This shadow." She took Deacon back a few frames, into shot again. "It's not there now, but as he goes forward..." She sent him on, one frame at a time.

There, at the very edge of the screen, just as he stepped out of view, part of the wall darkened. Something had obscured the light. "A pulse?"

"No, the timing's wrong. Sir, I think someone was down there with him."

"No-one else is on the cameras."

"I know. I'm not sure how, but whatever caused that shadow must have been right in front of him." She stood up. "Sir, we've got to go down there and look."

"Agreed. But I need you on the bridge."

"Colonel—"

"Major, I know you and Deacon were friends. But I need you keeping an eye on that storm. Don't worry, I'll find him."

She hesitated for a moment, then gave in. "All right. But please let me send a team of marines down to meet you there."

"Wouldn't have it any other way."

Once he was in corridor nine, Ellis found it even harder to

see where Deacon might have gone. It stretched ahead of him, wide and blank-walled. There didn't seem to be anywhere to hide.

Still, appearances could be deceptive. The corridor was clean and uncluttered compared to some of the smaller access-ways—in less central areas of the ship, corridors were little more than spaces between compartments, and were often narrow and tangled with systemry. There were places where two men simply could not get past each other for all the ducting on the walls, and if any crewmember met another coming the other way in such a place, they would have to agree as to which of them would back up to a wider point.

This corridor, running along the ship's spine between the upper hull and the roof of the bomb bay, was kept free from such obvious obstructions. But in many places the wall panels could be removed to reveal storage areas, equipment lockers, access to systems. If Deacon had, as was looking increasingly likely, been attacked, he could quite easily have been concealed in such a place.

The marines Meyers had assigned to Ellis had already been briefed on that possibility. There were four of them, all armed, all carrying tactical lights clipped to their weapons. The emergency lighting made the corridor gloomy, a flat, grayish twilight that made details vanish. Ellis was as glad of the extra illumination as he was of the firepower.

"All right, this is where the camera last picked Deacon up," he told them, pointing a few meters up the corridor. "We know he didn't come back past this point, or at least not until the ship broke out. We'll start here and move forward."

The squad leader's name was Spencer. He moved a couple of steps past Ellis, then turned back to him. "Colonel, we'll run a fast sweep of the corridor first, make sure nothing's obviously screwy. If it all looks clean, we'll come back and start taking the walls down. Agreed?"

"Sounds good."

Spencer gestured for the squad to follow him, then moved cautiously off down the corridor. Ellis took up position behind them, his own firearm drawn and held high. He would have liked to have gone ahead of the marines, but there were protocols to be observed. Putting himself in harm's way to look good in front of a marine squad would have not only been foolish, but would have put others in jeopardy. The marines were here to search for Deacon, not to project him while he did the job himself.

He stayed close, though. There was no way he was simply going to hang back and watch them work.

Spencer had reached the next camera. "Colonel? He never made it to this one, am I right?"

"You are."

"Not much of a blind spot."

"Big enough. Needs redesigning, as soon as we get back. Anyway, my gut feeling is that whatever happened, happened here."

The marine nodded. "Well, there's only about six of these panels that will come off. If he's here, it won't take long to-"

"Sir!" One of the other marines was beckoning him to the far side of the corridor, closer to the first camera. "There's something here."

Ellis followed Spencer over. The marine who had called out was down on one knee, his taclight aimed at the floor. "I almost slipped up on this, Sir. Thought it might be blood, but it's not…"

There was a fluid on the floor, but the marine was right; it wasn't blood. Ellis could see a faint glisten along the edges of two floor panels, as though something had seeped up between them. He crouched, and drew his finger along the line of wetness.

It was slightly warm, and greasy. When he brought it to his nose it smelled faintly of meat. "What the hell?"

"More over here, sir!"

Spencer walked over to look at the new find. As he did, Ellis saw the marine closest to him put his hand on the panel to push himself upright, and freeze. "Hey, what?"

"What is it?"

The marine shook his head. "Sir, I'm not sure. I can feel… Here, you try." He drew back.

Ellis touched the center of the panel. "Everybody hold still."

"Sir?"

"Just stop walking!" He got lower, spread his hand out on the panel. There was a faint vibration there, rhythmic, a repetitive shudder from under the metal floor. Like an engine, pistons moving down there maybe. Or…

"Get this panel up," he snapped. He stood up, stepped back, found himself wiping his hand reflexively on his jacket.

The panel was about a meter square. There were recessed screws holding it down, and fold-up handles in case engineers needed to reach the crawlspace below. One of the marines stepped forwards with a small powered screwdriver and bent over the panel.

In half a minute, the screws were free. Ellis watched the marine grab one of the handles and, as the lights dimmed in their regular pulse, hauled it up.

It resisted him, as if something sticky was holding it down. The man strained, cursed, and then the panel came free with a wet tearing sound, like the shell being ripped from a live crab. Off-balance, the marine stumbled sideways, taking the panel with him and exposing what lay beneath it to the light.

Beside him, dimly, Ellis heard one of the marines give vent to a choking curse.

The space under the floor panel was full of tissue, crimson and glistening wetly. For a moment Ellis thought that some creature had been butchered down there, had exploded from some ghastly internal pressure and spread it's flesh and organs among the underfloor wiring. But there was simply too much of it. Almost the whole square meter was covered, a glossy, vein-shot mix of muscle and membrane, and what wasn't flesh was metal—bright, new metal, impossibly polished, woven into and through the tissue like roots in soil. It was as though some unholy fusion of meat and steel, sinew and wire, ridged tracheal pipe and fluted silver cable had grown under the floor, a sickening, pulsing biomechanical tumor skulking and swelling beneath the shell of the corridor.

And it was alive. Ellis had felt the beat of it through the

panel.

He stepped closer, transfixed by horrified fascination, and as he did so a dozen eyes opened in the morass and rolled around to look at him. He saw the pupils contract as they met the light.

The corridor groaned. Beneath his feet, the floor shifted.

He heard the metallic double-click of a P90 being primed, but whoever had done so never got the chance to fire it. In the next instant the floor erupted upwards, panels shrieking as they were torn free of their moorings. The corridor went dark, the fluorescent tubes shattering into dust and shards as the walls buckled. In an instant, the entire space was a chaotic nightmare of spinning taclights, sparks, the shouts of men and the thin, hissing bellows of whatever was squirming its way to freedom from under the floor.

Ellis was on his back. He'd been bowled clean off his feet by the churning corridor, the pistol flung from his grip. He scrabbled at the walls, trying to right himself, but they were slick and warm. There was a haze in the air, a drizzle of grease and blood. It was like being inside a lung.

The marines were still yelling. Ellis heard a scream, choked, cut short by a crunching, meaty impact. A P90 spun past him and he grabbed it, aimed it up the corridor as he rolled over and staggered to his feet.

He saw only chaos. Everything was moving, a ceaseless, whipping motion surrounding a vast and impossibly complex bulk that reared up from its hiding place, huge and strong and reeking of meat and oil. In the stark beam of the taclight, it shone as it rose.

It had already killed one of the marines: Ellis could see the man crumpled against the wall, eyes open and lifeless. Another marine scrambled in, trying to retrieve his comrade, but before Ellis could yell a warning an arm-thick mass of cable and tendon lashed out of the darkness with impossible speed.

The impact was sickening. The marine flew a dozen meters before he struck the deck.

The thing was almost at the ceiling now. Ellis still couldn't get a grip on its shape—its outline was unstable, seething, writhing like a nest of crimson snakes. As it rose it juddered and shook like an ill-kept machine, as if multiple joints and cables and pistons were dragging it up, protesting, into position. Ellis couldn't tell if any part of it was flesh or metal, plastic or gristle. It was organic and mechanical, bloody and glittering, and in the heart of it was something crucified, something that lolled forwards, skeletal, and turned its heavy, malformed head towards him to scream out its defiance and pain.

That something had the face of Kyle Deacon.

CHAPTER ELEVEN

Lock and Load

She awoke, suffocating. The sheet was tangled around her, spinning her to the narrow bed, and the darkness pressed down around her like wet sand. There was a noise close to her head, a shrill buzzing that scratched at her ears, but she couldn't identify it nor reach out to silence it. The depth of her sleep, and the suddenness of her waking, had nailed her down.

She fought the pressure, the crushing fatigue, convulsing sluggishly on the bed until, finally, some measure of control returned to her deadened body. She got an arm free, flailed until she found her headset, and shut off its insistent whirring.

Carter sat up in bed, not remotely awake, and pressed the headset into her ear. "Wha?"

"Colonel? Is that you?"

"Teyla? What… What's going on?" She swung her feet free of the sheet and stood up, swaying a little. According to the clock next to her bed she had been out for no more than a few minutes. Just long enough to fall really, soundly asleep, which made waking all the harder.

There were noises coming through the headset; scuffling, panting, as though Teyla was running. Another voice, too far out of pickup range to identify. Something that sounded like sobbing.

"Colonel, something has happened. We were attacked, the lights have failed—"

"Attacked? Lights?" Carter rubbed her eyes, trying to shake the edges of fatigue away. "Where are you?"

"We are near to the Ancient's lab. Colonel, we were attacked by two of the marines guarding him. I do not think they are human."

"We? Who—?" Carter stopped in mid-sentence, aware that

she was doing nothing but asking random questions. "Okay, let's start again. Are you injured?"

"*I am not. Radek is fine too, but Alexa Cassidy is in extreme shock.*"

A thin tone broke through the Athosian's words; another call coming through on the headset. "Teyla, hold on a moment, I just need to switch channels." She keyed the new call in. "Carter."

"*Colonel, this is Palmer in the control room. We've got a serious situation here. Looks like an entire section of the west pier has gone into some kind of lockdown.*"

"I'll be right up." Carter switched channels again. "Teyla, get yourselves up to the infirmary, as quickly as you can. I'll meet you there in a few minutes."

She dressed quickly, in the dark, something she had done so many times that she could let her body deal with the task while her mind went elsewhere. The west pier was, of course, where McKay had chosen to set up Angelus' lab. That was no real surprise to her—in fact, it had a kind of sickening inevitability. Despite all her efforts to keep the situation with Angelus under control, all her hopes of dealing with the Ancient's plans peacefully, through diplomacy and reason and common sense, the whole thing had slid out from under her. Now she was getting wild calls in the middle of the night and Fallon was going to have her skinned alive.

Carter was out of her quarters no more than three minutes after she had first woken, and within five was striding into the control room. "What have we got?"

Palmer was waiting for her, standing next to the sensor terminal. The screen showed a vector image of the city, a broad, angular snowflake drawn in threads of pastel blue. A red circle pulsed ominously on one of the piers. "It's here," he told her. "We picked it up just a few minutes ago."

"Can you zoom in on that?"

He did so. The picture of the city spread abruptly, making Carter feel like she was swooping uncontrollably down into its complexities. In a few moments the pier filled the screen, and the red circle now centered around a rectangle of the same color.

Carter looked at it warily. "Okay, what am I seeing here?"

"Basically, nothing. It's a hole in the city—not a *physical* hole, but we're no longer getting any returns from it at all. No external lights, no communications in or out, and no sensor readings of any kind. There's a whole bunch of functionality at its edges we can't identify, as well."

"Functionality?"

"Systems we weren't previously aware of activated at the same time the section went dark."

"Right," said she quietly. The Pegasus expedition had been occupying the city for years, now, and they were still finding new pieces of kit to trip over. Even in a structure as large and as complex as Atlantis, she couldn't help but wonder how the previous administration had been spending its time if there was still 'functionality' here that no-one could identify. "Give me a minute."

There were times, Carter thought ruefully, as she opened the doors to the balcony, that being in command was no fun at all. In principle, it was what every soldier strove for; promotion after promotion, the recognition of one's superiors, the inexorable climb up the ladder of command.

But damn, things were a hell of a lot easier when she had someone to tell her what to do.

She walked out onto the balcony, letting the doors slide closed behind her. The air was cold, almost freezing, the sky above her clear and bright with stars. The planet's two visible moons were up, neither full, but each casting a silvery light across the ocean. She could smell brine, and, if she listened hard past the soughing of the wind, could hear the far-off, rhythmic rushing of the sea.

There was a cold beauty to it, although at that precise moment Carter would rather have been in bed.

She looked down, out across the city. Little of its actual structure could be seen, given the altitude and the darkness, just silver-blue edges caught in moonlight and a constellation of golden lights. The sight was strange, surreal, made even more so by the missing part of it.

On the west pier, far to her left, was a very regular rectangle of pure darkness.

Palmer's diagram had been informative enough, but the true enormity of the situation didn't hit her until she saw that black space for herself. It was shocking as a missing limb.

She looked out at it for a long minute, until the bite of the night wind began to hurt her, then she spun on her heel and marched back inside. "All right, as of now the city is on full alert status."

Palmer was at the communications terminal. Carter saw him punching buttons, and a few seconds later the lights in around her rose to their daylight levels. The same would be happening everywhere else, too; inside living quarters, corridors, public areas, labs... Within minutes, the city would be awake.

Whether or not the same could be said if the locked section, she couldn't say. Effectively, that was now no longer part of the city. It was a sovereign state, answerable to no-one. What, if anything, was occurring in there was a mystery to which she would have to devote all her efforts.

Right now, nothing else mattered. Not Fallon, not the IOA, nothing. The dark space was her only concern.

"Palmer? I'll need city-wide comms. And how long do you think the rest of the control staff will take to get here?"

"Fifteen minutes?"

"Call them individually, tell them they've got five." She walked a couple of steps away from him, taking a deep breath, readying herself. Then she switched her headset on. "Pegasus expedition, this is Colonel Carter. As you are probably aware by now, the city of Atlantis is on full alert. All active personnel are required to go to their duty stations, all others please make yourselves ready and await further instructions."

She let the echoes of her own voice die away, then said: "In addition, it's possible there may be non-human intruders in the city. Please be as vigilant as you can."

With that, she closed the connection. "I take it there's been no response from *Apollo*?"

"Not a word, Colonel. I've been sending out hails every fifteen minutes..." He gave her a small, helpless shrug. "So far, nothing."

Carter nodded briskly. She'd have been alerted if Ellis had reported in, that was certain, but she'd still had to ask. Just to make sure that things were as bad as she thought they were. "Keep trying. Palmer, are you going to be okay up here on your own until the rest arrive?"

"Sure. Are you not going to be here?"

"I'll be back shortly. There's some things I need to do first. Oh, and one more thing… Now that it's all just hit the fan, Andrew Fallon is probably going to be looking for me. If he asks, tell him I'm in the ZPM room."

"Is that where you'll be?"

"No. But tell him anyway."

The lights in the infirmary were up very high, higher than normal by some considerable degree. The brightness struck Carter as soon as she came in, and her made wince. She still didn't feel truly awake. A mug of furiously strong coffee was helping slightly in that regard, but she couldn't shake the strange feeling that she was lagging behind the rest of the world by about a quarter of a second.

Keller looked up as she heard Carter come in. "Colonel," she said, very quietly.

"Morning, Doctor." Carter kept her voice at the same level. She had been warned to do so before she'd arrived. "I think this just about counts as morning, doesn't it?"

"Only just." Keller got up. "If you're looking for Teyla and Zelenka, I stashed them in the lab next door."

"Were they okay?"

"I checked them out and they seem fine. Just a little shaken up."

Carter gestured over to a screened-off area. "Is Cassidy in there?"

"Yeah. I gave her a sedative. She was in quite a state when they brought her in, poor kid." Keller hugged herself nervously. "Some of the stuff she was saying… Jesus."

"Can I talk to her?"

"I'd rather you didn't." Keller glanced back at the screened-off area. "Colonel, is what they were saying true? Teyla and

Zelenka?"

"I have no idea. All I know is that we've lost an entire section of pier, and that Fallon's going to have my hide."

"What are you going to do?"

"I'll let you know when I've woken up. In the meantime, take care of Cassidy."

"I will. She's sleeping okay at the moment, as long as I leave the lights on full. If I try to lower them, well…" She sighed. "Let's just say it doesn't matter how much sedative I give her."

Carter thanked her, then went into the adjacent lab. Teyla Emmagan was there, pacing in the small space. Zelenka was busying himself with a data terminal. He looked up as she came in. "Hello Colonel."

"Hi Radek, Teyla. How are you both doing?"

"Physically, we are both well," Teyla replied. She was practically bouncing with nervous energy. "Colonel, you need to post guards around the affected area."

"I already have." Carter had spent the journey down to the infirmary on her headset. "I've got a full marine squad on their way, and more standing by if needs be. Don't worry, nothing's going to get in or out of there until we give the word."

Teyla looked unconvinced. "From what I saw, leaving is not their intention."

"Blast doors," said Zelenka helpfully. "I'd not seen them before, but they looked thick, heavily armored. They shut the corridor off just before the lights went out."

"Okay…" Carter found a seat, a high lab stool, and perched on it. "Teyla, exactly what happened down there? You said you were attacked?"

"That is correct. Radek and I had both decided separately to observe Angelus, and we met in the gallery. While I was there, I noticed that the marines on guard were acting in a strange way."

"They'd both left their post when I arrived," Zelenka cut in. "Teyla saw them go and come back. But then that poor girl screamed…"

"Cassidy?"

"That is correct," said Teyla. She had a haunted look to her now, remembering. "We found the guards trying to force her back into the lab. She was terrified of something there, and would not return. When we intervened, the marines turned on us. I shot Lieutenant DeSalle."

Carter stared at her. "You *shot* him?"

"In the head. However, he did not seem unduly concerned."

Zelenka stood up. "Colonel, I know that part sounds hard to believe. But it happened right next to me. DeSalle should have been dead before he hit the ground, but he was acting as if nothing had happened. That was when the blast doors closed and all the lights went out."

Before Carter could answer, her headset crackled. "*Colonel Carter, this is MacReady.*"

Major MacReady was leading the marine squad she had sent down to observe the dark section. "Good to hear from you, Major. What can you tell me?"

"*I've had my people do a full sweep. Looks like every corridor in is blocked by armored doors—tried to run a bypass on a set of 'em, but got nothing. And the lights are out to a perimeter roughly ten meters outside the doors in all directions. Colonel, that section of pier is nailed shut like a cheap coffin.*"

"Thanks, Major. We'll need each set of blast doors guarded, two marines per. Stay in constant contact—if anyone tries to go in or come out, I want to know about it." She caught a glimpse of Teyla's expression. "Oh, and Major?"

"*Yeah?*"

"There's a possibility that there could be non-humans inside that area, masquerading as our people. Be careful—normal weapons fire might not bring them down."

"*Understood. MacReady out.*" The man's tone of voice hadn't changed, as though bullet-proof shapeshifters was something he dealt with on a daily basis. Carter couldn't help but allow herself a wry smile at the thought of that.

"Looks like you were right about the blast doors," she told Zelenka. "They've come down in all the access corridors to the lab. Could Angelus have activated some kind of security protocol?"

"It's possible. He is an Ancient, after all. If anyone could, it would be him."

"If you found what he'd done, could you undo it?"

"Again, it's possible. I'd need to track down the exact proto-col he'd used first. That might take some time."

She took a sip of her coffee, but it was getting cold. "Get right on it. Oh, and before you get set up, can you find someone on your team to get down there with some cutting equipment? If the high-tech approach doesn't work, we'll need some brute force instead."

"Absolutely. Norris knows how to use a oxy-acetylene torch. I'll call him and Bennings up when I get to the ZPM lab."

"Fine, I'll see you there later…" Something behind him had caught Carter's eye. She stepped aside as he went for the door, not taking her eyes off it. Suddenly, half the pieces in her mys-tery folder had just arranged themselves into new and terrible configurations.

"Teyla, can you go up to my office and meet me there? I need your help with something."

"Very well."

"Actually, can you wait ten minutes? I need to check on something first, but I don't want Fallon to catch you up there without me around. He's probably on the warpath right about now."

Teyla raised an eyebrow. "I am not afraid of Mr Fallon."

"Neither am I. But I'm afraid *for* him." She gave the Athosian a brief smile. "I'll see you up there."

"Very well." With a final, slightly puzzled look, Teyla fol-lowed Zelenka out of the door.

When she had gone, Carter walked slowly up to what she had seen; a row of empty sample tubes, racked for storage above one of the lab's benches.

Blood, she thought.

She went to the door and poked her head out. Keller was still there, but now a few of her nursing staff were bustling around as well, readying the infirmary in case of injuries. And to Carter's surprise, Alexa Cassidy was awake; the physicist was sitting up, the screen partially drawn back, sipping at a cup of something that steamed. There was a nurse with her, standing alongside the bed.

The lights were still very bright, and it was obvious that Cassidy could still not be left alone.

Carter waved at attract Keller's attention, then beckoned her over. "Doctor, can I ask you something?"

"Sure."

"One of your nurses sent in a report a couple of days ago. There was a screw-up with some blood samples?"

"Er, yeah. That was Neblett—she's over there with Cassidy."

"So what happened?"

"You can ask her yourself. Hold on a second." Keller went over to join Cassidy and the nurse. A few words were exchanged; Carter saw the nurse nod, then get up. Keller took her place.

When Cassidy looked over at Carter, she gave the physicist a wave and a reassuring smile. She hoped it would do some good.

"Colonel Carter?" Neblett was somewhat shorter than Carter, with dark hair tied back. "Is there a problem?"

"No, not at all." Carter gently drew her away, out of Cassidy's view. "I just wanted to follow up on that report you sent me. The blood samples?"

The woman's expression changed, very slightly. As if she had been reminded of something she had been trying to forget. "Colonel, I don't know what to say about that. I guess someone could have been playing some kind of a trick, or—"

"Really, it's okay. I just need to know what happened."

Neblett paused, gathering herself. "Well, like I said in the report, I'd put the samples in a TCL for storage—"

"Sorry, TCL?"

"Temperature-controlled locker. If the blood needs to be kept for long periods we'll freeze it down to minus eighty, but we were planning to re-analyze it after forty-eight hours, so I just locked it up at four degrees C."

That sounded like reasonably standard procedure to Carter. "Go on."

"Well, when I went back to check it the next day, the blood

was gone."

"All of it?"

"Yeah, every drop."

"But the sample tubes were intact."

Neblett nodded. "Colonel, I swear the tubes hadn't been tampered with. The locker was still shut tight, too."

"Can you show me?"

"Sure. It's right in here." Neblett led her back into the lab. "This is the locker. I've not put anything in it since. It's just how I left it."

Carter peered at the thing: it was thoroughly unremarkable, a stainless steel cube with a pull-twist handle and a small temperature LCD above the door. She touched the surface of it, felt a slight warmth through the metal. All the heat taken out of the interior had to go somewhere, after all.

She twisted the handle and pulled the locker open.

Sure enough, a small rack of empty sample tubes stood on the top shelf, very much like those that had reminded her of the report. Carter lifted one of the tubes; it came up with a very slight resistance, as though it had part-frozen to the rack, but in all other respects it was exactly as she had expected it to be.

Including the label, which had the name 'Angelus' printed on it.

Carter put the tube back in the rack, and carefully closed the locker door. "Rhonda?"

"Yes?"

"I'm going to send someone to collect this locker. In the meantime, don't touch it."

"Is there something wrong?"

"Probably not. I'm just allowing myself a little paranoia right now." She backed away from the locker, and turned to leave.

Then she paused. "In fact, come to think of it, it might be better if no-one comes in here at all until this is sorted out. Is there a lock on this door?"

Once Carter was out of the infirmary, she called a couple of marines in to seal the medical lab. Still wary of Cassidy's fragile state of mind, she asked them to do so in civilian clothing.

As she had told Neblett, it was probably nothing. A mistake, or an act of theft. Maybe Angelus had spirited his own blood away somehow, unwilling to have it subjected to further tests; she had no real idea of the extent of his powers, if he had any at all.

But still, in these troubled times, she felt it best to take no chances.

She must have been a little early getting to the control room: Teyla was nowhere to be seen, but Andrew Fallon was already waiting for her. To her relief, though, he looked more concerned than angry.

"Colonel," he said politely. "You can be hard to find, sometimes."

"I'm sorry. As you might expected, these aren't exactly normal circumstances."

"Oh, I'm well aware of that." He walked over to the sensor terminal, eyes fixed on the map and its pulsing circle. "I take it there's been no change?"

"None at all. I've posted guards around the blast doors, just in case, but right now it's completely locked down."

"So basically we don't know what happened in there, or what's happening now."

"Well, I've been told what *happened*—"

"Yes," he muttered. "That news traveled quite fast, I can assure you."

She shouldn't really have been surprised at that. "You don't believe it?"

"That Teyla Emmagan shot a man in the head and he didn't die? I have to admit I have a difficult time with that element of it, yes. In all the zombie movies I've seen, a shot in the head normally does the trick."

"This isn't a movie."

"More's the pity. I'd probably know who the bad guys were if it was." He went over to stand in front of the balcony doors. He didn't open them, just stood there, looking out through the glass. "Colonel, how well do you know Teyla?"

"Not well at all," she replied, after some hesitation. "But I like to think I'm a pretty good judge of character. I've seen nothing to make me think she'd cook something like this up."

"There's only three explanations," he said. "She's telling the truth, she's lying, she's mistaken. Until we find out which is which, all we're doing is chasing our tails."

"What do you suggest?"

"Well, if she's telling the truth, I guess that's your ball game. If she's lying, it's mine. Even if she's just mistaken, it still leaves us with why she and Zelenka were down there in the first place, and why Alexa Cassidy is acting so spooked." He glanced over at Carter. "Teyla and Zelenka aren't a couple, are they?"

Carter eyebrows rose. "I'm pretty certain they're not."

He gave a slight shrug. "Just a thought."

"Mr Fallon, Alexa Cassidy hasn't shown any sign of mental weakness prior to this. If she had, she'd not be in Atlantis. She's not just acting, believe me. Something frightened the hell out of her down there."

"Look, Colonel…" He turned away from the doors, leaned back against them with his arms folded. "My first responsibility is to Angelus and his project. If your people went down there, and caused him to lock himself in for whatever reason, then trust me, there will be trouble. On the other hand, if they're telling the truth about what they saw, then I consider that a direct threat to Angelus too. You've already said that the Replicators have tried to kill him—what if they've infiltrated Atlantis?"

Carter frowned. "There's no way they could do that."

"How much are you willing to bet? Colonel, right now, priority number one is that we find out what's happening behind those doors. Let me talk to Angelus."

"He's not answering. We've tried."

"*You've* tried. I haven't. It's possible he sees you as an enemy now."

Carter mulled this over for a moment. If Zelenka couldn't convince the blast doors to open from the outside, maybe Fallon could talk Angelus into reversing whatever protocol he had invoked to lock the section down. And then, she thought, she would take great satisfaction in throwing the Ancient right back where he had come from.

Wherever that was.

"I guess it couldn't hurt," she told him. "I'll give you full access to the comms system. I hope you have better luck than us."

"So do I. In the meantime, please keep Teyla and Zelenka away from Angelus. I don't want him thinking anyone else is going to get shot in the head."

Once she had set Fallon up at the communications terminal, Carter went to her office. Teyla joined her a few minutes later.

Carter sat the Athosian down and, over the next few minutes, outlined what it was she needed Teyla to do. She had wondered at first whether the woman was the right person for the job, whether she should simply have drafted in a technician instead. But Teyla had been in the corridor when the blast doors had slammed shut. She knew what to look for. And she knew John Sheppard well.

Besides, having Teyla in the office allowed her to keep an eye on Fallon. And Fallon, seeing Teyla there, would hopefully be less troubled by thoughts of her trying to inconvenience Angelus.

The fact that she would be doing exactly that, right under his nose, was neither here nor there.

Once Teyla had started work, Carter set off to find Zelenka. As expected, he was in the ZPM lab. Stepping from the transporter there gave her an odd, uneasy sensation—the memory of those sinister noises Zelenka had conjured from his computer were still fresh in her mind, and remembering them made her shudder.

It was an eerie feeling, going back.

Zelenka had four terminals open at once; three were displaying complex rotating graphics, the fourth streams of raw numerical data. He looked up as Carter came in. "Colonel," he said. "I'm glad you're here."

"Have you had any luck?"

"Depends how you define luck." He leaned back, and tapped the screen of one terminal. "I have managed to access a partial database of emergency protocols. I can't tell how partial, and right now I'm only certain what about twenty percent of the ones I have found do—if Rodney was here, I'm sure he'd be able to identify them far more readily than I."

"And he'd enjoy rubbing it in your face, too." Carter gestured at the screen. "Come on, Radek. McKay's not here—it's you I'm relying on right now. What are we seeing?"

"Well…" He pointed at a graphic. "These are the protocols, in 3-D form. Basically, they present as virtual crystals."

"That makes sense."

"Identifying the purposes of the crystals gives us clues as to what the protocols do. This one right here, this is to do with the transporters—I think it would re-route all transporter traffic to a central location. This one here, though, is purely decorative. Flashing all the city lights in sequence."

"Pretty," said Carter. "Have you found any that reference the blast doors?"

"No, I haven't. I have found some that reference local power nodes, though."

"That's great! How many?"

He looked glum. "About six hundred."

"Damn," Carter muttered.

"Oh, and one other thing. Just in case you weren't feeling quite futile enough." He nodded at the screens. "So far I have no evidence that *any* of the city protocols have been activated, apart from the alert status."

"That doesn't make sense," Carter breathed.

The lockdown, as she understood it, would require many processes to occur at once. Activating those processes one at a time would be no great feat—anyone with enough knowledge of the city's systems could cause a door to close and lock, to interrupt communications along a limited path, to extinguish an exterior light, and so-on. But in order to set off an entire series of those processes, like raising all the city's internal lights when the alert status was sounded, would require a large set of programmed instructions keyed to a single command. A protocol.

If no protocol had been activated, how had Angelus been able to close and lock all the blast doors at once? To shut down all communications in the section? It was impossible.

"It must be one you've not found yet," she told Zelenka.

"There's no way he could do that without a protocol."

"I'll keep looking," he said. "There's something else. Around the edges of the lockdown zone, there's some kind of activity."

"What do you mean? Where?"

"Everywhere. Well, not exactly… What I mean is, all the systems around the lockdown are showing this activity. Power, sensors… It's something I've not seen before, like a set of new functions being applied."

That rang a chime in Carter's memory. "Hey, you know Palmer? In the control room… He said there was unidentified functionality around that area. Could it be those armored doors you saw?"

Zelenka weighed this up for a moment. "It could be. On the other hand, it does seem to have some similarities to the signal pattern I detected earlier. Or it could be nothing at all."

"I guess…" Carter shivered slightly. A coldness had moved across her, a terrible sense of things moving into place. For a moment, it felt to her as if everything that was happening now had been somehow set in motion long ago, that tonight was the end result of some vast and dreadful process. That rectangle of darkness out on the west pier was merely the final domino toppling over: hidden hands had tipped the first one at some distant point in the past, knowing exactly when and where the ultimate impact would occur.

Behind her, something moved, and a shadow fell across the lab.

Carter turned around, and saw Teyla Emmagan in the doorway. She was about to welcome her in, glad of the extra company, but then she saw the distraught look on the woman's face. "Teyla? What's wrong?"

Teyla remained very still. "Colonel, I did as you asked."

"Jesus, Teyla, you look terrible. Get in here and sit down." Carter drew a seat out for the Athosian, who walked slowly in and dropped onto it. "What happened?"

"The cameras… Most of them are malfunctioning. There was very little footage. I saw…" She fell silent.

"What?" whispered Zelenka. "What do you mean?"

"I had Sheppard install a surveillance suite before Angelus

moved into the lab," Carter told him. "He gave me the access codes. I was hoping Teyla could download what they'd been recording, but—"

"Maybe he found the cameras," Teyla said bleakly. She reached into her jacket pocket and pulled out a USB thumbdrive. "All I saw is here."

Carter took the drive from her, found an unused terminal and plugged it in. Together, the three of them watched what Sheppard's cameras had recorded earlier that night.

Later, Carter found herself back in her office with only the vaguest recollection of how she had gotten there.

After she had seen the surveillance footage, there seemed to be almost no words that could be exchanged between her and Teyla. Zelenka had been shocked into silence too, apart from a few half-hearted denials. But in the main, the film on the thumbdrive had robbed them all of voice.

Since returning to the office, Carter had seen the film three more times, perhaps hoping for some hint of insight with each successive viewing. But each time was the same.

The footage was not good quality: the picture was grainy, monochrome. An annoying diagonal scratch of interference hovered around one corner, and dark specks danced distractingly across the screen every few moments. There was no sound. However, the scene, and the players in it, was unmistakable.

Rewinding the footage back to its start, Carter once again found herself looking into the corridor that led to Angelus's lab on the west pier.

The camera had been set high, near the ceiling, probably in an air vent or close to a light panel for concealment. It was aimed back towards the gallery, with the end of the corridor a skewed rectangle of black at one side of the picture.

In the center was a small knot of people. Closer to the camera lens, with their backs to it, were two men in marine uniform; Kaplan and DeSalle. Facing them were Zelenka and Teyla, with Alexa Cassidy off to one side.

Teyla had a gun pointed at DeSalle's face.

Carter hit the Play control, and the picture shivered into

motion. Cassidy was backing away, hands to her mouth. Zelenka was looking at Teyla with a shocked expression on his face. Teyla was shouting, enraged, the gun centered on DeSalle's forehead.

She watched as Kaplan turned to the wall, began working at a control panel there. The picture shuddered, and then diagonal slabs of metal appeared at the corners of the corridor. The blast doors, sliding smoothly towards each other, the space between them a rapidly-shrinking diamond.

Teyla must have seen the doors rising between her and the marines. She stepped back and fired. Carter saw the flash from the muzzle, pixilated fuzzy white on the screen.

DeSalle ducked away from the shot, turned, his face a mask of shock, and then dropped to the floor. He lay there while the blast doors rose up. And then, once they had closed, he rose and turned back down towards the corridor. He shouted something.

The footage froze in mid-shout, DeSalle's mouth open, hovering between two final frames. Juddering endlessly.

There had been no attack on Teyla Emmagan. DeSalle had evaded the bullet she had fired, unprovoked, at him. The doors had been activated by the two marines for their own safety.

Teyla's story, backed up by Radek Zelenka, was a lie.

Carter leaned back in her seat, rubbing her eyes. There was no sense she could make of this. Unless Teyla and Zelenka were suffering from some kind of shared hallucination, the only other possible explanation was that they had deliberately concocted the story.

No wonder Angelus had locked himself away.

An insistent buzzing from her headset broke into her thoughts. If she was honest with herself, she rather welcomed the distraction. "Carter."

"*Colonel? This is Andrew Fallon.*"

She leaned across her desk to peer along the gangway. There was a man at the communications terminal, but it wasn't Fallon. "Where are you?"

"*I'm with Major MacReady, down by the gallery blast doors. Angelus has agreed to let me in.*"

"Good grief…" Carter found herself quite stunned. "You spoke to him?"

"While you were away. I'm afraid it looks like your people have been stringing you along, Colonel. Angelus says that DeSalle's alive and well, despite Teyla trying to shoot him when the blast doors started to close. She was threatening Angelus, and they closed the doors to keep her from carrying out those threats."

"Mr Fallon, can you ask him to open the doors and return that section to our control?" Carter was looking at the picture on her terminal, but not really seeing it. The two frames still shuddered one to the other, everything on screen shaking back and forth, over and over. Only the corner scratch stayed stable. "I can guarantee his safety."

"I've already asked that, Colonel. Angelus no longer trusts you, I'm afraid. He knows you've been working to obstruct his project."

"Fallon? Tell him…" Carter fell silent, frowning. Something about the picture in front of her was familiar. It nagged at her, itched like a bug in her ear… "Wait. Hold on. Don't do anything."

She slid her seat back to get to her desk drawer, opened it and pulled her mystery folder free. Her hands were trembling slightly—fatigue, she told herself—and she fumbled with the folder, scattering its contents across the desktop.

"Colonel? The doors are opening."

"Wait!" The top few sheets were reports. She slid them aside, the paper elusive under her dry fingertips. Under them, photographs. Scans from Keller's examination of Angelus.

A side–on x-ray of the Ancient's skull. Down in the bottom right, a diagonal scratch of interference.

An oblique false-color CAT scan of the skull and spine. In the corner, the same scratch.

Her eyes darted up to the screen. The line of bright, random pixels along the bottom right corner was identical. "Fallon? Don't go in there! For God's sake, don't go in! *He can fake images!*"

There was no answer. Only a soft, rhythmic rushing that sounded, if she listened very hard, like the rise and fall of distant voices.

CHAPTER TWELVE

By the Sea

The puddle jumper had been out of Atlantis for just over a day and a half when McKay told Sheppard and Ronon Dex that they could not complete the mission. "There isn't enough power," he said.

Sheppard, who was at the controls, looked back over his shoulder at him. "You're kidding me."

"Nope. I wish I was. Using the cloak both times we went into orbit put a drain on the reactor that I wasn't expecting. And even if it hadn't, I still don't know if we'd have had enough."

Sheppard took his hands off the joysticks and turned fully around in his seat. "So let me get this straight. We're halfway through the mission, twenty light years from Atlantis—"

"Twenty seven."

"Twenty *seven* light years away from Atlantis, and you're saying we're running out of gas."

McKay, who was standing at the hatch, nodded. "That's about it, yeah."

"Have we got enough to get back?" Dex asked. His voice was flat, but Sheppard detected a very slight warning note there. McKay either didn't hear it or simply chose to ignore it. Instead he drew himself up to his full indignant height. "Of course we have," he snapped.

"Then what's the problem?"

"I'm not saying there's a problem. I mean, it's not like I've stranded us out here or anything. We just don't have enough power to visit the other two origin sites and *then* get home."

Sheppard let out a long breath, and returned his attention to the jumper's controls. In front of him, through the forward viewport, a misty globe rotated slowly against a backdrop of stars: M2L-374, the second of McKay's designated origin points that they had visited, and the second to have turned up nothing.

Of the dozens of planets Angelus could conceivably have launched from, only four were capable of supporting human—or indeed Ancient—life. The first, and closest to Atlantis, had turned out to be seething with living things; its jungles rife with beasts, its plains lush, its oceans blue and bright with fish. Had the mission been to seek out and study new forms of flora and fauna, that world might have kept an army of scientists busy for decades—even its skies were full, so much so that Sheppard had found himself flinging the jumper around just to avoid the creatures that flew or floated there. But there was no way Angelus could have started his voyage from this planet. It was a primitive world, free from intellect. Nothing with a mind walked on those plains or fished those oceans. Life there was new, and violent in its youth. It was not Eraavis.

Neither was this second planet, but for very different reasons. Beneath that covering of cloud lurked a world that should, given its composition and distance from its sun, have been Earthlike. But something had gone very wrong in the planet's distant past. Pollution, possibly, or an excess of volcanism. Some growing taint in the air. In any case, it's atmosphere had turned from a source of life to a suffocating blanket, a chemical wall that no heat could escape. M4T-638 had a surface environment so hot, so corrosive and pressurized and thick that it had almost wrecked the jumper. Sheppard had been forced to engage the vessel's emergency thrust and power it out of that hellish atmosphere, long before McKay had finished his scans. Had he waited any longer, the vile stuff would have eaten through the hull.

Which left two more worlds. And, McKay was telling him, not enough power to visit them.

"So what you're saying," growled Dex, "is that this has been a complete waste of time."

"That's a matter of opinion."

"In this case, it's the only opinion that matters." The Satedan folded his arms. "You should have let me ask Angelus where he came from. Would have been a lot quicker than this."

"I don't think torturing the guy was really an option."

"Who said anything about torture?"

"You didn't need to."

"Okay, you two! Knock it off!" Sheppard put his head in his hands, briefly, then straightened and shook himself. Either Dex or McKay, alone, might have been tolerable companions for the duration of the mission, but together they were making his head hurt.

"Rodney," he said firmly. "Straight answer time, okay?"

"Er, sure."

"Do we have to turn around and go home right now?" *Please say yes*, he thought silently. *Please, please say yes.*

"No," McKay replied.

Dammit. "What else can we do?"

"There's two more planets on the initial list. We can check out either one of them before we need to head back and recharge."

"You're sure of that?"

"Well, as sure as I am of anything. I mean, this hyperdrive is hardly standard equipment. I'm not entirely sure why is doesn't blow up every time we try to use it, let alone how much power it eats. But so far, it's been consistent. As long as it stays that way, then yeah, I'm sure."

"'No' would have been quicker," Dex told him.

"But it wouldn't have been as accurate."

"Guys," warned Sheppard. "Come on, I don't want to be out here any more than you do. Probably a lot less. Let's pick our last planet and get going, yeah?"

"Sounds good," Dex replied. "What are our choices?"

McKay had a laptop jacked into the jumper's systems. He hit a control and a stylized star map appeared on the HUD. "Here," he said, pointing. "M1Q-432. And here, M7Y-119."

Dex snorted. "You people chose the galaxy's most confusing way of naming worlds."

"Hey, come on," said Sheppard. "There's a lot of planets. All the good names get used up really fast, and then you have to visit some colony and tell them you've called their planet 'X' or 'New New Jersey'."

"Still beats naming them after... What are those things on

cars?"

"License plates," said McKay. "And trust me, I know what you mean. Back in the Milky Way we at least started them with P for planet and M for moon, but somehow even that got screwed up."

"Fine," said Sheppard, pointing at the two planets in turn. "Chunky Monkey and Rocky Road. Which one do we go for?"

McKay leaned close to the HUD, rubbing his chin. "Rocky Road's closer to the biozone sweet spot. If I was an Ancient, that's the kind of temperature range I'd want to be living in."

Dex blinked lazily. "The Monkey's closer to us."

"Sorry Rodney." Sheppard grabbed the controls and concentrated on the jumper's engines. The boards lit up under his hands. "Chunky Monkey it is."

"Banana and walnuts?" McKay screwed his face up. "Please."

He was wearing the same expression all the way into hyperspace.

Conventionally, puddle jumpers were not hyperspace-capable. Their engines were as efficient as any other piece of Ancient technology, but they had never been designed to bridge the gap between universes. If it hadn't been for one very important feature, the jumpers would have remained nothing more than rather cramped shuttlecraft.

The feature that transformed the puddle jumpers were their cross-section. With the engine pods retracted, the ships were just small enough to fly through a Stargate.

Obviously, that had been enough for the Ancients. They had possessed armadas of starships, after all, each of them fitted with hyperdrives among their many wondrous technologies. There had never been a need for them to upgrade the jumpers to handle superlight velocities. It would have been like fitting a rowing boat with wings.

However, for the members of the Pegasus expedition, a hyperspace-capable puddle jumper was nothing short of a holy grail. It was just a pity there was only one.

And that it didn't work very well.

The jumper-scale hyperdrive had been designed by Rodney McKay. Unfortunately, he had not been himself while designing it—an encounter with a piece of Ancient technology had caused a massive acceleration of his mental capacity, among other powers. Luckily, he had been able to reverse the process before it killed him, but it left him with several new designs that he could barely understand. He had been so much more intelligent when he had created them.

Out of those designs, the engine presently hurling the jumper through hyperspace was one of the more comprehensible, now that his intellect was back within human ranges. He had even made it work, after a fashion. But despite continually tinkering with the hyperdrive, McKay still had little faith in it. As a result, neither did anyone else.

If Carter had been able to contact *Apollo*, she would not have entertained the idea of sending anyone out in the jumper. But Ellis had missed his deadline, and *Apollo* could not be raised on subspace comms.

That, to John Sheppard, was a cause for concern. Ellis wasn't the kind of man who missed things if it could possibly be avoided. There could be any number of reasons why he might not have reported in, and for why the ship could not return communications hails. But for both of those circumstances to arrive at the same time required reasons that were far more rare.

Sheppard couldn't think of any good ones.

His first thought had been to take the jumper out and use it to look for *Apollo*, but Carter had vetoed that immediately. There was no direct evidence that Ellis was in trouble, for a start, and of course no indication of where the battlecruiser might actually be. That, coupled with the more immediate threat of Angelus and his project, was enough for Carter to requisition the jumper for a recon mission.

And so Sheppard found himself piloting a ship no bigger than a compact Winnebago through the silver-blue vortices of hyperspace, in search of a planet named after a flavor of ice-cream, while Dex and McKay did their best to bicker throughout the entire length of the trip.

Sheppard had a bad feeling about Chunky Monkey as soon as he saw it, and when McKay came forward from nursing the hyperdrive, he said so.

"Well," McKay replied, "I'll admit it's not pretty."

"Not pretty?" Sheppard squinted down at the planet, trying to see something appealing about the surface. "I've seen prettier Wraith. What the hell's wrong with it?"

Once again, he was sure they had not found Eraavis. The planet seemed ill-equipped to support life of any kind, let alone Angelus and his subterranean children. And while it was ugly, the world did not show any obvious signs of heavy orbital bombardment. On the contrary, rather than being attacked, it looked more as if it had been left alone to rot.

What he could see of the land masses were a roiled, greyish brown. There didn't seem to be any surface vegetation at all, which of course would rule out a breathable atmosphere. Oxygen is a highly reactive gas, and left to its own devices will bind to other chemicals as fast as it is able. In order for a world to sustain breathable air, there needs to be something keeping the oxygen in circulation. On most worlds, that was green plants.

On Chunky Monkey it was vast, slimy mats of sea-borne algae.

"Pretty small diameter," McKay read, staring at his laptop screen. "Gravity's a shade higher than Earth normal, though, so it must have a dense core. Atmosphere is… What do you know? You could breath it."

"I'm not sure I want to." From altitude, the seas looked sludgy and toxic. Only the country-sized algal colonies gave them any color at all, and that color was a sickly, phlegmy green. "Look, Rodney, this place is a dump. Angelus wouldn't have come from here, would he?"

"Sheppard's right," said Dex. He was leaning forwards in his seat, looking at the world's surface with a slightly queasy expression. "This is still a waste of time."

Behind him, McKay started. "Oh my God," he breathed.

"Guys? Maybe this one isn't a bust after all."

"What do you mean?"

"There's a power signature. Something down on that slime-ball is generating power!"

The energy trace McKay had picked up was faint and inter-mittent, and when Sheppard flew the cloaked jumper in a high, slow pass over the site of it there seemed to be nothing about the rocky landscape below to suggest its source; just the wrin-kled, wattled ground, a ragged curve of coastline and the oily, thick wash of algae-riddled sea.

A lower, slower pass once again failed to reveal anything unusual. It was only when Sheppard hovered the jumper just a hundred meters up could he make out any signs of structure, and then only hints, blurred by rain that sluiced down from the mud-colored clouds and ran in streams off the viewport.

McKay's scans revealed nothing more concrete. "I'm just not picking up enough to get a fix on," he complained. "There's something down there, but I've got no idea what."

Dex peered out of the viewport, studying the ground. "Angelus said his people lived underground. Maybe it's an entrance."

"They lived underground to hide from the Wraith. Leaking a power signal like that… It's like leaving the front door open."

"Or having the front door blown off," the Satedan replied grimly. "I can see blast marks."

Sheppard stood up, trying to get closer to the port, to see past the distorting rain. "I can't see anything."

"We'll have to land."

McKay blinked, his eyes wide. "Really? I mean, actually land?"

"You got a better idea?"

"We've got no idea what's down there!"

"And we never will if we stay up here." Dex grinned wolf-ishly at him. "What are you going to do? Head back for home and when Carter asks if you found Eraavis, tell her 'maybe'?"

"He's right," said Sheppard. "Nothing else for it. Trust me, Rodney, this place gives me as bad a feeling as it does you, but

I don't think we've got the choice." He gripped the controls again, taking the jumper up higher, and then edging it slightly inland. The ground rose there in a series of twisted, bonelike formations, but behind them was a relatively flat area of something very like shale. He aimed for that, letting the jumper turn like a falling leaf as it dropped, finally settling onto the wet ground with its rear hatch facing the site of the power leakage.

There was an ugly sliding sensation as the ship put its weight down. The shale must have been slightly unstable, slick below the jumper's belly, but after a final, jolting twist it became still.

Sheppard throttled back the drives, eased the power down until only enough to run the cloak filtered from the generator. The interior of the jumper darkened slightly, and the noise of its workings, so constant and pervasive that he had quite forgotten it was here, faded to nothing.

The three men sat, quite still, listening to rain patter on the viewport.

"Anyone bring an umbrella?" said McKay, after a time.

"If it really worries you, there's rain cloaks in the survival kit," Sheppard told him. "But I don't intend to be out in it for that long. We're about two hundred meters from that trace. We'll double-time over to it, see what we're looking at and go from there, okay?"

"Well, if you think there's no other way..."

"Yeah, sorry." Sheppard got up, and began pulling a black tactical vest on over his uniform. He'd already checked it a dozen times during the trip, when Dex and McKay were arguing over some impossible point and he'd needed to go to a quiet place in his head. Going over the vest, making sure its multiple pouches contained all the ammo and equipment that they should do, testing the webbing and the reinforced stitching, positioning the custom-reinforced slabs of Kevlar... It had been like a mantra for his hands, a muscle-memory he could retreat into.

It also meant that he could pick up the vest at any time and be sure it was ready.

In the aft compartment McKay was readying his own gear, stuffing the laptop into a backpack already filled with gadgets and spare batteries. And several MRE ration packs, Sheppard noticed, allowing himself a wry grin. He'd lived off the things himself often enough in his life, but he had no love for them. McKay, in fact, was about the only person he knew who would eat MREs by choice.

Dex had no such concerns. If the prospect of hiking in the driving rain bothered him, he didn't show it. He simply checked that his blaster was fully charged, shook his dreadlocks out of his face and got up from his seat. "I'm ready."

"You're always ready."

Dex seemed to weigh this up. "Pretty much. Anything wrong with that?"

"No, no…" Sheppard finished strapping up the vest and twisted himself this way and that, making sure it was snug but didn't restrict him. "Just spare a thought for us slower folks, okay?"

He moved to the back, past McKay, to where the weapons were held. He thought about taking one of the M4s, but he wasn't sure if he'd need to be fighting in a confined space. The P90 was a lot shorter, so he took that, along with a pair of grenades and as many spare clips as he could fit into the vest. "Rodney?"

"I'm good." Sheppard glanced over to see that McKay already had a P90 held across his chest.

"Remembered the ammo this time?"

McKay glared. "Yes!"

"Just asking." He threw a grin back over his shoulder at Dex, and then keyed open the rear hatch.

Almost the entire aft wall of the ship hinged downwards, folding outwards to form a ramp. Sheppard heard it's top edge crunch into the shale. "Guys? Watch your step on that stuff, okay? Even if it wasn't raining, it sounds unstable."

"So unstable *and* slippery, right, got it." McKay walked nervously down the ramp, stopping just below the rear overhang of the jumper's hull. "Wow."

Sheppard joined him, frowning up at the muddy sky. There was no wind at all, and the rain was coming straight down, a merciless, unceasing wash of grimy water spattering and bouncing off the rocks and the broken ground and the far edge of the ramp. He could smell it in the air, a swampy musk, like the wet fur of a dead animal. Ahead of him, the rocks twisted up into eroded lumps and mounds, eaten through by the rain into a maze of glistening holes, and in the distance, past the hiss and spatter of rain, he could hear the sea, sluggish and thick, slapping aimlessly at the bleak, colorless shore.

"God almighty," he breathed. "What a dump."

"You sure this isn't toxic?" Dex was hanging back, slightly. "Seriously, what is that smell?"

"Rotted algae," McKay replied. He stuck a hand out into the rain, and quickly pulled it back in, shaking it. "Warm," he muttered, then brought his palm up to his nose to sniff it. His nose wrinkled. "Aw crap."

"Oh, what the Hell." Sheppard ducked his head and trotted down the ramp.

A blood-warm fug of rain washed over him, coating him almost instantly. It wasn't heavy, like a monsoon or the sudden thunderstorms of home, but it was continuous. It felt almost artificial, like a chemical shower. There was a greasiness to it that made him want to wash.

"Come on, will ya?" He beckoned to McKay and Dex, who were still under the overhang. "Let's get this over with!"

Grudgingly, heads held low, they followed. Dex keyed the hatch shut as he stepped off the ramp, and in a moment, the jumper had vanished.

No, not quite. Sheppard couldn't help but smile as he looked back towards the ship, a hand cupped over his eyes to protect them from the rain, and saw the upper surface of the cloak outlined in greasy sparkles. The rain was bouncing right off it.

Not even the Ancients, it seemed, could beat the weather.

It took them longer than Sheppard would have liked to reach the power trace. As he had predicted, the going was treacherous—where the ground hadn't been pulverized into multiple layers of shifting, razor-edged shale, it was granite-hard and slippery with rain and algal grease. The three men had to plant their feet carefully, making sure their boots had grip on each step before moving onto the next. To cross the two hundred meters from the jumper to the trace took them almost ten minutes.

By the time they got there, Sheppard was soaked through. "You know something? I am really not looking forward to being locked up with this smell all the way back to Atlantis."

"Be glad it's only half a day," Dex growled. His dreadlocks were soaked onto his head. "But I swear, if McKay's got his numbers wrong again and we end up stranded, having to breathe this stink until we're rescued?"

"Don't think about it," Sheppard advised him. "Really, it's best not to."

They had reached the foot of a low hill. On any other world it might have been impressive, soaring, but Chunky Monkey's incessant rain had beaten it low; its hunched peaks were almost invisible through the wet air, the shattered, powdery margins of its slopes shelving messily into the ground until it was almost impossible to see where it began.

Dex had been right about the weapons fire, though. From close up, Sheppard could see where the shale had been scooped away by blast effects in a dozen places along the slope. The weather had disguised much of the damage—in such a naturally broken landscape it was difficult to tell which craters were the result of erosion and which of explosion. Like a hurried murderer, though, the rain hadn't covered everything. There was evidence enough of some bloody crime, here.

Sheppard stooped to pick up a chunk of shale. It had another piece fused onto it, the two rocks welded into one by the intense heat of some violent energy discharge. He showed it to Dex, who nodded silently, then threw it away.

The rock clattered eerily as it struck ground, the vibration of it sending rivulets of jagged pebbles rustling and skittering down the slope. It must have startled McKay, because he popped up a few meters down-slope, clutching a PDA in one hand and the P90 in the other. "What was that?"

"Nothing," Sheppard called back to him. "Found anything?"

"Yeah. This way." He turned away and began trudged along the edge of the slope. Sheppard swore under his breath and began to follow him, picking his way as quickly as he could on the treacherous ground.

A few minutes later, he stopped. McKay was standing near a bulge in the hillside, a ragged swelling that emerged from the slope like a blister. "It's here," he said. "Can you see that?"

"See what?"

"That shape!" McKay pointed at the blister.

Sheppard covered his eyes again, blinked rain from his lashes and tried to see what McKay was talking about. For a moment it eluded him, but then he saw an edge—fractured and crumbled, half covered by broken rock and rivulets of streaming water, but unmistakably an edge.

Once he had seen that, the outline emerged from his confusion like the solution to a puzzle. Seconds later, he couldn't understand why he hadn't been able to see it.

There was a structure emerging from the side of the hill. A broad shape, flat and faceted, maybe thirty meters across, ten high. It had been clad in the same gray, sodden stone as the rest of the landscape, but here and there parts of the covering had fallen away, revealing a dark smoothness beneath.

Large parts of it had been blasted open, too. The violence Sheppard had noticed further along the hill must have been concentrated here.

"Rodney? You getting any residuals off these blast patterns?"

"I kind of wish you hadn't asked that."

"Why?"

"Because then I wouldn't have had to tell you this was done by Replicator weapons."

Sheppard snapped the P90's fire control selector down from safe to semi-automatic. Behind him, he heard Ronon's blaster charge with a thin whine. "Any idea what this place is?"

"Not a clue."

"I was afraid of that. Okay, let's start looking for a way in."

"Hm?" McKay gave him a quizzical look, still squinting against the rain. "Oh, I've already found one of those." He stumbled a few steps closer to the structure, and pointed. "See?"

Past a jumble of broken rock and twisted metal, an uninviting wedge of gloom. An explosion had opened up a rift in the structure's wall, a piercing wound that went deeper than Sheppard could see, and wide enough to crawl through.

The prospect was far from enticing. "Well," he muttered, mostly to himself. "It'll be out of the rain."

He stepped towards the wound and leaned inside. He heard water, a cacophony of echoing drips and rushes, and he could smell metal and something burnt.

There was no light. He reached into one of his vest pouches and took out a tactical light, flicked it on and shone the beam inside. The light caught water first—streams of fat droplets cascading from the fractured, leaking ceiling, and filling the floor ankle-deep. Past the initial meter or two of rubble Sheppard could see that the wound opened up into some kind of tunnel or corridor, walled with repeating slabs of grayish metal. What little he could see looked functional, utilitarian.

It also looked oddly familiar.

"Okay, it widens out in there. We're going to get our feet wet, though."

"My feet are already wet," McKay griped. "See anything else?"

"No." Sheppard gripped the edges of the wound and pulled himself up, putting his boots in first and lowering himself past the opening. He had to slither down an incline of debris, and carefully. Not all of it was rock—twisted spars of metal, their edges ragged, poked through the mess in several places.

Finally, he splashed down into the corridor. He froze as soon as he was able to stand, letting the echoes of his entry die away, keeping the beam of the taclight focused on the end of the corridor.

Nothing. The darkness ahead of him stayed as impenetrable as before, and the tunnel noiseless save the constant pat and splatter of water. "Clear," he called back. "And watch your way in. There's sharp stuff."

McKay followed next, rather more quickly than he would have expected, and with several choice curses. It took Sheppard a moment to realize that Dex had probably picked him up and dropped him through the opening. The Satedan followed close behind, and within a few seconds the three of them were standing up to their ankles in warm, moving water.

Dex flicked his own flashlight on, and scanned it around. "See the walls?"

McKay had taken a plastic headband from his pack, and settled it down over his hair. Sheppard saw him tighten it, then switch on two tiny halogen lamps, one at either temple. It looked slightly ridiculous, but the light wasn't much less than that from a standard-issue taclight and it left his hands free.

He looked around, the twin beams following his gaze. "Oh yeah. Carbon scoring."

"There was a firefight in here," said Sheppard. "Energy weapons, lots of 'em." He clipped the tactical light to the Picatinny rail on the P90's receiver, then set off down the corridor, moving his boots slowly through the water. "Looks like somebody had to fight their way in."

"You want to know what else is weird about the walls?" McKay splashed up behind him.

"Well, they look kind of familiar."

"Oh, you noticed too."

They moved on without speaking for a few meters. The leaks in the ceiling lessened as they made their way further into the hill, the sound of water dropping away behind them. Sheppard welcomed that: the splattering had been random, like static. It made listening difficult.

Ahead, so far, was only silence.

Abruptly, the corridor ended. There was no door, just a dark expanse of open space behind it. Sheppard noticed that the water was getting shallower as he neared the end, and looked down to see it spiraling down into vents in the floor. As he walked into the open space, he left the last of it behind.

There was a glossiness to the floor in front of him that had nothing to do with water, a greenish tint to the walls he knew but couldn't immediately place. The room he now stood in was oddly shaped, all angles, set with several doorways and tall, glassy panels that would probably have supplied light if there had been power in the building.

There were no curves anywhere. He was in a world of straight, hard lines. "Rodney," he said slowly. "Tell me I'm wrong."

McKay had his PDA up, the light from its screen a hazy block on his face. "Trinium, refined titanium, superdense polymers... Oh man."

"What?" said Dex.

"You don't want to know."

The Satedan raised an eyebrow. "I think I do."

"Yeah, well, you'll wish you hadn't asked," Sheppard told him. He gestured ahead with the barrel of the P90. "This is Asuran technology."

"*Replicators?*"

"Uh-huh. We've walked right into the goddamn lion's den."

CHAPTER THIRTEEN

Immortal Remains

In some ways, the revelation made perfect sense. In others, none at all.

Now that he knew what he was looking at, Sheppard could see the work of the Asurans everywhere. The structure wasn't a direct copy of any Replicator buildings he had seen, but its design aesthetic was identical. The doorways, although gaping open in the darkness, were of the same proportions as those on Asuras and in Atlantis, each with the same tubular activation sensor set alongside. The walls had the same repetition of form, the angles at which they met suggested the interior of some great prism rather than a conventional building. With knowledge as well as torchlight to illuminate him, he could see it quite clearly now. McKay was right.

But by the same token, McKay *couldn't* be right.

Ronon Dex obviously had the same idea. "That's crazy," he growled. "You said the weapons fire was from Replicators."

"It is."

"Replicators don't shoot each other, Rodney." Sheppard scanned the P90 around, letting the taclight beam come to rest on a nearby doorway. "They're part of a collective, remember?"

"I know that! I didn't say I could explain it."

Sheppard walked over to the doorway. There was something there, something reflective, sending his light back out in a complex interplay of overlapping beams. He drew closer, peered inside, and for an awful second saw a face looking back out at him. But it was only his own reflection, and he recovered from the start quickly enough for the others not to notice.

As he stepped through the doorway, he heard Dex ask McKay if he could hear ticking.

He was in a small chamber, maybe a couple of meters across, perfectly hexagonal. One of the six walls was open, the doorway at his back, but the others were set with transparent panels, and behind the panels were narrow spaces, cells, the back wall of each a slab of incomprehensible technology.

Sheppard moved close to one of the cells, touched the panel with his fingertips. It wasn't cold, more a neutral temperature. Maybe a kind of plastic, then, rather than glass.

He scanned the taclight up, and saw nothing. Then he scanned it back down, and with a start of raw horror saw what was tangled in the bottom of the cell.

A curse ripped its way out of him.

The corpse was naked, its limbs pale sticks, its skin white and papery in the beam of the flashlight. It was crumpled up and facing the wall, and for that Sheppard was grateful. The back of it, that shriveled rack of ribs and spine with their covering of withered skin, was quite enough for him. He had no desire to see its face.

Its head had been shaved.

Not wanting to, knowing he had to, he moved the flashlight around. And as he had feared, each cell was occupied.

There were three men in the chamber with him. There was a woman. There was a child. All were naked, shaved, crumpled like driftwood in the floors of their cells. Some had turned away from the glass as death overtook them, but not all. One of the men had died trying to get out. His face, a shrunken nightmare, was pressed against the cell door.

The transparency in each compartment was smeared with long, bloody marks. The fingertips of each corpse were worn down to the bone.

McKay must have heard him shout. "Did you say something? Ronon says he can hear—"

He stopped in the doorway. Sheppard heard him swallow hard. "What the hell?"

"They were trying to get out," Sheppard said flatly. "They tried to break the glass, but it's not glass and they couldn't break it…"

"Sheppard—"

"There's a goddam kid in there, Rodney!"

"I know, I can see." McKay put a hand on his shoulder, pulled him gently away from the cells, towards the door. "You can't do anything for them."

Sheppard turned, and pushed past him. As he stepped out into the open room, Dex emerged from another doorway. His face was dark with rage.

"More?"

"Bodies?" The Satedan nodded. "Yeah. Locked in and left to die."

McKay joined them. "Look, there's two more chambers I can see from here. We don't need to go into them all."

"I guess not. Whatever happened here, we missed it."

"Right. But that energy trace is still active, and Ronon can hear something coming from that corridor over there." He pointed. "Much as I'd really like to head back to the jumper right now, I think we've got to check this out."

Sheppard looked back into the chamber doorway once more, trying not to imagine how long the occupants of those unbreakable cells had pounded and scraped at the not-glass. How long can a human survive without water?

Too long, sometimes.

He walked away, over to the corridor McKay had indicated. "In here?"

"Yeah." McKay fell into step alongside him, and he heard Dex's catlike tread following behind.

"Have you seen anything like this before?"

"From Replicators? No." McKay shook his head, the beams from his halogens dancing wildly. "If anyone was going to wall people up it should be the Wraith, and they, well…"

"Eat them?" Dex chimed in helpfully. McKay grimaced.

"Okay, I wasn't actually going to go there, but yes."

The new corridor was as dark as the rest of the structure. From its position, Sheppard guessed he was now some distance under the hill itself. The thought made him want to stoop, to duck under the weight of rain-sodden rock scant meters above his head. He wasn't usually claustrophobic, but the fate of the people in the cells had sparked a horror in him that only open sky could dispel.

But he couldn't go back. Not yet. He needed to know what had happened here. If he left without an answer, if the reason those wretches had died their dry, lonely death remained a mystery, then their withered eyes would haunt his dreams.

He had to go on. Besides, now he was in the corridor he could hear ticking too.

It wasn't regular. It was staccato, random, like the clicking of a bug on its back. Faint, but unmistakably mechanical. McKay's power source was here, and something connected to it was moving.

"This place smells," said Dex.

"Oh God," muttered McKay thickly. "Oh no, I just got a sniff of that. Something's died in here too, hasn't it."

The corridor ended in a corner. Sheppard rounded it, and put a hand to his mouth on reflex. The stench of rot, suddenly, was sickening.

There was a room in front of him, narrow, widening towards the far wall. A long structure, flat and waist-high, dominated the center of the chamber, while the walls were lined with what looked like murky fishtanks.

A fitful light, bluish and dull, fluttered under the surface of the long structure, a sputtering electrical glow. "I guess that's your power source."

"No, I don't think so." McKay was studying the screen of his PDA. "Whatever's in here is just trace energy, some kind of backup battery. The main source is somewhere else."

"Great." Sheppard walked in, slowly, and drew closer to the structure. It was a table, like a long bench but deep, faceted and paneled in smooth white and gleaming steel. Hinged arms were attached to it at one end, dozens of them, folded back on themselves like the limbs of a waiting mantis. Sheppard could see a continuous rail around the table, the arms mounted on it so they could reach any part of its surface with the knives and claws and razored spindles that tipped them.

The arms twitched, clicking one against another, as if eager to be at work.

Sheppard leaned over the glassy surface of the table, just far enough to see what lay in the cavity beneath it. After a moment, he grimaced and looked away.

McKay was staring at him. "What? What's under there?"

He gestured back at the glittering metal arms. "What do you think?"

"Oh." A queasy realization crossed McKay's face. "Oh. Okay."

Dex raised an eyebrow. "Dead?"

"Very." For longer than the prisoners in their glass coffins, Sheppard guessed, although it was hard to be sure. The arms had done their work well, and enthusiastically. What lay in the cavity was still shaped like a man, but only just.

"Rodney? Anything else you need to see in here?"

McKay shook his head emphatically. "Believe me, I've seen more than enough."

"So okay, at least we know why they were keeping people in cells," Dex whispered a few minutes later, as they prepared to go back into the exit corridor. They had paused at the edge of the water to let McKay investigate some random technological anomaly he had spotted.

"We do?"

"Yeah, to do experiments on them."

"Oh, right." Sheppard nodded. "Yeah, we know what they were doing. But *why* were they doing that? The Asurans have got access to pretty much all the Ancients knew, haven't they? What would they need to know about humans that they couldn't just get from a book?"

"And here's another one." Dex made a sweeping gesture. "What's Angelus got to do with all this?"

"You got me there. Hell, maybe this has got nothing to do with the guy. He's not a Replicator—Ellis would have spotted that the moment he set foot on *Apollo*. Besides, the Replicators were trying to kill him."

Dex shrugged. "Maybe he saw this, and that's why they were after him. To keep him quiet?"

For a moment, that seemed almost plausible, but Sheppard found himself having to dismiss it too. Mainly due to the outrageous arrogance of the Asurans. If they had decided to go picking people apart to see how they worked, they wouldn't have let a witness bother them. Replicators did whatever was best for Replicators. Why would they fear exposure?

He shrugged. "It's got me beat. Maybe Rodney can get some answers out of all the readings he's taken. I don't think there's much more to see here."

"Or that we want to." Dex looked away. "I don't know, John. I've seen a lot of bad things. They don't usually bother me. Death's just something you get used to. But this?"

"Yeah, I know what you mean." He slapped the Satedan's shoulder and moved past him, towards the spot where McKay had been working. "Hey Rodney! Come on, we're outta here."

There was no answer. Come to that, there was no McKay, either.

Sheppard aimed the taclight at the spot. There was another corridor exit there, equidistant between the waterlogged entrance and the way to the dissection rooms. McKay had noticed something unusual there, and the last time Sheppard had seen him he had been crouching at the entrance to the corridor, taking more readings with his custom PDA.

There was no sign of him now.

"McKay?" Sheppard's voice echoed eerily as he called out. But once the echoes had gone, there was only silence.

And then a strangled cry, followed by the stuttering hammer of a P90.

Sheppard hurled himself into the corridor, Dex on his heels, the barrel of his own gun nosing for a target. The corridor was short, just an angled opening into another open space.

Beyond it, McKay was standing rigid, his gun raised with the butt jammed into his shoulder. There was a square of dim light spinning down on the floor: the PDA.

"Rodney?"

"Replicators," he hissed.

"What? Where?"

"Over there. On the ground."

There was no other sound in the chamber, no movement Sheppard could detect. He moved ahead of McKay, lowering his weapon slightly, scanning the taclight beam left and right.

What he saw made no sense. "What the hell?"

McKay had been right. There were indeed Replicators in the chamber—Sheppard counted a dozen, maybe more. Their uniforms were unmistakable.

But the Asurans were on the floor. They lay sprawled like dead men.

Sheppard glanced quickly across at McKay, seeing the man's knuckles still white around the P90's grip. "Were they moving?"

McKay's eyes met his for an instant. "Not as such."

"So you fired because…"

"It's dark, okay?" McKay lowered the gun. "I just saw a face, and…" He gestured angrily at a perforated Asuran.

"And you panicked," said Dex.

"I did not panic!" McKay snapped. "My reaction-time got the better of me, that's all."

"It's okay," Sheppard told him, "I don't think he's going to lodge a complaint." He moved further into the room, keeping his finger lightly on the trigger, using the taclight beam to illuminate the crumpled Replicators one by one.

The Asurans weren't the only thing littering the ground. There was debris, too; random chunks of stone and metal were scattered across the chamber floor, increasing the further right he looked. Sheppard could see that the ceiling there was open, a gaping maw fanged with twisted shards of metal and dangling braces. What must have been several tons of debris littered the chamber below it, forming a treacherous slope, and several replicators lay pinned beneath its margins. Others were scattered around a complicated ball of machinery on the far side of the chamber, almost as though they had been fighting for possession of it before they had fallen.

Sheppard knelt gingerly next to one of the fallen Asurans, and poked it with his gun barrel. It didn't move, just lay there, open eyes staring sightlessly at the ceiling.

"What's wrong with them?" he asked, his voice a whisper.

"They look dead," McKay replied.

"That's impossible. Dead replicators are just piles of dust."

He saw the beams of McKay's halogens swing around at him. "Well, they're not exactly up and dancing, are they? Lucky for us... And what the hell's wrong with their faces?"

"I don't know..." Sheppard prodded the Replicator again. It was hard to tell in the taclight beam, but the Asuran's face looked strange; pallid and sunken, almost pasty. Around one temple and the corners of the mouth were something that looked like lesions.

The Replicator looked *diseased*.

Dex had wandered past him, and was surveying the drum of machinery by the far wall. "Are you sure they're Replicators? Not dead people dressed up?

"No, I'm picking up traces of nanite code." McKay crossed the chamber to join him. He had retrieved the PDA. "Back in the main chamber? I noticed something odd about the walls near this corridor, it was like the surface of the metal had started to break down. There's more of it in here, too. And these guys just lying around like corpses..." He crouched down next to the ball. "Well hello, what have we got here?"

"I give. What have we got?"

"Our power source." McKay was leaning around the ball, twisting himself to see it from all sides. "But it's not connected to anything. Weird."

Sheppard got up, and moved back to the corridor. Sure enough, the wall there was corroded, blistered, patches of it stretched like melted plastic. "Weapons fire?"

"I doubt it. That stuff's a trinium-reinforced polymer compound. You'd need, oh, shipboard weaponry to melt that. Maybe a drone..."

"You know something?" Sheppard stalked back into the center of the room. "I am getting pretty damn tired of wandering around this chamber of horrors and not having a clue what's happened here."

"You and me both," said McKay, shrugging out of his pack. "But maybe we don't have to now. Sheppard? Do me a favor?"

"What?"

"Find me a Replicator. One that's really good and stuck

under something."

"Huh?"

In answer, McKay just looked around at him, mouth set and eyebrows high, stabbing a finger towards the rubble pile.

Sheppard shook his head in despair, and turned away. When Rodney McKay got an idea, it tended to fill his mind to the exclusion of all else. Including manners, social skills... "Here's one. He's about halfway under. Is that okay?"

McKay scurried over, his hands full of equipment and the laptop jammed under one arm, and surveyed the Asuran Sheppard had chosen. It was a male—although that distinction was entirely cosmetic—and had the same doughy look to its skin as the others. Its left leg, left arm and the lower part of its torso were covered with broken chunks of stone, and a thick metal brace was lying across it, crushing the right shoulder. "Perfect."

He knelt down, setting the laptop on the floor with one hand and flipping it open. Sheppard watched as he spread out the rest of the gear he had carried over. "What are you doing?"

"I am going," said McKay, beginning to tap command strings into the laptop, "to power this guy up."

There was a click and thin whine as Dex's blaster came to life a hand's width from the back of McKay's head. "I don't think you are."

"Would you get that thing out of my ear?" McKay glared up at him, eyes narrowed between the halogens. "He's not going anywhere—what's he going to do, drag himself out from under a couple of tons of rubble? Look, he's trapped and dead. All I'm going to do is reactivate some of his nanite code, specifically the parts relating to memory and recording. Under the right instructions from me those nanites will start downloading into the laptop, and once I've decoded that data I'll know everything he knows."

Sheppard blinked. "Is that even possible?"

"I hope so. To tell you the truth, since we've never encountered a Replicator in this state before I really can't be sure exactly what's going to happen, but as long as I can get into this guy's memory files I don't really care." He looked up at the pair of them. "Don't worry, he's not going to wake up or anything."

"Fine," Dex snarled. "But if he starts acting up, I'm blasting him."

"Be my guest." McKay had connected a portable power pack to a small switch box, from which he drew a length of multi-colored ribbon cable. The end of the cable plugged into a probe array, a spidery mass of wires each tipped with a crocodile clip or an insulated needle. Sheppard had seen him use similar gear when trying to bring Ancient technology back to life.

The Replicators were, basically, Ancient technology. By that token, he thought, perhaps McKay's strange plan actually had some merit.

"Okay, here we go…" McKay took two of the sharper steel probes, touched them to the Replicator's scalp and then, with a sudden twisting push, forced them both deep into its head.

Sheppard grimaced, hearing the probes crunching through layers of alien matter as they slid inwards. If the Replicator had been human, those needles would have been driven clear through the skull and several centimeters into brain tissue. The Asuran, as a coherent mass of microscopic nanites, should have been the same hazy metallic stuff all the way through, with no complex structures under its skin at all. But if that was the case, why did the probes sound as if they were being forced into frozen hamburger?

McKay took another pair of probes and rammed them in alongside the first, then returned his attention to the laptop. "Okay… No response to the probes."

"It didn't work?"

"I haven't switched him on yet." He pressed a key on the power pack, and Sheppard saw a row of LEDs on its front face start to glow. "I'll give him a hundred microvolts. That shouldn't be enough to fry anything vital."

He touched a control. There was a soft bleep from the pack, and then silence.

"Okay, okay, that's…" McKay sighed impatiently. "Disappointing. Charging to two hundred microvolts."

Sheppard raised an eyebrow. "Should I be shouting 'Clear!'

at this point?"

"No, you should be making sure Ronon's still aiming at Bishop here and not at me." He stabbed at the control again.

This time, there was a reaction. But not the one anyone had been expecting.

The Asuran jolted into life: Sheppard saw its whole body jerk, twist sickeningly under the rubble. Its face worked for a moment, eyes flicking wildly around, the head lifting and then snapping back down to impact the floor. Its free leg kicked and scuffled.

And then its mouth opened, very wide, and it began to scream.

CHAPTER FOURTEEN

Dead Metal

The scream was continuous, nothing at all to do with breath. It was metallic and filtered and atonal and utterly horrifying. Sheppard resisted the temptation to cover his ears. "Jesus, Rodney!"

"I have no idea why it's doing that!" McKay was tapping frantically at his laptop, face screwed up in discomfort. Even Dex, Sheppard noticed, had stepped back from the Replicator and its awful shriek.

"Can you stop it?"

"Frankly, I doubt it."

"Try," Dex growled. "Or *I'll* stop it."

McKay scowled. "Look, just plug your ears or something, okay? I'm starting to get data on this thing."

The Asuran twisted suddenly, in a weird mechanical parody of pain. Sheppard knew it was incapable of true sensation: he was looking at a device, a robot made of self-replicating nano-machines, an artificial intelligence that walked on two legs only in honor of its lost creators. But seeing the stricken thing at his feet, writhing under its tomb of rubble and howling an endless note of pure electronic misery, it was difficult not to see the Replicator as being in terrible distress.

"Rodney, how long is this going to take?"

"I don't know…" McKay peered at the laptop screen, still wincing at the noise, his voice raised to make himself heard over it. "There's a lot of code coming through here. Even with the upgraded storage I've got all kinds of compression routines going just to avoid a complete overload." He shrugged. "What can I tell you? It's ready when it's ready."

The scream stopped.

It was sudden, totally without warning. Sheppard glanced

down at the Replicator, expecting to see it inert, but it was still moving, scrabbling weakly at the rubble. Its head was twisting left and right, but not in the random spasms it had exhibited earlier. It looked, for all the world, like the Asuran was conscious and trying to free itself.

Sheppard wasn't the only one surprised to see it behave in such a lifelike way. McKay was stabbing frantically at his laptop keys. "It shouldn't be doing that. There is no *way* it should be doing that."

"Kill me," gasped the Replicator.

Sheppard stared. "Say what?"

"Kill me." The voice was rough, still metallic and synthesised, but it sounded far more human than that awful screaming had done. "I am… Compromised…"

Dex made an angry rumbling noise in the back of his throat. "You said you were just going to get its code."

"Code," repeated the Asuran. "You are downloading me. Stop."

Sheppard had his P90 aimed at the Replicator's forehead, the beam from his taclight illuminating its agonized face. "No can do, feller."

"Destroy me. I am compromised. The collective…" The Asuran shifted violently under the rubble, straining against the weight. Sheppard saw Dex step back, bring his blaster up to fire. "Hurts…"

"What did you say?" gaped McKay. "It hurts?"

"You are bleeding me of everything that makes me what I am," the Replicator snarled. "My motor functions are destroyed. My core programming is compromised. I am cut off from the collective. Human, it hurts more than you can comprehend!"

If the Asuran was telling the truth about being cut off from the collective, Sheppard thought, that was the first piece of good news he'd heard all day. If he had thought there was a chance the thing was going to revive in the way it had, he would have vetoed McKay's plan to reactivate it immediately. An active Replicator would have instant access to the Asuran collective, would know what they knew, see what they saw. If this one hadn't been cut off from its network, Sheppard would be looking into the eyes of every Replicator in the galaxy right now.

"What's wrong with you?" he snapped.

"You'll learn nothing from me." It twisted again, trying to tear itself free, and actually made sounds of pain as it contorted. "If there is a scrap of mercy in you, human, destroy me now."

"Well, let's just say for the moment that there isn't."

"Curse you!"

Sheppard lifted his foot and rested it on one of the slabs holding the Replicator down. He severely doubted that his weight would add anything significant to that of the rubble, but it was an effective gesture nonetheless.

"We can make it hurt more," he said quietly.

"Or," McKay cut in, angrily, "we could make it hurt *less*."

Sheppard glared at him, then returned his attention to the Asuran. "Your call."

It said nothing, just kept struggling. Sheppard leaned closer to it. "Listen buddy, we've got spikes in your head. Right now we're turning your brain into MP3s, and when we're done we'll put on our iPods and listen to it all the way home. I'm giving you a chance to make things easier on yourself—the more you tell me right now, the less we'll have to rip out of your skull, okay?"

The machine ceased scrabbling, and fixed him with a look of unremitting hatred. "Your species is a stain on the universe," it muttered.

"Is that a yes?"

The Asuran's mouth opened, and it made a strangled metallic cry of pain and anger. "Yes, human. Ask your questions while you turn my mind into qubits."

"Quantum bits," said McKay, wearily answering Sheppard's question before he asked it. "Go on, just interrogate the poor bastard, will you?"

"You and I are going to have a serious talk on the way home, Rodney," Sheppard told him, then returned his attention to the Asuran. "What's your name?"

"The entity I used to be was called Laetor. That will suffice."

"Used to be?"

"I told you, human. I am compromised. I am no longer what I was, *who* I was. I have no name."

"Compromised by what?" asked Dex.

"The chimera," Laetor spat. "The hybrid."

Sheppard sighed. "Wanna be a little more specific?"

"A weapon, human. That is all you need to know. We·came here to destroy it… It was too dangerous to be allowed to continue."

That sounded familiar. The Replicators had a policy of obliterating weapons they thought too dangerous, it seemed, along with everything around them. Although the level of destruction here paled into comparison with what they had wrought on Eraavis. "But it got to you before you could destroy it, right?"

"We sacrificed ourselves to destroy the hybrid." The Replicator, jerked its head to the side, its face contorting, then appeared to relax again. "We brought an autonomous pulse emitter. It destroyed the chimera and shut us down. Until you wrenched me back in to this parody of existence!"

Something about that struck a chord with Sheppard. He shone the taclight over towards the ball of machinery he had noticed on the way in, the one that even now was surrounded by dead and contorted Asurans. "Autonomous… That thing over there?"

"Your perception does you credit," Laetor sneered.

"Ronon, have you got this for a minute?"

Dex grinned wolfishly. "Oh yeah."

Sheppard stepped over the Replicator and tapped McKay on the shoulder. "Come on."

"Hey, what? I'm downloading here!"

"It's going to do that anyway." He pointed at the ball. "I want to have a look at this thing, but without you I'm not going to know what the hell I'm looking *at*. So take a break, okay?"

With McKay somewhat reluctantly in tow, he picked his way across the corpse-scattered chamber and over to the emitter. Approaching it, he could see that his initial impression had been right: the Replicators had been fighting for possession of this thing up until the moment it killed them.

But fighting who? All the bodies in the room were Asurans.

There was no sign of anything he might have thought of as a chimera.

He shifted a couple of the inert Replicators aside, and crouched down next to the emitter. It was large, maybe a meter and a half wide, and formed from blackish, faceted metal. Dozens of pipes and vanes studded its surface, and although it looked at first glance like a random mess he could see on closer inspection that it had a weird, twisted symmetry.

He'd been right. He didn't have a clue what he was looking at.

"What do you think?" he said to McKay, his voice low. He checked back on Dex as he said it, but the Satedan still had Laetor firmly in his sights. "Any of this make sense to you?"

"Not much." McKay was aiming his PDA at the emitter, peering at it intently. "This is Replicator tech, same as the rest of the base. What did he call it, an autonomous pulse emitter?"

Sheppard smiled. "So we can call it an APE, huh?"

"Yeah, that's... That's really clever," muttered McKay dismissively. "EMP generator. Probably tuned with these arrays here, capacitors here. Charge it up from its own power core, set it off and say goodbye to your cellphone."

"Powerful enough to take out Replicators?"

"Enough to take out the whole base. Why d'you think there's no power?"

"Is it charged?"

"I think so." McKay took another reading with the PDA. Sheppard saw his eyes widen slightly. "Okay, that's a yes. It's on standby now, but there's a couple of million volts in this thing."

"Whoah." Sheppard edged away. "Rodney, let's not play with the ball right now, huh?"

"Oh, I think it's safe." McKay stood up. "But this still doesn't explain anything. Replicators shooting up a Replicator base? Human dissections? A weapon called a hybrid that makes Replicators sick but that gets taken down with an EMP?"

"A hybrid..." Sheppard thought about what they had found in some of the other chambers, and felt slightly queasy. "Oh man. I think—"

"Yeah, me too." By the distasteful look on his face, McKay had obviously come to the same conclusion he had. "Let's not go there at the moment, huh?"

"Suits me. Let's get finished up with Laetor."

McKay nodded. "Go ahead. I'm just going to set something running on this…" He began tapping at his PDA again. Sheppard got up and left him to it, rejoining Dex on the other side of the chamber.

The Satedan was standing just as he had left him, with the wide barrel of his blaster aimed directly at the Replicator's head. As Sheppard walked up to him he said: "It's been looking at me."

"Laetor, stop trying to stare Ronon down. Trust me, statues blink first."

The Asuran made no reply. It had stopped moving, and now lay completely inert on the littered floor. Only its eyes moved, flicking over to Sheppard as he approached and following him.

"Rodney? He doesn't look so hot."

"Yeah, well I think he's pretty much empty." McKay came over and crouched down next to his laptop, scanning the screen. "And this is full. Okay, I think we're done with the torture."

Thinking about the desiccated corpses in their cells, Sheppard found it difficult to be sympathetic to the machine. For all its howling, it was only a mechanism, after all. What it called pain could only be a signal telling the Replicator it was being damaged. He had seen Asurans exhibit a vague kind of emotion once or twice, but in general they were no more individual than ants in a nest.

He reached down and switched off the power unit. "Goodnight, sweet prince."

The row of LEDS on the power unit went out, one by one. As the last one faded, Laetor's eyes became still.

Its expression remained frozen, a mask of hatred. Weirdly, for all the ruin that had been inflicted on it, this Asuran had been the most lifelike—the most human—he had seen. Perhaps its distress had lessened its mechanical nature, he wondered. Brought it closer to being alive.

The idea that pain was the closest Replicators could get to life was an unsettling one. Sheppard shook it away. "Anyone want to say anything?"

"How about 'Goodbye'?" replied Ronon, finally letting his blaster down.

"Sounds about right. Rodney, how long do you think it'll take to read that data?"

"Could be a while." McKay had folded the laptop closed and was stuffing it into his backpack. "I'll have to decompress it first, then get it onto a secure server so I can run decryption routines on it... Believe me, you do not want this stuff running around an unsupervised system."

"I'm sure Sam will be happy to set you up when we get back."

"We're leaving? Already?"

Dex snorted. "If you're starting to like it here, we can leave you."

"Yeah," grinned Sheppard. "If you get lonely, you can just power up a new friend for a while."

McKay had his mouth open to reply when he was interrupted by a faint electronic chirrup from the darkness. An alert from his PDA, Sheppard guessed. "Aha!"

"What?"

"I set up a routine to try and hack some of the APE's nanite code." McKay stood his backpack against Laetor's head and checked the PDA screen. "Yes! I just got a return!"

Sheppard eyed him warningly. "Rodney, didn't we just agree not to play with the ball?"

"Don't worry, I'm not going to set it off."

"Yeah?" said Dex flatly. "Like you weren't going to wake up the Asuran?"

McKay chuckled and aimed the PDA at the emitter. "You want to see something really cool?" He pressed a control. There was a moment's silence, and then the emitter lit up.

Sheppard brought the P90 up reflexively. Thin lines of blue light had appeared on the APE's surface, outlining a complex series of panels. As he watched, the panels suddenly snapped free of the main body of the ball. They hinged outwards, unfolded, rotated around each other.

The APE extended three angular legs and stood up.

Sheppard looked slowly around at McKay, and at the smile of quite unbelievable smugness that he had on his face. "You are so proud of yourself right now, aren't you?"

McKay shrugged. "Who wouldn't be?"

Dex walked closer to the APE. "Can you make it walk?"

"Yeah, I think so. It's part of the same subroutine. I figured that they'd need to be able to deploy it somehow, but it would have been too big to carry down those corridors, even if the Asurans were strong enough to haul it about."

"And you knew it had legs?"

"Actually no. I thought it was going to float. What do you think, it should fit in the jumper?"

Sheppard blinked. "You're thinking of taking it back with us?"

"Why not? Any anti-Replicator weapon has got to be a good thing, right?"

"Not when it's charged up with about a million volts and is sitting inside a spaceship!" Sheppard gestured wildly around him. "Have you forgotten we're in the dark here? What if you get your subroutines mixed up and it goes off inside the jumper? Or in Atlantis?"

"Did you hear something?" asked Dex suddenly.

"No!" Sheppard growled. "To both questions. Rodney, shut it down—*carefully*—and leave it here."

"Hey, McKay." That was Dex again. "Your pack fell over."

"So what?"

"You had it resting against the Replicator."

McKay frowned, puzzled, and walked over to where his backpack lay on the floor. Sure enough, it had toppled over. "That's odd."

Sheppard joined him. "Maybe he twitched."

"He can't 'twitch'. I checked the output before I closed the laptop down, there was nothing in there. No power, no code. The guy's a paperweight."

Laetor's right hand snapped out, insect-quick, and grabbed McKay's ankle.

McKay gave a shout of shock and pain. He tried to drag his leg away but the grip was too strong. He overbalanced, howling, and crashed to the ground.

The Replicator was trying to twist its way out from under the rubble again.

Sheppard grabbed McKay under the arms and tried to pull him away. Even with McKay helping him, his free foot planted against the side of the Asuran's chest, he couldn't get away. "Ronon!"

Dex leapt forwards, stamped his boot down solidly on Laetor's wrist. He brought his blaster up.

"I meant use a goddamn knife or something!"

"Cover your eyes," Dex said, and pulled the trigger.

The blaster went off with an electric snarl and a blinding orange flash. Sheppard, who hadn't had a chance to look away, saw the energy bolt strike Laetor in the shoulder, blowing free a fist-sized chunk of matter. The Replicator made an incoherent sound, a buzzing metal scream, but the hand around McKay's ankle stayed firmly clamped on.

McKay screamed. "It's biting me!"

"What do you mean, it's biting you?" Sheppard was trying to kick the hand away. "Ronon, do it again! Blow it's damn arm off!"

"Way ahead of you." Dex took aim again, let off another two shots. The chamber lit up fire-yellow with each of them, and white-hot gobs of molten matter spattered into the air. Sheppard felt some of the stuff hit his skin, and winced as it burned him.

Laetor's arm came off at the elbow, the ragged end of it glowing, sizzling like frying meat. McKay tumbled, still yelling. Sheppard leaned down to him, held him still and wrenched the Asuran's disembodied hand free from his ankle.

The hand came away bloody. In the wild light from McKay's halogens he saw fat threads of something shining dart back onto the palm, like startled sea-creatures whipping back into their dens. "What the hell?"

"Just get rid of that thing!" McKay cried. He struggled up and clamped his own hands over where Laetor had gripped him. "Ow! First Angelus' ship and now this!"

"Are you okay?" Sheppard threw the arm across the chamber, half expecting it raise itself on its fingers and scuttle back towards him. It didn't.

"Of course I'm not okay!" McKay offered a hand, and Sheppard hauled him up by it. "What the hell's happening here?"

"Looks like Laetor was just taking a nap."

"No way. There was no active nanite code in there." McKay was on one leg, gingerly testing his weight on his injured ankle. "And his goddamn hand was biting me! I could feel something trying to get through my skin…"

"It's still alive," said Dex. He was pointing his blaster at Laetor. "Something's happening to it."

Sheppard looked more closely. "No way…"

Laetor, or the entity that had once called itself that, was convulsing under the slabs and the metal brace that crushed its right shoulder. The burned stump of its arm flailed, slapping the floor, and its head turned left and right, eyes wild, as if trying to find a way to get free.

There was something mindless about the way it moved, something queasily animalistic. There seemed to be none of the Replicator's previous intellect there at all. "Rodney, look at that."

"Yeah, I can see it." McKay was supporting himself fully on his injured leg now. "It shouldn't be doing that."

"You downloaded it's whole brain," said Dex, leaning down to look closely at Laetor. "Maybe this is what's left."

"Look at the arm," breathed Sheppard.

The Asuran's arm, horribly truncated by Dex's blaster shots, was still flapping. But the ragged end of it was sprouting a nest of glistening worms, part crimson, part silver, writhing and extending and swarming over each other as they slicked out of the stump.

Sheppard aimed his taclight at the wound in Laetor's shoulder. That was erupting too, sewing itself together with gouts of what looked like gristle and liquid metal. "This is not good."

"John?" That was McKay, his voice dull with fear.

Sheppard looked up, and followed McKay's terrified stare.

Across the chamber, one of the other Replicators was hauling itself upright.

"Oh crap," he muttered.

A second later, the air was hot with weapons fire. Sheppard opened up on the Asuran with his P90, hammering a ragged hole into its chest. Dex leveled his blaster and put a bolt into the thing's face, swinging it around, then blew its head into ragged shreds. It fell.

Sheppard could hear scuffling sounds from all around the chamber. Where there had been only a still silence, now the place was coming to horrible, shuddering life. Everywhere the beam of his taclight touched seemed to be moving, the Replicator corpses dragging themselves up, heavy and unco-ordinated.

"I think I've seen this movie," he grated. "Rodney, get your stuff. We're outta here."

"How many?" Dex said quietly, swinging his blaster left and right.

"About fifteen."

"We can take them."

"Don't be too sure." Sheppard focused his taclight on a Replicator on the other side of the chamber; the one Dex had blasted a few seconds earlier. It was dragging itself erect again, the stump of its neck a medusa of whipping tendrils. He aimed low, the P90 clattering as it sent a stream of lead into the Asuran's left ankle, and the awful, headless thing tumbled as the foot came free. But a moment later it was trying to get up again.

There was no sound from the Asurans other than the scrape of their limbs on the floor: they rose in eerie, inhuman silence.

McKay had retrieved his backpack and his own weapon, and was looking wildly about. "Where's my gun?"

"Where did you leave it?"

"By the APE..." He started towards it, but stopped mid-stride. He must have realized there were simply too many Replicators between him and the weapon. "Sheppard?"

"Leave it!" Sheppard heard a scrape to his left, snapped around and put a burst of fire into the face of a Replicator just a few meters away. The shots knocked the Asuran back, ripped half its head off, but it righted itself almost immediately, its wounds sprouting as he watched. "Just get to the door!"

He saw McKay go past him, still holding the pack. "I'm out!"

"Get back to the exit!" He fired again, stepped back, pulled the trigger and found the gun empty. "Ronon, you too," he yelled, slapping in a fresh magazine and snapping the charging handle back.

Dex's blaster was going off almost continuously. Each shot sent a Replicator sprawling, but they were recovering faster with each passing second. Sheppard could see the way they moved was smoother, more natural, as if they were regaining functions they had lost as they lay like corpses on the floor. Whatever these things had become, they were waking up.

It was time to be gone. He shot out the throat of one Replicator, turned to blast away the face of another, then began to back away. "Ronon!"

"I'll follow you!"

"Follow the damned order!" The P90 clattered empty again. "Ronon, behind you!"

A Replicator was within a meter of the Satedan, reaching out to him, its fingers elongating into oozing spines. Sheppard saw Dex spin around, raise his blaster and fire it point-blank into the Asuran's face, but he was too close to it. The Replicator staggered back, its head an exploded mess from the jawline upwards, but the backblast had flipped Dex over too. He fell away, covering his eyes, snarling.

Sheppard raced over to him, gabbed him by one arm. "You okay?"

"I will be when I can see!"

"Now will you listen when I tell you to do stuff?" Sheppard righted the man, then sent him with a shove towards the door. "Go on, I'm right behind you!"

Dex hit the wall, found the doorway with his hands, and ducked into it. Sheppard turned, fired a long, street-sweeping burst into the advancing Replicators, then followed him.

The two of them ran through the short corridor and out into

the first chamber. McKay was there waiting for them, near the exit. Sheppard could hear the sounds of water coming from the ceiling there, and almost smiled. He could even see natural light issuing from the other end. "Everyone okay? Ronon?"

The Satedan was blinking. "Yeah, I'm okay. Give me a minute."

"I don't think we've got a minute." Scuffling, slapping sounds were coming from behind him. When he looked around, the taclight beam fell on a corridor that was a seething mass of Replicators.

"I've got an idea," said McKay suddenly. "Where's my PDA?"

"In your damn bag." Sheppard shoved him towards the exit corridor. "How's this for an idea? Just run!"

"No time, they'll catch us trying to get through that hole. Just wait…"

"Rodney!"

McKay was tapping at the PDA screen. "I can control the APE from here."

"Can you set it off?"

"No," McKay shook his head, not taking his eyes off the screen. "But I can do *this*."

The scuffling grew louder, turned into a cacophony of impacts, crunches, sickening scraping and crushing noises, and a moment later something dark and bulky erupted from the corridor. The Replicators in front of it were bowled aside; Sheppard saw one crushed down and impaled by the APE's spindly leg, another torn in half in a gout of crimson and silver.

Next to him, McKay made a flourish on the PDA screen, and in response the APE spun, pirouetting wildly. Another pair of Asurans were knocked flying, limbs ripped free.

McKay gave a nervous laugh. "I've missed having a pet."

Sheppard slapped him on the shoulder. "Right now, I'm probably almost as proud of you as you are. Ronon, get your blind ass down to the exit! I need you to drag us out fast!"

"I'm not blind," the Satedan grumbled, splashing off down the corridor. Sheppard stepped aside to let McKay in after him, then followed the pair of them, letting the APE spin its wild, uncontrolled dances at the corridor mouth. Some of the Replicators were already scampering past it, but it had bought them a precious few seconds.

The corridor was just as he had remembered it; dank, crumbling, ankle deep in stinking water. After the nightmares he had just witnessed, though, it felt absurdly welcoming. He followed the light from McKay's PDA all the way out, turned and dropped to one knee to fire bursts back along the corridor as Dex hauled McKay out into the open, then as soon as he saw daylight flood past him he stopped firing and began to scramble out of the hole.

Rain, heavy and slippery-warm, sluiced down over him as he emerged. The murky, grayish light felt searing, making his eyes blink and water. It had been cool in the Replicator base, the heat of the air leached away by the weight of rock above it, but out in the open it felt muggy and hot.

Still, compared to the alternative, it was practically paradise.

Sheppard heard splashing behind him, the scrape of flesh on stone. He unclipped a grenade from his belt. "Better stand back, I'm gonna blow this—"

A Replicator erupted from the hole.

In an instant, it had him, one hand around his throat, the other clamped iron-hard over the grenade in his right hand. The Replicator had given up all pretence at humanity: whether it was one of the creatures he had seen decapitated by weapons fire he could not tell, but what bobbed on the end of its neck was not a head. It was a seething cluster, a mass of eyes and mouths and the waving needles of sensory antennae. Part metal, part meat, all hunger.

The Replicator was appallingly strong. Sheppard couldn't even shout.

Dimly, through the pain in his throat and the reddening in his vision, he could see Dex next to him, trying to yank the thing away, hacking at it with one of his many knives, but the Satedan was wasting his efforts. He was opening superficial wounds at best.

And then, without warning, something washed over him.

At first he thought it was death, but then the ground came up and hit him in the back. There was an awful feeling in the air, a million crawling itches scuttling under his skin, a hissing, crackling sound in his ears. A dry, wavering heat drawing steam from the rain.

A stink of ozone. McKay had set off the APE.

Sheppard struggled to his feet. The Replicator was hanging halfway out of the hole, inert, lifeless. Horribly, it was starting to disassemble as he watched: the machine parts of it shrinking away like severed tendons, the fleshy elements breaking down, liquefying into a thick, ruddy soup that oozed down onto the broken stone, carrying a myriad of silvery fragments and threads.

The pain in Sheppard's throat was lessening, almost to the point where he thought it might be possible to start breathing again. He gave it a try, sucking in a mouthful of the reeking air, but it caught in his chest. He coughed, spat, straightened himself up and tried again. This time it worked, more or less. "Oh, man…"

"Are you okay?" That was McKay, the PDA still in his hand. Sheppard nodded.

"Finally hacked that part too, eh?"

"Well, I didn't want to let all that voltage go to waste." McKay blinked sorrowfully at the PDA. "Well, that's the end of that."

"You break it?" asked Dex. McKay tossed it to him.

"EMP cooked it. It was beefed up with Ancient technology, and that's what the APE was tuned to, I guess. I'm just hoping the laptop survived. It was powered down, so it shouldn't have blown the storage…" He raised his arm and pulled his sleeve back. "Hey, my watch is okay!"

"Wonderful." Sheppard saw that he still had the grenade in his right hand. He clipped it carefully back onto his belt. If the Replicator had been a second later in grabbing him, he would have had the pin out of the thing. It would have gone off when he fell.

Come to that, a stray spark from the electromagnetic pulse could have cooked off either grenade, or the ammo in his vest…

He suddenly thought just how close he had come to obliteration. "Guys, can we get out of here now?"

"With pleasure," McKay said emphatically. "This place makes me want to take a shower. I more ways than one."

The walk back to the jumper gave Sheppard time to think about what he had seen. But his thoughts were circular, chasing each other around in his tired head and ultimately making no sense at all.

He had almost worked out the sequence of events at the Replicator facility, although there were still a few puzzling gaps. The biggest of which was the idea of two groups of Asurans working at cross-purposes to each other, even to the point of one group shooting its way into the other's facility and setting off a suicide weapon there. If there had been more light in the base, would he have seen scatterings of metal dust on the floor of that corpse-strewn chamber? It was impossible to say. The APE had rendered the compromised Replicators inert the first time it was used. The second time, at least given what he had seen of the one that had grabbed him, it had broken their structure down entirely.

A structure that was, quite obviously, part Replicator, part living tissue.

A chimera. A hybrid.

Too many pieces to the puzzle, he thought wearily. Too many gaps in the picture. He couldn't put it all together just yet. Especially where Angelus was concerned. How the Ancient fitted into all this was a mystery beyond his capacity to solve.

Maybe when he was back on Atlantis things would become clearer. Right now, all he wanted to do was get back into the jumper and go home.

They had almost reached the landing site. Sheppard was first in line as they rounded the rocks, with McKay in the middle and Dex last. So it was Sheppard who first saw the puddle jumper.

He stopped in his tracks. "Aw crap," he muttered.

McKay heard him, increased his pace on the slippery ground, and scrambled up alongside him. "What? What's wrong."

Sheppard gestured at the jumper. "I think we've got a problem," he said.

"It looks okay to me."

"Yeah," said Dex, stopping a few meters away. "But when we left, the cloak was on."

McKay stared at it for a second, then looked back over his shoulder. "What, you don't think…?"

"Tuned to Ancient technology," Sheppard replied. "Congratulations, Rodney. You just cooked our ride home."

CHAPTER FIFTEEN

In the Zone

Outside the city, dawn was breaking.

Cold, clear sunlight was skating across the ocean, broken into misty shafts by the spires that dotted the piers and rose, clustering like admiring acolytes, around the control tower to form the city core. Carter had seen the sun come up from the balcony, as she had waited for the senior staff to congregate in the conference room. Those few minutes leaning on the angled rail, watching night turn into golden day, had been the first rest she had allowed herself since Teyla's call had roused her in the night.

Now, with the conference room's multiple doors closed, and the only light coming from the half-globe that hugged its ceiling, Carter missed the sun. Surrounded by identical rust-colored panels and the expectant faces of the Atlantis senior staff, she felt entombed here. Trapped.

She was very tired, and she wanted to be away.

Still, those feelings were a weakness, and there was no place for them now. She pushed the fatigue and the fear aside, shut them away within herself. Later, when all this was done, she would deal with them at her own pace—for now, ruthless efficiency was the order of the day.

"Okay," she began. "Thanks for getting down here so quickly. I'll keep this as short as I can; we've all got other things to be doing. So, first things first—I think it's safe to assume that Mr Fallon isn't coming back."

"There has been no answer at all from him?" asked Teyla. Carter shook her head.

"Nothing. He went in to meet with Angelus, oh…" She checked her watch. "About four hours ago, and there's been no word at all since then. I've had people trying to get in touch with him and with Angelus periodically since that time, and they've had no response."

"Won't that just be due to comms being out in the lockdown area?" That was Major Lorne, who was standing in for John Sheppard, representing the city's military contingent. MacReady was still at the lockdown. "Maybe he's just trapped, unable to respond."

Zelenka, who sat across the table from Teyla, shook his head. "That's just the point—the communications aren't out, not in any conventional sense. Fallon proved that when he got in touch with Angelus. Try connecting to anyone who's still in there, and listen. You'll get a return, just no answer."

"Actually, don't," Carter cut in, grimacing. "Trust me, it's one of the creepiest damn sounds you'll ever hear."

"Creepy how?" Jennifer Keller was right opposite Carter, looking slightly more nervous than usual, if that was possible. "What is it, static?"

"Not exactly," muttered Zelenka. He obviously remembered the eerie sounds he had amplified for Carter in the ZPM lab. "Put simply, something has infiltrated the comms net. We don't know what—a computer virus, maybe, some kind of nanite infection—but that's the noise it makes. It's part of the same pattern of interference that's been draining power out of the grid every forty-one seconds."

"And the false images on the surveillance cameras and the medical scanners," Carter went on. "The pattern interferes with some of our compression codecs, sets most of the picture just slightly out of phase, so you get that diagonal—"

"*Jesus!*" hissed Keller, and tugged the headset out of her ear. She had gone quite pale. "Sorry."

"I *said* don't," Carter told her, smiling grimly. "Look, what this means is that we can't trust the comms network any more. From now on, any communications that could possibly be of tactical advantage to Angelus can't go via the city net."

"What else have we got?" Lorne wondered.

Teyla raised a hand. "Colonel, I can organize a team of message runners. It would not be unlike the system we used on Athos—all I will need are some volunteers who are quick on their feet."

Carter nodded. "That's a great idea. Get together with Major Lorne. I'm sure you can rustle up a few sprinters."

"Count on it," grinned Lorne. "But Colonel, you mentioned information being of tactical use to Angelus. Does that mean we're treating him as an enemy now?"

"Absolutely." Carter glanced around the table. "He can fake images, project false test readings, everything. He somehow managed to conjure up twenty seconds of surveillance camera footage specifically designed to sow distrust and paranoia among us... Basically, we can't be sure of *anything* we thought we knew about him. It's probable that he's not only been lying to us since he arrived, but that all the medical tests we did on him showed false results too."

"So he might not be an Ancient?"

"That's right. Everything we thought we knew about him is thrown out as of now. We operate on the following assumptions: *something* hostile has infiltrated the city and locked itself into an area of the west pier. It's drawing power from the grid, it's hacked into the communications network, and it might well have subverted whatever Atlantis personnel are in there with it—from what I've been able to get out of Cassidy, the techs I assigned to Angelus are..." She paused, trying to translate the physicist's terrified story into something she could use here. "Are probably no longer human."

Lorne sat forward. "So what do we do?"

"Our priority is to get into the lockdown area and neutralize whatever threat we find there. Right now we've got two ideas about that, but I'd welcome more."

"What two have you got?" asked Keller.

"Firstly, we've got a team of engineers trying to cut their way in through one of the blast doors. According to Major MacReady the oxy-acetylene torch hasn't even scorched them, but we're rigging up a high-density plasma unit right now."

"It's a little difficult," Zelenka said, "because the power is out around the lockdown area, as opposed to just inside it. But we're setting up a naquadah generator to run the plasma torch, which should give us a real chance."

"And if that doesn't work, we've managed to identify a possible way in through an inter-level crawlspace." Carter wished she'd brought the systems diagram Zelenka had printed out for her earlier. It would have made her look more confident, if nothing else. Given her something to do with her hands. "MacReady has a team ready to go in through one of the ventilation flues and into a space between the lab ceiling and the deck above it."

"Colonel," frowned Lorne, "we did a security evaluation of the interfloor spaces about six months ago, when they were first discovered. There's really not a lot of room in there."

"I know." Carter had studied the diagram in great detail: the crawlspace, where it existed at all, was cramped, barely tall enough to lie down in and criss-crossed with power conduits, atmospheric ducting and all manner of unidentified systems. "Believe me, it's not a job I'd want. But if we can't cut our way in, we've really got no choice."

"Colonel Carter," said Teyla. "Perhaps it would be better to send someone into the crawlspace while the doors are being cut. The attempt to burn through would make a useful diversion."

"Actually, that's worth a try." Carter stood up. "I'm heading down there right now. I'll tell MacReady to proceed with both at the same time. Anything else?"

"There's one more thing," said Zelenka, hesitantly. "We've recently been monitoring the city's seismic detectors—they're normally used to detect undersea quakes, as an advanced warning against tsunami. But with the gain up, we've gotten some vibration from inside the lockdown zone."

"What kind of vibration?"

"I'm not sure," the scientist said. "But it almost sounds like hammering."

Someone handed Carter a tactical vest when she reached the gallery. She shrugged into it, sealed it up over her jacket, feeling the integral slabs of Kevlar pressing into her from its pockets. It was a safety measure, just in case anyone did come out of the lockdown zone shooting, although something told

Carter that was just about the least likely thing that could happen. Besides, with the number of armed marines MacReady had stationed around the blast doors, anything that did try to come out and cause trouble would be shredded by weapons fire before it could blink.

There was no harm in taking care, though. By the same token, Carter had recently taken to wearing her sidearm all the time.

MacReady was waiting for her at the end of the gallery. He was a wide, blocky man, with rough features and graying hair under a battered forage cap. The battledress jacket he wore under his tacvest made him look bulky, almost clumsy, but Carter knew that was an effect he cultivated on purpose.

"Colonel," he said flatly, nodding a greeting. "I've spread the word about the comms net. We'll be passing notes like schoolgirls from now on in."

"Now there's an image," smiled Carter. "Is the plasma unit ready to go?"

"Almost." He led her over to the end of the corridor, now plugged with the burnished silver slabs of the blast doors. There was an irregular burn mark marring the metal surface to one side, but when he brushed at it the carbon simply wiped away. "I've got to say, Colonel, I don't even think a plasma torch is gonna to mark this."

He was almost certainly right, Carter thought. Many of the corridors and walls in Atlantis were lined with a superconducting alloy, and the blast doors didn't appear to be any different. If that was the case, heat from any kind of cutting equipment would simply be absorbed and shunted away quicker than it could ever be poured in. Somewhere in the lockdown a heatsink of some description had probably warmed up a little in response to the technicians' efforts, but nothing else would have changed.

Hopefully, though, Angelus would notice the attempt to cut in. And it might draw his attention away from the three marines already clambering into the nearest ventilation flue.

They were being helped in even as Zelenka's technicians returned with their plasma torch. All of them were small, slender; one was a man, the other two were women. There had been more than three volunteers to start with, but not many on MacReady's watch could have fitted into the crawlspace.

Carter couldn't see their faces. Although they had stripped out of their tacvests and uniform jackets, they all wore sets of night-vision goggles with headset communications links. Each had a pistol duct-taped to one thigh, and the sleeves of their t-shirts had been taped down too. Hopefully, that would reduce the chances of the marines becoming snagged as they struggled through the crawlspace.

Just watching them made Carter feel slightly claustrophobic. She didn't envy them their task one iota. "Major, they know not to use those headsets, right?"

"They know."

"Unless they really have to."

"Colonel, they *know*," he said gently. "I don't like the thought of it either. Hell, if I went where they're going I'd get stuck like a tick."

She nodded silently, then turned her head slightly away as the plasma torch lit up. One of the technicians—Norris, she guessed, although both men wore full-face welding masks—was aiming the anode at the door's surface, bringing it close. The tiny ball of searing blue light at its tip flared as he increased the power, sending hard-edged stripes of light and shadow fluttering around the gallery.

The last of the three marines was fully inside the vent, now. Carter could hear distant thumps and scuffles past the electric fizzing of the plasma. As they faded, she found herself hoping that they would sound less loud inside the lockdown than they did in the gallery.

"We were gonna put headcams on them," MacReady told her, looking at the vent with just a raised hand between his retinas and the unbelievable light of the plasma torch. "Then we remembered the output would have to come through the comms net just like voice."

"So that could end up hacked too…" Carter wasn't sure whether she was displeased about that or not. Given her experience with the surveillance footage, she wondered if she could have actually trusted anything the head-mounted cameras might have shown. Not only that, but the thought of watching the marines as they inched their way through the flat maze of pipes and cables made her ribs feel tight.

On the other hand, now that the three were away inside the crawlspace, no-one had any idea of exactly where they were or what they were doing. If they did get into danger, how would anyone know?

"Maybe we should have tied something to them," she muttered. "Had a mic cable running back to the vent…"

"Would have gotten snagged."

"I guess." Carter took a deep breath, partly to remind herself that she could. "Okay, I'm going to head back up to the control room. If we hear anything from *Apollo* or Sheppard's team I'd like to be—"

Several hard, flat bangs issued from the vent.

"That's a goddamn Colt," yelled MacReady, running towards the blast doors. Carter followed him, protecting her eyes with her hand until the light of the cutting torch went out. More shots sounded as she got close, sounding short and metallic through the confined space. Some of the shots were so close together that they must have come from more than one weapon.

And then Carter heard voices.

Shouts at first, their actual words lost to distance and the crawlspace's multiple obstructions. Sounds of impact, more shots. Carter found herself staring at MacReady, him at her, as they both strained to hear what was going on above the lockdown zone.

Something large moved past her, inside the vent.

She started as she heard it: the sound of its passing was unmistakable. It was a brushing, a slithering, a succession of metallic rings and tears as whatever moved did so without allowance for the obstructions in is path.

A scream echoed out of the vent, faint and shrill.

In an instant, Carter was listening to an unholy cacophony from inside the crawlspace. There were no more shots—the marines must have emptied their weapons in that first fusillade, and there was no room to reload—but there were more screams, shouts, hammering impacts. A high, unearthly bellowing.

"My God," whispered MacReady. "What is that?"

Abruptly, the sounds ceased. Carter strained to listen, but only heard the sighing sea and the beat of her own rapid pulse in her ears.

"They're gone," she breathed.

Beneath her feet, the floor moved.

She jumped back. Something had slid under her, like the back of some great beast; she had felt its vibration, its heat. She heard a long, mournful groan of overstressed metal, saw MacReady's eyes widen as he realized what was happening, and then the gallery erupted into shouts and movement.

"Get out of here!" she yelled. "Everyone, drop what you're doing and go!"

There were five marines on the gallery with her, as well as MacReady and the two technicians. Most were on Carter's side of the gallery; she stepped aside to let them go past ahead of her, hurrying them with hard slaps as they went past. Once they were gone, she and MacReady bolted after them.

She could feel the floor moving as she ran, could hear shuddering impacts against the walls. There wasn't just one source of it, but many. It felt like the very stuff of Atlantis was springing to violent life around her.

The two technicians had moved to the other side of the gallery, along with one marine. The three of them were actually ahead of Carter on their way out: she saw them flinging their welding masks aside as they ran, the marine shouting at them, telling them to move faster…

The floor ahead of them burst like trodden fruit, splitting upwards in shards. From within came something whipping, a blur of movement, a great nest of mindless, thrashing serpents, looping and coiling and lashing too fast for her to see. Norris skidded right into the heart of it, and was gone in an instant. Behind him, Bennings and the other marine went scrambling back the way they had come.

Carter hadn't realized she had stopped to watch until MacReady dragged her out of the way. She felt herself being shoved bodily into the corridor, the Major taking up position in front of her, dropping to one knee and firing his P90 back into the gallery. She saw the flailing things struck, sparks and fragments whipping away over the rail.

She snapped her own sidearm up, flicked off the safety and emptied the gun into the mass.

Bennings and the last marine were running up the other side of the gallery. Carter could feel the drumming of their feet as they ran.

And then she remembered that the deck was far too solid for her too feel that. Something else was making the floor shake.

From the corners of her vision, metal appeared.

"Blast doors! Everybody get back!"

The end of the corridor was shrinking, cut into an octagon by the sliding doors. Bennings was almost there, she could see his terrified face as he saw the octagon contract into a diamond ahead of him. If he dived for it, Carter thought wildly, he might make it. He might almost make it.

He wasn't going to make it.

A gout of matter splashed from the wall beside him, ripping the metal as it vomited out into the air. Carter saw it shine wetly in the morning sunlight for a split second; it was a limb of raw flesh and pulsing metal, of silver and gristle, and it had Bennings off his feet before he could scream. It lashed at him, coiled around him, wrenched him off the deck and into mid-air.

He reached out to her, in those final seconds before the blast doors met, hands clawed, face imploring. Had there been breath in his lungs he would have shrieked, Carter had no doubt of that, but the limb was around him too tight. All he could do was flail and squirm, twist in its awful grip as it dragged him away.

And then he was gone, sealed away behind the smooth, silver wall of the blast doors. All Carter could see now was her own reflection, white with horror.

It was some time before Macready could pull her free of its gaze.

Up in the control room, several minutes later, Carter and Zelenka stood at the sensor terminal and watched Palmer's city map swoop towards the lockdown zone again. It stopped swooping a lot earlier this time.

"It's grown," he told them quietly. "Almost exactly doubled in size. And that unknown functionality we detected has increased as well."

"What about the…" Carter searched for suitable words, ones stripped of emotion. "What's in there?"

"It seems quiet now. Nothing on visual."

"A runner from my lab says that the vibrations have dropped back to their previous levels," said Zelenka. "So really, all we did was get its attention."

"Maybe." Carter undid the straps on the tactical vest and shrugged out of it, glad to be free of its weight, its constriction. "On the other hand, maybe it was about to do that anyway. Expand its territory, I mean."

Zelenka frowned. "That's a scary thought. If the lockdown area has doubled in size in about… How long has it been? Five hours? If it's a geometric progression, that would mean…"

"Oh God," Carter muttered. "Thirty hours. It would enclose the city core in thirty hours."

There was no way that could be allowed to happen. The core contained everything that allowed Atlantis to function—the control room, the ZPMs, even the infirmary and most of the living quarters.

And the Stargate.

"We'd lose control of the city," she whispered. "Everything. This… *Tumor*, would take Atlantis right out from under us."

"What can we do?"

Carter thought for a moment, then tilted her head towards the internal balcony overlooking the Stargate. "Out here."

He followed her, plainly puzzled. "Colonel?"

"Sorry. I didn't want to say this in there, not yet." She walked up to the rail and leaned on it, looking down to the smooth, raised floor of the gate room. "Radek, how much explosive force would we need to blow off the west pier?"

There was a moment of pure silence. Then: "I'm sorry?"

"Look, I know that sounds extreme. It's a worse-case scenario, but right now I'm having trouble thinking of anything else. I wasn't kidding when I called that thing a tumor—this city has a malignant cancer, eating away at us from inside the lockdown zone. It's infiltrated our vital systems to feed itself, it can defend itself against us, and it's growing. We don't have much time left."

"So, to continue the medical analogy, you're talking about amputation."

"I guess I am."

He puffed out a long breath. "Well... Back when we thought the Wraith were going to take the city, I modeled the effect of the self-destruct system on Atlantis. That broke the whole city into pieces, though..." He rubbed his chin, deep in thought. "Seriously, I don't think you could remove a pier with anything less that ten kilotons."

"Seriously?" Ten kilotons would only be a little less explosive force than that of the Hiroshima bomb. Letting something the size of Little Boy off inside the city wasn't something she wanted to do. "That would wipe us out."

"Almost certainly. The piers are tough, you see... Atlantis is constructed of fantastically strong alloys. It has to be, to hold together in flight. If they were made from conventional materials, all the piers would still be on Lantea. They'd never have survived the takeoff stress."

"Damn," she said. "Could we shrink the shield? Activate it, but draw it in until it covers the city core and leaves the piers exposed?"

"It's possible. The last time that happened was when we left Lantea, an automatic response to the power drain. I suppose we could try to contract it intentionally this time." He put his hands into his jacket pockets, looking uncomfortable to even having the conversation. "But Colonel, what are you going to use as a bomb?"

"Drones," she said. "A massed drone launch, take them straight up and then right down onto the pier. If we hit it hard enough, we could sever the entire structure."

"You know, I'd never thought about using drones against *ourselves* before." His eyes were a little wide, but she could tell he was mulling it over. "Perhaps you wouldn't even need to remove the whole pier. If you launched enough drones, aimed them right at the lockdown zone… With the shield to protect the city core, we could cut structural loss down to no more than six, seven percent of the city."

"That's great!" smiled Carter. Then the smile fell away. "Oh my God, what am I saying? That's not great at all… I've been in Atlantis three weeks and already I'm going to blow six percent of it apart…"

There was a movement behind her. She looked back and saw Palmer there. "Colonel? Something's happening. We've got an incoming wormhole."

"What? Have you got an IDC?"

"It's a jumper."

As he spoke, the gate activated.

There was a hissing, a liquid metallic growl that filled the gate room. A ring of glittering quantum foam appeared at the inside edge of the gate, whirled inwards to form a membrane that erupted out into the gate-room, a billowing horizontal splash. The splash paused, then recoiled, dragged by its own field stresses into a vertical mirror, a rippling plane of tension a billionth of a millimeter thick and untold light-years long. The event horizon.

The gate was open. A few seconds later the angled nose of a puddle jumper split the mirror.

The jumper decelerated smoothly, coming to a halt in the middle of the gate room. Behind it, the event horizon lost cohesion and spun away to nothing, the gate suddenly a dark, empty ring once more. Carter caught a glimpse of John Sheppard through the jumper's viewport just before the ceiling irised open and the craft fled upwards and out of sight.

"Radek," Carter said bleakly. "What am I going to tell them?"

"Everything," he said. "And as quickly as you can. Like you said, we don't have much time left."

CHAPTER SIXTEEN

Phage

Rodney McKay felt thoroughly sick.

His nausea wasn't the result of the unending smell of Chunky Monkey's algae-laden rain, although the quick shower he had taken had done little to get the reek of the stuff out of his clothes and skin. Surprisingly, it also had little to do with the thought of what was lurking out on the west pier, in the center of what people were calling the lockdown zone. The thought of that was terrifying, certainly, and McKay wouldn't argue that there was a queasy sense of violation in the thought of something so cancerous, so vigorously alive insinuating itself into the city's structure. But no, what really had his stomach roiling was the two days he had spent in the center of that enclosed, diseased area, working on what he had thought of as the cutting edge of high energy physics.

Setting up to translate the nanite code he had downloaded from Laetor helped him forget that, for periods of several minutes at a time. But every now and then, while he worked, some train of thought would lead his mind back to that time, and a wash of nausea would sweep over him and leave him in a cold sweat.

It was only a matter of time, of course, before Zelenka saw it happen. "Rodney?"

"What?"

"Is everything all right? You don't look so good."

He waved Zelenka away. "I'm fine. Just keep… Doing whatever it is you're doing."

"What I'm *doing* is monitoring the unknown functionality around the lockdown zone," Zelenka snapped. "For your information, while you were out doing whatever it was *you* were doing I've located a series of antiphase pulses that—"

"Yeah, yeah." McKay swallowed hard a couple of times. The server he was setting up for the nanite code was almost complete; the stack of high-capacity drives installed, the decompression and translation routines ready. His main concern now was with the output—normally he would have downloaded all the translated information to the Atlantis main servers for storage, then sorted through it by relevance later. But things were a lot more difficult now. Not only couldn't he use a networked server for the raw nanite code, but he couldn't even have the output go anywhere online either. There was the constant suspicion, now, that Angelus had hacked into the network and was watching the city's data traffic. McKay couldn't discuss important information over the communication system, and he couldn't send important data, either. It was immensely restricting, having to work in whispers and mime.

He sat back, running his hands through his hair and clasping them at the back of his neck, trying to get some of the kinks out. Being cooped up in the puddle jumper for so long hadn't done his spine any good at all.

Zelenka was still looking at him. "Dammit, what?"

"Are you ill? Maybe you should get Keller to check you out."

"I'm not ill, okay? It's just been a rough couple of days…" He glared at Zelenka. "What the hell are you looking at me like that for?"

Zelenka shrugged, and returned his attention to the program he was working on, an algorithm for restructuring the shield in case Carter went ahead with her plan to launch drones into the lockdown zone. "I don't know."

"Yes you do! You think I'm one of those things, like you and Teyla saw."

"I didn't say that."

"You didn't have to!"

"Would I be sitting here if I thought you were?" Zelenka didn't take his eyes off the screen, just kept typing out his command strings. "I just asked if you were okay. You look a little…" He flicked a glance over at McKay. "Peaky."

Yeah, well. You'd look peaky too if you'd—" He broke off

and jerked upright, almost knocking his seat over. "Jesus, what was I doing down there?"

"Rodney—"

"No! Okay?" He pointed a feverish finger at Zelenka. "No! You didn't spend any time down there… I was working with Angelus for two days, and we were *doing* stuff! I'm sure of it… The algorithms he was generating were just, I dunno, magnificent! Okay, I know it was only preliminary modeling, but in terms of compression rations, the encoding…" He trailed off, his eyes widening. "Oh my god."

"What now?"

"Carter was saying he can project false images… In the briefing, those medical scans she showed us. What… What if he was doing the same thing to me?"

Zelenka gave up on what he was doing and spun his seat around to face McKay. "What are you babbling about?"

"What if all my experiences down there were fake?"

"That's ridiculous… Rodney, I studied the surveillance footage myself—it's just image manipulation of an extremely advanced kind. Pixels, that's all. There's no way that he could create a false memory."

"Are you sure?" McKay felt short of breath. The lab, with its gloomy lighting and flickering terminals, was closing in on him like a vice. "Those marines you saw. What if they didn't know they weren't real?"

"Rodney, you're being ridiculous." Zelenka frowned. "I think you're also hyperventilating. You need to sit down."

"Ridiculous, huh?"

"Yes. There's no telling what happened to the marines—you said in the briefing that you encountered Replicators who had been altered, infected by this chimera, this hybrid. Not copied as evil clones. What happened to those marines was probably the same thing."

McKay blinked at him. "You think so?"

"If you're worried, get Keller to check you out." He went back to his workstation. "If there's a diagonal scratch on your x-ray film, then you'll know."

"Did she check Cassidy? She was in the with Angelus for

a while."

"Not as long as you. And yes, Keller checked her out. She's fine." Zelenka's expression darkened for a moment. "Physically."

"Okay…" McKay took a couple of deep breaths. "Okay, you may be right. And yeah, I could go down to the infirmary, might put my mind at rest…"

"Unless there's a printer malfunction," said Zelenka, his voice devoid of emotion. "Something that puts a scratch on the film somewhere."

McKay narrowed his eyes. "You're an evil little man, did you know that?"

Zelenka didn't reply. McKay stood where he was for a moment, then retrieved his chair and sat back down. "Maybe you're the fake instead. Angelus built you specially just to make me nervous."

"In which case," said Zelenka, giving him a nasty sideways look, "it's working really well, isn't it?"

There came a time, when McKay started to download the nanite code from his laptop, that he no longer had anything to do. He realized that it probably wouldn't be for long, but until the translated information started to build up in his output store, all he'd be doing down in the lab would be staring at swathes of raw code coursing down a monitor screen and trying not to get into a fight with Zelenka.

Oddly, the thought of some time to himself was no respite. He didn't want to be alone with his thoughts, and neither did he want to waste the slack period on useless make-work, not while the hybrid was no doubt busy with its own loathsome projects at the heart of the lockdown zone. So instead of going to the mess hall, or having a bath to try and rid himself of some of the Chunky Monkey smell, he went to find Sam Carter.

She was in the control room, which was no great surprise. Since returning to the Atlantis McKay had learned just how different life there had become for everyone: the city had been taken to a state of alert and had remained that way. There was no downtime any more. All marines were active and either on guard duty or inducted into Teyla Emmagan's army of message runners, while the science staff were all working on problems that related, directly or indirectly, to the thing on the west pier. Even the support personnel were involved in emergency procedures.

And Carter was coordinating them all. The pressure on her must have been immense.

McKay almost felt guilty about intruding on her, but as soon as she saw him she gave him a tired smile and beckoned him over, and he decided he might well have been providing a welcome break for her.

They went out onto the internal balcony, overlooking the Stargate. Across the open space McKay could see that Sheppard and some of his marines were in the conference room, talking animatedly. The multiple doors were still open. "I guess he's not discussing anything private," Carter ventured.

"Either that, or it's because of the smell," said McKay sniffing his own sleeve and grimacing. "This stuff doesn't come off."

"What was it again?"

"Rotted algae. I tell you, I've been to some weird places since taking this assignment. But that planet has got to be one of the most, I dunno, *yucky* that I've ever seen."

"Yucky," repeated Carter, smirking.

"You know what I mean. We've been to all kinds of planets. Most of them are pretty nice, considering. I mean, the Ancients didn't put many Stargates on worlds that weren't habitable. And there are some that are dangerous, or really harsh, or whatever... Chunky Monkey wasn't any of those things. It just rained all the time and it smelled bad."

"Let's hope it was worth a few showers," Carter replied. "How's it going with the nanite code?"

"It's translating. It won't be too long before I can start sorting through it for clues."

Carter turned away from the gate and leaned back against the rail. "Anything we find out could help us. If the lockdown expands again, or if anything else happens, I'm going to have to launch the drones."

"Really? You're actually going ahead with that?"

"I hope I don't have to. We'd have to saturate the pier with them, and I don't even want to think about how much damage that could do."

"It would be one hell of a risk, Sam. You do realize that the explosive power of a drone has never been accurately measured? From what I've been able to model in the past it's got more to do with the power source in its control than in the drone itself—when we used naquada generators to power them they didn't pack anything like as much punch as they do with a ZPM in the chair." He shook his head. "Get it wrong and you could blow the city in half."

"So give me alternatives. Tell me about the APE."

"Oh, that. Well... Talk about a two edged sword..." He gave a wry chuckle. "Put it this way, if it hadn't worked so well I'd be able to build you one right now. All the readings I took on it were in my PDA, and the pulse cooked it."

"Yeah, Sheppard said it affected the jumper, too."

"Only the cloak. Everything else was powered down..." He paused. "Okay, not only the cloak. It kind of screwed up the lifters too. And the sensors." He looked away and cleared his throat. "And the hyperdrive."

"So everything, really."

"Well, yeah, pretty much. But the stuff that was powered down just needed rebooting. I managed to get it all working okay with a little tinkering."

Carter raised an eyebrow. "I guess your definition of 'okay' is different from John's."

"Ah, picky. So using the hyperdrive was like riding a jackhammer all the way home... I can fix it."

"I wondered why you used a gate to get back."

"Yeah, we just found the nearest one and dialed back. It was probably a short cut, anyways." He made a dismissive gesture. "Look, the important thing is that the Replicators brought the APE with them specifically to kill the hybrid. Laetor and the other infected Replicators were shut down by the pulse when it went off, so he couldn't know it hadn't worked. The hybrid got away."

"And pretended to be Angelus?"

"Maybe. If that's what happened, I still can't figure out why… We've still only got half the picture right now. But Sam, if the plans to the APE were in Laetor's head—and if he was part of the Asuran collective at any time I can't see why they wouldn't be—then I bet you any money I could beef it up."

She leaned a little closer to him. "Could it work?" she asked quietly. "Honest answer, Rodney. If what we've got here is the same as what you found in the Replicator facility, could the APE kill it?"

"Honest answer?"

"Please."

"I don't know."

She sagged. "Okay. Guess there's no way you could."

For a moment, he could see, the pressure had almost gotten to her there. And McKay realized, in that instant, why the thought of his time with Angelus was making him sick. It wasn't that he could have been killed by the hybrid at any time, if Angelus was indeed the Replicator's feared chimera. It wasn't that the physics he had been so engrossed in, so seduced by, had been stolen from him again.

It was because he had let everyone down.

He had been closer than anyone to the Ancient, and hadn't noticed anything amiss. If he'd seen something earlier, he could have warned them. People might not have died.

But he had been so in love with the science that he hadn't even spotted the fact he was working with a monster.

"Sam? Let me go through what I've gotten from Laetor. If the APE is in there, I can build it for you, I swear to God."

I won't let you down again, he thought. Although he could never bring himself to say it out loud.

The contents of Laetor's head, in terms of nanite code, were immense. The laptop's storage, even with the massive increase it had gained by McKay's installation of an Ancient data crystal, was filled with a solid mass of supercompressed data. Each fragment of code had to be extracted from that mass, run through a decompression routine to expand it back to its original size, recombined with all the nearby fragments in order to form viable blocks of data and then finally sent through a series of translation protocols to turn the data from pure nanite code to something readable by human beings. It was a mammoth task, and if McKay hadn't set all his routines up to be extremely selective in what they extracted and expanded, one that could easily have taken years.

There was, however, just one area of information that the programs were interested in. They still vomited out terabytes of data, but at least it was a manageable amount. Before too long McKay was able to start filtering it by relevance to the hybrid.

The rest of the information, that which didn't have any direct relevance to Laetor's experiences on Chunky Monkey, would have to stay in storage for now. McKay hoped that, once this present crisis was over, he would be able to return to it and add it to the Atlantis database. One could never know too much about an enemy, and certainly not one as dangerous and implacable as the Asurans.

He was alone in the lab when he first found something helpful. Zelenka had finished his run of simulations, and had gone to find Carter and give her the results. From the look on his face when he left, they hadn't been entirely what he was hoping.

What McKay had started seeing wasn't exactly what he had been looking for, either. In the data blocks he was first able to read there was little or no mention of the APE, and nothing at all in the way of specifications for it.

What he did find, however, were some very interesting facts about the hybrid itself.

Interesting enough to have him running out of the lab, so fast that he collided with a junior technician on the way in. The tech had a mug of coffee in her hand, no doubt trying to stay alert after a long night's work. The coffee wasn't as hot as it might have been—presumably the tech had carried it all the way down from the mess hall—but it still made McKay yelp as it soaked through his shirt.

"Ow! Son of a—" He stepped back, batting at himself. "Ooh, hot… What the hell are you doing?"

"I'm sorry, doctor," the woman stammered. "I was just—"

"What? Just what? You know I'm scalded, don't you?" She was looking at him in utter horror, and seeing that, he relented slightly. There could be no-one in the city who wasn't on an edge of tension at the moment, even though the exact details of what had been occurring hadn't been completely disclosed. "Screw it, just forget it, okay? Look where you're going from now on, yeah?"

She nodded.

McKay started away, then paused. "Were you looking for me?"

"No doctor. I was just going in to use my workstation."

"Really?" McKay blinked. "You've worked in here?"

"Yes."

"While I've been here?"

"Yes." Maybe she saw that he was looking bewildered, because she said: "It's all right, doctor. I don't think we've ever spoken."

"Oh, okay then…" He gestured vaguely upwards. "I've got to, uh… Upstairs. Control room."

She gave him a shy smile. "Do you want me to lock up when I'm done?"

"No, no. I'll be right back." The woman was quite attractive. Had he really not noticed her before? "Sorry, what did you say your name was?"

"Solomon. Gina Solomon."

"Well, pleased to, er…" He waved her into the lab. "Carry on."

With that, he carried on, more slowly now, and rather lost in thought. He stayed that way until he got up to the control room.

There was a marine stationed at the entrance, standing at ease to one side of the door. He nodded to McKay as he came in. McKay returned the greeting on reflex, then paused. "What, we need guards on this place now?"

"I'm sorry? Oh, no doctor. I'm a message runner."

"Oh, I see! I thought things had gotten worse." He glanced past the man, into the control room, but he couldn't see any-one there but the usual technicians. "Ah, is Colonel Carter around?"

"Out on the balcony."

"Thanks." McKay left him there, crossed the control room and opened the balcony doors.

Carter was there, near the rail, looking up into the sky with a pair of binoculars. Zelenka was there too, standing nearer to the wall, and Sheppard was right up against the rail, looking upwards with a hand cupped over his eyes.

"Hey," McKay said warily. "What are you looking at?"

"Major Lorne," Sheppard replied.

"Up there?"

"He's in a jumper," said Carter. "Doing a flypast of the lockdown zone."

"Oh, I see…" McKay looked up, but couldn't see anything. "Observation, or target acquisition?"

"Bit of both." Sheppard pointed. "There he is!"

McKay joined him at the rail, and followed the line of his finger. As he did so a metal splinter raced up from his far right, catching the sun as it skimmed low over the west pier. "He's moving fast."

"He started off slower," said Zelenka, sounding unhappy. "Something reached up and tried to grab him."

"Holy…" McKay turned his attention to the pier itself, shielding his eyes from the high sun. For a few moments he saw nothing, but then, between two structures, something moved convulsively. "Okay, that's nasty."

"Third pass," Carter muttered. "He should be coming in now. Hi Rodney."

The jumper sizzled past again. "Okay," said Sheppard, with an edge to his voice. "Fourth pass."

"He's probably, you know, just being thorough." McKay turned away from the view. "Look, guys? I've managed to translate some of Laetor's head. You might want to hear this."

Zelenka looked puzzled. "Laetor?"

"The zombie Replicator we interrogated on Chunky Monkey. Didn't I tell you his name?"

"You don't tell me anything."

"Yeah, well." McKay waved him away. "The important thing

is, I think I know what we're dealing with here. The hybrid."

Carter lowered her binoculars and turned to him. "Go on."

"It's a weapon," he said proudly.

There was a few moments when no-one spoke. Then Sheppard said: "We know."

"You do?"

"Er, that's what Laetor called it, remember?"

"What? Oh, that!" McKay shook his head. "No, I mean now I *really* know."

"I would have thought it was pretty obvious!"

"Would you just listen to me for a minute?" McKay waved a hand out towards the lockdown zone. "That is *not* what it's supposed to be doing!"

"If we told it that," ventured Zelenka, "would it stop?"

McKay gave him the sour eye, but didn't answer him. "It's a pet project of Oberoth's. I'm guessing part of an instant arms race we kicked off when we screwed with the Asuran base code."

Sheppard raised a hand. "Hold on, Oberoth directly?"

"Oh yeah, his name's all over the code. Figuratively. Anyways, the original plan for the hybrid wasn't that mess over there. What it's supposed to do is make more Replicators."

"That doesn't make any sense at all," said Zelenka.

McKay made an exasperated noise. "Of course it does! It makes perfect sense… Listen, the Ancients lost the war with the Wraith because they were outnumbered, yeah? So the Replicators design something they could, I dunno, get into a hive ship, or drop onto a populated world, whatever. It disguises itself, uses all kinds of ninja tricks to avoid getting caught, and quietly starts grabbing people and turning them into new hybrids. Two become four, four become eight… Wouldn't be too long before the whole planet's full of Replicators."

"Replicators can't reproduce like that," said Zelenka.

"That's why it needed to be a hybrid. Living tissue can be infectious—this thing isn't part Replicator, part human. It's part replicator, part *disease*."

"My God," breathed Carter. "That's just…"

"I think the word you're looking for," Zelenka muttered, "is 'disgusting'."

"You defeat your enemy and increase your own forces at the same time." Sheppard gave a low whistle. "Holy cow."

"Yeah. Except it doesn't work."

"Seems to be doing okay to me."

"What?" McKay nodded out to sea. "That? We know all about *that*! Sure, it's got the upper hand at the moment, with all the ninja tricks it knows, but as a stealth weapon it's blown its cover big time."

"And you know why, don't you," smiled Carter. "C'mon, Rodney. You so want to tell us…"

"Ah, you know me so well," he grinned. "As a matter of fact, I do. It's hungry."

He looked at the three of them, and was met by three blanks stares. "Oh, for goodness… The Replicators must have made an error in the design. *Hugely* underestimated how much power it would take to keep the nanites and living tissue functioning together. The hybrid works, but it's energy-poor. It's starving, in a way we can't even comprehend. It's mad with hunger—that's what drove it beyond its programming."

"And the Replicators found out what it was capable of," Carter said, very quietly. "Once it went mad. They knew they couldn't control it. They had to destroy it."

"Hold on…" Sheppard had a hand at his headset, no doubt taking a call. McKay hoped it wasn't anything important—even though the hybrid was insane with hunger, it was still startlingly intelligent. And not only that, it was imaginative, a complex function that that had probably evolved from the stealth techniques programmed into it by its creators.

This wasn't just artificial intelligence, he thought. It was artificial *cunning*.

And that made the hybrid, in its present, imperfect form, even more dangerous. In order to satisfy its insatiable appetites the chimera could be capable of almost anything, the full range of action from stealth to huge and overt violence. It would hide in the shadows and strike like an assassin in the night, and in the next instant would unleash unimaginable fury and brutality right out in the open. It was unpredictable and ruthlessly efficient and completely terrifying.

No wonder the Replicators had sacrificed an entire starship to destroy it. The hybrid would consume anything, Asuran and Wraith and human alike. It had to.

"Lorne's down safely," Sheppard reported a moment later. "I'd better get in there and see what he's got."

"I'll come with you," said Carter. She walked across to the doors and waved them open. "Rodney, that was good work."

"I thought so."

"At least we know what we're dealing with now…" Closer to him now, she sniffed. "Is that coffee on you?"

"Yeah, a tech threw it at me. I think it was a sign of affection."

"Keep thinking that," Zelenka told him, then turned to Carter. "Colonel, should I give up on the shield deformation? With what Rodney has discovered, surely the pulse emitter has got to be our best option."

She shook her head as she went through into the control room. "No, keep on that. The more options we have the happier I'll be."

"We might still need to do both," said Sheppard, looking grim. "The APE didn't work for the Replicators, not all the way. It escaped."

"At least part of it did." McKay followed Carter through the doors. "But yeah, we might have to zap it more than once. Or…" He trailed off. Gina Solomon, the technician who had spilled her coffee on him, was standing at the entrance door. She waved to him nervously, as if to try and attract his attention without drawing any to herself.

McKay gave Zelenka a nudge. "'Keep thinking that', huh?" he murmured, then strode over to her, smiling. "Doctor Solomon, what brings you up here?"

"I was trying to find you." She glanced nervously around, and paled slightly as she saw Carter and Sheppard there. When she next spoke, her voice was very low. "Something's happened."

His smile dipped. "What kind of something?"

"Well, I was in the lab, where I met you? I set up what I

needed to and left the program running, and then when I was coming out, another tech came in. He didn't say anything, and I didn't really look at him…"

Carter had obviously overheard, despite Solomon's hushed voice. She walked quickly over to join them. "Is there a problem?"

"I'm not sure, Colonel." Solomon was looking deeply uncomfortable. "I… I'd forgotten my mug, so I went back to get it. But the lab door was locked from inside."

McKay's stomach lurched. "Locked? Somebody locked themselves into my lab?"

She nodded miserably. "I think it might have been Doctor Norris."

"Norris? But isn't he… Oh no." McKay put a hand over his face. "Oh no nononono!"

"Colonel Sheppard," said Carter. "Get a squad down to Doctor McKay's lab. Get that door open. Blow it off its rails if you have to."

"On it." He raced away. McKay almost went after him, then thought how futile it would be. "Damn it, Solomon," he hissed. "Didn't it occur to you that Doctor Norris might not exactly be himself right now?"

"I'm sorry," she whispered. "I didn't—"

"Oh, this is perfect!" McKay snarled. "Everything we got from Laetor will be trashed by now…"

"Doctor, calm down," Carter snapped. "It's obvious we've got a change in situation here. Where's Clarke?"

"Who?"

"The runner, he was just here."

McKay glanced around. The marine he had seen on the way in was gone. "Maybe he had to use the bathroom or something."

"I sure hope that's it…" Carter suddenly dipped her head, putting a hand to her headset.

"That's not a good sign," McKay moaned, watching as she nodded and muttered her end of a terse conversation. "That's not supposed to happen."

Zelenka looked around, suddenly. "Do you hear sirens?"

McKay listened hard. Sure enough, from somewhere else in the tower, an alarm had begun to hoot mournfully. A moment later they were joined by chimes from one of the workstations, more musical but identical in pitch and rhythm.

One of the techs, Palmer, sprinted to the workstation screen, scanning its readouts. "Colonel?" he called. "Alert in the hangar—someone activated an alarm, and I'm also picking up weapons fire."

"The ship," groaned McKay. "Angelus' ship… What, is he trying to fly out of here or something?"

Carter was already running past him. He followed her, with Zelenka on his heels. "Sam?"

"Not now!"

"Was that call you got about Angelus' ship?"

She was clattering down the stairs to the next level, drawing her sidearm. "No. That was MacReady—he's lost another two marines. Looks like one set of blast doors opened up and they got attacked before they could even call in." She skated to a halt outside the doors to the hangar, waved her hand over the control. "The hybrid's gone on the offensive. Something tipped it off."

The doors opened onto utter chaos.

When McKay had last been here, the hangar had seemed cavernous, dark and quiet around the golden ship. Now it was an assault on the senses; the stuttering glare of muzzle-flashes, the deafening hammer of machine guns, the reek of blood and cordite. McKay yelled in shock at it, clapped his hands over his ears to shut out the din, squeezed his eyes shut to block out the sight. It was insane, hellish.

He felt someone grab him, pull him down into cover. It was Carter, he saw as he opened his eyes again, her pistol leveled, her head turned slightly away from the gunfire. He hadn't even known that there had been guards stationed around the golden ship—from what he could see now, peeking over a tumbled crate, there had probably been about a dozen of them, armed with everything from conventional firearms to anti-Replicator guns. What formation they had taken around the starhopper he could only guess, because those still on their feet were now clustered at the long sides of the hangar, taking cover behind the piled equipment and stores that the ship had displaced.

They were firing almost continually at the starhopper, or what the hopper had now become. The noise was insane, an earsplitting racket of stuttering machine guns, the whining snarls of ARGs, the hooting of the alarm.

There were screams, too. Some of the screaming came from injured men. Most issued from the towering, writhing tangle in the center of the hangar.

The golden ship was gone. McKay could see elements of it in the mass—a fin here, the glossy globe of a viewport there—but even those last fragments were unraveling before his eyes. It was as if the entire vessel had turned to fluid, risen up into a great column of liquid metal veined with pulsing flesh, connecting floor and ceiling and lashing out in every direction with a thousand whipping, squirming tendrils.

The noise it made, that cacophony of whistling shrieks and metallic, bass bellows, was simply astonishing.

Carter was firing her pistol into the thing: McKay saw her empty the magazine, the slide locking back, the empty mag falling to the floor and another in its place before it struck. She opened fire again, squeezing off shot after shot, placing each one. She was testing the hybrid, McKay saw, not just firing randomly but planting each bullet in a different location, seeing if any of them had an effect.

Zelenka was just behind him. He shouted something, but McKay couldn't hear him over the noise. He looked back. "What?"

"Up!" Zelenka pointed frantically. "It's trying to go up!"

McKay turned, and saw that Zelenka was right: there was now less of the mass on the floor than there was spreading out over the ceiling. It was hauling itself upwards like an inverted tree, sending out thousands of pulsing metal roots that locked into the panels above and dragged it, hissing and howling, off the ground.

A marine ran forwards, dropped to one knee a few meters in front of the doorway. He had a weapon over one shoulder, some kind of rocket-launcher. He shouted a warning over his shoulder; behind him, marines covered their heads.

He never fired it. McKay saw the man correct his aim slightly, angling the launcher upwards, and then a limb of metal snapped down towards him. It coiled around him with insane speed, enveloping his chest and head before he could loose a cry, let alone a missile. The launcher tumbled from his grasp as he was whipped up into the air.

McKay saw the launcher fall, strobe-lit by weapons fire. Reflexively he went to grab it, desperate to stop the impact setting the missile off. But he was too far away; it skidded out of his grasp.

It hit the floor end-first, bounced, toppled. Swung back towards the doorway.

Carter snatched it up, dropped to one knee and fired it in a single action.

There was an almighty sound, so loud and so vast that it was almost beyond noise. McKay felt it like a punch over his entire body. It had him off his feet. The light, a blast of searing flame in the center of the hangar, lit up everything.

There was an instant of almost pure peace. For a fraction of a second McKay saw nothing but light, felt nothing but heat, heard nothing past the wall of silence in his ears. He was alone, gliding backwards. Nothing could touch him.

The floor came up and smashed into him rump-first, so hard his teeth snapped together. The air was full of smoke and water, and everything was on fire.

The hybrid had stopped screaming.

McKay, his vision blurring and clouded with spots, could just about make out what had happened to the chimera. Carter's missile had struck it a third of the way down, blasting it entirely in two. There was a foaming, burning mess of it on the floor, leaping and convulsing in eerie silence, while the part on the ceiling was a gigantic inverted crater, ringed with ragged tendrils, shrinking in on itself as it retreated.

There were bits of it everywhere. Most of them, McKay saw to his horror, were still moving.

He scrambled to his feet. Oddly, he was soaked through; when the launcher had gone off a back-blast of hot brine had covered him from head to foot. There were small secondary fires on whatever tarpaulin hadn't been saturated, and a couple of marines were batting out minor flames on their uniforms.

The smoke was clearing, slowly. McKay saw Zelenka getting up, his hair plastered to his head and his glasses knocked askew. Carter was curled up on the floor with her arms over her head.

McKay went over to her and helped her up. "Nice shot," he said, his own voice dim in his ears.

"Did I get it?" She was blinking fiercely, trying to focus.

"Oh yeah."

The hybrid was mostly gone, now. The part that had been on the ceiling was sucking itself up into whatever crawlspace existed between the hangar and the level above. The lower section, that which wasn't scattered in chunks around the floor, was making a similar escape. The last of its tendrils, ridged like silvery worms, vanished out of sight as he watched.

There was something broken in its actions, though. It was running, not attacking. The explosion, while far from fatal, had done enough to drive the thing into full retreat.

It had left some objects behind, McKay noticed. Getting closer, he could see that at least one of the objects had been a marine, although it was hard to tell. But there was machinery too: something that looked like a stretched car engine married to a series of coils, twisted and scorched by the explosion. Other parts that were even less identifiable.

Zelenka was close by. "This looks like Replicator technology," he said, pointing at the largest section. "A hyperdrive?"

"Maybe." He rolled it over with his foot. "It was pretending to be a spaceship, but it still needed an engine. Must have stolen it from the Replicator landing party."

He went back to Carter. She was tending to a wounded marine, tying a tourniquet around the ragged mess that had been his right leg. "Medics are coming," she told him. "Just hold on."

"Sam?"

"Rodney." She glanced up from her work. "Are you okay?"

"What, apart from drowning?" He waved around at the

mess. "Look, we need to collect some of these fragments. I can test them and use the data to get the pulse frequencies for the APE."

"Sure. I'll get a couple of guys on it."

"Yeah…" He gazed around, at the chaos, the fires, the scattered chunks of hybrid and human. "I just thought of something else."

"Let me guess. Something bad."

"Could be. Remember how I told you the ship had lost weight? And that I didn't know what that meant?" He spread his hands, encompassing the mess all around him. "Now I do. There's still about fifty kilos of hybrid on the *Apollo*."

CHAPTER SEVENTEEN

Open Season

There was a sound on the bridge of the *Apollo* that Ellis had never heard before. It was a thin, high rushing, a continuous crackle that, although it wasn't loud, seemed to pervade the entire space. In itself, the sound wasn't unduly disturbing. But Ellis knew what it was, and he didn't like it at all.

The sound was that of millions of ammonia crystals hitting *Apollo* at high speed. Sharpe had taken the battlecruiser high, as high as she dared, a long parabolic arc that took it almost entirely out of the water layer and into the frozen skies above.

It wasn't a course that could be maintained for long. The friction of the ammonia crystals would slow *Apollo* even more than the water layer had—the ship was a creature of pure vacuum, built for the airless reaches between worlds. It was too big to be comfortable in an atmosphere; too blunt, too heavy. In the spaces between power drains Sharpe had poured as much energy into the drives as she dared, sending the ship up into what might be its last climb.

When *Apollo* reached the highest part of the arc, began to slide back down the other side and deeper into the water layer, there was a very good chance that the power drains would be too severe to allow the engines to restart. If that was the case, *Apollo* would begin one last maneuver: an unstoppable dive into the heat and gravity and crushing pressure of the jovian's heart.

For the moment, though, the ship rose. Ellis hoped it would give him enough time.

"Meyers," he said. "Give me a countdown. Twenty minutes mark."

"Mark," she acknowledged, setting the clock running on her PDA. "Do you want me to count you down at all?"

"Best not. I might need to sneak around." He got up, walked between the two consoles and right up to the viewport. He could see almost nothing; Apollo was on the dark side of the jovian, so even this high there was no filtering sunlight. All he could see was powdery crystals washing against the viewport in random waves, a supercooled blizzard hammering at his ship. Robbing him of speed, of altitude. The planet wanted *Apollo*, wanted to drag the vessel down into its terrible interior.

Ellis allowed himself a grim smile. The planet wasn't the only thing that wanted to eat his ship at the moment. But with luck and a following wind, he would deny both the jovian and the awful thing shrieking and squirming in corridor nine.

"Not today, you sons of bitches," he muttered under his breath. "Not today."

There were marines on guard near the corridor, around the corner and out of sight of the creature. They hugged P90s to their chests like totems, although the weapons had proved to be largely ineffective. After the initial encounter with the creature there had been an abortive attack on it, after which Ellis had basically banned anyone from trying to shoot the thing. Missed shots and ricochets were not something he wanted to happen inside a spaceship—even if there was little chance of a shot puncturing the armored hull, there were just too many vital systems around to risk another firefight. Besides, the shots that did hit the creature had little effect on it.

It was also quite capable of defending itself. Its tentacles could lash out several meters, faster than a man could move, and with brutal, impaling force. And if it took a dislike to anything further away, it had weapons taken from the two marines it had killed. Somehow, those guns had become part of the creature, partially absorbed into it in much the same way as it had infiltrated the ship. Whatever it was, wherever it came from, it seemed to have an instinctive affinity for machinery.

In addition to the two marines killed in the first attack, there was another in the ship's sickbay with serious gunshot wounds. Ellis wasn't about to risk anyone else if he could help it.

As he greeted the marines on guard he heard footfalls

coming up behind him, and turned to see Major Spencer and Copper, the bridge tech. He waved them down, and then tentatively peeked around the corner.

The creature was still there, filling the space, as raw and unearthly as he remembered. The skeletal likeness of Deacon still jerked and shuddered at its heart, as if driven by poorly-maintained engines. Ellis wondered if there was anything left of his helmsman in the creature at all, or if his shape was just some vestige, an unthinking, unfeeling image of the man.

Ellis guessed he'd probably never know, but he hoped it was the latter.

The Deacon-face turned towards him, glittering and ravaged, and its jaw unhinged to vent a whistling scream. Ellis ducked back, hearing a shot and a whine of ricochet as he did so. Had he remained still, the creature would have put a hole though his forehead.

Its aim was remarkable. Luckily, though, its reflexes were not much better than human.

"Any change?" Copper asked him. Ellis shook his head.

"Just as ugly and pissed-off as before. What have you got for me?"

"Managed to print these off in forty-second chunks," Spencer said, producing several battered-looking sheets of paper. "Schematics of this area, the bomb bay and the bridge sections above."

He spread them out on the deck. Ellis leaned close, studying the various levels of systemry the plans displayed. Dozens of trajectories and reflection angles had been drawn onto the paper, along with copious notes in Copper's neat handwriting. "This looks thorough."

"I'd have preferred another few run-throughs," said Copper, "but there really isn't time. I guess we're out of options."

"Pretty much. What about McKay's sensors?"

The tech nodded. "They'll be up to the job. I've been double-checking the specs, and my team's almost got them wired up. We're ready to go."

"That's good to hear. I'd hate to have to come up with a backup plan this late in the day."

Spencer frowned. "There *was* a back-up plan."

"What was it?"

"C-4. Wouldn't have been pretty."

"Something tells me this one's not going to be a bundle of laughs." Ellis checked his watch. A hair less than fourteen minutes. "Right, let's get down there. Getting the timing right on this one is going to be a bitch, and we're not going to get any second chances."

The lack of power meant that Copper hadn't been able to reliably lower the launch racks. The team he had assembled were clambering around near the roof of the bomb bay, several meters up and lit only by flashlights and portable spot lamps. Ellis gazed up at them, wondering how long it would take them to get down again. He couldn't afford to have anyone still in the bomb bay when he put the plan into operation.

Copper looked worried. "Sir, I'm not sure we're going to be able to get them all wired in time."

"Then just make sure we've got enough. How's the circuitry going to hold up?"

"In this heat?" The bomb bay was actually cold, almost uncomfortably so, but compared to the deep space it was an oven. "I wouldn't trust it to last more than an hour."

"Lucky for us we've only got a few more minutes, then," said Spencer. Copper ran a hand nervously back through his hair.

"Yeah. Lucky us."

"Copper, I don't think there's much more you can do here. Get back up to the reactor—if this works, I'll need you on the restart."

The tech nodded, took one more long look at the spiderweb of cable tangled above his head, and then went for the hatch.

Ellis had to admit, the job being done on the stealth sensors was one of the most haphazard-looking kludges he had ever had the displeasure to witness. McKay, had he been around, would have thrown a royal fit, there could be no doubt of that.

Every one of his sensors had been activated early, their generators brought online while they were still tethered to the launch racks. Those that had been successfully modified had been levered open, force-fed a new set of instructions, then connected by lengths of scavenged fiber-optic cable to a central controller. The controller was powered by batteries, as was the remote to operate it, and of course the sensors had their own internal naquadah generators. Hopefully, the entirely network was independent of the power drains, and the obscene creature that was causing them.

None of the sensors would ever be fit for their original purpose again. Over the past couple of hours, every one of them had been systematically wrecked. Still, thought Ellis, if the plan worked, the sensors would be giving themselves for a noble cause.

Hell, if he made it out of the jovian alive, he'd even buy McKay a drink.

Spencer was starting to order some of the techs down. It was a slower process than Ellis would have liked; he was intensely aware of time ticking away. As one man started to clamber down from the rack there was a hefty clanging sound in his wake, and Ellis actually winced. "Careful up there, damn it!"

The tech looked down at him, over one shoulder. "Sir, that wasn't me…"

"Then what the hell was it?"

"Not sure…" He moved another meter along the rack, heading for the lowest point so he could jump down.

Above him, the noise came again. A solid metallic impact.

"Aw crap," muttered Ellis.

A section of the bay roof crashed out of its moorings, spinning down to the deck; Ellis saw Spencer duck aside to avoid being bisected. A moment later something darted from the hole left by the panel, an oozing congeries of eyes and mouths on the end of a sinuous limb. The limb swung about, its movements convulsive, lashing like an injured snake while the eyes blinked and the mouths opened and closed, tongues tasting the air. They looked sickeningly human.

The creature had been breeding tissue for hours, ever since it had devoured Deacon. It had used him as a template, an incubator, a biofactory as it had spread and grown into the ship, and now it had copied his senses to find out what was happening directly below it.

It was using Deacon's eyes to look everywhere at once. And it didn't like what it saw.

The tech Ellis had shouted at gave a hoarse scream as the thing lunged at him, and batted it away. As he scrambled along the rack a thin tendril dropped down alongside the sensory cluster, hung for a second, and then cracked like a whip. It was so fast that Ellis didn't even see where the last couple of meters of it had gone, but when it recoiled it had the man in its grasp.

Instantly, the bay was a chorus of screams. The techs that were already on the deck scrambled for the exits; those that weren't jumped for their lives. Ellis heard bones break as some of them hit, and then he was in the midst of them, dragging the injured onto their feet.

Above his head, the tendril snapped again, and the tech's body crashed with shattering force into a sensor.

Ellis drew his pistol and snapped off a series of shots into the bundle of eyes. He saw three of them burst wetly before the thing snaked back into the ceiling, squealing and hissing. He kept firing, shots caroming off racks and the roof panels, before the slide locked back and he threw the weapon down. "Spencer! We're done here!"

Spencer was still over at the controller, aiming at the tendril with his P90 and squeezing off tightly controlled bursts at its root. As Ellis shouted he snatched up the remote and tossed it over to him. "Catch."

Ellis grabbed it out of the air, purely on reflex. "Get over here!"

"Can't…" Spencer emptied his weapon, dropped the mag and slammed in a new one. "If it gets this we're all done for."

Another sensor came apart in a rain of sparks and broken metal. Ellis took one more look at Spencer, cursed, and went for the hatch. Behind him, the tendril snapped, and Spencer's P90 fired and kept firing, emptying itself into the ceiling.

Ellis keyed the hatch closed without looking back. When it was shut he sprinted past the shocked and injured techs, heading for the stairs. "Get out of here!" he yelled back. "Now!"

He hit the stairs at a run, triggering his headset as he began to climb them three at a time. "Meyers?"

"One minute fifty, sir. And we've got a problem."

"Another one?"

"I think that last burn was too hot. Three Wraith cruisers just entered the ammonia layer."

"Nothing we can do about that now. Get ready." He was at the top of the stairs. He grabbed a rail, using his own forward momentum to haul himself into the corridor. Around the corner from him, the creature was screaming like a burning zoo.

Ellis rounded the corner and stopped. He waited until the thing looked around at him again, that metallic copy of Kyle Deacon's agonized face lolling towards him with a look of deranged malevolence in its glittering eyes.

It saw him. The mouth opened, and it hissed.

"Got something for you," said Ellis quietly. He raised the remote, just long enough for the creature to notice it, and then thumbed the trigger.

Somehow, while he was putting the plan together, he had managed to convince himself that the communications lasers would be silent. He had probably been imagining them in normal operation, sending pulses of coherent light across thousands of kilometers, allowing the sensors to talk to each other, stay in formation without giving themselves away. In space, of course, the lasers would be soundless and invisible.

Inside *Apollo*, all firing at maximum power through the roof of the bomb bay and into corridor nine, they were unimaginably loud.

The noise that almost deafened him permanently was, he would learn later, that of air exploding in the path of the laser beams. He didn't hear the floor of the corridor flash apart, or the creature erupt in a whirling cloud of fluid and spinning fragments; it was all part of the same gigantic noise, and after that his eardrums were frozen in shock.

The final part of the plan was for him to call Meyers, tell her to trigger the bay doors, but that was beyond him. Luckily, the noise and the impact of the lasers had been enough for her to hear all the way up in the bridge. She opened the bomb bay without waiting to be told.

There was no vacuum outside *Apollo*. The atmosphere around the ship was only a little thinner than that inside, although its composition was very different.

No, what sealed the creature's fate was not differential pressure, but simple gravity.

With the bay doors closed, the ship's artificial gravity was kept at a constant Earth normal. Even when they were open, the corridor above maintained its own 1G field. Or it would have done, had it not just been blown open by several high-energy communications lasers.

The jovian was a very big planet. Its surface gravity was at least four times that of Earth.

Burned, pulverized, and bleeding, the creature suddenly found itself being dragged downwards by its own mass. Ellis saw it peel off the wall, the tendrils and roots that anchored it ripped away as it was hauled towards the floor. Had he not been temporarily deafened, he thought, he would have heard it screaming as it was torn free, but he heard nothing. He didn't hear the groan of the corridor floor beginning to give way, either.

He felt it, though, through the soles of his boots. A frightening bass rumble of stressed metal tearing, shearing through its fixings, and then a sudden springing impact as an entire section of it surrendered to gravity and dropped away, rushing down into the darkness. A moment later the creature went too, a last few tentacles hanging on for an agonizing second before they split apart under the stress.

Even through his deafness, Ellis heard it crashing through the launch racks.

Apart from a few squirming fragments of meat, the thing was gone, spiraling away into the hydrogen layer. Its fall would take it into areas of the jovian no ship, no probe had ever explored, into regions of gas so massively compressed by gravity that it became fluid, then solid, then something even beyond those states. By the time the creature with Kyle Deacon's face had gone a thousand kilometers it would be hammered into nothing.

Ellis was alone in the corridor, and Meyers was yelling at him though his headset.

By the time he got back to the bridge he could hear a little, although sounds came to him as though he was listening through layers of thick cloth. "Okay people, listen up. Things got pretty loud back there, so if you could face me when you're talking to me for the next few minutes, I'd appreciate it."

He dropped into the command throne, suddenly aware that he was spattered with fluids. Large areas of his green uniform had been turned an oily black. When Meyers turned around to him she saw it too, and grimaced. "Are you okay?"

"I'm fine."

"Did you get it?"

"It's gone. Good work, people." There was a muted cheer from the bridge crew, but Ellis ignored it for now. There was still a long way to go before they were out of this. "Meyers, get the bay doors closed. Once we're back online send a team to the corridor. There may be some scraps of that thing left lying around."

She nodded, and turned back to her console. As she did so, Ellis glanced upwards on reflex, waiting for the power drain. That dip in the lights, the groan of the air systems winding down and then spinning up again, the flickering of computer screens as they lost voltage was so much a part of him now that he could have set his watch by it.

When it didn't happen, he didn't quite know what to feel. "Sharpe, what's our status? Where are we?"

She answered, then stopped herself, turned around in her seat. "Sorry sir. We're almost out of the water layer. Main power's still offline. Unless we can get restarted we'll be past bingo in about two minutes."

"The Wraith?"

"Not far behind us," Meyers told him. "I'm not picking up any weapons fire yet, but as soon as they get close enough to realize what we are, things are going to get bad."

"I hear that." He switched his headset to ship-wide communications. "All decks, brace for an increase in gravity. We'll be pulling about four gees, so you have roughly ten seconds to not be standing up any more."

He glanced around the bridge. "That means you too, people. This is out of our hands, so get ready."

Behind the tactical map, the technical crew got down onto the deck. Meyers and Sharpe settled themselves back in their seats, and Ellis followed suit, trying to relax into the contours of the command throne. Then he turned the volume on his headset up as loud as it would go. "Copper?"

"Right here, sir."

Ellis took a deep breath. He'd been secretly dreading this part. "Lieutenant, you have permission to disengage the power system. Shut her down."

"Yes sir," Copper replied, and even though his hearing was still muzzy Elllis could tell he didn't really like the idea either. "Shutting down in five, four—"

"Just do it."

The bridge lights went out.

Ellis didn't hear the air system shut down; his hearing was still too affected. But he could feel a sudden stillness in the air, a deadness in the structure of the deck and the command throne and the very walls surrounding him. Within a few short moments, all energy and motion leached out of the bridge, leaving it dark and almost completely silent.

There was no light, barring a few laptops and PDA screens. No sound loud enough for him to hear. Only his own breathing and the thump of his heart as he waited for the jovian to reach out and grab him.

It took a few seconds for the artificial gravity to die, but when it did the increase was frighteningly abrupt. Ellis had been expecting a slow rise in his own weight, but instead he found himself being crushed into the throne mid-breath. He sucked in a lungful of air, and it was hard, four times harder than it should have been. His limbs felt as though they were full of wet sand.

He clamped his stomach muscles down hard, just as he would do in a high-gee flight maneuver. It kept the air in his lungs, the blood in his head. Everyone on the ship would be doing the same thing. Basic Air Force training.

No light, no sound, hard to breathe. It was like being buried alive, thought Ellis grimly. Copper, just as planned, had not only shut down all output from the reactor, but all the emergency power circuits and auxiliaries too. Even the capacitor banks had been taken offline.

Apollo was dead metal, plunging through the water layer on the downward slide of its arc, unassisted, uncontrolled, heading for the hydrogen and certain destruction. And there wasn't a damn thing Ellis could do about it. His life, everyone's life, rested in the hands of a slender technician who, just a few hours before, had suffered a serious head wound and almost passed out.

Ellis blinked into the darkness, his eyelids heavy. He hadn't thought of that. What if Copper blacked out under the high gee? "Meyers?"

"Here sir." He heard her, this time. His hearing must have been improving, because there was no way she could turn around right now. Her words came out from between clenched teeth.

"Time."

"Twenty... Seconds."

Had it only been that long? Ellis dragged in another breath. In aircraft, high-gee turns seldom lasted this long. Still, he'd endured more than this in the centrifuge, hadn't he? Unless he'd gotten old flying the battlecruiser, gotten weak. He should be able to do this...

There was an odd feeling. He was being dragged backwards, not just down. "Sharpe... What's that?"

"We're ass-heavy," she grated. "Tilting."

Apollo's prow was rising, the weight of the engines and the reactor and the 302 bays pulling the rear of the ship down faster. That would rob them of even more speed. At this rate, the ship would hit the hydrogen layer too fast. *Apollo* would shear in two.

As he thought that, the bridge came alive.

In an instant, he was balloon-light, almost out of the throne with the sudden loss of weight. The lights around him came up to full brightness, a painful glare after all those hours in the gloom, and every panel chirruped with start-up routines.

Copper had done it. The reactor was back online, the generators pumping out power. Now, if they could only keep doing so for more than forty-one seconds Ellis would be a happy man.

"Sharpe, what's our status?"

"One second, I'm just re-booting…" She got up from her seat, ripped the laptops free from her console and dumped them onto the deck. "Main drives are in warm-up. Thrusters are online. Capacitors beginning charge cycle."

"Get us level. Meyers?"

"Most systems are still in calibration, sir. Passive sensors indicate the Wraith are accelerating to within weapons range. We've got nothing to hit them with, and no shields. Comms and active sensors are down."

"How long until the main drives are back up?"

"At least a few minutes, sir—"

The ship jolted, a sledgehammer blow from behind. "Wraith are in weapons range, sir. They're firing."

"I gathered." Ellis thought fast. There was no way to outrun the three cruisers, not on thrusters. *Apollo* could maneuver now, even leave the ammonia layer and climb into empty space, but doing so would simply get them closer to the rest of the Wraith fleet. Without weapons or shields the battlecruiser was an easy kill. He couldn't even use the 302s—their launch racks wouldn't be fired up yet either.

So all he could do was fly. But where? The Wraith ships were bigger than *Apollo*, fast, armed with multiple weapons and protected by energy shields and the bone-like armor of their hull carapaces. There was no contest.

Something nagged at him, a moment in the past, before the creature in corridor nine had taken up all his thoughts. What had *Apollo* got, even now, that the Wraith did not?

A stream of energy bolts hosed past the bridge, lighting up the viewport as it lanced away into the water layer. Ellis saw it illuminate the jovian from the inside for a few seconds before it faded.

In the far distance, blue-white light fluttered and was gone. The storm.

"Sharpe, full evasive. Give it everything you've got. Meyers, what's the status on that storm front?"

"About a five hundred kilometers dead ahead. We can avoid it now that we've got the thrusters fully online, though."

"I don't want to avoid it. Sharpe, get us in there."

"Damn it," muttered Sharpe, tapping frantically at her board. "I knew I should have gone home when I had the chance."

"Sir?" Meyers turned to face him. "I'm sorry, I don't mean to tell you your business, but flying this ship into the storm is nothing less than suicide." She grabbed at her console as *Apollo* slewed violently to port, one of Sharpe's evasive maneuvers. "Without shields we'll be a kite in a hurricane."

"I appreciate your concern, Major. And believe me, I'm aware of the risks."

The ship dropped several hundred meters. Energy bolts screeched overhead, audible in the jovian's atmosphere. "Sir, I don't understand."

"Faraday," Ellis told her. "Now give me the best course you can through that storm front. All we have to do is survive until the main drives fire up."

Meyers went back to her console. Ellis wasn't sure if she understood the reference, but right now it wasn't necessary that she did. As long as she could fly *Apollo* into the storm without getting the ship torn apart between the convection cells, then they had a chance.

The storm was approaching fast, now: Ellis could see flashes of lightning ahead, a continuous series of sparks snapping between the ammonia sky and the hydrogen layer. Each of those sparks, tiny in the far darkness, was a hundred kilometers long. The energy contained in them made the Wraith blasts seem small, attenuated.

Ellis got up, went to stand by Meyers. "Where are the cruisers?"

She tapped out a command, and on his side of the console a screen flipped from data readout to a tactical view. The cruisers were still in formation behind *Apollo*; one slightly ahead, the others further back and to either side. Pulsing red indicators showed which were charging weapons and which were unleashing streams of lethal energy towards the battlecruiser. So far, their aim had been appalling, their sensors possibly confused by the conditions inside the jovian. Ellis was surprised by that, but relieved. The cruisers should have had an advantage, at least in terms of maneuverability. Despite their size, they were almost aerodynamic.

Lightning snapped down to *Apollo*'s starboard. Ellis felt the ship judder as the atmosphere around the bolt exploded with heat. They were in the outer edges of the storm, now, and the going was starting to get rough.

It was going to get rougher. "Hold onto something, people."

"Sir?" Meyers didn't look up from her board, but her voice was urgent. "Shields are coming online. Should I raise them?"

"No." The Wraith would have their shields up. And with all this electricity flowing around, pouring more energy into the mix might not be the best idea.

The Replicator weapon, the one they had tried to kill Angelus with, had been mostly lightning. It had carved through *Apollo*'s shields without trying, but the damage had been minimal. And that, plus the biomechanical nature of the Wraith ships, was exactly what Ellis was betting on.

It was a sizeable gamble, he knew, maybe the biggest of his life. But what else could he have done? If he failed, if he died, at least it would be in a blaze of glory.

There were worse ways to fall.

Lightning lit the bridge again. It was close, close enough for a fork to lick *Apollo*'s hull. Again the ship rocked as the atmosphere around it roiled, and again as another bolt came close, and another... The shuddering was constant, as were Sharpe's course corrections. She was flinging the ship around as hard as its structure would allow, following Meyers' flightplan, adding violent evasive maneuvers of her own. So far she had avoided the worst of both the storm and the Wraith firepower, but it couldn't last.

It didn't. The next lightning bolt struck *Apollo* directly in the center of the upper hull.

The ship bucked. Ellis saw the lightning flash down, painfully bright, splashing out into a million coursing forks over the hull. For a few seconds *Apollo* was alive with sparks, the air in the bridge greasy with static, and then just as suddenly it was over.

One of the Wraith cruisers vanished from the tactical screen.

Ellis switched to a rear camera view, just in time to see the stricken vessel tumbling away, trailing fire and debris. The camera view dissolved in static for a moment as another lightning blast hit *Apollo* and coruscated over the hull, but when it came back one of the two remaining Wraith ships was climbing, fast, up into the ammonia layer and away.

The last ship accelerated, got close, and fired all its weapons at once.

In an instant the space around it was riddled with electricity. The plasma pouring from the Wraith ship was acting as a conduit for the lightning, focusing it straight into the heart of the vessel. Ellis saw it swell, split, break apart in a great cloud of fire that dropped back and down, gone in a final few seconds.

"Sharpe, take us up. Fast. We've been lucky so far, let's not overplay our hand."

The storm began to drop. Meyers let out a long sigh. "Sorry sir. Forgot my physics."

"Sometimes there are advantages to being inside a metal hull." Ellis went back to the command throne and slumped into it. "Do we have main drive yet?"

"In the next few seconds," Sharpe reported.

"As soon as we clear the atmosphere, full thrust away from the Wraith fleet. At this range we should be able to outrun them until we can get the hyperdrive back, unless that last cruiser tries anything funny."

If the Wraith had even made it out of the jovian, he thought tiredly. Its hull, comprised of the strange, biomechanical armor the Wraith used for all their vessels, would not have acted like *Apollo*'s trinium hull in the midst of the storm. The battecruiser, clad in metal, had acted like a Faraday cage, in just the way airliners in the skies of Earth were struck by lightning every day—the electricity had simply conducted around the ship.

Certainly there had been some damage; scoring and blown systems due to static, plus the awful effects of the storm's titan winds.

The Wraith ship, partially alive, could never have survived such a strike.

In front of Ellis, the clouds whipped away, thinned to nothing, and opened up into a black sky full of glittering stars. And he felt *Apollo* leap forwards, eager to be away.

Me too, he thought. *So let's go. Anywhere but here.*

CHAPTER EIGHTEEN

Resistance

Carter was on her way to the ZPM lab when Sheppard caught up with her. She had been walking fast, lost in her own racing thoughts, and had not heard him calling her. He had to put a hand on her shoulder before she noticed he was there.

The contact made her jump slightly. "Damn it, John. Don't do that."

"Sorry." He was wearing a tactical vest over his uniform, and had a P90 cradled against his chest. All the city's military personnel were on full combat alert, and most were armed and armored in the same way. "I was yelling from halfway back there."

"Is something wrong?"

"No more than usual. Where are you headed?"

"ZPM lab. Zelenka's got some new data to show me. I think McKay's down there too—he's been in and out of there since Norris trashed his lab."

"Yeah, he wasn't happy about that. Said I'd 'dawdled'." He nodded down the corridor. "Shall we?"

"Sure." She set off again, and he fell into step alongside her. "So, what's the news?"

"Right now, nothing good. No-one's seen Clarke. He's officially AWOL."

Clarke was the marine who had been working as a message runner from the control room. He had vanished at the same time the hybrid had launched its offensive. "So either something's grabbed him, or…"

"He guarded Angelus for a while. Same as Kaplan and DeSalle."

"Chances are he's hybrid too, then. Who was he partnered with on that, Bowden?"

"Also missing."

"Well, if he turns up and he still acts human, throw him in the brig. Tell him it's for his own protection."

The corridor branched; Carter headed for the nearest transporter. As she did the lights dipped noticeably, and Sheppard looked warily up at the ceiling. "Has that been getting worse?"

"Yeah. Whatever the hybrid's up to, its definitely drawing more power."

"Still hungry, eh?"

"Always, according to McKay."

There was silence for a few meters. Then Sheppard said: "Sam... How are you doing?"

"I'm fine," she smiled, slightly surprised to have been asked.

"Okay," he replied. "I'll try again. How are you doing? Really."

She didn't answer immediately. The question wasn't an easy one to answer; ever since the hybrid had gone on the attack she'd barely had time to think. Organizing the city against the creature had been difficult enough when it was skulking in the lockdown zone. Now that it was active, the job was doubly hard.

So far, apart from the awful thing in the hangar, there had been no other violent attacks. But it was obvious the creature was testing her defenses. It was as if the thing was probing her; acting in a certain way to see what she would do, then changing tactics. Prodding her, testing her responses. Keeping her on edge.

After the hangar incident, and the destruction of McKay's lab by the Norris replica, things had gone quiet for a short time. Then a report had come in from the medical lab, the one in which Angelus' blood samples had mysteriously vanished—an element of the hybrid had been discovered there by some of the nursing staff. The lab had been sealed, but the thing inside had been crashing about, obviously trying to attract attention. It had been driven off without injury, thankfully, but the whole incident had resulted in considerable disruption to the running of the infirmary.

The missing blood, Carter guessed, had been nothing of the kind. Tiny fragments of the hybrid, they had crawled out of the sample tubes and gone on to assimilate part of the locker.

Since then there had been more sightings of replicas, isolated attacks, and several attempts to hack into vital systems. For some reason the hybrid hadn't been able to disrupt the water supply, the transporter system or the ventilation network, despite having tried to do so on several occasions. It seemed, thankfully, that there were still parts of the city it hadn't figured out yet.

Still, it was keeping Carter on her toes. At the moment she considered the situation a stalemate, but she had the uneasy feeling that it couldn't last. She was being too reactive. Sooner or later, in the next day, the next hour or minute, the hybrid would make a new move and tip the balance.

That was how Carter was. Fearful, frantic, worried, overstretched. Angry and sickened. Violated and exhausted. Almost at the limits of her endurance, and completely unable to stop, to falter, to give in. To do so would be to hand Atlantis over to the hybrid, and there was simply no way she could do that. It was beyond her.

What to tell Sheppard, then?

"Really, I'm okay," she said.

"Tired?"

"No, I'm so hopped up on coffee I can barely see straight." She glanced sideways at him as they reached the transporter. "What about you?"

"Me? I feel like I've been hit by a truck. Why'd you ask?"

The transporter doors slid apart. Once the two of them were inside and the doors had closed again, Carter selected the nearest transport point to the ZPM lab, six levels down from the gate room. There was a brief flash, a fizzing sensation and a moment's disorientation, and then the doors opened onto a different scene.

Carter stepped out. "By the way, did you get a look at Lorne's flypast scans?"

Sheppard made a face. "Sure did. Apart from the ones with the scratch in one corner they were pretty… What's the word

I'm looking for?"

"Informative?" Carter suggested, heading into the ZPM lab.

There were few words to properly describe what the jumper's flypast had revealed. Barring the first few images, which showed nothing awry and were quite obviously fake, the scans had shown an area of the city that was almost completely taken over the by the hybrid. Not only had the creature grown vast amounts of new flesh while it hid in the lockdown zone, it had also started to assimilate the structure of Atlantis itself. Parts of the pier had changed, become ridged and rippled and twisted into disturbing new formations, as if the chimera had learned the trick of manipulating the very stuff of the city.

The pictures that stuck in Carter's mind, though, were the ones showing, however briefly, that while Lorne looked down on the hybrid from the air, something very like a vast, unblinking eye had been staring back up at him.

She looked quickly around the ZPM lab as she went in, but McKay was not in sight. Zelenka sat at a workstation, his back to her, and a couple of other technicians were busy at other parts of the lab.

He glanced around as she entered. "Ah, Colonel. Sorry, Colonels, plural. Any more developments?"

"Nothing that wouldn't give you nightmares." She moved next to him and sat down. Sheppard stayed behind them both, arms folded. Guarding as well as watching. "Where's Rodney?"

"I'm not sure. He said there was something he needed to work on, but he wouldn't tell me where. Maybe something to do with his new pets, I don't know."

Carter hid a grimace. Some of the pieces of hybrid McKay had salvaged after the hangar encounter had remained alive, and he was keeping them in an isolated lab under constant guard. She had reports of certain tests he had performed on them—she hesitated to use the word *experiments*—and while she could summon no sympathy for the hybrid or its works, the idea of McKay vivisecting squirming chunks of protean bio-matter made her stomach roil.

She pushed the thought aside; there were more pressing matters at hand. "So what do you have for us?"

"Okay." He tapped at his keyboard, bringing a map of the city up on the workstation monitor. "Firstly I've been able to verify the output of the biometric sensor. I thought the hybrid had hacked it, but I've run some sequence tests and I'm pretty sure it's one of the systems it can't get into yet."

Carter felt the word 'yet' settle in her gut like a ball of cold stone. "What does that show us?"

"This." Zelenka hit a key, and the map was overlaid with a series of crimson shapes. "I took some readings from one of McKay's new friends and re-tuned the sensor. You can see the lockdown zone here—obviously, most of the activity is confined to that area. But we've also got incursions in the tower." At the press of another control, the map turned, revealing itself to be a 3D model of the city. The virtual viewpoint zoomed in on the control tower, and as it drew close two red splotches appeared most of the way up. "This lower one hasn't moved, but this one here has spread itself thin between the hangar ceiling and the gate room."

"Damn," Carter breathed. "I hadn't realized it was still there... What do you think it's doing?"

"Could be trying to hack into the control room systems. Maybe even the gate."

"Why the gate?" asked Sheppard. "It's not trying to go anywhere, is it?"

Zelenka shrugged. "The gate has direct power connections to the ZPMs. Maybe it's trying to get a better source of energy."

Carter leaned closer to the monitor. "It's only a few levels away. Why not try to go for the ZPMs directly?"

"I'm not sure." He sat back. "There are a number of systems it hasn't gotten into yet, and I don't know why. I have a theory... McKay shot it down in flames, of course, and he might be right. But there do seem to be some essential elements of the city's function that I would have expected the hybrid to take over first. Now that its out in the open, why not shut down the transporters? Poison the air or the water?"

"It wants us alive, maybe?" Sheppard stepped closer, peering at the map. "Maybe we taste better fresh."

"What's your theory?" Carter asked. "Forget McKay—what do *you* think?"

"I think it's possible there's a connection between the unaffected systems and the unknown functionality we've been seeing. There's a signal component to the activity that seems to be in antiphase to the hybrid's pattern…" He sighed. "I'm sorry, I don't have much more than that."

Carter gave him a smile. "Don't worry. It's certainly worth looking into. In the meantime, this biometric data is a godsend. If we can use it to track the hybrid elements…" She squinted at the map. "Can it show us the replicas?"

"It's not quite tuned that finely yet, but I'm working on it. Oh, and there's one more thing. The seismic detectors are showing even heavier vibration in the lockdown zone. It's still hammering away in there."

"That's so odd." Carter looked over her shoulder at Sheppard. "Building something?"

"Doesn't seem like the constructive type. If I had to lay money down, I'd say it was probably ripping the pier apart and eating it piece by piece."

"That makes a depressing kind of sense, actually." Carter straightened up. "Although I still don't get why it's obsessed with increasing its mass when what it's short of is power."

"Fat guys don't stop eating. It's kind of a vicious circle, I guess."

"Actually, it's a little more than that." McKay walked into the room, a laptop under his arm. "Hey everyone. Did I miss anything?"

Carter pointed at the workstation. "Zelenka's found out how to track the hybrid."

"Really?" McKay gave the screen a cursory glance. "Yeah. That's, ah, really interesting." He put the laptop down and flipped it open. "Anyways," he went on, bringing the machine off hibernation. "The hybrid's mass. The bigger it gets, the more of its own power it can generate. It's working towards a point where it'll be self-sustaining."

Zelenka looked up at him, blinking. "How did you find that

out?"

"Oh, you know. A little applied science, a little raw genius." He brought up a graphic on the laptop screen. "Here you go. I've been analyzing those sections we saved, you know, from the hangar? And the mass to power ratio has got a definite curve. Extrapolating, I can tell within a fairly thin margin when it will have reached a big enough mass to not be hungry any more."

"That's great," said Carter. "Maybe, if we just find the thing enough to eat, it'll get full."

"Okay, two problems with that," McKay told her. "Firstly, there's no guarantee that it will stop—just that it will be self-sustaining and no longer tied down to draining power from the grid. And secondly, I don't think we'll be able to find it enough to eat."

"Why, how much will it need?"

"About half the city."

Carter sagged. "Damn. I thought we actually had a piece of good news."

"Yeah, sorry about that." McKay rubbed the back of his neck. "Ouch. That thing you fired in the hangar... I tell you, ever since that, my neck's been killing me."

"You were pretty close to it," said Zelenka, not unkindly. "Maybe you sprained some muscles when you landed."

"I was in the air?"

"Oh yes. I watched you."

"Wow. I thought that was just an out of body experience." He looked around at Carter. "And what was with all that water, anyway?"

"Confined-space version," she told him, rather impatiently. "There's a saltwater countermass to dampen the backblast. Rodney—"

"'Dampen' being the operative word."

"Hey," said Sheppard. "At least you weren't on fire."

"Okay guys, come on." Carter folded her arms. "Focus. Rodney, are we any further on the APE?"

His gaze dipped. "Not so much. Without the data we got from Laetor I'm kind of groping in the dark. I've not been able to tune a pulse that has any effect on the hybrid. Not the pieces of it I've got in the lab, anyway."

"Radek?"

"There's no immediate way to deform the shield, not with the hybrid's pattern interfering with the power grid. Sorry."

Carter suppressed the urge to swear. "John?"

"I've got nothing."

"Great." She raised her hands to her face, cupped them over her eyes to block out the world for a moment. The respite was welcome, but momentary. "So we've got a giant tumor in the west pier that's not going to stop before it's eaten half the city, a bunch of zombie clones of Atlantis personnel that we have no way to track, carnivorous biomass in the crawlspaces under the gate room and who-knows-where else, and Rodney's got a bad neck. Anything else?"

There was a long silence. Finally, Sheppard said: "I think that covers it."

For a moment, just a heartbeat, Carter almost lost control. A wave of anger and despair hovered over her, like the crest of some dark breaker about to surrender to its own mass and slam down on her, sluicing her away.

It didn't last long. Carter had never been a woman to give in to such feelings, even when all hope was gone. But the temptation to rage and howl and quite possibly pick up the laptop and shatter it over Rodney McKay's head was a very real one.

Embrace despair, someone had once told her. Turn it into anger. Use anger as energy.

"Okay," she said, her voice very calm. She pulled a seat out from under the workstation bench and sat down. "If what we've been working on so far has gotten us flat nothing, what else can we work on?" She glanced up at McKay. "How do you cure a smart disease?"

"Maybe you should be talking to Keller."

"Could be…" She frowned, thinking hard. "The tumor's metastasized. It's spread to other areas of the city, set up new infections there… It's acting just like a cancer, but a cancer that knows all about us. How does it know so much?"

"I think that's pretty obvious," said McKay, his voice low.

"Rodney," replied Sheppard, a note of warning in his voice.

"Don't go there."

McKay rounded on him. "What, you think you're going to make it not true by not saying it?"

"It doesn't need to be said!"

"There's no way she could have kept anything back!" He slammed the laptop screen down in sudden anger. "John, you know as well as I do that they had everything as soon as Oberoth stuck his damned hand into her head!"

"Shut up!" Zelenka had jumped to his feet. "All of you! *Just be quiet!*"

"He's right, " Carter began. "There's no need—"

"No, you too." Zelenka had a wild look in his eye, but it wasn't anger. "I'm sorry, Colonel, but I need everyone not to be talking right now. In fact, it might be best if you and Colonel Sheppard had something else to do."

"You're throwing us out?"

"Yes. Rodney, you have to stay. We've got a lot of work to do. Everyone else…" He pointed to the two other techs in the room. They were staring at him incredulously. "No, you stay too."

Carter stood up. "Radek, what's going on?"

"I think I know how you cure a smart disease," he told her. Then he waved at the door. "I'm really, really sorry, and you can fire me later if you like. But for now, *go.*"

Carter had a lot to think about on the way back up to the control room, and she wasn't disturbed in her thoughts. Although Sheppard accompanied her, he wasn't saying anything.

He was probably lost in his own reverie, she decided. He had been close friends with Elizabeth Weir, and having to abandon her on Asuras must have been harder on him than anyone.

From what Carter had read in various reports, Weir had been critically injured in the Replicator attack on Lantea. McKay had hinted at it when she first spoke to him about setting up a lab for Angelus—the beam weapon that had carved down through the city, scoring the tower. Weir had been caught by an edge of the blast, and that had almost put an end to her. For a while, she had not been expected to survive.

However, some time previously Weir had been infected with Asuran nanites, and by reactivating those microscopic machines McKay had been able to save her life, reprogramming them into replacing the damaged tissues in her body and brain. In effect, Weir had become a hybrid herself, although—as her purpose was not to replicate herself endlessly through violent assimilation—she bore nothing in common with the intelligent disease writhing out on the west pier. In fact she had worked actively against the Asurans, helping Sheppard and McKay to steal a ZPM from their homeworld to repower Atlantis and save everyone within.

But in doing so, she had sacrificed herself. Discovered by the Replicators, Sheppard had been forced to abandon Elizabeth Weir to them.

Once they had broken down her mental defenses and stripped her mind of its memories, the Asurans would have incorporated them into their own collective database. Although they did not know where Atlantis had relocated to, they knew everything else about it.

And, being part Replicator itself, so did the hybrid.

It would have known how to find *Apollo*, and how best to disguise itself in such a way as to be taken back to the city. It knew the strengths and weaknesses of the expedition staff. It knew how to make people trust it.

It knew where to hide.

Finally, Carter thought, her mystery file was complete. All the pieces had been arranged into the correct order, and the picture was plain to see.

Unfortunately though, the image it showed was one of unremitting horror.

Carter hadn't even gotten as far as the transporter when her headset crackled. That alone was enough to tell her that something bad had happened—the prohibition on sending anything but the most urgent information over the communications network hadn't been lifted.

She didn't break stride, but raised a hand, letting Sheppard know something was awry. "Carter here."

"*Colonel, this it Teyla. Ronon has been attacked by the hybrid.*"

"Is he okay?"

"*He is in the infirmary.*"

"I'll be right down. Teyla, where was he attacked?"

"*He was patrolling with some marines in the lower accommodation level.*"

"Thank you." She cut the connection and turned to Sheppard. "John, get back to the ZPM lab. I don't care if Zelenka tries to throw you out again, just see if the biometric sensor picked up any activity on the accommodation levels. Ronon and the hybrid got into it down there."

"Ronon?" Sheppard's face hardened. "Is he—?"

"He's alive, I'm just going to check on him. Go on." She shooed him away, then ran to the transporter.

When she got to the infirmary, a few minutes later, she heard Dex before she saw him. His voice was carrying out into the corridor, and he didn't sound pleased.

"I'm fine," he snarled.

"You're an idiot." That sounded like Keller. "Since when did having a dislocated shoulder count as 'fine'?"

"I've had worse. Just pop it back in."

"There's tendon damage. It won't 'pop back in'."

"Then hit it with something."

"You're insane!"

"All right, *I'll* hit it with something!"

There was a yelp, and then sounds of a struggle. Carter increased her pace, and got to the infirmary door in time to see Dex trying to haul a medical lamp off its base with his left hand, while Jennifer Keller held onto his forearm with her entire weight. By the looks of things, he was doing a fair job of lifting both Keller and the lamp.

"Ronon, what are you doing?"

"Hey," he said, sounding unconcerned. "Keller won't let me fix my arm."

Carter smiled. "Put her down. Please."

He met her gaze for a moment, just a token defiance, then gave a shrug and set Keller back on her feet. He handed her the lamp. "I've done this before," he told her. "That's all I'm saying. Hit it hard enough, it'll pop back in."

"If anyone's going to do any surgical hitting," Keller replied, straightening up and sweeping a few stray strands of hair out of her eyes, "it'll be me."

"Colonel, I need to get back out there," Dex said. "Sorry, but those marines don't know much about fighting Replicators."

"They haven't had a lot of practice." Carter walked over to him, surveying the Satedan's injuries. His right arm almost lifeless, and when she got closer she could see that long bruises had darkened the right side of his face. He was sitting slightly askew, as well. "Did you crack a rib?"

"Yeah, I guess. Hi Teyla."

"Ronon." Teyla had appeared at the doorway, and walked quickly into the infirmary. "Doctor, how is he?"

"Dislocated shoulder, broken rib, a lot of bruises," Keller replied. "He'll be out of action for a while."

Teyla smiled briefly. "I do not think you know Ronon Dex very well, Doctor."

"Okay," said Carter. "What happened? Ronon?"

"Are we gonna do anything about my arm?"

"In a minute. I need to know what happened."

"Huh." He shrugged again. Carter could see him hide a spike of pain as he did so. "I was on one of the accommodation levels. Some marines were following me around… Anyway, a man came up and asked me where you were."

"A man?"

"I didn't recognize him. Anyway, I said I didn't know and then he hit me."

"He was knocked through a wall," Teyla said, interrupting. "It was a hybrid replica."

Dex nodded languidly. "Well, I knew he wasn't human."

"How?" Carter asked, before she could stop herself.

"Because I ripped his arm off," said Dex. "He didn't seem all that bothered."

"Colonel," said Teyla. "It was Fallon. I heard gunfire and came to help. As soon as Fallon saw me, he ran. I followed, but I lost him."

Carter shook her head, puzzled. "Why would he ask for me?"

Dex made a sound in the back of his throat, as if the answer had been obvious. "You're the leader."

To Carter, that made no sense at all. She didn't feel much like a leader of anything, at the moment, and even if the hybrid disagreed, what reason would it have to target her specifically? Surely the science staff would have more chance of harming it, not her.

Then again, sowing discord was one of its talents. "Teyla, can you do me a favor?"

"Of course."

"Go to the ZPM lab. Sheppard should be there with McKay and Zelenka. Tell John to start posting guards with the science personnel—if the hybrid is starting to go after us individually it might try to take them out too."

Teyla nodded, and ran quickly out of the infirmary. Carter turned back to Keller. "Doctor, is there—?"

From outside in the corridor there was a sudden cry, and the sound of something heavy hitting a wall.

Carter drew her pistol. "Teyla?"

Behind her, Dex got up, and from the corner of her eye Carter saw Keller backing away, the lamp still clutched incongruously in one hand. "Teyla, if you can hear me, answer."

A heartbeat later, someone came in through the door. But it wasn't Teyla.

Andrew Fallon, or at least something that looked very much like him, was striding across the infirmary towards Carter. He was fast, far faster than any human should have been: Carter only managed to get three shots into his face before he back-handed her across the room.

She tumbled into the side of a bed, rebounded and crashed onto the floor. The pistol spun out of her grasp, skittering away. She made a futile grab for it, but it was already out of reach, and Fallon's hand was snapping down to grab her.

She ducked back, rolling under the bed, came up on the other side of it. Her ribcage was singing with pain, the whole side of her face numb from the shock of the blow. Fallon was not unharmed; her shots had unsewn his skull. What remained of his face was twisted in a kind of twitching, mechanical rage.

He reached for her again, but as he did something whipped sideways in a blurring arc from behind. The lamp Keller had been holding; Dex had it now. The blow flipped Fallon clear around, sent a portion of his ruined head flying away. The injury didn't slow him, though, and Dex didn't get a second chance. Fallon ripped the lamp from his hand, grabbed the Satedan's face and simply flung him out of the door.

Carter dropped to her knees, flailed until she found the gun, and then dived past Fallon. As he spun to follow her she fired again, taking off his jaw, then emptied the rest of the bullets into his torso. It was a useless gesture, she knew. Fallon was no longer using eyes to see her. He was no longer anything that could be slowed by the kind of damage that would kill a human—if she tore him in half with weapons fire, both the halves would come after her.

The pistol's slide locked back. Carter dropped it, looking wildly about for something to fend Fallon off with, but there was nothing within reach, and the replica was already on her. It took her around the neck with one hand, held her up. She felt her feet leave the floor.

The Fallon-thing's head no longer looked even remotely human. It was changing as she watched, eyes and mouths bubbling up out of the mess her bullets had made, whipping rootlets emerging from its opened skull to flail at the air. The other hand extended towards her, the fingers impossibly long, claws and needles erupting from the tips, and Carter remembered Bennings in the gallery, snatched by such a limb and dragged off to an unseen fate.

Was this what had happened to him, she wondered? There was a scientific curiosity that wouldn't leave her, even though her throat was crushed shut over her final breath and the hybrid's tendrils were worming through the air to spear her. Was this how the process took place? And in time, would a version of her walk the corridors of Atlantis?

She slapped the limb away, but the pain and lack of air had made her feeble. The Fallon-thing didn't even notice the blow.

And then it froze. She felt a jolt go through it.

The thing on the end of its neck opened all its mouths and screamed.

A second later, she was released. She fell, limp, a stringless puppet. Crumpled on the floor, it was all she could do to roll back and watch the Fallon-thing stagger away from her.

McKay was behind it, holding some piece of equipment in his hands. There was a thick cable extending from it, and the probe at the end was buried in the Fallon-thing's back.

The replica was still screaming, a single, breathless note of rage and agony. It was an awful noise, a whistling like escaping steam, suddenly liquid, then dry and whispery like the crunching of old leaves. And then, as suddenly as it had started, it stopped.

The replica dropped to its knees. The very structure of it was breaking down in front of Carter's gaze. She scrambled weakly away from it as it dissolved, the crimson flesh of it splitting and peeling and rotting as she watched, the metal of it dripping and running like mercury. The Fallon-thing swayed on its knees for a few seconds, then its multi-eyed head dropped forwards, and the whole body simply fell in on itself.

Heat, and the reek of spoiled meat and old metal, washed over Carter. She gagged, but the awful stench gave her the impetus to move again. She started to get to her feet, and then Keller reached down to help her.

Dex was already up again, and standing over the thing. Teyla was at the doorway, looking groggy, holding onto the frame for support. And McKay...

Rodney McKay raised a fist in victory. "*Yes!*" He hissed.

"And *that*, ladies and gentlemen, is how you fight a smart disease!"

CHAPTER NINETEEN

Kill or Cure

By the time Sheppard got to the infirmary, the remains of the Fallon replica had been largely cleared away. A couple of the medical staff were disposing of the last scraps, watched over by armed marines, and an orderly was on his hands and knees with a scrubbing brush and a bucket. The replica's dissolution had left a stain on the flooring, as though a vat of medical waste had been tipped out there and left to rot. Sheppard stepped carefully past it on his way to see Carter, trying not to breathe in too hard. What he had experienced of the hybrid close up had been less than fragrant when it was intact. Dead, it stank.

Carter was already on her feet, looking pale and bruised. Her jacket was off, and he could see the outline of bandages under her vest—from what Keller had told him, she had been knocked around quite badly in the fray.

When she saw him approaching she managed a weak smile. "John," she said. "I guess you heard we had some fun down here."

"Sorry I missed it." He glanced around, at the other patients. Several marines were being treated around him, mostly minor injuries from various encounters with the hybrid. He knew there were more serious wounds being dealt with as well, but those were hidden from sight. He couldn't see Dex or Teyla. "How is everyone?"

"Ronon's going to have a sore shoulder for a few days, but he'll deny it, of course. Teyla's fine. Fallon just knocked her out of the way. He was after me."

"It wasn't Fallon."

"I know." She tilted her head around, flexing her shoulder and wincing. "Even the clothes melted when Rodney jabbed him. But the likeness was frightening."

Sheppard stepped aside to let nurse Neblett go past him. She had what looked like a partially melted human jaw clasped in a pair of biohazard tongs, her arm outstretched and a look of complete disgust on her face. "Oh," he muttered. "Nice."

"I shouldn't be surprised, really," Carter went on. "Clarke was running messages for us for, oh, how long?"

Sheppard nodded. "I hear you. The replica situation is one I've tried to keep under wraps as much as possible. I don't like keeping secrets from people around here, but there have been some incidents…"

"What kind of incidents?"

"Just paranoia. But it's one thing to have a giant squishy monster on the west pier, people can deal with that. Not knowing if the guy standing next to you is human or not affects them in a whole different way."

"All the more reason to finish this quickly." She reached for her jacket, but the movement made her gasp quietly. Sheppard picked the garment up and handed it to her. "Thanks."

"Are you sure you're okay?"

"I'm fine. I've got to be." She shrugged carefully into the jacket. "John, we've all been knocked around. You too, and I don't see you resting."

That was a point he had to concede. The very thought of slowing down, of stopping to rest or tend his injuries hadn't even occurred to him. Compared to some, he had come through the events of the past few days largely intact, although his jaw still throbbed from the beating Dex had given him, and there was a tiredness in him that went into his very bones. But Carter was right—to rest for a minute would be to allow the hybrid an advantage, and that was a concept that bordered on the terrifying.

Especially now. The creature knew it was under threat.

"So," he asked, stepping around the stain again. It didn't appear to be coming off all that easily. "Have you spoken to McKay since then?"

"Not really." She looked a little embarrassed. "I sort of lost consciousness for a bit after that. When I came around he was already gone."

"So you don't know exactly what he's been up to either?"

"Not precisely, no. But he's up in the control room, I know that. Hopefully he can fill us in when we get there."

"Hopefully?" Sheppard gave her a wry smile. "Do you actually think he'd be able to resist?"

Carter could not have been out of action for more than thirty minutes or so, but it had been a busy half hour for John Sheppard. Ever since McKay had destroyed the Fallon replica, the hybrid had been reacting with a new ferocity. Although he would not admit it, Sheppard had found himself honestly believing that the creature was now on the verge of overwhelming all human efforts to resist it.

The loss of the Fallon-thing must have alerted it to the fact that it was in real danger. Sheppard wasn't certain how McKay had done what he had—he had been in the ZPM lab when the scientist had run out with his PDA, yelling cryptic technobabble about antiphase pulses and immune systems—but whatever he had done had been at least as effective as the APE on Chunky Monkey. In response, the hybrid had doubled its efforts.

Zelenka's seismic detectors had gone berserk; the thing in the lockdown zone had started to thrash with rage, its hammerings tripling in frequency and strength. The marines stationed at the blast doors had reported terrible sounds from within; shrieks and bellows the likes of which they had never heard before or wished to again. Two technicians observing from a higher structure had been studying the zone with binoculars, but after the increase in activity they had left their posts and refused to look back into that nightmare place again. Neither would discuss what they had seen, and Sheppard had decided not to press the matter. There were some things he simply didn't want to know.

There had been other reactions, too. Sheppard had been told of alterations to the structure of the city itself; in certain areas, the walls had started to blister, the blisters flowing together into strings as though roots were spreading behind the panels. A marine had been trapped between two sliding doors in a storage area, his arm crushed. Part of the ceiling in the hangar had opened and grown teeth.

And according to Zelenka, the fractal pattern of disturbance pervading the city's systems had increased massively. The hybrid was unleashing every weapon in its arsenal in its efforts to turn Atlantis into more of itself. And from where Sheppard was standing, it was very likely to succeed.

When Sheppard and Carter got to the control room, McKay was already hard at work. Two of the consoles were open, their crystalline innards exposed, glowing with multicolored light. Palmer and Franklyn had been banished to the edges of the room, but from what Sheppard could see they were only too pleased to be away from their posts; dozens of cables had been plugged into the consoles and were snaking across the control room floor in a confusing tangle. Most of the cables were thin, fiber-optic lines for transferring data at high speeds, but there were some big power leads in the mix too.

It looked, at best, desperately unsafe.

As Sheppard stepped through the doorway McKay popped up from behind a cable. "Sam!" he smiled. "You're okay!"

"More or less. Rodney, what the hell?"

"Give me a minute." He raised a hand to his headset. "Zelenaka, how's the water? Warm?"

Carter gave Sheppard a look, and mouthed *water?* at him. McKay caught it, and raised his hand a little higher. "Rolling boil. Oh lovely. I'll get back to you."

"It's code, obviously," he told them, once the connection was cut. He lifted a cable, checked a plug at the end and fitted it into the console. There was a spray of sparks. He jerked back on reflex, then studied the connection he'd made and nodded. "Mm-hm. Zelenka's monitoring the hybrid's interference pattern. I don't have time to have people running about with messages, so we're using a code instead."

"Will that work?" Sheppard asked him. McKay shook his head.

"I very much doubt it. Its just what Eliz- Just what *I'd* expect."

Carter was peering into a console, supporting herself on its open frame. "This is a patch into the communications network, right?"

"Among other things. Did Zelenka talk to you about this?"

"No-one's talked to me about this."

"Really?" McKay seemed surprised. "I thought someone would have filled you in."

"No. I haven't heard anything since Zelenka threw us out of the ZPM lab. Next thing I know, you're stabbing Fallon with a PDA and he sort of…" She made a face. "Melted."

"In fact, if I remember rightly," said Sheppard, "it was Zelenka who said he knew how to fight this thing."

"Hey hey hey…" McKay raised his hands. "Credit where it's due, please. Okay, maybe Zelenka came up with the seeds of the idea, but do you see him up here risking his neck in a sea of high-energy re-routes? No, I didn't think so." He picked up another cable, a data-line this time, then picked his way through the mess to the other opened console. "It's one thing to follow a medical analogy through. I'll give him that, some of his imagery was useful…"

"Medical?" Carter tilted her head slightly, the way Sheppard had seen her do when she was working out some complex problem. "We were talking about smart diseases, the way the hybrid's acting like a metastasizing tumor… Then he…" Her face lit up. "Oh, you're kidding me…"

"The antiphase pulse was clustering around the protected systems as well as the edges of the lockdown zone. One of us was going to work it out eventually."

"You're just jealous he got there first," Carter grinned.

"Sam?" Sheppard leaned towards her and lowered his voice. "Am I being especially dense here, or—?"

"No, no…" She got up from the console. "When the hybrid first shut itself into the lockdown zone we noticed there was something happening around the zone's edges… I remember Palmer called it 'functionality'. Basically a system no-one had seen working before had come online. Zelenka spotted it too, it was like a pattern that was interacting with the hybrid's control attempts."

"Is this to do with the systems it couldn't get into, like the transporters?"

"That's right. I'm guessing, but I think what Rodney's saying is that the city has something like an immune system."

"What, like antibodies? Against disease?"

McKay had gotten close enough to overhear. "It's only a very rough analogy," he said. "But yeah, when the city got infected it activated a set of new functions to stave off the infection. Read the hybrid's pattern, created opposing systems and set them working. Tried to protect essential systems as long as it could, while fighting the disease."

"Power's an essential system."

"Yeah, but power is the hybrid's number one priority. That what it's built to consume; or really, what its builds *itself* to consume. And anyways, the city's immune system isn't all that hot. It might have been built for something other than Replicator infiltration, I don't know. But the hybrid was going to overwhelm it sooner or later."

Sheppard heard a faint crackling sound from the cables near his feet, and stepped gingerly away from them. "So what's this you're doing now? Boosting the immune system?"

McKay nodded. "By a factor of about a thousand, yeah. Same principle as the APE."

"I thought the APE was an EMP emitter."

"So did I. That's why it didn't work when I tried to recreate it here: the EMP was a carrier wave for the antiphase pulse, not the pulse itself. If you hadn't let Norris trash my lab I'd have gotten that from Laetor."

Sheppard glared at him, but decided not to press the matter further. The crackling was getting louder. "Should we even be in here? Something sounds like it's going to catch fire."

McKay was about to answer when there was another loud crackle from the floor, and almost immediately another one directly above. Sheppard looked up.

"Aw crap," he muttered.

The ceiling above his head was deforming slowly, a series of welts rising in the metal to form a long, branching track. It looked as though something was growing there, roots or veins, splitting and dividing and inching forwards to form a slow, inexorable network above their heads.

"The hybrid," said Carter quietly. "It's infiltrating the control room."

McKay had a hand to his headset. "Ah, Radek? Just a point, but how's the water in my immediate vicinity, hm? Warm yet? Oh, hissing and spitting. Thank you so much." He looked up at Sheppard. "We're in trouble," he said.

"Is that more trouble than a minute ago?"

Behind him, down in the gate room, there was a grinding noise, a deep, gritty scraping. Sheppard ran onto the internal balcony and looked down in time to see a section of the floor bounce up, as though something massive had slammed into it from below. A moment later, that section of floor began to deform too. "Rodney, maybe you could speed things up a little here?"

"Yeah, I've not exactly been taking my time on this, you know!" Sheppard saw him look up from his console, hands filled with cables. "What's happening?"

"Let's just say you've got its undivided attention!"

He looked back. McKay was frantically plugging cables together, and Carter was taking calls on her headset. He couldn't hear what she was saying, but from her movements and the tone of her voice he guessed she was taking multiple reports.

The root-like deformations were on the outside of the control room now; Sheppard saw one accelerating along the frame of one of the big windows, spreading out to cover the metal surface. A second later the window transparency itself shivered and split, detonating an instant later in a shower of razored shards. He ducked away as they crashed down past him, onto the gate room floor.

Something down there, beneath the balcony, was issuing a thin, whistling scream.

"Damn it." He marched back into the control room. "We haven't got long."

"It's all over the city," Carter told him. "I think it's breaking through the immune system."

"So we're too late?"

"Don't panic," muttered McKay. "I'm already panicking, so more panic would not be good. There." He snapped two final cables together, then scampered across the control room to the center console. He lifted something up, a small slab of metal connected to several thin cables. A PDA, Sheppard saw.

"Is that it? Are you ready?"

"Yeah." McKay frowned at the PDA. "You know, for something this momentous, you'd think there'd be a bigger switch."

"Rodney, just for once, will you please take your ego out of gear and *do this thing?*"

"Fine, fine. Kill the moment." He tapped the PDA screen with a fingertip.

Sheppard felt something pass through him, up through his boots and down through the top of his head. It wasn't like the APE going off—that had been a surge of raw electromagnetic power. This was different, somehow more subtle but at the same time far more unpleasant. It sang over his nerves, through his bones. He felt it in his teeth, the backs of his eye sockets, down his spine, in his fingernails. It crawled through his hair like a nest of ants, made the fillings in his teeth shiver. It was horrible.

"God almighty," he yelled, cringing. "What is that?"

McKay had his eyes closed, his face screwed up. "The antiphase," he answered through gritted teeth. "Broadcasting…"

Out in the gate room, the thing under the balcony was shrieking. Sheppard staggered out, leaned over the rail. As he touched the metal he felt static electricity bite him, crawling pains eating into his fingertips. He ignored it, searching for the source of the screams.

Below him, something lurched into view, shedding parts of itself as it stumbled towards the Stargate. It was impossible to tell what it might have once looked like; now it was sagging apart as he watched, dripping gouts of liquescent flesh and metal, sloughing down into a droozing pile that shuddered once, tried to rise, and then collapsed. When it hit the floor, crimson slime spattered a meter out from it in every direction.

A thin reek rose from it, rot and vomit.

Sheppard backed off in disgust. The deformations in the control room ceiling were crumpling in on themselves, some sections smoothing back out, others dripping like mercury, leaving open scars in the metal.

The hybrid was dying. McKay's signal, rippling out through the city on a wave of energy, was attacking it like a human immune system attacks a disease. Where before the antiphase pulse only had the strength to keep the hybrid's infiltrations from attacking the most vital systems, now it had been copied and turned into data and broadcast in a massively amplified form. It was killing the hybrid just like the APE had killed the hybridized Replicators on Chunky Monkey, but without the destructive electro-magnetic pulse. Atlantis had the immune system built-in. It was designed to carry it.

The physical effects of the signal were lessening now, Sheppard realized. Either that, or he was becoming inured to them. He went back into the control room, trying not to touch any metal. "I think it's working," he said. His mouth still felt like it was full of tinfoil, but it was nothing he couldn't deal with for now. "How long do you need to keep it going for?"

McKay shook his head. "I have no idea. The smaller sections of hybrid will be dead pretty soon, but I'm not sure how much of this the main part will need. I'll have to call Zelenka, see if he can get—" he broke off, suddenly, looking over Sheppard's shoulder.

Sheppard turned. Zelenka was there behind him, totally out of breath. He looked like he'd just run the six flights of stairs from the ZPM lab.

"What the hell?" McKay scowled, putting the PDA carefully down onto the console. "Why aren't you monitoring the hybrid?"

Zelenka didn't speak for a few seconds, just stood holding onto the doorframe and gulping air. Finally he pointed at the doors to the external balcony. "Problem," he gasped.

"What do you mean, problem? It's working."

"Seismic," said Zelenka, quite white. "Something's wrong…"

Sheppard ran for the balcony doors. As they hissed open he

went straight for the rail, looking out towards the west pier. He was groping for the folding binoculars in his tacvest when he realized he didn't need them. The problem, as Zelenka had so succinctly called it, was perfectly visible from where he was standing.

The lockdown zone was in turmoil. There were clouds of dust rising from it, so big they were easily definable from two kilometers away. Sheppard could hear distant crashing noises from within, howls and roars, softened by the distance but still horrifying. As he watched, a chunk of debris whickered out from the dust clouds, high into the air, catching the light for a second before it topped its arc and fell end over end into the sea.

The sound of its splash reached him a second after he saw it.

McKay was next to him, hands clamped tight onto the rail. "Is it dying?"

"I don't think so…" Sheppard cupped a hand over his eyes. The sun was high, and coming from the relative gloom of the control room had made sparks swim his vision. There was something happening past the dust and the debris, but he couldn't make it out. He took the binocs out of his vest anyway, flipped them open and focused on the lockdown zone.

For a moment, he still saw nothing but clouds. Then a great form rose from behind the dust, unfolded, slammed down out of sight.

"Whoah," he whispered. Whatever that object had been, it was big, truck-sized. And fast. Debris had flashed up from its impact with the pier.

"What can you see?" said Carter. "John?"

The dust was clearing. Behind it Sheppard caught an unidentifiable darkness, like a great shadow… Then his perspective shifted, and he was looking into a hole. Almost the entire upper surface of the lockdown zone was gone, collapsed inwards and open to the sky.

And the hybrid was climbing out of it.

Sheppard lowed the binoculars. "We are *so* boned."

Now he knew why the hybrid had been hammering, hidden in the lockdown zone; what it had been doing for these past days. It had been preparing for this very moment, building what it would need to protect itself should the puny, fleshy creatures infesting its new food source gather enough of their wits together to do it harm. It had built a body for itself, armored it, protected it, and set it clambering on massive, articulated limbs out of the lockdown zone and onto the pier.

Its shape was impossible to completely make out: it was shifting, protean, great panels of curved metal sliding over raw flesh, tendrils swarming from it, new segments erupting and old ones sucking back into the mass. There was something of a spider to it, or a great crab, but it was far more complex and far less elegant than that. Its legs rose out of sequence, reaching out to grind down into the metal surface of the pier so the whole vast weight of the hybrid could drag itself forwards. It was like a crippled thing on pistoning crutches. Despite its size, its power, there was a sickening, fetal vulnerability to it.

It was heading for the control tower.

Sheppard couldn't help himself, even in the face of this nightmare. He turned to McKay. "*Now* look what you did!"

"What?" McKay gaped. "I didn't know it was going to do that! How the hell could I know it was going to do that?"

"Well, now you've turned it into a giant spider and we're all going to die."

"John," warned Carter. "Don't tease him." She turned to Zelenka. "Radek, can you confirm that the rest of the hybrid is gone?"

"I'll run up the biometric sensor," he replied, and vanished back into the control room.

Carter touched her headset. "This is Colonel Carter to all military personnel. We have a hostile lifeform on the west pier—trust me, you can't miss it. Do not approach it closely, but hit it with everything you've got. I'd recommend AT-4s if they can be set up in time. Carter out."

The hybrid was almost mid-way long the pier already. In spite of its bulk and the shambling way it dragged itself forwards, it was deceptively fast. Sheppard found himself trying to gauge how long it would take before it reached the tower. At the rate it was moving, he thought, not all that long.

A rattling sound rose over the city, distant and faint, but growing steadily louder. Gunfire.

The hybrid was still too far away to see the effects, if any, that the bullets were having. Most of the fire was invisible, but Sheppard saw a stream of tracer spring from a building partway along the pier. It was joined by another, and a third, far enough away for him to see the faint curve they made as gravity pulled them down.

Those must have been heavier weapons, he thought. M60s, emplacement-mounted to protect the city against air assault by Wraith darts. He could hear the difference in the tone of those weapons, the deeper rattle of their fire as opposed to the high, rapid stutter of smaller guns. The first people to open up on the hybrid had used P90s and sidearms.

As the tracer began to strike the hybrid's flanks, it hesitated, as if waiting to see if any damage was inflicted. A moment later, though, it moved on. "It's not working," Sheppard breathed. "Got to get something bigger down there."

"Give them time," Carter replied.

As she spoke, something in the city flashed, and a trail of smoke reached out to touch one of the hybrid's legs. There was a spark of yellow fire, a cloud of smoke whipped away by the wind. Fragments of debris spun away, arcing down like metal rain over the city. Another rocket lanced up, striking the main body of the thing. Two more.

The hybrid was being hit from all sides by machine gun fire and AT-4 missiles, but it still wasn't slowing. Sheppard could see pocks of damage on it now, scorch-marks from rocket explosions, small fires burning on its armor. But the effect was minimal. "It's too damn strong."

"Something's happening," said McKay suddenly, pointing.

Sheppard followed his finger, and saw that a part of the hybrid's forward body had opened up. An instant later, a thread of impossible brilliance connected the opening to a building that had been firing tracer rounds; the entire upper floor of it simply turned to fire, expanded, blasted apart in a shattering explosion of metal and glass. Sheppard heard the thump of it, felt the blast in his guts, watched burning pieces of debris carving tracks of smoke through the clear air.

The thread went out, vanished as abruptly as it had appeared. "Holy God," Sheppard whispered. "Where did it learn to do that?"

"It knows everything the Replicators know," groaned McKay. "It knows how to build beam weapons, everything."

"Yeah," spat Sheppard. "And we gave it a goddamn lab and all the time it needed, didn't we?"

"I should have told *Apollo* to stay," Carter whispered. "If I hadn't sent them away we'd have 302s, railguns…"

"You couldn't have known."

"I should have done," she replied, her voice dead. "I should have known."

Sheppard couldn't answer. She was in charge. This had happened on her watch. He knew there was no blame to be appointed here, but how could he tell her that? If he could not convince himself that he had not brought this on Atlantis by abandoning Elizabeth Weir to her fate, how could he comfort Carter in this dark hour?

There was no comfort to be had. He turned away, ran to the doors.

Carter called after him. "John? Where are you going?"

"Up," he told her. And kept on running.

CHAPTER TWENTY

Old Friends

After spending so long in the hyperspace-capable jumper on his way to and from Chunky Monkey, Sheppard had hoped not to be inside one of the machines for a while. Still, few of his hopes came to fruition these days; he was rapidly coming to terms with that.

And so, as he took a standard jumper up and out of the bay, he did not allow himself to hope.

In the time that he had taken to get there and take off, the hybrid had moved another few hundred meters. It had used its beam weapon again as well—another building was a raging inferno from the middle levels upwards. Seeing it, Sheppard cursed. Buildings could be repaired, he knew; at times, structures within Atlantis had been returned to pristine condition within startlingly short periods of time. But the lost lives horrified him. People were dying down there, in that great metal city, people he had spoken to, known, liked. In one single flare of energy, lives were being snuffed out.

As a soldier, death in battle was a fact he was intimately aware of. But he knew that it was not something he could ever fully accept. Human lives had their worth, he had decided long ago. And any one of them was worth more than the ravenous ambitions of the abomination stalking towards the city core beneath him.

He brought the jumper round in a long, swooping arc, testing his flight path above the hybrid. It grew in the forward viewport, the full awful shape of it spread out in front of him, then it whined away beneath him and out of sight. He wrenched the controls about, bringing the ship around for another pass.

His communications board lit up. *"What the hell are you doing?"*

"Sam, I'm going to drone this thing. It's too close to the core to use drones from the launchers, but if I can come in low enough there shouldn't be too much damage."

There was a pause. He knew her instincts would be to order him back, but there was no point to that and she knew it. Besides, he was right. "*I'll send out some more ships.*"

"Wait until I give this a try. I'd like to be the only thing in the sky at the moment."

"*Don't take too long.*"

The hybrid was almost in his sights again, the center of a web of tracer fire and rocket trails. He thought a drone into life, and as he did so the comms board lit up again. "*Sheppard.*"

He didn't immediately recognize the voice. "Get off the damn line, I'm busy."

The board went dark. Sheppard gave the mental command to launch the drone, sent it hissing away from the craft. Instantly his mind opened to encompass it; in one version of himself he was hauling the jumper up and over the hybrid's bulk, in another he was guiding the drone right towards it. There was no conflict involved, no effort. The Ancient gene he carried had attuned him to the technologies involved as completely and accurately as he was attuned to his own fingertips.

He spun the jumper around in a turn that made his chest ache, in time to see the drone strike the hybrid squarely in one leg. There was a sheet of flame, a globe of brilliant light expanding into a bubble of debris, and the leg sagged away. The material above and below the strike point was white-hot, glowing liquid like magma, and as it cooled into yellow it stretched, softened. The leg broke away, the clawed end of it striking the deck below, catching, so the entire severed limb stood, tilted, crashed down like a tree.

"Not bad," he grinned. "Not too bad at all."

The hybrid's beam weapon seared up at him and hammered into the side of the jumper.

The machine slewed wildly sideways. Sheppard's hands were ripped from the controls by the impact, and his seat spun, almost tipping him out. He dragged himself back to the controls in time to see the city core racing up to meet him, grabbed the yokes and hauled them back. The jumper leapt under him, climbed sickeningly fast. Something hit its belly, a deafening screech of metal on metal, and then he was in the air again and heading for the sky. He leveled off. "Okay then. Complacency in combat situations: not good."

An incoming communication crackled through his speakers. "*Sheppard, you cannot win this.*"

It was the same voice as before, but this time he recognized it. "Go to hell, Angelus."

"*I am there already. In order to finish this, you need to join me.*"

Sheppard didn't answer. The hybrid was ahead of him again. It was in the city core, among the buildings. He slowed, looped the ship around. There was too much structure in the way. "Come on," he found himself murmuring. "Incey wincey spider, get up that damned water spout…"

The beam lashed out again. It missed the jumper, but it was close; he felt the fizz of static from its passing, and the ship rocked under him. He increased speed, took the jumper a couple of kilometers out to sea, then around in a long, wave-skimming turn.

The hybrid was climbing the tower.

It was a hundred meters up, reaching out with one leg, spearing its clawed foot through the shell of the tower before doing the same with another. It would have been slow progress had each stride not been fifty meters long. Sheppard watched it grow in his viewport, marveling at the strength of the thing. It was one thing to drag itself across the pier with those titan limbs, quite another to haul itself vertically up a smooth surface.

Still, it was in the open now. He thought up another drone, launched the brilliant thing towards the hybrid's body. If it fell from the tower, the buildings below would suffer terrible damage, but what else was there to do? He could only attack this armored nightmare, and keep on attacking it, until one or the other of them was no more.

The drone sliced through the air, completely on target.

Sheppard smiled as he thought it through the last hundred meters, half a second...

The hybrid whipped a limb back, insect-quick, a car-sized piece of tower wall still impaled on the end of it. The speed was enough to fling the debris directly into the path of the drone. The explosion atomized the chunk of plating, washed the jumper in fire as the ship went right through it. Sheppard was battered back into his seat and then forward with massive force into the controls. He hauled the yokes back, a cry of fury ripping out of him.

Water sprayed up. He was out to sea, slicing the tops from waves. The jumper had a limited automatic pilot, he knew: either it had cut in at the last moment, or he was an even better flyer than he thought he was.

He turned the ship around again, but something was wrong. The controls were loose in his hands, the engine note wavering behind him. He checked the drones mentally and came back with no returns. The weapons were offline.

And the hybrid was most of the way up the tower. Almost at the level of the ZPM room.

If it used its beam weapon to cut into the tower, it could shut the city down in a second. Or strike a ZPM and send most of Atlantis into orbit in pieces no larger than a suitcase.

There was only one thing left to do, Sheppard realized. And the less time he had to think about it, the better.

He aimed the jumper at the hybrid, brought the engines up to maximum power, and locked the controls.

Maybe the creature simply didn't believe what he was trying to do, or maybe it was so close to the source of power it craved that it had forgotten him in its lust. In either case, it didn't try to defend itself. The jumper struck it between the upper joints of two legs, in its open flank.

The impact was gigantic. Sheppard's last conscious memory was seeing the rear door of the jumper racing up towards him, a dreadful sense of tumbling, free-fall, and then all was noise and darkness.

"Sheppard?"

There were no words in him, no breath, no thought. He was

still, and unable to be other than still.

"Sheppard?"

He couldn't move to wave the voice away. It pained him in ways he could not describe, but all he could do was endure it.

"*Lieutenant Colonel John Sheppard.*"

"G'way," he mumbled. His mouth was full of something coppery and foul. He opened his aching jaw and let some of it fall out. He felt it splash warm on his chest.

Light filtered in through closed eyelids, and there was a rocking sensation. Somewhere above him, a deep, organic groan. The sound was massive, heavy, like a great boulder poised above his head. He didn't like it at all.

"You have to open your eyes."

He did. Doing so was an effort, and it hurt. And when he had them open, what they saw still made no sense.

He was looking at chaos; a twisted, mangled space of deranged complexity. Part of it close to his head was metal, some recognizable and some completely alien to him. Other parts were pulpy, fleshy, crimson and pulsing. There was as dreadful smell in the air, like the inside of a rotting carcass, and the space around him was hot and foully damp.

He tried to move, and found that he couldn't. A mass of pulsing silver tubes was running over and around him, holding him against a wall of debris. As he watched they slowly retracted, slid away, and he fell, gently onto something that had once been a puddle jumper floor.

"Get up," the voice said. "We don't have much time."

"Until what?"

"Until the hybrid wakes up."

He knew the voice, now. "Angelus, you *are* the goddamn hybrid." He looked around, still trying to make sense of the cramped space around him. "Okay, I'll bite. Where am I?"

"Partly inside the hybrid. Partly in the crater it made in the southwest pier when it landed. Partly in the remains of your ship. John Sheppard, I commend your bravery, but not your common sense. Did you really think that a simple mechanical impact would destroy this creature?"

"It always works in the movies."

"As Colonel Carter said to another man recently, this is not a movie. Sheppard, you have only stunned the creature. I was able to take back some measure of control when your ship struck it, and managed to cushion your fall. And I can talk to you now. But this situation is not one that will last once the hybrid regains control of its core functions. When that occurs, the space you are in will collapse, you will die and then everyone in the city will die soon after that."

Sheppard got to his feet. Every part of him hurt. "I don't understand. Why are you even talking to me? Why don't you just eat me and get on with chewing up the city?"

"That can be explained more easily if you step through the hole to your left. Between the jumper's engine module and that section of flooring."

Sheppard peered to his left. In the dim, ruddy light pervading the space, he could see an irregular patch of darkness. "If I don't?"

"My fate is sealed in either case."

Above him, the hybrid groaned again. Sheppard muttered a curse under his breath and clambered through the hole.

Beyond it was another space, no less jumbled. The floor here was steeply angled, part of the crumpled deck of the pier. The impact of the jumper must have knocked the hybrid a considerable distance, Sheppard realized. Not just down from the tower, but clear of the city core altogether. If he ever made it out of here, he decided, he would love to see film of that. He hoped a security camera had been pointed in that direction when the jumper hit.

There was something on the far wall of the space, moving fitfully. It was high up, and embedded in a wall of tangled debris and pulsing biomechanical organs. Sheppard peered at it, but couldn't make out its shape in the meager light. He searched around in his tacvest pockets and found a small LED penlight. Luckily, it had survived the fall in better shape than he had.

In the bright beam of the light, Angelus looked down at him.

The false Ancient was far from the man he had once been. There was little more than a tattered remnant of him up in the wall; a curl of spine, a distorted cage of ribs, a few other sundries that shook and twitched among the wreckage. Most of the remnant's frame was not bone, but glistening metal, the same bright, liquid silver of the hybrid's internals, but there were a few shreds of Angelus' face adhering to the nodding skull.

In the midst of the glitter, a single eye looked down at Sheppard, and the ragged frame of an arm moved in fitful greeting.

"I apologize for my appearance," Angelus said, although the voice didn't come from his ruin of a face. It issued from everywhere. Sheppard didn't want to think about the mechanism that formed it. "I was almost completely absorbed. This is all that I've been able to reconstruct in the time I've had."

"I've been in better shape myself." Sheppard felt at his hip.

"Your sidearm is elsewhere," the remnant said, a slight sigh in his voice. "I thought that removing it would save the time otherwise spent by you emptying it into my face."

"Can't blame me for wanting to."

"Indeed, I cannot. I brought untold ruin to your door. But there is no time for recriminations. You have to destroy the hybrid."

"Yeah, you know what? I'd love to!" Sheppard looked around for a weapon to hit Angelus with, but there was nothing loose in reach. That was no accident, he was sure. "But I'm kind of out of options here!"

"Only because you will not listen. Together, you and I have the means to end this, but you must trust me first."

The word stopped Sheppard in his tracks. "*Trust?*"

"Sheppard, I am not the hybrid, not in the sense you believe I am. It made me from itself, but I have only recently become aware of that."

"What the hell are you talking about?"

"Listen to me. Who makes the best liar?"

Sheppard shook his head, helplessly. The surreal nature of

his situation was rapidly robbing him of reason. "I give."

"The best liar is one who believes his lies. Sheppard, when I came to you I was Angelus. Everything I told you was true…" The Ancient's voice was strange, almost wistful… There was a sorrow to it that stabbed at Sheppard, despite the derangement all around him. "My history, my origins, my children. Everything."

"It wasn't true. That's bull. You didn't come from that planet!" He pointed upwards, a random direction. "There's no way you could have made it from there!"

"Of course not. Sheppard, don't you understand? The hybrid needed to get to Atlantis. It needed to be left there, alone and undisturbed for long enough to regain its strength after the Asurans damaged it. While it was escaping its birthplace, it accessed the memories of Elizabeth Weir and used them to create the perfect bait, the perfect cover story. It invented Angelus!"

Sheppard stopped looking for a weapon. He turned, slowly, to look back at the remnant. "Are you telling me you didn't *know*?"

"Angelus was a construct from beginning to end, a pretty prize that your people couldn't help but take into their arms. A Trojan horse, to use a human phrase… It learned what to do from Doctor Weir's uploaded mind. Her memories are part of the collective's database." The arm waved sluggishly. "But in order to deliver that prize, it built me from itself. Gave the memories and form of the Ancient called Angelus to me. I sought out the *Apollo* believing I was who I said I was. That what my memories told me had happened had really happened."

Sheppard stared. "That's… That's insane."

"Can you imagine? Discovering that you are a monster, that everything you believed is a lie? That you were not born ten thousand years ago, but extruded from a biomass a week before? Can you *imagine*?"

The hybrid shifted, moaned a long, mournful bellow. There were other sounds too, distant thumps and bangs. People were still shooting at the thing, Sheppard realized. If they were still around when the hybrid awoke, it would kill them all.

"Do you know what hurts more than anything?" Angelus asked him. "I can still remember Eraavis. My children. The cities… Oh, Sheppard, if you could have seen the cities! Soaring under mountains…" The awful head dipped. "The fact that all those memories are utterly false is something I cannot bear to fully comprehend."

"We saw a planet," Sheppard breathed. "Burning…"

"The Asurans attacked that world. To test planetary bombardment techniques. There was no human life there."

"Target practice?" It was too much. Sheppard was reeling, his aching head full and pounding. How could he believe this, in such a place? It was a reversal of everything he had known.

But then, if Angelus was telling the truth, wasn't he in the same situation? And if he was lying, why was Sheppard even alive?

"Okay, just in case we're not both crazy right now, what do I do? To kill the hybrid."

Angelus lifted his unmade head. "I have control over a few of the hybrid's most basic functions for the moment. I was able to build myself this vessel and regain what little individuality I ever had… I can introduce an infectious element into its system. Before it regains control. A vaccine."

"Vaccine?" Sheppard shook his head. "Something this big? I don't—"

"Sheppard, the hybrid is comatose. It is defenseless. It is a made thing; not an evolved creature, but a construct. It has no immune system other than its own conscious defenses. If we infect it now, it will be poisoned before it can recover."

"What do you need?"

"Something external. Something alien to the hybrid. You."

"Me?"

"Not all of you. Some blood… A little of the Ancient gene. I am a part of the hybrid, and so I can use its weapons against it. In the same way it grows flesh, I can grow a poison. Give me your arm."

Angelus reached out. The metal bones of his hand were suddenly alive with silvery worms, their tips needles.

Sheppard had seen those glistening tendrils before, when he had pulled the Replicator's hand free of McKay's ankle in the weapons facility. Carter had seen them tear a man inside-out, make a replica of him. He jerked back in horror. "Not a chance!"

"Sheppard, we *have* no more chances!" The arm turned slightly, the hand outstretched. "I do not know what happened to Elizabeth. The hybrid was made soon after she arrived on Asuras... Her fate is unknown to me. But if she knew of this... Her memories, used as a weapon against her friends... Would she want you to hesitate?"

Sheppard stared up at the remnant for a long moment. The hybrid could still be lying. Maybe it needed a jolt of blood to kick-start its recovery. Maybe everything Angelus had told him was more lies.

But if it was true, then Angelus was right. Elizabeth should not be used this way.

He stepped forwards. "Do it."

The hand clasped his. The metal of it was warm, and the needle-tips of the worms frighteningly sharp. "This will cause you pain," Angelus told him gently. "I am sorry."

The worms slithered into the flesh of Sheppard's forearm.

He cried out, tried to yank his hand away on reflex, but Angelus was holding him too tight. The remnant's arm, for all its frail appearance, was machine-strong. Sheppard could no more have pulled himself free of that gleaming hand than he could from locked handcuff. All he could do was sink to his knees, staring at the pulsing worms sliding deeper and deeper under his skin.

His flesh was alive with them. He could feel them draining him, gnawing at him, drawing his blood away into their metal throats. Angelus had lied, he thought wildly. He was a vampire, sucking down one last draught of hot blood...

The worms snapped back, out of him and away. He fell.

"Sheppard?"

He rolled onto his back, staring up at the pulsing ceiling.

He penlight was spinning on the floor, strobing crazy shadows.

"John? It is done. You have to leave now."

Sheppard struggled up, onto his knees. "I don't think I can."

"You can." The Ancient's voice was weaker, thinner. It sounded as though it were coming from far away. "I'll help."

The hybrid had already started to die when Sheppard made it out. Angelus had taken control of some more of its structure, opening a way for him in the same way as it had cocooned him for the fall from the tower. The false Ancient's control failed in the last few meters, leaving him to struggle out though a liquefying mass of flesh and metal before he finally reached a gap in the armor plating and freedom.

He emerged, according to what he was told later, in front of several terrified marines, covered in bloody slime and making incoherent bubbling noises. It was only by luck, and the fact that he had collapsed unconscious almost immediately, that he hadn't been shot dead on sight. If he had continued towards the marines, they would have thought him some kind of birthing from the stricken hybrid, and ended him.

It took the hybrid a long time to die, and even longer to fully disintegrate. While Sheppard lay insensate in the infirmary, Carter had the nauseating mass pushed close to the edge of the pier, so that its oozings could drain off into the ocean. It was pollution of the worst kind, but there was nothing else to be done. Hopefully the ecosystem of M35-117 was pristine enough to recover from such a slight.

As it was, the slick of dissolved hybrid was visible for days, and the reek of it drove the inhabitants of Atlantis to stay inside with the windows closed for longer than that.

Gradually, Sheppard recovered. Angelus had taken more than two liters of blood from him, which was a worrying amount, and he had suffered multiple injuries from the crash and the fall. Under Keller's care, though, he became himself again, and within a short time was finding the enforced bed-rest distasteful. It was then, Keller told him, that she had known he was going to be all right.

Later, his friends and colleagues came to deliver news to him and to wish him well. McKay arrived and told him that the hangar space was damaged beyond repair, and would have to be welded shut. Not only that, but the city's antibody system had shut down completely after it had been boosted by McKay's signal, and could no longer be reactivated. That might have been because there was no longer a threat, or because it had been overloaded and destroyed. No-one knew.

Teyla brought him a portable DVD player and a selection of movies to watch, and told him that contact had been re-established with the *Apollo*. Ronon Dex challenged him a to stick-fight as soon as he was fit enough, and let him know that the Atlantis security protocols were being revised completely in view of what had occurred. There would be a lot of work for them both when Sheppard's stay in hospital was done.

Eventually, when she had a free moment, Carter arrived.

They spoke of many things, some pleasant, many somber. The casualty figures had to be discussed—twenty-eight dead, thirty-six injured, not counting casualties that had occurred on the *Apollo*. Apparently, McKay's fears for the ship had been justified. Ellis had suffered a hybrid outbreak of his own.

There were also some personnel for whom the experience had been too much. Nineteen members of the Pegasus expedition were ending their tours early. Alexa Cassidy was going home on medical leave. There were high hopes for her recovery, but she would not be returning to Atlantis.

Finally, Carter brought up the subject of Angelus. "So, he was telling us the truth after all."

"What he thought was the truth, sure." Sheppard closed his eyes for a moment, but all he could see was the pain in the Ancient's tattered face, so he opened them again. "Poor bastard. He lost them twice."

"Hm?"

"The Eraavi. He lost them when the Replicators killed them all, then again when he discovered they were never real in the first place." He sighed. "Sam? How the hell do we tell people he wasn't the bad guy?"

She shook her head. "We don't, not the IOA. It's too risky. If we tell them the truth about him, they might be more inclined to believe the next fake Ancient that turns up on our doorstep." She smiled. "Besides, I know for a fact that most of them just wouldn't get it."

"Yeah, well. It's pretty hard to get. I keep thinking, all the different things he told us... He believed them all, and none of them were true." Another memory jolted him. "Hey, that's it. The weapon he was going to build... What was he actually doing down there?"

Carter shrugged. "Most of it was lost when the lockdown happened. McKay saved some of it—a big chunk of the science looks like stuff the Replicators already knew, and there was a lot of random gibberish."

Sheppard laid back, staring up at the ceiling. "Rodney's gonna hate that."

"Yeah, he does." She stood up. "Anyway, Keller says you're ready to be discharged tomorrow. I'll leave you to your final night of peace."

"Why'd you say that?"

"Because one of the buildings that got cooked was right outside your quarters. You're going to be hearing the repairs crews there for weeks." She went to the door, and waved as she stepped out. "Goodnight!"

"Thanks a bunch." He settled back.

Slowly, the stillness surrounded him, settled on him like a membrane.

Even now, out in Atlantis, panels were being replaced, walls repaired, wiring checked and fixed. The city would, over a period of weeks, return to how it had been before. The gaping holes in the west and southwest piers would be covered. The events of the past few days would pass into history, just like the people that had been lost to them.

Which was worse, he wondered: killing twenty-eight people, or killing an entire planetary population that had never existed? To him, the former, without question. To Angelus?

He didn't know. And he found that he could not speak for the man, even though he too had never been. A false man mourning false children. The death of a lie breaking the heart of a man who was only a lie himself.

It was beyond him, a paradox without answer. Maybe, one day, he might be able to ask the opinion of the only person he felt might know its solution.

Until he found her, though, he would have to let the matter rest.

EPILOGUE

Fire from Heaven Redux

Apollo was different. There was a strangeness to the vessel now.

Ellis had felt it as soon as the ship had fled the jovian. At first he had put it down to the effects of damage, or the hammering meted out to both *Apollo* and its crew. Then, for a time, he had simply been too busy to dwell on it: as soon as the battlecruiser left the shadow of the gas-giant it had been detected by the Wraith fleet, and Ellis' attentions had been fixed very firmly on not getting *Apollo* blasted to atoms before it reached the safety of hyperspace.

It had been a tense time. Several Wraith vessels had altered vector and given chase, and without shields or weapons *Apollo* had been in no position to do anything but run. The pursuit had stretched halfway across the system, each vessel under constant acceleration, and there had been a time when Ellis had become convinced that they weren't going to make it. The hyperdrive had taken far longer than expected to reboot and run through its auto-calibration routines, almost allowing the Wraith vessels into weapons range before Sharpe was finally able to make the jump.

Had the main drives taken a similar time to reheat, or had the third Wraith cruiser from the storm been waiting in orbit as Ellis had feared, *Apollo* might never had escaped. Even when the hyperdrive had returned to normal function, using it had been something of a leap of faith. There was no time to check whether the system had accurately recalibrated. If there had been any significant error in its startup routine, all the crew's efforts to rid the ship of its intruder and the pursuing Wraith would have come to nothing.

Any fears Ellis might have had on that matter were

unfounded, thankfully, and the ship had leapt away without further incident. And once it was gone, the Wraith had not attempted to keep up their pursuit. Either they hadn't recognized the significance of the battered spaceship that had entered their staging area, or else they simply had other fish to fry. In either case, once *Apollo* had jumped, it was safe.

After the trauma, then, the recovery. A quiet system in which to nestle the ship close to an uninhabited moon, and time to make the best repairs possible and to re-establish contact with Atlantis.

Later still, perhaps, a chance to mourn the dead.

For now, Ellis was content to supervise the repairs. He was in the bomb bay, watching the launch racks being disengaged and lowered onto the bay doors; they were useless now, tangles of broken gantry and dangling cable. The creature—what Colonel Carter had referred to as the *hybrid*—had partially ripped them apart as it had attacked McKay's stealth sensors. Its path through them on its way out of the ship and into the jovian had finished the job.

Past the racks, steel plates were being welded over the hole in the ceiling. The fluttering blue-white glare of welding torches lit the bay, reminding Ellis uncomfortably of the lightning storm. Above that, another crew was working in the corridor, but nothing was being welded there. Corridor nine was largely off-limits, and only temporary coverings had been set down. One of the first instructions Ellis had given upon breaking out of hyperspace had been to order a crew of engineers, plus a squad of marines, into the corridor to pull away every panel from the floor, walls and ceiling.

Unsurprisingly, fragments of the hybrid still remained. Most were dead, including all of the vein-like tubules that had infiltrated the ship's control cabling and power lines. Those were easy to remove; since the demise of their host they had already begun to rot and peel.

A few of the pieces had tried to crawl away from the light, and one had even been discovered in the process of trying to infiltrate a wiring conduit again. Engineers had used arc welders on the tenacious mass of tissue until it had shriveled, and then dumped it unceremoniously out of the airlock along with all the other pieces.

Ellis couldn't shake the nagging feeling that they might still not have caught all the hybrid's last scraps, but that wouldn't be determined until the ship could be dry-docked. Hence his reluctance to order anything more than temporary coverings to be placed in the site of Kyle Deacons death. They would be lifted and the systems under them checked at regular intervals until he was sure.

If he could ever be sure.

That, he had decided, was part of the ship's strangeness. Like a man who has recovered from a tumor no longer trusts his own body, Ellis was finding it difficult to trust *Apollo*. In a way that was unfair—the ship had not turned against him of its own volition. But now he could not watch a screen glitch on start-up, or hear a stutter in the air system, or see the merest hint of a flicker in the internal lighting without wondering if part of the hybrid was once again in the process of infecting *Apollo* and eating it away from the inside.

He hoped it was a feeling he would be able to shake, in time. For now, he was getting used to the vessel all over again.

After a while he left the bay and returned to the bridge. It was time for *Apollo* to jump into hyperspace again.

Both Meyers and Sharpe were back at their consoles; Ellis had ordered them away to rest while the ship orbited the silent little moon. Whether either of them had slept at all was anyone's guess—there was probably a sizeable proportion of the crew who would prefer to rest with the lights on for a while. However, now that they were back at their stations Ellis knew the ship was in the safest of hands.

The lack of Kyle Deacon was something else he would need to get used to, though.

"Status report," he barked, settling himself into the command throne. "What are we missing?"

"Nothing essential." Meyers was tapping rapidly at her board, running test routines almost continuously. "Weapons are up, shields at eighty percent strength. Long-range sensors are showing some calibration errors, but short-range and passive are fine. I think we're about as good as we're going to get."

"Sharpe?"

"Course laid in, sir. As long as we keep the jumps short for now, I think we'll be okay. Hyperdrive could do with a little fine-tuning, but nothing that can't wait."

"Very well. Let's do this."

Sharpe worked her console, and within a few moments there was a throaty grumble from somewhere deep in the ship's interior. Ellis found himself listening to it, feeling it through his boots, through the throne arms. He could sense himself waiting for it to fail.

The gray bulk of the moon slid away and out of sight as the ship accelerated smoothly out of orbit. "Jump in ten seconds," Sharpe announced. "All systems nominal, capacitors charged. Hyperdrive at max power in three, two, one."

Blue light whirled out from the darkness, reached out and dragged *Apollo* into its maw. A second later all Ellis could see outside was the spiraling tunnel of hyperspace.

He had seen far less pleasant sights. He stood up again. "Sharpe, call me when we get close."

"Yes sir. Five minutes out?"

"That'll be fine."

He stood at the end of the corridor, watching the engineers checking under the floor panels and then tacking them down again with beads of silicone sealant. They were using powerful spotlamps to hunt for anomalies; wide-lensed halogens fed by thick power cables. Ellis found himself studying the lights for flickers, and shook the thought away. "Damned fool," he muttered.

"Sir?"

He turned. Copper was there behind him, the bandage around his head replaced by an adhesive patch. He looked wan, but Ellis was coming to realize that he always did.

There was a haunted air to him, though, that hadn't been there before. And little wonder, thought Ellis. Seeing what the hybrid had done down in the bomb bay would be enough to haunt anyone. "What brings you up here, airman?"

"I wanted to run some integrity checks on the cabling." He held up a small aluminum briefcase. "Just to make sure there's no stress fractures, really."

"Really?"

"Yes sir." The man's gaze dipped slightly. "And to check for power drains."

That wasn't on the repair schedule, but Ellis decided to let it slide for the moment. People needed their own reassurances after something like this. "Okay, Copper. Carry on."

Copper nodded, then looked past him, along the corridor. "This is where he was?"

"Who?"

"Major Deacon."

"No, airman." Ellis shook his head. "That thing wasn't Deacon. Part of it looked like him, but believe me, that was just a scam."

"So there was no way we could have…" The man trailed off, helplessly.

"Could have what? Saved him? No, not a chance. Like I said, Copper, he wasn't even here." Ellis slapped Copper's shoulder. "Report back to me once you've checked things out. The more I know about this corridor the easier I'll sleep."

"You and me both, sir."

Ellis walked away, left Copper opening up his tool case. He had brushed off the man's notion of saving Deacon, but in truth it was a thought that had plagued him, too. It was foolish; he knew that logically, from what he had seen and from what Carter had told him about the situation in Atlantis, Deacon never stood a chance.

The Ancient's ship—or rather, the part of the hybrid that had disguised itself as a ship—had left a section of itself behind when the puddle jumpers had lifted it free. Some fifty kilos of something half nanite, half tissue had crawled away into the dark spaces of the ship, found a place to hide and proceeded to send its rootlets into the power and control cabling than ran along corridor nine. It had sent false images to the test equipment used to hunt down the power drains it caused; the engineering crews had probably walked back and forth over it a dozen times.

It was good at hiding. It had even jammed *Apollo*'s communications, back when it had first appeared as the Ancient and his starhopper. Ellis had thought the Replicator vessel had done that, but of course it was the hybrid. It couldn't have risked the Asurans telling Ellis what they were pursuing.

Only later, when it was strong enough, had it emerged from its lair and attacked Kyle Deacon.

The helmsman's death, while not entirely painless, would have been swift. The hybrid was a predator, not a sadist. Down there under the floor panels it had taken Deacon apart and built itself among his ruins. Nothing of the man had survived. Only his tissues, copied and incubated to increase the hybrid's mass, had remained. And only a tattered image of him had fallen away into the jovian.

If there was some measure of comfort in that, however small, Ellis was prepared to take it.

As he reached the stairs, his headset chimed. "*Sharpe here, sir. We're almost at the target point.*"

"I'll be right up. Tell Meyers to go weapons hot."

Apollo broke out of hyperspace as Ellis reached the bridge. By the time he was in the command throne the ship was in stable orbit around Chunky Monkey.

Despite the whimsical name Colonel Sheppard had given it, the planet was as unlovely as he had described, sludge-gray and pocked like a rotted melon. No complex life existed there, which made Ellis' job a lot easier. As it was, he would have no compunction about boiling a few square kilometers of that greasy globe.

It would probably be an improvement. "Meyers, have you got the target co-ordinates?"

"Yes sir. Locked in and ready to fire on your command…" She paused, then straightened in her seat. "Hold on."

Ellis sat forward. Something was badly wrong. "Talk to me, Meyers."

"Hyperspace signature," she said quickly. "Something's

jumping in."

"Shields up, max power." Ellis stood and walked towards the viewport. He could see a star where no star should be, a point that suddenly erupted into a billowing cloud of azure light and a flood of elemental particles.

A hundred kilometers from *Apollo*'s prow, the angular bulk of a Replicator warship slid into view.

"Crap," snarled Ellis. "If it's not one thing it's the goddamn other…"

The ship was big; he didn't need sensors to tell him that. A battleship, twice the size of *Apollo* or more, black as night and bristling with gun ports. It slowed, decelerating smoothly from the hyperspace emission, and then swung about to face *Apollo*. Ellis watched its silhouette shrink into a looming cross-section.

The Asuran was hard to see. For all its bulk its surface seemed to suck light in. Only the endless rows of lit viewports along its flanks gave it away.

"They've charged their weapons, sir. Shields are maxed out too…" Meyers paused. "Colonel? It looks like they're locked onto the same co-ordinates we are."

"What the hell?"

Sharpe looked up from her console. "Comms request coming in, Colonel."

"Firewalls up, then put it on screen." Ellis strode back to stand next to her, looking down at the comms panel on her board.

It flickered, then lit up. From the Asuran ship, a Replicator glared back at Abe Ellis with a look of cold contempt and waspish intelligence.

The Asuran's face was familiar—older than the norm, the hair receding and closely cropped, the eyes deep-set, the mouth a grim line. Ellis had seen it on file more than once.

"Oberoth," he said quietly.

"Indeed," the Replicator replied. "And you are Colonel Abraham Ellis."

"I'm flattered."

"Don't be. To us, one target is very much like another."

Ellis glanced back at the ship. The fact that it wasn't already spitting fire in his direction gave him a small measure of hope.

He turned his attention back to the screen. "On the subject of targets, I notice that your weapons are locked onto the planet."

"As are yours."

"Which leads me to believe our missions may not be entirely incompatible."

Oberoth was silent for a moment. He looked like he was weighing the situation up.

"Look," Ellis continued. "We know what's down there. We had a little taste of it after it got away from you, but we managed to finish the job." He nodded down towards the planet. "We're just here to make sure it doesn't happen again."

The Asuran raised an eyebrow, very slightly. "And we," he replied, "are here to make sure it never happened *at all*."

"In which case, how about we both just prosecute our respective missions and then go home?"

There was a pause, and then Oberoth smiled. It was a chilling sight.

"A logical suggestion. Perhaps there is hope for you yet."

The screen went dark. Ellis straightened up and let out a long breath. "Meyers, have they changed status?"

"No sir. All their active weapons are still aimed at the facility."

"Good. Target that base and open fire."

As he spoke, streams of energy lapped from the Replicator ship, a concentrated broadside that lanced down at the surface of the planet with unimaginable ferocity. Under it, the rainclouds shrank away, and the ground boiled.

As if in answer, missiles darted up from *Apollo*'s launch tubes, angled themselves down at the same spot and accelerated into the maelstrom. Ellis saw the planet grow a spot of impossible brightness, like the rising of a minor sun.

It was a brief moment of grudging co-operation, nothing more. But for those few seconds, humans and Asurans brought light to the surface of a dark world.

And when they were finished, they turned their backs to each other once again, and were gone.

ABOUT THE AUTHOR

Peter J Evans made his professional writing debut in 1992. Since then he has worked on a broad spectrum of projects, including over two hundred articles and reviews for various entertainment magazines. He has worked as features editor on several publications, and in 1995 he co-wrote the award-winning Manga Video *Collectors Edition* catalogue.

His first novel, *Mnemosyne's Kiss*, was published in 1999 under Virgin Publishing's science fiction and fantasy imprint, Virgin Worlds. More recently Evans has co-written the novel *Judge Dredd: Black Atlantic* for Black Flame, which was recently re-printed as part of the *I Am The Law* Judge Dredd Omnibus. His latest novels have been the five part *Durham Red* cycle, also for Black Flame.

During daylight hours Evans does something terribly complicated involving navigational radar. He lives near Croydon in southern England, and rather wishes he didn't.

STARGATE

SG·1

STARGATE
ATLANTIS

**Original novels based on
the hit TV shows,
STARGATE SG-1 and
STARGATE ATLANTIS**

AVAILABLE NOW

**For more information, visit
www.stargatenovels.com**

STARGATE ATLANTIS: NIGHTFALL

by James Swallow
Price: £6.99 UK | $7.95 US |
$9.95 Canada
ISBN-10: 1-905586-14-0
ISBN-13: 978-1-905586-14-1

A terrifying weapon threatens the Pegasus galaxy

STARGATE
ATLANTIS.

NIGHTFALL

James Swallow

Based on the hit television series created by
Brad Wright and Robert C. Cooper

Series number: SGA-10

Deception and lies abound on the peaceful planet of Heruun, protected from the Wraith for generations by their mysterious guardian — the Aegis.

But with the planet falling victim to an incurable wasting sickness, and two of Colonel Sheppard's team going missing, the secrets of the Aegis must be revealed. The shocking truth threatens to tear Herunn society apart, bringing down upon them the scourge of the Wraith. Yet even with a Hive ship poised to attack there is much more at stake than the fate of one small planet.

For the Aegis conceals a threat so catastrophic that Colonel Samantha Carter herself must join Sheppard and his team as they risk everything to eliminate it from the Pegasus galaxy...

Order your copy directly from the publisher today by going to www.stargatenovels.com or send a check or money order made payable to "Fandemonium" to:

USA orders: $10.82 ($7.95 + $2.87 P&P). Send payment to: Fandemonium Books, PO Box 2178, Decatur, GA 30031-2178.

UK orders: £8.30 (£6.99 + £1.31 P&P). **Rest of the World orders:** £9.70 (£6.99 + £2.71 P&P). Send payment to: Fandemonium Books, PO Box 795A, Surbiton KT5 8YB, United Kingdom.

Or check your local bookshop – available on special order if they are out of stock (quote the ISBN number listed above).

Past, present, and future — nothing is what it seems

STARGATE
ATLANTIS

MIRROR MIRROR

Sabine C. Bauer

Based on the hit television series created by
Brad Wright and Robert C. Cooper

Series number: SGA-9

STARGATE ATLANTIS: MIRROR MIRROR

by Sabine C. Bauer
Price: £6.99 UK | $7.95 US |
$9.95 Canada
ISBN-10: 1-905586-12-4
ISBN-13: 978-1-905586-12-7

When an Ancient prodigy gives the Atlantis expedition Charybdis — a device capable of eliminating the Wraith — it's an offer they can't refuse. But the experiment fails disastrously, threatening to unravel the fabric of the Pegasus Galaxy — and the entire universe beyond.

Doctor Weir's team find themselves trapped and alone in very different versions of Atlantis, each fighting for their lives and their sanity in a galaxy falling apart at the seams. And as the terrible truth begins to sink in, they realize that they must undo the damage Charybdis has wrought while they still can.

Embarking on a desperate attempt to escape the maddening tangle of realities, each tries to return to their own Atlantis before it's too late. But the one thing standing in their way is themselves…

Order your copy directly from the publisher today by going to www.stargatenovels.com or send a check or money order made payable to "Fandemonium" to:

USA orders: $10.82 ($7.95 + $2.87 P&P). Send payment to: Fandemonium Books, PO Box 2178, Decatur, GA 30031-2178.

UK orders: £8.30 (£6.99 + £1.31 P&P). **Rest of the World orders:** £9.70 (£6.99 + £2.71 P&P). Send payment to: Fandemonium Books, PO Box 795A, Surbiton KT5 8YB, United Kingdom.

Or check your local bookshop – available on special order if they are out of stock (quote the ISBN number listed above).

STARGATE ATLANTIS: BLOOD TIES

by Sonny Whitelaw &
Elizabeth Christensen
Price: £6.99 UK | $7.95 US |
$9.95 Canada
ISBN-10: 1-905586-08-6
ISBN-13: 978-1-905586-08-0

Things couldn't get worse–or could they!

STARGATE ○ ATLANTIS.

BLOOD TIES

Sonny Whitelaw &
Elizabeth Christensen

Based on the hit television series created by
Brad Wright and Robert C. Cooper

Series number: SGA-8

When a series of gruesome murders are uncovered around the world, the trail leads back to the SGC—and far beyond…

Recalled to Stargate Command, Dr. Elizabeth Weir, Colonel John Sheppard, and Dr. Rodney McKay are shown shocking video footage—a Wraith attack, taking place on Earth. While McKay, Teyla, and Ronon investigate the disturbing possibility that humans may harbor Wraith DNA, Colonel Sheppard is teamed with SG-1's Dr. Daniel Jackson. Together, they follow the murderers' trail from Colorado Springs to the war-torn streets of Iraq, and there, uncover a terrifying truth…

As an ancient cult prepares to unleash its deadly plot against humankind, Sheppard's survival depends on his questioning of everything believed about the Wraith…

Order your copy directly from the publisher today by going to www.stargatenovels.com or send a check or money order made payable to "Fandemonium" to:

USA orders: $10.82 ($7.95 + $2.87 P&P). Send payment to: Fandemonium Books, PO Box 2178, Decatur, GA 30031-2178.

UK orders: £8.30 (£6.99 + £1.31 P&P). **Rest of the World orders:** £9.70 (£6.99 + £2.71 P&P). Send payment to: Fandemonium Books, PO Box 795A, Surbiton KT5 8YB, United Kingdom.

Or check your local bookshop – available on special order if they are out of stock (quote the ISBN number listed above).

The first victim of warfare is the truth

STARGATE ATLANTIS

CASUALTIES OF WAR

Elizabeth Christensen

Based on the hit television series created by
Brad Wright and Robert C. Cooper

Series number: SGA-7

STARGATE ATLANTIS: CASUALTIES OF WAR

by Elizabeth Christensen
Price: £6.99 UK | $7.95 US
ISBN-10: 1-905586-06-X
ISBN-13: 978-1-905586-06-6

It is a dark time for Atlantis. In the wake of the Asuran takeover, Colonel Sheppard is buckling under the strain of command. When his team discover Ancient technology which can defeat the Asuran menace, he is determined that Atlantis must possess it — at all costs.

But the involvement of Atlantis heightens local suspicions and brings two peoples to the point of war. Elizabeth Weir believes only her negotiating skills can hope to prevent the carnage, but when her diplomatic mission is attacked — and two of Sheppard's team are lost — both Weir and Sheppard must question their decisions. And their abilities to command.

As the first shots are fired, the Atlantis team must find a way to end the conflict — or live with the blood of innocents on their hands…

Order your copy directly from the publisher today by going to www.stargatenovels.com or send a check or money order made payable to "Fandemonium" to:

USA orders: **$10.82 ($7.95 + $2.87 P&P). Send payment to: Fandemonium Books, PO Box 2178, Decatur, GA 30031-2178.**

UK orders: £8.30 (£6.99 + £1.31 P&P). **Rest of the World orders:** £9.70 (£6.99 + £2.71 P&P). **Send payment to: Fandemonium Books, PO Box 795A, Surbiton KT5 8YB, United Kingdom.**

Or check your local bookshop – available on special order if they are out of stock (quote the ISBN number listed above).

STARGATE ATLANTIS: ENTANGLEMENT

by Martha Wells
Price: £6.99 UK | $7.95 US
ISBN-10: 1-905586-03-5
ISBN-13: 978-1-905586-03-5

When Dr. Rodney McKay unlocks an Ancient mystery on a distant moon, he discovers a terrifying threat to the Pegasus galaxy.

Determined to disable the device before it's discovered by the Wraith, Colonel John Sheppard and his team navigate the treacherous ruins of an Ancient outpost. But attempts to destroy the technology are complicated by the arrival of a stranger — a stranger who can't be trusted, a stranger who needs the Ancient device to return home. Cut off from backup, under attack from the Wraith, and with the future of the universe hanging in the balance, Sheppard's team must put aside their doubts and step into the unknown.

However, when your mortal enemy is your only ally, betrayal is just a heartbeat away…

Order your copy directly from the publisher today by going to www.stargatenovels.com or send a check or money order made payable to "Fandemonium" to:

USA orders: $10.82 ($7.95 + $2.87 P&P). Send payment to: Fandemonium Books, PO Box 2178, Decatur, GA 30031-2178.

UK orders: £8.30 (£6.99 + £1.31 P&P). Rest of the World orders: £9.70 (£6.99 + £2.71 P&P). Send payment to: Fandemonium Books, PO Box 795A, Surbiton KT5 8YB, United Kingdom.

Or check your local bookshop – available on special order if they are out of stock (quote the ISBN number listed above).

STARGATE ATLANTIS: EXOGENESIS

by Sonny Whitelaw & Elizabeth Christensen

Price: £6.99 UK | $7.95 US

ISBN-10: 1-905586-02-7

ISBN-13: 978-1-905586-02-8

When Dr. Carson Beckett disturbs the rest of two long-dead Ancients, he unleashes devastating consequences of global proportions.

Series number: SGA-5

With the very existence of Lantea at risk, Colonel John Sheppard leads his team on a desperate search for the long lost Ancient device that could save Atlantis. While Teyla Emmagan and Dr. Elizabeth Weir battle the ecological meltdown consuming their world, Colonel Sheppard, Dr. Rodney McKay and Dr. Zelenka travel to a world created by the Ancients themselves. There they discover a human experiment that could mean their salvation...

But the truth is never as simple as it seems, and the team's prejudices lead them to make a fatal error — an error that could slaughter thousands, including their own Dr. McKay.

STARGATE ATLANTIS: HALCYON

by James Swallow
Price: £6.99 UK | $7.95 US
ISBN-10: 1-905586-01-9
ISBN-13: 978-1-905586-01-1

In their ongoing quest for new allies, Atlantis's flagship team travel to Halcyon, a grim industrial world where the Wraith are no longer feared—they are hunted.

Horrified by the brutality of Halcyon's warlike people, Lieutenant Colonel John Sheppard soon becomes caught in the political machinations of Halcyon's aristocracy. In a feudal society where strength means power, he realizes the nobles will stop at nothing to ensure victory over their rivals. Meanwhile, Dr. Rodney McKay enlists the aid of the ruler's daughter to investigate a powerful Ancient structure, but McKay's scientific brilliance has aroused the interest of the planet's most powerful man—a man with a problem he desperately needs McKay to solve.

As Halcyon plunges into a catastrophe of its own making the team must join forces with the warlords—or die at the hands of their bitterest enemy…

Order your copy directly from the publisher today by going to www.stargatenovels.com or send a check or money order made payable to "Fandemonium" to:

<u>USA orders:</u> $10.82 ($7.95 + $2.87 P&P). Send payment to: Fandemonium Books, PO Box 2178, Decatur, GA 30031-2178.

<u>UK orders:</u> £8.30 (£6.99 + £1.31 P&P). <u>Rest of the World orders:</u> £9.70 (£6.99 + £2.71 P&P). Send payment to: Fandemonium Books, PO Box 795A, Surbiton KT5 8YB, United Kingdom.

Or check your local bookshop – available on special order if they are out of stock (quote the ISBN number listed above).

STARGATE ATLANTIS: THE CHOSEN

A little knowledge is a dangerous thing

STARGATE ATLANTIS

THE CHOSEN

Sonny Whitelaw & Elizabeth Christensen

Based on the hit television series created by Brad Wright and Robert C. Cooper

Series number: SGA-3

by **Sonny Whitelaw & Elizabeth Christensen**
Price: £6.99 UK | $7.95 US
ISBN-10: 0-9547343-8-6
ISBN-13: 978-0-9547343-8-1

With Ancient technology scattered across the Pegasus galaxy, the Atlantis team is not surprised to find it in use on a world once defended by Dalera, an Ancient who was cast out of her society for falling in love with a human.

But in the millennia since Dalera's departure much has changed. Her strict rules have been broken, leaving her people open to Wraith attack. Only a few of the Chosen remain to operate Ancient technology vital to their defense and tensions are running high. Revolution simmers close to the surface.

When Major Sheppard and Rodney McKay are revealed as members of the Chosen, Daleran society convulses into chaos. Wanting to help resolve the crisis and yet refusing to prop up an autocratic regime, Sheppard is forced to act when Teyla and Lieutenant Ford are taken hostage by the rebels…

STARGATE ATLANTIS: RELIQUARY

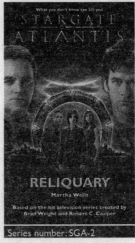

by Martha Wells
Price: £6.99 UK | $7.95 US
ISBN-10: 0-9547343-7-8
ISBN-13: 978-0-9547343-7-4

While exploring the unused sections of the Ancient city of Atlantis, Major John Sheppard and Dr. Rodney McKay stumble on a recording device that reveals a mysterious new Stargate address. Believing that the address may lead them to a vast repository of Ancient knowledge, the team embarks on a mission to this uncharted world.

There they discover a ruined city, full of whispered secrets and dark shadows. As tempers fray and trust breaks down, the team uncovers the truth at the heart of the city. A truth that spells their destruction.

With half their people compromised, it falls to Major John Sheppard and Dr. Rodney McKay to risk everything in a deadly game of bluff with the enemy. To fail would mean the fall of Atlantis itself—and, for Sheppard, the annihilation of his very humanity…

Series number: SGA-1

STARGATE ATLANTIS: RISING

by Sally Malcolm
Price: £6.99 UK | $7.95 US
ISBN-10: 0-9547343-5-1
ISBN-13: 978-0-9547343-5-0

Following the discovery of an Ancient outpost buried deep in the Antarctic ice sheet, Stargate Command sends a new team of explorers through the Stargate to the distant Pegasus galaxy.

Emerging in an abandoned Ancient city, the team quickly confirms that they have found the Lost City of Atlantis. But, submerged beneath the sea on an alien planet, the city is in danger of catastrophic flooding unless it is raised to the surface. Things go from bad to worse when the team must confront a new enemy known as the Wraith who are bent on destroying Atlantis.

Stargate Atlantis is the exciting new spin-off of the hit TV show, Stargate SG-1. Based on the script of the pilot episode, Rising is a must-read for all fans and includes deleted scenes and dialog not seen on TV — with photos from the pilot episode.

Order your copy directly from the publisher today by going to www.stargatenovels.com or send a check or money order made payable to "Fandemonium" to:

<u>USA orders:</u> **$10.82 ($7.95 + $2.87 P&P). Send payment to: Fandemonium Books, PO Box 2178, Decatur, GA 30031-2178.**

<u>UK orders:</u> **£8.30 (£6.99 + £1.31 P&P).** <u>Rest of the World orders:</u> **£9.70 (£6.99 + £2.71 P&P). Send payment to: Fandemonium Books, PO Box 795A, Surbiton KT5 8YB, United Kingdom.**

Or check your local bookshop – available on special order if they are out of stock (quote the ISBN number listed above).

STARGATE SG-1: HYDRA

by Holly Scott & Jaimie Duncan
Price: $7.95 US | $9.95 Canada |
£6.99 UK
ISBN-10: 1-905586-10-8
ISBN-13: 978-1-905586-10-3

Rumours and accusations are reaching Stargate Command, and nothing is making sense. When SG-1 is met with fear and loathing on a peaceful world, and Master Bra'tac lays allegations of war crimes at their feet, they know they must investigate.

Series number: SG1-13

But the investigation leads the team into a deadly assault and it's only when a second Daniel Jackson stumbles through the Stargate, begging for help, that the truth begins to emerge. Because this Daniel Jackson is the product of a rogue NID operation that spans the reaches of the galaxy, and the tale he has to tell is truly shocking.

Facing a cunning and ruthless enemy, SG-1 must confront and triumph over their own capacity for cruelty and violence in order to save the SGC – and themselves…

Order your copy directly from the publisher today by going to www.stargatenovels.com or send a check or money order made payable to "Fandemonium" to:

<u>USA orders:</u> $10.82 ($7.95 + $2.87 P&P). Send payment to: Fandemonium Books, PO Box 2178, Decatur, GA 30031-2178.

<u>UK orders:</u> £8.30 (£6.99 + £1.31 P&P). <u>Rest of the World orders:</u> £9.70 (£6.99 + £2.71 P&P). Send payment to: Fandemonium Books, PO Box 795A, Surbiton KT5 8YB, United Kingdom.

Or check your local bookshop – available on special order if they are out of stock (quote the ISBN number listed above).

STARGATE SG-1: DO NO HARM

by Karen Miller
Price: $7.95 US | $9.95 Canada | £6.99 UK
ISBN-10: 1-905586-09-4
ISBN-13: 978-1-905586-09-7

Stargate Command is in crisis—too many teams wounded, too many dead. Tensions are running high and, with the pressure to deliver tangible results never greater, General Hammond is forced to call in the Pentagon strike team to plug the holes.

But help has its price. When the team's leader, Colonel Dave Dixon, arrives at Stargate Command he brings with him loyalties that tangle dangerously with a past Colonel Jack O'Neill would prefer to forget.

Assigned as an observer on SG-1, hostility between the two men escalates as the team's vital mission to secure lucrative mining rights descends into a nightmare.

Only Dr. Janet Fraiser can hope to save the lives of SG-1—that is, if Dave Dixon and Jack O'Neill don't kill each other first...

STARGATE SG-1: THE BARQUE OF HEAVEN

by Suzanne Wood
Price: $7.95 US | $9.95 Canada |
£6.99 UK
ISBN-10: 1-905586-05-1
ISBN-13: 978-1-905586-05-9

Millennia ago, at the height of his power, the System Lord Ra decreed that any Goa'uld wishing to serve him must endure a great trial. Victory meant power and prestige, defeat brought banishment and death.

On a routine expedition to an abandoned Goa'uld world, SG-1 inadvertently initiate Ra's ancient trial – and once begun, the trial cannot be halted. Relying on Dr. Daniel Jackson's vast wealth of knowledge, Colonel O'Neill must lead his team from planet to planet, completing each task in the allotted time. There is no rest, no respite. To stop means being trapped forever in the farthest reaches of the galaxy, and to fail means death.

Victory is their only option in this terrible test of endurance – an ordeal that will try their will, their ingenuity, and above all their bonds of friendship…